PRAISE FOR

GENERATION LOSS

"Hand expertly ratchets up the suspense until it's at the level of a high-pitched scream near novel's end." —*Milwaukee Journal Sentinel*

"A terror tour-de-force that testif[ies] to the power of great fiction to disturb and provoke." —*Publishers Weekly* (starred review)

"Hand combines elements of the traditional amateur-sleuth mystery with a visceral story of personal redemption, and her pulsating prose smacks us in the face with frank, fascinating discussions of sex and drugs . . . The utterly compelling protagonist, whose self-loathing competes with her hatred of life to see which can beat her into submission first, wins us over almost in spite of herself. Brilliantly written and completely original, Hand's novel is an achievement with a capital A." —*Booklist* (starred review)

"This novel crackles with energy: it is alive." —Nicholas Rombes, author of *The Ramones* and *New Punk Cinema*

"A lucid and beautifully rendered tale of an aging and damaged punk photographer's journey from the safety of the streets of New York into the wilds of Maine. Great, unforgiving wilderness, a vanished teenager, an excellent villain, and an obsession with art that shades into death: what else do you need? An excellent book." —Brian Evenson

GENERATION LOSS

a novel by

elizabeth hand

A Harvest Book
Harcourt, Inc.
Orlando   Austin   New York   San Diego   London

Requests for permission to make copies of any part of the work should be submitted online at www.harcourt.com/contact or mailed to the following address: Permissions Department, Harcourt, Inc., 6277 Sea Harbor Drive, Orlando, Florida 32887-6777.

www.HarcourtBooks.com

An excerpt of this book appeared in 2005 in *Gargoyle 50*, edited by Lucinda Ebersole and Richard Peabody.

Camera Lucinda: Reflections on Photography by Roland Barthes, translation by Richard Howard, translation copyright 1981 by Farrar, Straus and Giroux, Inc. "sister morphine" from *Babel* by Patti Smith, copyright ©1978 by Patti Smith. Used by permission of G.P. Putnam's Sons, a division of Penguin Group (USA) Inc.

First U.S. edition published by Small Beer Press in 2007.

Library of Congress Cataloging-in-Publication Data
Hand, Elizabeth.
Generation loss/Elizabeth Hand.—1st Harvest ed.
p.   cm.
A Harvest book.
1. Women photographers—New York (State)—New York—Fiction.   I. Title.
PS3558.A4619G46   2008
813'.54—dc22   2007044645
ISBN 978-0-15-603134-9

Text set in Centaur MT

Printed in the United States of America
First Harvest edition 2008
K J I H G F E D C B A

For David Streitfeld,
who asked for a letter from Maine

I then realized that there was a sort of link (or knot) between Photography, madness, and something whose name I did not know.
—Roland Barthes, *Camera Lucida* (trans. by Richard Howard)

ART NEEDS LIGHT
look at the lack of it.
—Patti Smith, "sister morphine"

part one
BURNING IN

1

THERE'S ALWAYS A MOMENT where everything changes. A great photographer—someone like Diane Arbus, or me during that fraction of a second when I was great—she sees that moment coming, and presses the shutter release an instant before the change hits. If you don't see it coming, if you blink or you're drunk or just looking the other way—well, everything changes anyway, it's not like things would have been different.

But for the rest of your life you're fucked, because you blew it. Maybe no one else knows it, but you do. In my case, it was no secret. Everyone knew I'd blown it. Some people can make do in a situation like that. Me, I've never been good at making do. My life, who could pretend there wasn't a big fucking hole in it?

I grew up about sixty miles north of the city in Kamensic Village, a haunted corner of the Hudson Valley where three counties meet in a stony congeries of ancient Dutch-built houses, farmland, old-growth forest, nouveau-riche mansions. My father was—is—the village magistrate. I was an only child, and a wild thing as the privileged children of that town were.

I had from earliest childhood a sense that there was no skin between me and the world. I saw things that other people didn't see. Hands that slipped through gaps in the air like falling leaves; a jagged outline like a branch but there was no branch and no tree. In bed at night I heard a voice repeating my name in a soft, insistent monotone. *Cass. Cass. Cass.* My father took me to a doctor, who said I'd grow out of it. I never did, really.

My mother was much younger than my father, a beautiful Radcliffe girl he met on a blind date arranged by his cousin. She died when I was four. The car she was driving, our old red Rambler station wagon, went off the road and into the woods, slamming into a tree on the outskirts of town. It was an hour before someone noticed headlights shining through the trees and called the police. When they finally arrived, they found my mother impaled on the steering column. I was faceup on the backseat, surrounded by shattered glass but unhurt.

I have no memory of the accident. The police officer told my father that I didn't cry or speak, just stared at the car's ceiling, and, as the officer carried me outside, the night sky. Nowadays there would have been a grief counselor, a child psychologist, drugs. My father's Irish Catholic sensibility, while not religious, precluded any overt emotion; there was a wake, a funeral, a week of visiting relatives and phone calls. Then my father returned to work. A housekeeper, Rosie, was hired to tend me. My father wouldn't speak of my mother unless asked, and, forty-odd years ago, one didn't ask. Her presence remained in the framed black-and-white photos my father kept of her in his bedroom. While Rosie vacuumed or made lunch I would sit on his bed and slowly move my fingers across the glass covering the pictures, pretending the dust was face powder on my mother's cheeks.

I liked being alone. Once when I was fourteen, walking in the woods, I stepped from the trees into a field where the long grasses had been flattened by sleeping deer. I looked up into the sky and saw a mirror image of the grass, black and yellow-gray whorls making a slow clockwise rotation like a hurricane. As I stared the whorl began to move more quickly, drawing a darkness into its center until it resembled a vast striated eye that was all pupil, contracting upon itself yet never disappearing. I stared at it until a low buzzing began to sound in my ears. Then I ran.

I didn't stop until I reached my driveway. When I finally halted and looked back, the eye was still there, turning. I never mentioned it to anyone. No one else ever spoke of seeing it.

My sense of detachment grew when I started high school, but as my grades were good and my other activities furtive, my father never worried much about what I did. Our relationship was friendly if distant. It was my Aunt Brigid who worried about me on the rare occasions she paid us a visit.

Brigid was like my father, stocky and big boned and red haired. I resembled photos of my mother. Tall and angular, narrow hipped, my mother's soft features honed to a knife-edge in my own. Pointed chin, uptilted nose, dirty-blond hair, and mistrustful gray eyes. If I'd been a boy I might have been beautiful. Instead I learned early on that my appearance made people uneasy. There was nothing pretty about my androgyny. I was nearly six feet tall and vaguely threatening. I wore my hair long but otherwise made no concessions to fashion, no makeup, no lipstick. I wore my father's white shirts over patched blue jeans or men's trousers I bought at the Junior League Shop. I wouldn't meet people's eyes. I didn't like people looking at me. It made me feel sick; it reminded me of that great eye above the empty field.

"She looks like a scarecrow, Dad," Brigid said once when I was sixteen. She and her husband were in Kamensic for a rare visit. "I mean, look at her—"

"I think she looks fine," my father said mildly. "She's just built like her mother was."

"She looks like a drug addict," Brigid snapped. She was sensitive about her weight. "We see them out where we live."

I pointed out to the bird feeder at the edge of our woods. "What, like the chickadees? We see them too," I said, and retreated to my room.

Several months later I had this dream. I was kneeling in the field where I'd seen the eye. A figure appeared in front of me: a man with green-flecked eyes, his smile mocking and oddly compassionate. As I stared up at him, he extended his hand until his finger touched the center of my forehead.

There was a blinding flash. I fell on my face, terrified, woke in bed with my ears ringing. It was the morning of my seventeenth birthday. My father gave me a camera. I sat at the breakfast table, turned it in my hands, and remembered the dream. I saw my face distorted in the round glass of the lens, like a flaw; like an eye staring back at me.

I took an introductory photography class in high school and was encouraged to take more.

I never did. I quickly learned what I needed to know. I liked a slow lens. I liked grainy black-and-white film and never worked in color. I liked the detail work of creating my own photographic paper, of processing then developing the film myself in the school photo lab. I loved the way the paper felt, soft and wet in the trays, then the magical way it dried and turned into something else, smooth and rigid and shining, the images a mere by-product of chemistry and timing.

I didn't care if the pictures were over- or underexposed, or even if they were in focus. I liked things that didn't move: dead trees, stones. I liked dead things: the fingerless soft hand of a pheasant's wing, mouse skulls disinterred from an owl pellet, a cicada's thorax picked clean by tiny green beetles. I liked portraits of my friends when they were sleeping. I've always watched people sleep. When I occasionally babysat, I'd go into the children's rooms after they were in bed and stand there, listening to their breathing, waiting until my eyes adjusted to the soft glow of night-light or moonlight. I liked to watch them breathe.

When I was seventeen I fell in love with a boy from a neighboring village. He was a year younger than me, fey, red haired, with sunken, poison green eyes: a musician and a junkie. I'd hitch to his town and sit on the library steps across the street from his big Victorian house and wait there for hours, hoping to see him but also wanting to absorb his world, clock the comings and goings of his younger siblings, parents, his golden retriever, his friends. I wanted to see the world he knew from inside his junkie's skin, smell the lilacs that grew outside his window.

One day his sister came out and said, "My brother's inside. He's waiting for you to come over."

I went. No one else was home. We crawled underneath the Steinway Grand in the living room and I sucked him off. Afterward we sat together on the front porch while he smoked cigarettes. This pattern continued until I left high school. One night we broke into the village pharmacy and stole bottles of Tuinals and quaaludes before the alarm went off then ran laughing breathlessly back to his house, where he pretended to sleep while I hid in his closet. We weren't caught, but I was too paranoid to ever try it again.

I liked to watch him sleep; I liked to watch him nod out. I took pictures of him and got them processed over in Mount Kisco. At night in my room I'd look at those photographs—his eyes closed, cigarette burning in his hand—and masturbate. I told him I'd do anything for him. A few years later, he got caught burglarizing another drugstore up in Putnam County. His parents bailed him out and he wrote to me, desperate and lonely, while he was awaiting sentencing. I never wrote back. His family moved to the Midwest somewhere. I don't know what happened to him.

He was the only person I ever really cared about. I still have those photos somewhere.

In 1975 I graduated from high school and started at NYU. I had vague plans of studying photojournalism. That all changed the night I went over to Kenny's Castaways to hear the New York Dolls.

The Dolls never showed, but someone else did, a skinny chick who screamed at the unruly audience in between chanting bursts of poetry while a tall, geeky guy flailed around with an electric guitar.

After that I quit going to classes. I took up with a girl named Jeannie who waitressed at Max's Kansas City. For a few months she supported me, and we lived in a horrible fourth-floor walk-up on Hudson Street. The toilet hung over a hole in the floor; the claw-foot tub was in the kitchen. We put a sheet of plywood over the tub and on top of that a mattress we scrounged from the street. I didn't tell my father I'd been suspended from NYU. I used the checks he sent to buy film and speed, black beauties, crystal meth. There was a light that fell on the streets in those days, a light like broken glass, so bright and jagged it made my eyes ache, my skin. I'd go down to see Jeannie when she got off work at Max's and take pictures of the people hanging out back. Some of those people you'd still recognize today. Most you wouldn't, though back then they were briefly famous, just as I was to be. Most of them are dead now.

Some of them were dead then. I shot an entire roll of film of a kid who'd OD'd in the alley early one morning. No one wanted to call the ambulance—he was already dead, why bring the cops down? So I stood out there, shit-colored light filtering from the street lamp, and photographed him in close-up. I was nervous about bringing the film to the place I usually went to. I had a friend at the university process the film there for me.

"This is sick stuff, Cass," he said when I went to pick it up. He handed me the manila envelope with my contact sheets and prints. He wouldn't meet my eyes. "You're sick."

I thought they were beautiful. Slow exposure and low light made the boy's skin look like soft white paper, like newsprint before it's inked. His head was slightly upturned, his eyes half-open, glazed. You couldn't tell if he'd just woken up or if he was already dead. One hand was pressed upon his breast, fingers splayed. A series of black starbursts marred the crook of his bare arm; a white thread extended from his upper lip to the point of one exposed eyetooth. I titled the photo "Psychopomp." I decided it was strong enough that I should start assembling a portfolio, and so I did, the pictures that would eventually become part of my book *Dead Girls*.

People used to ask me what it was like to take those photographs.

"'How do you think it feels?'" I shot back at the guy from *Interview*. "'How do you think it feels? And when do you think it stops?'"

He didn't get it. No one does. I can smell damage; it radiates from some people like a pheromone. Those are the ones I photograph. I can tell where they've been, what's destroyed them, even after they're dead. It's like sweat or semen or ash, and it's not just a taste or scent. It shows up in pictures, if you know how to catch the light. It shows up in faces, the way you can tell what a sleeping person's dreaming, if they're happy or frightened or aroused. I don't know why it draws me; maybe because I dream of leaving this body the way other people dream of flying. Not flying to a sunny beach or a hotel room, but true escape, leaving one body and entering another, like one of those wasps that lays its eggs inside a beetle so a wasp larva grows inside it, eating the beetle until the new wasp emerges.

It sounds creepy, but I always liked the idea of disappearing then becoming something new. That of course was before I disappeared.

But taking a picture feels like that sometimes. When I'm getting it right, it's like I'm no longer standing there with my camera, with my eye behind the lens, looking at someone. It's like it's me lying there and I'm seeping into that other skin like rain into dry sand.

Sometimes it happens with sex. Once I brought a sixteen-year-old boy back to the apartment. I'd picked him up at a club, dark eyes, curly dark hair, a crooked front tooth, tiny scabs on the inside of his arm where he'd been popping heroin, still too scared to mainline.

The tooth is what got me. I'm still sorry I didn't shoot him. He was beautiful, one of those Pasolini kids who absorbs light then shines it back into your eyes and blinds you. But I left my camera on the floor, and instead I just fucked him, more than once. Then I lay awake and watched him sleep. When he woke in the morning he looked at me, and I saw what had happened to him: his mother's death, the small apartment in Queens where he lived with his father and sister, the after-school job at a pet shop. Cleaning fish tanks, measuring out birdseed. He told me all this, but I already knew; I could see the light leaking from his eyes. I wanted to photograph him, but suddenly I felt real panic. I gave him coffee and money for a cab and literally pushed him out of the door. The look he gave me then was crushed and confused, but that I could live with. What I couldn't deal with was the knowledge that he was so close to dead already. The only thing that had made him feel alive was fucking me.

I tried to explain this to Jeannie. She looked at me like I'd spit in her face.

"You're crazy, Cass. You're, like, a nihilist. You're in love with annihilation."

"Yeah? So is that a bad thing?"

She didn't think that was funny. She left me soon after and got a job at a massage parlor. I didn't care. I stayed in the apartment. By then I'd gotten messed up with a rich girl from Sarah Lawrence who liked slumming with me. She split when the school year ended, by which time my father had figured out what was going on—that I'd been kicked out of school and was no doubt spending the checks he sent on drugs. He was surprisingly calm. He made sure I knew he wouldn't give me another dollar until I straightened out and earned enough to put myself back through school, but he also let me know I was always welcome back home. I thanked him and kept in touch intermittently, usually by postcard.

I bought a tripod and began doing a series of pictures, black-and-white photographs of me dressed and posed like women in famous paintings. I called the series "Dead Girls." There was me as Ophelia, wearing a thrift-shop bridal gown and ribbons, floating in a tenement bathtub filled with black-streaked water—dye bled from the ribbons so that it looked as though blood flowed from my dress. There was me topless, sprawled in a Bowery alley on my back as Waterhouse's dead *St. Eulalia*. For Munch's *The Day After* I lay on top of my plywood bed with empty wine bottles scattered around me. I used a similar setup for Walter Sickert's *The Camden Town Murder*.

It took me five months. I got a job at a wino's liquor store on the Bowery to get by. There were twenty-three photos when I was done, enough for a show.

My central image derived from a lithograph from Redon's "La Tentation de Saint-Antoine": a life-sized human skeleton, a plastic model I had a friend borrow for me from the NYU art department. I draped it with a white sheet and posed beside it, naked, my hand clutching its bony plastic fingers. I set the shutter so that the image was so underexposed as to be almost indiscernible, deliberately out of focus. All you saw was the skeleton, seeming to fall forward through the frame, and floating beside it a face suggestive of a skull: mine. I translated the drawing's original caption into English.

> Death: I am the one who will make a serious woman of you; come,
> let us embrace.

I added these to my portfolio, and a few portraits I'd done of Jeannie and her friends hanging out in the apartment and the back room at Max's. The pictures were harsh and overlit, but they had a scary energy, most of it supplied by Jeannie herself in torn fishnets and smeared eye makeup, her works on the floor beside her, the glare of a naked hundred-watt bulb making Gillette blades glow like they were radioactive.

It didn't hurt that some of the figures lurking in the background were starting to get written about. Back in January I'd begun seeing flyers stapled to telephone poles around town: PUNK

IS COMING. I bought the first copy of the magazine for fifty cents at Bleecker Bob's not long after. A month later, the first copy of *New York Rocker* came out, and I bought that too. When I got off my night shift at the liquor store I'd walk over to CBGB's and get trashed and dance. I'd take my camera and shoot whatever was going on, speed, smack, sex, broken teeth, broken bottles, zip knives. People laughing while blood ran down their face, or someone else's. Some people didn't like getting their picture taken while having sex or shooting up. I got good at throwing a punch then running. I started wearing these pointy-toed black cowboy boots that weren't good for dancing, but I could kick the shit out of someone if he lunged for me and be gone before his knees hit the floor. I loved the rush of adrenaline and rage. It was as good as sex for me.

"Scary Neary!" Jeannie shouted when she saw me coming. By then people were getting used to me. And other people were starting to take pictures too. *Punk* and *New York Rocker* didn't create the scene, but they gave it a name, and we all knew where it lived.

By now I'd made some contacts in the city's photography scene. I brought my photos to the director of the Lumen Gallery, and he agreed to give me a small show in the back room. Three years earlier, Robert Mapplethorpe had begun to win a following among Warhol acolytes and some prescient art-world types. The same thing was happening now with the downtown scene. I sent out a hundred xeroxed invitations to everyone I vaguely knew and scattered another hundred at the clubs where I hung out. I made sure all the musicians knew they were featured in the photos. Then I bought myself a bottle of Taittinger Brut, got smashed, and went to my opening.

It was the right place at the right time. "Dead Girls" bridged the gap between two camps, photography and punk, my staged self-portraits and documentary images of the downtown scene. The dreamy kitsch of photos like "St. Eulalia" melded into the shock of seeing Jeannie nod out while the lead singer of Anubis Uprising masturbated onto her face. I could hear the buzz as I stumbled into the back room at Lumen.

I was a hit, and I wasn't yet twenty years old.

WHO ARE THE MYSTERY GIRLS? ran the *Voice* headline a week after my show opened. CASSANDRA NEARY'S PUNK PROVOCATIONS. They used a detail of "St. Eulalia," cropped so you could see my bare foot and the Canal Street sign. It looked like a crime-scene photo. This wasn't a bad take, since I was being castigated in the press for everything from pornography to drug dealing.

I didn't care. I was safe behind my camera at CBGB's. I loved the rituals of processing film. I had an instinctive feel for it, how long it would take for an image to bleed from the neg onto emulsion paper. I loved playing with the negs, manipulating light and shadow and time until the world looked just right, until everything in front of me was just the way I wanted it to be.

But best of all I loved being alone in the dark with the red safelight, that incandescent flare when I switched the lights back on and there it was: a black-and-white print: a body, an eye, a tongue, a cunt, a prick, a hand, a tree; drunk kids racing through a side street with their eyes white like they'd seen a ghost with a gun.

This is what I lived for, me alone with these things. Not just knowing I'd seen them and taken the picture but feeling like I'd made them, like they'd never have existed without me. Nothing is like that: not sex, not drugs, not booze or sunrise off the most beautiful place you can imagine. Nothing is like knowing you can make something like that real. I felt like I was fucking God.

You read a lot of crap about photographic craftsmanship in those days, and technique; but you didn't hear shit about vision. I knew that I had an eye, a gift for seeing where the ripped edges of the world begin to peel away and something else shows through. What that whole downtown scene was about, at least for a little while, was people grabbing at that frayed seam and just yanking to see what was behind it; to see what was left when everything else was torn away.

My story was picked up by the *Daily News.* Then the *Sunday Times Magazine* interviewed me for a very brief piece. And there were the "Dead Girls" photos, and there was me, smoking a Kent and wearing beat-up black jeans and red Keds and an MC5 T-shirt fili-greed with cigarette burns, my hair a dirty blond halo around a pale face with no makeup. I looked like what your mother dreams about in the middle of the night when you don't come home.

I was actually a little worried about what my father would think. He finally called me after the *Times Magazine* story ran. He made it clear that he had no interest in seeing the show—a relief to both of us—but he also wanted to make sure I wasn't in any legal trouble.

"Anything comes up, call Ken Wilburn over in Queens," he said and gave me the number. "He represents some guys, they'll help you out if you get into trouble. I don't know how the hell you can make money out of this stuff, Cass, but I hope to God you do. Especially if you need Wilburn."

I never did need to call Wilburn. But I didn't make much money, either. The *Times* article did its business, and all the photos sold; but I had only set the price at seventy-five bucks a pop. Jeannie bought most of them—God knows where she found the money—but about six months later they were destroyed when her apartment flooded. The girlfriend of Anubis Rising's lead singer bought the picture of him with Jeannie then proceeded to set it on fire with her Bic lighter in the gallery, screaming "Fucking cunt!" until someone threw her out. John Holstrom bought a picture that had Johnny Thunders in the corner.

And the last photo went to Sam Wagstaff, which is how I got a book deal. I'd met a literary agent at my opening, a petite red-haired woman in a red latex miniskirt named Linda Kalman.

"This is very interesting," she said, peering at "Psychopomp." She was older than most of the people at the show, in her mid-thirties, and wore expensive gold jewelry and stiletto-heeled boots. I pegged her for a socialite slumming among the barbarians. She glanced at the crowd drinking white wine in plastic cups, Jeannie and her friends hooting raucously as a reporter took notes. "Do you know which one's the artist?"

I dropped my cigarette and stubbed it out with my sneaker. "That would be me."

"Really." Her eyes narrowed. She gave me a small smile then extended her hand. "Linda Kalman. I'm working on a book right now with Chris Makos. Do you know him?"

"Yeah," I lied and shook her hand. "Cass Neary."

"Cass. Are you with a gallery?"

"No."

"Mmmm." She looked at me sideways, opened a little red clutch purse. "Well. Here. Take my card. Call me. Let me know who buys your pictures. And good luck."

As it turned out, she got in touch with me when she read the piece in *New York Rocker.*

"So." I could hear her drag deeply on a cigarette on the other end of the line. "Have you sold any photographs yet? Do you know who bought them?"

When I named Wagstaff, she sucked her breath in sharply. "Sam Wagstaff?"

"Yeah."

"You know who he is, right?"

"Yeah." A collector and curator with deep pockets; Mapplethorpe's lover, though I'd heard they were on the outs.

"Well, Cass. Are you interested in putting a book together? Because I have an editor who's very interested in what's happening downtown. She can get someone to write an introductory essay, I think she said Macey Claire-Marsden from the Eastman Foundation might do it. It's not huge money, but it would be good exposure for you."

She hesitated. "I think you should do it. Not just for me. This kind of opportunity doesn't come that often, Cass. Not for someone as young as you. You don't want to blow it."

"Let me think about it." I didn't say anything, didn't hang up. I counted to five then said, "Yeah, okay. Sure. I'll do it."

But you know what?

I blew it anyway.

2

A YEAR LATER *Dead Girls* came out and got good press. Good reviews, good coverage, and the first printing sold through, which for a fifty-dollar coffee-table book by an unknown twenty-one-year-old photographer was pretty decent. This was back when you'd see books by Helmut Newton and David Hamilton in the front windows of Brentano's and Rizzoli Books.

Now you started seeing *Dead Girls* too. I was written up in *Interview* and *WWW.* Word got out that I was funny: I got on the radio and even had a fleeting appearance on *The Merv Griffin Show.*

But I was fucking up big time. I showed up at interviews drunk. I insulted people. I came on to the women hired to talk to me, which pissed them off, and pissed off the guys too. A reporter referred to me as a lesbian photographer, and I reamed him out about it when I saw him a few nights later. I wasn't a lesbian; I wasn't straight. When it comes to relationships, I'm an equal opportunity destroyer. I fucked whoever I wanted to. Women just seemed able to put up with me better than men did. For a little while, anyway. The *SoHo Weekly News* did a story on what a mess I was, quoting liberally from the interview I'd given them. I thought I was a fucking rock star, I thought I was Iggy fucking Pop; but no one was paying to watch me fall off the stage.

Dead Girls never went into a second printing. Punk had crested; the violence of the scene made industry people nervous about even using the word "punk." They started slapping stickers on new EPs and 45s that said THIS IS POWER POP MUSIC! Farfisa organs began to dull the edge of guitars. Kids wearing skinny ties and wraparound shades were everywhere now. The scene got bigger, hipper, imploded then exploded. There were celebrities and celebrity suicides, and celebrity photographers to cover them. When I saw a seventy-five-dollar ripped T-shirt in a Fiorucci boutique with a brace of black-leather-collared miniature poodles tied to a meter outside, I knew that was it.

Punk's ugly little glittering perfect moment had ended. And so had mine.

I knocked around the city, at loose ends. People saw me, they recognized me, the skinny girl with ragged blond hair and chewed-up nails, striped boatneck shirt, and shaky hands. But no one wanted to be reminded who I was, and after a few years nobody remembered.

I still had the apartment on Hudson Street. I got a job working in the stockroom at the Strand Bookstore. This signaled to everyone that I was truly finished.

One other thing happened back then. On my twenty-third birthday I was down on the Bowery, leaving CBGB's, late, as usual. I was drunk, as usual. I was barefoot—I'd been dancing and left my shoes inside, even though it was late October and the streets were cold. I was alone, until a car pulled up alongside a broken street lamp. Someone was repeating my name, a low, insistent voice. Piecing it together later, I think he must have said "Miss, miss."

I heard *Cass. Cass.*

I stopped and turned. The car door was already open. There was a knife. It happened fast.

I don't remember much. Or no, I remember a lot, but it's all scattered, like those discarded photos you find strewn outside an instant-photo booth.

This is what I see: a burned-out vacant lot. Me on my knees. A cut on my bare heel where I stepped on broken glass. Blood above my pubis. Blood and semen on my thigh. Me running across chewed-up asphalt. A man's head protruding from a car window. Me screaming in the middle of the street. A police car.

I see these things, but I don't really remember them. I remember floating above the vacant lot and looking down on two shadows, one moving, the other still. I remember a car. There was a knife.

They asked me, did I fight?

I didn't fight. I couldn't describe him, or the car. My mind had been wiped clean. I don't talk about it much. It happened; I'm not in denial. I'm not ashamed.

But I know what that other set of photos would look like. The drunk young woman, the leather miniskirt, tight T-shirt, no bra, no shoes. That street, four A.M., late October. A bisexual punk who took pictures of dead boys. I didn't fight. My whole life since then, the only thing that matters to me is those three words.

I didn't fight.

You'll wonder what it's like to live with this. I'll tell you. It's like having a razor blade clamped between your teeth: you move your mouth too much, your tongue, you smile or talk or kiss someone, you cut yourself open. You could drown if you swallowed that much blood. You could fucking bleed to death.

3

I SHUT DOWN AFTER that. I didn't clean up my act, just went through the motions of behaving like a normal person, punched the clock, blew my paycheck at clubs and bars and bookstores. My dealings with most people had always been so ephemeral that no one took much notice when I stopped making even cursory efforts at emotional connection. I made no attempt to get a better job and little attempt to be civil to the Strand's customers. I had no interest even in getting promoted to stockroom manager. I went to work and opened packages and sorted books. I stole books as well, until store security got too tight. After a few years I got a tattoo incorporating the scrawl of scar tissue above my pubic bone into a frayed red banner with the words TOO TOUGH TO DIE emblazoned on it. I still took pictures, going to downtown gigs and occasionally selling my stuff to the *SoHo Weekly News.* When no one else would buy them, I gave my pictures to a D.C. fanzine called *Vintage Violence* in exchange for copies that I sold for a dollar a pop.

I continued to photograph things that moved me, which were mostly things that did not move. Pigeons flattened upon the curb; a corpse washed up on the shore of the East River, flesh like soft gray flannel folded into the mud; a stripper at a Broadway club sleeping between acts, her exposed breast like a red balloon where the silicone had leaked beneath the skin. I liked to think of my talent as something I'd honed to a point, a spike I could drive right into the eye of the viewer. You'd think that the 1980s vogue for decadence, for breaking taboos, would have created an audience for these pictures, but time and again they were dismissed. Too grisly, then too evocative of others' work—Mapplethorpe, Weegee, Nan Goldin's *The Ballad of Sexual Dependency*—then ultimately not evocative enough.

"It's too raw," Linda told me when, after six years, I had finally put together another portfolio, enough pictures for another book. "It's too much like being right inside someone's head."

I stared at her, the late afternoon sun in her uptown office, her gold jewelry and Armani jacket. "It *is* inside someone's head, Linda. It's the inside of my head."

She pushed the portfolio across her desk back toward me. "I know," she said. "Maybe you should show them to someone else, Cass."

I left. No one else wanted me.

Twenty years passed. I participated in a few group shows at hole-in-the-wall galleries. Now and then someone would buy one of my photos, and there was the occasional mention of *Dead Girls*, usually as a footnote to work by Cindy Sherman. When the time came, I didn't switch to digital. It wouldn't have been hard. Light is light, you just have to know how to find it, where to look for that slant of shadow, that moment when someone's eyes first open and you can't be certain if they're dead or asleep. I could have ditched my old Konica, just like I could have gotten another job or bought better clothes or gotten involved with someone.

This is what you have to understand about me: I could have changed. I didn't want to. I fucked people I'd meet at clubs: men, women. Nothing ever lasted long. Ravaged as I was, I was still good-looking enough. But I was a bad drunk. Eventually I could walk into most cafés in the East Village and watch every person hide behind a newspaper or laptop.

Despite that, in 1998 I got involved with a married woman named Christine Conti, a professor who specialized in the French Nouvelle Vague. She was thin, dark, chic, emotionally intense, a recovering alcoholic with issues. We were a good match sexually, but we argued a lot. After a while we argued constantly. I drank too much. Eventually Christine left her husband and got her own place, down near Battery Park, but it still didn't work out between us, not really. She said I wasn't a fully integrated person. I refused to quit drinking. I refused to go to an AA meeting. She refused to leave me.

Then I hit her. She called the police but then said she wouldn't press charges if I promised to get help. I suggested maybe she was the one who needed help, for staying with me, but I went. We saw a counselor. I sat there while Christine threw out words like *predatory, detached, obsessive.* The counselor came back with *dissociative amnesia, depersonalization, affective disorder.* The counselor recommended a psychiatrist, who put me on a regimen of lithium and antidepressants.

I took the medications for a week. They made me feel as though my brain had been shot full of strychnine. I refused to ever take them again. The doctor suggested other drugs, but I never went back to her.

"This is as integrated as my personality gets," I told Christine. "So get used to it or get out of here."

Christine, for whatever reason, continued to see me.

We didn't fight as much, but I still drank. My few other friends lived lives less marginal than my own. I think they kept me around as an eidolon of the sort of bleak bohemianism they'd lost—still listening to the same old music, still going to work with a hangover, still sleeping in my ratty rent-controlled apartment on a piece of plywood with a foam mattress on top.

Finally even Christine had enough. Gradually, I stopped seeing even my few remaining friends. I stopped going to clubs to hear live music. I shot fewer and fewer rolls of film and lost the few contacts I'd kept in the dwindling rock press. When I didn't have enough money to buy the photography books I wanted, I'd steal them.

Then Christine died. She'd called really early that morning and left a message: she was meeting someone for lunch at Windows on the World. Would I meet her for coffee first? We could talk things over. It might be better. It had been a long time. Maybe she was starting to get over some things. Maybe I had changed.

I hadn't changed. Not enough, anyway. I erased the message and didn't call her back. A few hours later the sirens started, the smoke. The sky was ice-blue. The phone rang, Phil Cohen screaming into my ear from Hoboken.

"Do you see it, Cass, do you see it?"

I looked out the window.

"Oh fuck," I yelled and dropped the phone.

When I stuck my head out, eddies of ash and paper were showering onto Hudson Street, the stink of jet fuel. People stared up with mouths open like they were catching snowflakes on their tongues. Shouting.

It was like being inside a breaking glass. Christine was already dead, though I didn't know that yet, didn't know she had gone down there anyway, early, thinking I might show up. Thinking I might have changed. You never know.

I lifted my face to where a single white contrail blurred into the rain of black grit and glass and ember. A charred fragment of paper fell onto the back of my hand and stuck there, damp, warm. I peeled it from my skin and read it.

For when first we

I smoothed the scrap against my palm then placed it upon my tongue. It tasted of petroleum, scorched metal. I swallowed it: a moment later began to vomit uncontrollably.

No one ever contacted me about a memorial service for her. I wouldn't have gone, anyway.

The wars began. I drank even more. For a while I saw flyers downtown with her face on them—her ex-husband and parents put them up. Every time I saw one I wanted to scream. I wanted to kill someone. Finally I began ripping them down, ignoring the angry looks I got from people on the street. Sometimes, alone in my apartment, I did scream. She was gone, it was all gone, there was nothing I could have done, nothing anyone could ever have done about anything. Why the fuck was I the only one who understood that?

That dead light that comes in late afternoon in winter, that light that makes everything look like it was cut from black ice—I could feel that light on me in the middle of summer; in the middle of the night. For a few months I got headaches, a blinding pain in my right eye, as though a spark had burned my retina. The ophthalmologist found nothing, but I could feel it, the hole left by a molten wire, a bit of ash or ember. I stared at my eye in the mirror, looking for a scar or scratched cornea, but there was nothing. It got so I had to drink three shots of bourbon just to get the nerve to pick up my camera.

I tried to forget I had ever been involved with Christine, or anyone else. Like the song goes, you can't put your arms around a memory. I was forty-eight, and my life had been over for decades. That was when Phil Cohen called me about Aphrodite Kamestos.

4

PHIL WAS AN OLD crony from the East Village who now lived in
Hoboken, a one-time drug dealer and music promoter who did
freelance work for various print magazines and websites, along with
writing a blog called Early Death. The rise of hip-hop and crap
pop had reduced his job security significantly, but his addiction
to speed had left him with admirable work habits, and he still got
me meth or black beauties when I needed them. He seldom slept,
he wrote compulsively, and he was constantly, obsessively, in touch
with anyone who might give him work. If the city were to be flattened by a nuclear bomb, Phil would be scrabbling in the ashes,
sending up smoke signals to other survivors in Hoboken. He resembled Don Knotts circa *The Incredible Mr. Limpet*, only not quite as
good-looking.

Still, Phil had always looked out for me, with mixed results. I
ran into him at a coffee shop one rainy morning in October.

"Hey hey hey. Cassandra Android, how you doing?"

"Phil. It's fucking great to be alive."

"I'm glad to hear that. Hey, look—I was going to call you.
Got a sec?"

We squeezed behind a table by the window. I sipped my coffee
and stared at him. A few months ago Phil had shaved his head. He'd
immediately realized this was a bad move and tried growing it back,

with the result that he now looked like what you'd get if Edvard Munch had painted Chia pets.

"So what's up?" I asked.

"So I think I got a job for you. I know this guy, editor for *Mojo*. That's a London music magazine. Print mag, not a webzine. He wants to do a story with photos. I thought of you, Cass. It's perfect for you, a real Scary Neary story."

"I know what *Mojo* is," I said. "Perfect for me? As in, 'Underemployed Losers and the People Who Hate Them'?"

"That's my girl! Close, very close! You know Aphrodite Kamestos?"

"Do I know her? Or do I know who she is?"

"Well, either." Phil's eyes widened. "You don't actually know her, do you? No, of course not," he said and quickly went on. "This editor, he wants to do some kind of old-time photography feature. 1950s, '60s . . . you know, Avedon, Diane Arbus, that kind of shit. I was telling him how I'd actually been up at Aphrodite Kamestos's place once. It was wild. So he wants a piece on her."

"So? You know her, you do it."

"I don't really know her," Phil admitted. "This guy she was involved with, he and I did a little business, back in the day. I still hear from him every couple of years. So I e-mailed him and asked could he maybe get me an in with Aphrodite Kamestos."

"Is she even still alive? She must be, what? A hundred?"

"Nah. Maybe seventy. But well preserved. She's got this place up in Maine, an island. There was a little commune there, that's how I got involved. I was their private dope peddler for a couple months. So I told this editor I have a contact, I could probably get someone up there again. The money's pretty good. Plus you'd be paid in pounds—good exchange rate."

I stared at my coffee and considered throwing it in his face. "Why didn't you suggest he do a story on me, Phil?"

"He said the fucking 1960s, Cass!" Phil looked hurt. "Christ, I'm trying to do you a favor!"

"Oh, right. A Phil Cohen favor—I almost forgot."

"I pitched you big time to this guy, Cass. I told him no one else on earth is as well qualified for this particular job as you are."

"Why the fuck would you say that?" I finished my coffee and pitched the cup into a trash can. "Again: why aren't you doing it?"

"I'm not a photographer!"

"So why doesn't this guy send a staff photographer?"

"Because I guess Aphrodite wanted someone they've never heard of. She's, like, crazy or paranoid or something. She wants an unknown."

He pinched his lower lip between thumb and forefinger. I started to laugh.

"An unknown? What'd she say? 'I need a total unknown—I know, let's get Cassandra Neary!'"

"Pretty much."

"Shit."

I sat and said nothing. After a moment, Phil shrugged. "Look, I was just trying to help you out some. I mean, she specifically asked for you, God knows why. But it could be an interesting gig. Remember how they used to say if you tipped the country on its side, everything loose would roll into California? Well, it's like they tipped it up again, only now everything that was *still* loose rolled back up into Maine. And these islands—Cass, it's your kind of place. 'The old weird America'—this is, like, the new weird America. You oughta think about it."

I sighed, then looked at him. "Really? She really asked for me?"

Phil shifted in his seat, staring at his cell phone. "Yeah," he said after a moment. "She did. Go figure."

"Okay. I'll think about it."

Phil glanced at his watch. "You've got, uh, five minutes."

"*What?*"

"I told the editor I'd call him back by three—three his time. Five hour difference. And it's almost ten."

"But I can't—I mean, how'd you even know you'd run into me?"

"I didn't. I was gonna call you—hey, I swear it!"

"But—Jesus, Phil. What, has this editor told her I'm coming?"

He shook his head. "No. I did. I promised I'd send you. Listen, don't think about it, okay? Just say yes, I can set it up. You got a license, right? A credit card? You're not a total fucking Luddite, right? You can still rent a car and drive?"

"Yeah." I gazed brooding out at the street. The rain had turned fallen leaves and blown newspapers to gray sludge. "Shit. Can they give me an advance?"

Phil looked as though I'd asked him to cook a baby.

"Well, is there a kill fee?"

"I'll get you a kill fee. If it doesn't go down, Cass, I'll pay your kill fee out of my own goddam pocket, how's that?"

"Tell me again why you're doing this?"

Phil ran a hand across his stubbled scalp. "Aw, man. You know, Cass, you are so fucking hardassed, you know that? I really did think it would be a great gig for you. The legendary Aphrodite Kamestos, the semilegendary Cassandra Neary—I mean, you could get close to her, you know that? I saw her place, that island. What you always used to talk about, all that bleak shit you like? Well, this is it. All these rocks, and the ocean, the sky."

He sighed. "And, I dunno, there was something about her. When I met you—you reminded me of her. You know?"

"The forgotten Cassandra Neary," I said. "The never-fucking-happened Cassandra Neary."

"Forget it." He glared at me, then said, "You know, I should know better by now. To try and do you a fucking favor." He picked up his phone. "I'll find someone else."

I shook my head. "I'll do it, I'll do it. I need the money. I need to get out of town." I glanced outside again. "So are you going to call me, or what?"

He opened the cell phone. "I'll call this editor. Then I'll call this other guy in Maine. I'll get him to set stuff up, bring you out in a boat or something. Then I'll call you."

"Well, that's suitably vague." I stood. "So I guess I'll wait for you to call me, or for some guy to do some stuff, or something."

Phil nodded. "Great. Hey, aren't you going to thank me?"

"I'll thank you when I get paid, how's that? I'll take you to dinner."

I leaned over to kiss his unkempt scalp.

"Thanks, Phil," I said, and walked home.

5

YOU'LL THINK I WAS leaving the city because I needed to escape from grief, or guilt, or fear: all the reasons people fled in those years, and a lot of them escaped to the same place I was heading.

But the truth is that when Christine had called me that morning, it had been almost two years since we'd last spoken. She couldn't bear the sound of my voice, she'd told me: it was like talking to a dead person. Or no, she went on, it was like that nickname Phil Cohen had given me. It was like talking to an android, something that mimicked human speech and affect but wasn't actually alive.

"The terrible thing is, I really loved you, Cass," she'd said on that last message. "I love you now."

I knew she wanted me to meet her, to say I loved her too. I knew she was giving me a chance to save her—to save myself, she would have said—but I couldn't lie. I can't lie about that kind of stuff. This isn't a virtue. It's a flaw, just as my seeing the true world is not a gift but a terrible thing. I've lived my entire life expecting the worst, knowing it will happen, seeing it happen. Making it happen, people used to think, then photographing it and making other people see it too.

People think they want the truth. But the truth is that people want to be reassured that it's only *there* that the horror lies, *there* on the other side of the television, the computer screen, the world. No one wants to look on the charred remains of a human corpse lying at their feet. No one wants to look on unalloyed grief and horror and loss. I don't always want to myself, but I won't deny that I do, and I won't deny that my photos show you what's really there. I can't look away.

6

I HAD VACATION TIME saved up at the Strand, so I gave notice that I'd be gone for a few weeks. They were surprised, but they also seemed relieved that I was doing something normal—it was the first time I'd taken off in about five years. I spent most of my last days there ferreting through the stacks, looking for anything on Kamestos.

I didn't find anything, except for that one iconic photograph of her in an Aperture volume on twentieth-century photographers, a black-and-white portrait taken by her husband, the poet Stephen Haselton, shortly after their marriage. I knew there were other images: a pencil drawing by Jean Cocteau that was on the dust jacket of the original edition of *Mors*, a sketch by Brion Gysin that looked like Jean-Paul Marat's death mask.

I assumed that when I googled her, I'd learn more. There was some stuff online, including Susan Sontag's repudiation of *Mors*, but little in the way of biographical information except for a thumbnail entry on Wikipedia. Despite her name, Aphrodite was as American as I was, a third-generation Greek who'd grown up in Chicago. But there were no details about her childhood, and only a fleeting mention of her marriage to Haselton.

I don't know anyone who looked less like her namesake. Aphrodite Kamestos was beautiful in the way a violent storm is beautiful, if you're watching it from a safe distance. In his photo,

Haselton must have caught her unawares. Her head is half-turned, her dark hair falling back from her face, her lips parted and eyebrows slightly raised. Her eyes are startlingly black against her white skin, and the light glances off her cheekbones. The gaze she shoots at the camera is direct yet impenetrable. She looks unafraid, but also unguarded, caught in that fraction of a second before she could compose her face into welcome or annoyance or desire or attack.

It was a strikingly beautiful face, but it didn't make me think of the Goddess of Love. It made me think of Medusa, someone whose beauty would be turned upon anyone stupid enough to mess with her. That was the power of the photograph. It didn't make you wonder what happened to her. It made you wonder what happened to the guy who took the picture. It's almost anticlimactic to know that he killed himself in 1976.

My Google search turned up some of her own images as well, but that was such a depressing experience I wished I hadn't bothered. I hate looking at bad reproductions of great photographs, and these online images were uniformly lousy. Generation loss—that's what happens when you endlessly reproduce a photographic image. You lose authenticity, the quality deteriorates in each subsequent generation that's copied from the original negative, and the original itself decays with time, so that every new image is a more degraded version of what you started with. Same thing with analog recordings. After endless reproduction, you end up with nothing but static and hiss.

This doesn't happen so much with digital imaging, but what I found online had been scanned from a 1970 pirate reprint of Kamestos's only two books, *Mors* and *Deceptio Visus,* first published in the late 1950s. Anyone who picked up that pirate volume could be forgiven for wondering how Aphrodite's photos ever saw the light of day. Unfortunately, those horrible reproductions were what had filtered onto the web. They were nothing like the images in the original editions of *Mors* and *Deceptio Visus*—I knew that because I owned both books—and those, of course, would be nothing like the original prints.

Her greatest images were vistas—islands, mountains. Highly
saturated blues and violets and magentas detailing an impossibly beautiful, distant archipelago that resembled a landscape by
Magritte: elusive, irrecoverable. I couldn't imagine those places were
real.

Only of course they were—the pictures were taken in 1956,
decades before computers made it possible to twist the world into
a pretty shape. That was the year Kodak started hyping the Type C
color process. Type C enabled photographers to produce their own
color negs without relying so heavily on a lab, and there was some
interesting color work done then by people like Nina Leen and
Brian Brake. I don't know if Kamestos was using Type C, but she
would have been picking up on some of the press it was generating.
You can see in her husband's photo how those eyes still burned,
though her hands looked as though they could handle a garrote as
easily as a camera.

It was a suspicion fed when *Mors* appeared: a catalog of places
where terrible things had happened. Suicide, a murder, sexual torture. These weren't like Weegee's crime scenes, or Bourke-White's
photos of Buchenwald. Kamestos's pictures lacked immediacy or
historical import; their sense of transgression was visceral because
it was so detached. When it first appeared, *Mors* was dismissed as
a form of malign spirit photography, and the 1970 pirate volume
only made things worse, with its over-the-top intro by Kenneth
Anger. It would be decades before that book's influence was ac-
knowledged by people like Sally Mann or Joel-Peter Witkin. And
me, of course. But no one was listening to me.

The thought of seeing those original photographs is what set
my heart pumping. More than the thought of money or escaping
the city. More even than the notion that Aphrodite Kamestos had
asked specifically for me, or that if I went up there, I might shoot
some decent work myself again.

Though I'll admit, I was curious—more than curious—about
what the hell had happened to her. A nervous breakdown? Failure

of nerve? Failed marriage? Her husband had been a minor poet, a kind of fringe person in the Beat movement, and my understanding was that he'd been gay. Kamestos met Haselton in 1955, and they married just a few weeks later. As a wedding gift, his wealthy father gave the couple a house on an island off the coast of Maine.

And that is where I was now headed: Paswegas Island.

I'd never known its name before. The thought gave me a weird feeling. It was like I was going off on some strange, creepy pilgrimage; like a Nabokov fan setting out to find the motels where Humbert Humbert slept with Lolita.

Because Paswegas was where Aphrodite shot the dreamscapes in *Deceptio Visus*. It was a place I'd thought and dreamed about for almost thirty years, a place I'd never quite believed was real. You know how you can look at a painting or picture and wish you could walk into it and just disappear? That's what I'd always wanted to do with those photos. Now I'd have my chance.

The night after I ran into Phil, I called my father. We hadn't spoken for a while, and as always, I could tell he was relieved to hear my voice: I wasn't dead.

"Cassandra. Good to hear from you. Everything all right?"

I told him about my conversation with Phil. "Didn't you used to go up there?" I asked. "Fishing or something?"

"Sure. Fishing and hunting. Up in the Allagash. I used to go with your grandfather. We'd stop in Freeport in the middle of the night and ring the bell at the little L.L. Bean store, and they'd let us in so we could buy our gear. Beautiful place, Maine. I haven't been since your mother and I made a few trips down east," he said, his voice suddenly sad. "That was before you were born."

"Do you know how to get there? I'm renting a car."

"Maine?" I heard the rattle of ice in his highball glass. "Sure. Drive to the New Hampshire border. Then turn right."

We spoke a little longer, catching up. Catching up with him, I mean. I had nothing else to report.

"Well, Cassandra, I wish you luck," he said at last. "Anything comes up, call Ken Wilburn. He's in South Salem now. Here, I'll give you his number—"

I wrote it down then said good-bye. Two days later I received a check for a thousand dollars, along with a note.

BUY YOURSELF SOME GUM BOOTS. LOVE, DAD

I blew a big chunk of the money on a pair of Hedi Slimane drainpipe jeans. I do have my little luxuries, and I figured the investment would pay off if I actually sold a story. The rest I stashed in my wallet.

That night I took out my copies of *Deceptio Visus* and *Mors*. I'd bought them cheap in a used bookstore in the city in 1978, when Kamestos's reputation was in deep decline. Now I thumbed through *Deceptio Visus*, hoping to find some hint as to what the island might be like in real life, or where.

It was like trying to get a compass reading from a postcard. So I went back online, poking around till I hit **www.maineaway .com, Your News for The Paswegas Peninsula And Beyond!** The site banner showed a scroll of cloudless sky and a windjammer racing across a cobalt sea. There were lots of pictures of romping Labrador retrievers, autumn foliage, children eating corn on the cob and lobster, snow-dusted spruce, healthy-looking couples in canoes, loons, and moose.

The headlines told a different story. A rash of teen suicides; support groups for people addicted to Oxy-C and Vicodin; two big heroin busts. Another bomb scare at the high school. Another confirmed case of West Nile virus. A missing persons alert for someone named Martin Graves, last seen August 29. The police log listed three arrests for domestic assault and another for possession of crack cocaine. A body washed up in Burnt Harbor had been identified as a fisherman lost at sea the previous winter. More bodies were missing from another boat presumed lost in a recent storm. There was also a feature, "The Facts About Bear Baiting," and notice of a Benefit Bean Supper for the Prout family, who had just lost their home to a fire. Someone was still looking for her husband, last seen driving home to Machias after work at Wal-Mart a month before.

So much for Vacationland, I thought, and went to bed.

7

IT WAS THE SECOND week of November; the beginning of the Maine winter. I was naive enough to think it was still fall.

For a couple of months I'd saved a small stash of crystal meth. Becoming an addict takes a certain amount of organization to dedicate yourself to your need to get high. In this as in other matters I'd lacked ambition. Crank was intermittently fun and useful, but I never could make a serious commitment to it. The afternoon before I left, I picked up my Rent-a-Wreck then went home and packed a map, the directions Phil had given me, a few clothes and my copies of *Deceptio Visus* and *Mors*, my old Konica, a few cassette tapes. I went to the fridge and opened the freezer, took out the small Ziploc bag of crystal and another, larger bag. In this was a piece of paper with blurred writing on it—JULY 2001—along with two plastic canisters of Tri-X film. The date was when I'd bought them; it was also the last time I'd done any serious shooting. They went alongside my camera in the chewed-up leather satchel I'd had since high school.

Even traveling light, there was room for more. Problem was, I didn't have much more. I had an old computer, but no laptop, no cell phone. No digital camera or iPod. I never had much spare cash, plus I just hated the stuff on principle: it made everything too easy.

"You're a fucking Luddite Looney Tune," Phil said once. "You got a microwave in that dump of yours?"

I shook my head. "I don't eat."

Now I went over to my old vinyl records and pulled out a portfolio wedged between *The Idiot* and *Fear and Whiskey*. It was filled with plastic sleeves holding dozens of black-and-white 8x10s. Not the pictures from *Dead Girls;* the stuff I'd been working on after that, the photos Linda Kalman had turned down. I still couldn't bring myself to look at any of them, just stared at the cover sheet, a white page with my name typed on it and the title I'd given the collection: *Hard To Be Human Again.* I put it back, turned, and found my bottle of Jack Daniel's. Very early the next morning, while it was still dark and I was still drunk, I began to drive north.

The buzz from the Jack Daniel's got me about an hour out of the city before it wore off. Just past the wooded exurban badlands where I'd grown up, I pulled over and snorted the remaining blue-white crystals from my stash, then shot back onto the interstate.

At some point I must've stopped for gas, but I didn't have another fully conscious thought until I looked up, blinking, and saw brilliant sun, the span of a bridge before me, and a broad, glittering blue sheet of water below. A sign at the highway's edge read LEAVING NEW HAMPSHIRE. I was halfway over the bridge, reading another sign—WELCOME TO MAINE, THE WAY LIFE SHOULD BE— before I began to wonder what had happened to Connecticut and Massachusetts.

That was my crossing into Maine. What little thought I'd ever given to the place was faintly contemptuous: Vacationland, snow. I didn't understand yet how this place works on you, how it splinters your sensorium. All I knew was that it was midmorning of a November day, and I was fucking freezing.

Somehow it had never crossed my mind that it might be cold. Back in the city it was Indian summer. Here it felt like midwinter. Even with the heat cranked, the little Ford Taurus exuded only a thread of warmth that smelled of antifreeze. The rear windows wouldn't close completely, and frigid air whistled through.

By the time I was fifty miles north of Portland my hands were numb. I pulled over and rummaged through my bag, pulled on a long-sleeved T-shirt, a moth-eaten black cashmere sweater, my battered motorcycle jacket. I replaced my sneakers with my old black cowboy boots. This was my entire wardrobe, except for socks and underwear, another T-shirt, and a backup pair of black jeans nearly indistinguishable from the ones I'd blown a small fortune on.

I had no gloves, no boots save my ancient Tony Lamas, no winter coat. Over the years, I'd spent a few Thanksgivings with my aunt's family in Boston, chilly days, nights warmed by firelight and Irish Mist. I figured Maine would be like that. I was wrong.

I drove for another hour before forcing myself to stop and eat at a convenience store. A table full of old men in flannel shirts and Carhartt jackets glanced up when I entered, then returned to low conversation. There was a sheet of orange poster board behind the cash register, two columns neatly written in Magic Marker:

Jeff Stonestreet	Buck
Missy Weed	Buck
Brandon Johnston	Doe
Barbara Johnston	Buck
Wallace Tun	Doe

"Hunting season?" I asked as I handed over my money.

The girl behind the counter stared at me. "That's right."

I bought a pair of heavy yellow work gloves. They made my hands feel clumsy and thumbless, and they weren't even very warm. But they were better than nothing. I bought a beer, too, then started for the door. There were a bunch of notices tacked to it: snowplowing, firewood, Little Munchkins child care, along with numerous photocopies for Lost Cats. Beneath the missing cats, someone had taped another photocopy, of a young man in a Nike T-shirt and woolen watch cap.

HAVE YOU SEEN MARTIN GRAVES?
LAST SEEN AUGUST 29 SHAKER HARBOR
REWARD FOR INFORMATION
PLEASE CALL 247-9141

I returned to the car, sat inside and drank my beer, watching as two guys in orange vests wrestled a buck from their pickup and weighed it on a hook outside the store.

"Supposed to have snow up to Calais," said one of them.

His friend lit a cigarette. "Good place for it."

I set my empty bottle on the ground and drove off.

The road began to veer east. After two wrong turns, I realized the MapQuest directions Phil had given me were useless. I pulled over and opened my map.

On the page, the road appeared to hug the coast. In reality the sea seemed distant and ghostly, hoving in and out of sight like mist. Now and then I saw the raw wood scaffolding of a McMansion-in-progress, its mammoth exoskeleton dwarfing the trailers and modular homes beside it, or mobile-home churches with signs reading DON'T WAIT FOR 6 STRONG MEN TO TAKE YOU TO CHURCH. TO BE AL-MOST SAVED IS TO BE TOTALLY LOST.

But after a while, even these reminders of the encroaching world disappeared. I finally found the turnoff and passed through a town consisting of a general store with a single gas pump, a shuttered antique shop, and an abandoned gas station. Two boys in baggy pants and T-shirts were riding a Toro lawn mower down the middle of the street. The boys pulled over to let me by, and I turned onto a pocked road with a sign that said PASWEGAS COUNTY LINE and another marked BURNT HARBOR.

That was when I really began to feel like I was driving off the end of the earth. Now, at last, there was the ocean. The coast fell away and the sea opened like a huge blue eye, lashed with black islands and rocky outcroppings. I switched the car radio on and picked up a weak signal that seemed to come and go with the waves, an alternative station playing snatches of odd music, requests, pleas for information about lost pets.

And that light! It gave a merciless clarity to everything, clapboards the color of dirty snow, trailers banked with trash bags, pyramids of lobster traps hauled out for the winter. Spruce and pines that looked like they'd been knapped from flint. The orange flare of a hunter on the horizon, the woods behind him black, endless.

It was as if layers of ash had been blown away until the true sky was revealed, a sky so pure a blue that it no longer seemed a color at all but an emotion, a desolation that tipped over into joy. The cold was like that too, the numbness in my gloved hands no longer something I felt but something I was, a character trait like stubbornness or generosity. I could see the peninsula before me, a ragged, four-fingered hand thrusting into the Atlantic. I hunched over the steering wheel, frozen but exhilarated, and headed toward the sea.

It was nearly four by now; nightfall. Burnt Harbor, the village at the tip of the peninsula—that was where I was supposed to find the guy who would bring me over to Paswegas Island. Everett Moss, the harbormaster. I didn't own a cell phone, so I drove until I found a gas station with an ancient pay phone outside. I hunched against the peeling vinyl siding and tried to keep my teeth from chattering as I fed coins into the slot.

There was another torn flyer taped beside the pay phone. No photo on this one, just the words HAVE YOU SEEN MARTIN GRAVES? LAST SEEN AUGUST 29, SHAKER HARBOR, PLEASE CALL WITH ANY INFORMATION. I shoved in the last coin and prayed the harbormaster was still around. The wind roared up from the sea so loudly that I could barely hear when someone answered.

"Is this Everett Moss?" I shouted. The phone reception was for shit.

"Hay-lo." The voice was brusque but cheerful. "Yes, it is."

"This is Cassandra Neary. Phil Cohen spoke to you about taking me over to Paswegas this afternoon?"

"Oh yes."

"I'll be there in about half an hour. I'm in—" I craned my neck. "Well, I don't know where I am, exactly, somewhere past Bealesville. Collinstown, I guess this is. So maybe fifteen miles away?"

"Oh yes, Collinstown, that's about fifteen miles. Well, that's very good, but I can't take you out today."

"What? Why not?" Cold and desperation made my voice crack. "I'll be there in what? Half an hour?"

"Well yes, but I'm afraid I couldn't do it then, neither. It'll be dark. Could probably do it first thing tomorrow. How's that?"

"Tomorrow?" I shivered, staring to where the ocean darkened from indigo to scorched steel. "Jesus! I don't even know where I am! Is there a place to stay between here and Burnt Harbor?"

"Well, yes there is," Moss boomed genially. "You just keep on heading this way, and when you get to just before the bridge, you'll see there on your right the Lighthouse Motel. He's open year round. Then first thing tomorrow, you come down here to the harbor and we'll get you taken care of. Say, six o'clock. All right?"

"What if he's not—"

"All right then!"

Click.

I stormed back to the car. My little by-blow of crank had long worn off. I wasn't hungry or tired yet, but I knew the crash was coming, and I didn't want to be stuck in a rented Ford Taurus when it did. That crystalline blue sky was now nearly black. Wind rattled the bare trees and sent dead leaves skittering across the parking lot.

I clambered back into the car and drove on. Once I crossed the bridge spanning an inlet of Hagman's Bay, I was officially on the Paswegas Peninsula.

Even in the near dark, I felt a wild sense of space, of sky, the smells of salt and balsam and rotting fish. Wood smoke pooled like fog above the marshes. I peered vainly through the twilight for any sign of the Lighthouse Motel. It was hard enough to see any houses, and when I did spot one it wasn't reassuring—a small, raised ranch house with what looked like a dog hanging above the garage door. That was weird enough, but it got weirder when I passed the next house and saw *three* dead dogs hanging alongside a shed. I slowed the car to get a better look.

They weren't dogs but coyotes. Big ones too. I decided that if the Lighthouse didn't show up in the next five minutes, I was going to turn around and drive back to Manhattan.

And then it appeared on a spur of land overlooking a small harbor, your basic American motel circa 1962. A one-story mock-up of a lighthouse, minus the light, stood beside a neat white clapboard building with green shutters, lamps lit within, a neon OFFICE sign. Three cars were parked in front of a row of attached motel units. A sign hung from a denuded maple.

> LIGHTHOUSE MOTEL
> BEST RATES IN MAINE ALWAYS
> YOUR HOST MERRILL LIBBY
>
> NO PETS NO GUNS FREE COFFEE
> VACANCY

That last word was the only one I cared about. I parked alongside the office, pulled my leather jacket tight against the cold, and went inside.

It was about what I expected, a room furnished in Early Knotty Pine, well-worn but clean. I couldn't tell if someone had repeatedly spilled coffee on the carpet or if this was a design decision that had never caught on in the lower forty-seven. Still, it was warm. Heat blasted from a propane monitor. I was so cold, I would have slept on that carpet. I hoped I wouldn't have to.

There was a little alcove at one end of the room, and here in a swivel chair a teenage girl, maybe fifteen, sat hunched over a computer. I drew close enough to catch a glimpse of a screen full of IM dialog bubbles. Then the girl looked up. A heavyset gothy kid with cropped hair dyed black, black-rimmed eyes, white skin beneath a flaking layer of pinkish foundation. She had a stud beneath her lower lip and what appeared to be a bunch of three-penny nails stuck through one earlobe. She wore a necklace made of the tabs from soda cans laced together on a leather thong and interspersed with bits of sea glass, a flannel shirt over jeans wide enough to double as body bags, disintegrating low-top sneakers.

She smiled shyly. That smile made her look about eight, that and the pink hearts she'd drawn on her wrist.

"You got a room?" I asked. "The sign says Vacancy."

"Oh, yeah—sorry."

She clicked off the IM screen and began rummaging around the desk. "We have *lots* of rooms. Um, non-smoking only, that okay?"

"Sure."

She pulled out a clunky old credit card machine and handed me a form. "You visiting someone?"

"Yeah. Nice piercing."

"Hey, thanks!" She was cute, in an early Exene Cervenka, bad hair kind of way. "I like your jacket. It looks . . . real."

"It is." I filled in the form and handed it back to her.

She read it then looked at me in surprise. "You're from New York?"

"Yeah. You'd fit right in there."

"I wish. I would love to go to New York."

"Yeah? Maybe I could fit you in the trunk on my way back." She laughed, then froze.

"Mackenzie! I told you, cash only!" A bleating, high-pitched voice echoed from the other side of the room. "No credit cards, sorry—tear it up! Tear it up!"

I've heard that pigs are among the most intelligent mammals. Seeing Merrill Libby, I could believe this was true. A short, bloated man who looked like he'd been carved from a slab of salt pork, he wore brown Dickie overalls and a flannel shirt that billowed around him like a deflated plaid balloon. He had small bright dark eyes, and his cheeks were an unhealthy pink against his white skin.

I gave the girl a quick sideways look, raising my eyebrow in sympathy, then turned back.

He waddled up beside the girl and elbowed her out of the way. "I told you, cash only," he repeated. "Go to your room."

Mackenzie started for the door. Her father stared at me balefully.

"All I want is a room." I pulled out two twenties and slid them across the counter. "Okay?"

He took the money and stuck it in a cashbox, keeping his cold little eyes on me the whole time.

"No smoking," he said. "Checkout's eleven. There are no telephones in any of the rooms."

By now I was just hoping there'd be heat and a flush toilet. I waited as he turned and began checking a row of keys. Just outside the doorway, Mackenzie stood and watched, her face half-shadowed so that all I could see was the glint of metal along one ear.

Poor kid, I thought. *If he was my father, I'd hammer nails in my head too.*

Merrill handed me a key. "Checkout time—"

"Eleven," I said. "One question—is there any place to eat around here?"

"This time of night?" Merrill looked as though I'd asked for directions to the local Satanic Hall. "No."

I wanted to point out it was only five o'clock, then recalled that I had not, in fact, seen anything resembling a restaurant for at least two hours. I hadn't seen anything resembling a motel, either, and all the B&Bs I'd passed were shut for the winter.

"That's okay," I said. "Thanks."

I went back outside and got my stuff from the car. The wind had picked up; my cheeks stung from the cold and salt mist. I hurried toward my room—Number 2—slammed the key into the lock and kicked the door open.

Inside was no warmer than out, but at least there was no wind. I shut the door and put on a light then located the electric heater, a pre-Sputnik deal with exposed heating coils.

Within seconds the coils began to glow. I huddled over them and warmed my hands and face until I felt like I could move without cracking. I did a quick room inspection—more knotty pine, a single bed with protective plastic beneath thin white sheets, a hundred-watt bulb in a lamp shaped like a lighthouse, Sears Kenmore television with rabbit ears. Propped atop the pillow was a small hand-lettered sign—

> Please DO NOT LEAVE
> Your Disgusting Germy Used Tissues
> Under The Pillows
> Thank You Your Host Merrlll Libby

I had just tossed the card across the room when there was a knock. I opened the door. Mackenzie stood in the dark, wearing a ratty wool poncho.

"Hi." She gave me that sweet shy smile, then glanced over her shoulder. "I just wanted to tell you—what he said about nowhere to eat? He's wrong—there is a place. Down in Burnt Harbor, on the waterfront."

"Wait, come in," I said. "It's freezing."

"Thanks." She stepped inside, and I shut the door. "It's warm in here, anyway."

"It'd be warmer if you left the heat on."

"Huh?" Her brown eyes widened. "You'd be paying to heat an empty room all winter."

"Right." I hadn't thought of that. "So there's a place in Burnt Harbor?"

"The Good Tern—it's right on the main street, you can't miss it. The only street," she added. "There by the water. The food is really, really good. They open for breakfast at five." She looked around and her gaze fell on my bag. "So you're really from New York? That must be really, really cool."

"Really, really different from here, I can say that." I rubbed my hands above the heating coils. "You work for your father? No child labor laws in these parts?"

Mackenzie shrugged. "Only part time. I go to the voc school up by Naskeag Harbor. I'm studying culinary arts. I want to be a chef. Or maybe make my jewelry and sell it."

"Good idea. You could come back here and open a restaurant."

"No way. I'm going to New York. Or San Francisco. I hear that's a sweet place."

I looked at her, the pink heart on her hand and the piercings that hadn't healed all that well; the way she stared at my leather jacket, like it was a shiny new bike or whatever the hell kids dreamed of up here—a snow shovel? I leaned forward to peer at her necklace, the sea glass glinting green and blue between the aluminum tabs. "Did you make that out of old cans?"

She fingered it and nodded. "Yeah. I like to do stuff like that."

She held out her arm to display more tabs and sea glass threaded with wishbones and broken seashells and dirty gray twine—beautiful and strange, like something you'd find buried in the sand. For a moment I thought she was going to say something else.

Instead, she went to the door. She looked at me, her face half-shadowed, and gave me that sweet kid's smile.

"Okay, bye," she said and left.

For a few minutes I sat on the bed and tried to warm up. The protective plastic crackled noisily every time I moved. I was afraid if I waited too long I'd end up stuck to the plastic, stuck here all night, hungry but still too buzzed to sleep.

Plus, I needed a drink. I peeled off my jacket and held it above the heater until the room started to smell a little bit too much like me, slung it back on and went outside.

I headed for my car, walking past Room 1. Without warning the door flew open. I ducked as a man stumbled onto the sidewalk. When he saw me, he backed up, smacking his head against the door.

"Hey, watch it," I said and edged away from him.

He rubbed his head and glared at me. "Goddamit, that hurts. What, are you lost?"

"No. I was leaving my room. I didn't know anyone else was here."

"Yeah, well you're sure acting like no one else is here."

He stared at me—a tall, lanky guy about fifteen years younger than me, with shoulder-length dark brown hair, a wide mouth, aquiline nose, wire-rimmed glasses. He wore corduroy jeans and a suede jacket over a white shirt, none of them very clean. After a moment he shoved his glasses against his nose and gave me a wry smile. It made him look younger but also oddly familiar. I had a spike of amphetamine panic. Could this guy know me?

Unexpectedly he laughed. There was nothing overtly sinister about that, but I felt such a powerful rush of fear—not just fear but genuine terror—that everything went dark: not just dark outside, but dark inside my skull, like there'd been an abrupt disconnect between my mind and my retinas. The only thing I can compare it to is what I felt the one time I shot heroin: a black wave that buries you before you even know it's there.

Damage. This guy reeked of it.

I backed away and glanced down at his hand. A scar ran from his middle finger to his wrist, as though someone had tried writing on his flesh with a knife. When I lifted my head, he was still staring at me.

"You don't belong here," he said.

His eyes were such a pale brown they were almost yellow. The left iris held a tiny starburst just above the pupil, emerald-green, rayed with black. It made me think of the trajectory a bullet makes through thick glass; it made me think of that scar on his hand, and how I'd seen it, him, somewhere.

But I'd never seen this man before. I knew that. My brain is hardwired for recalling bodies, eyes, skin; I absorb them the way emulsion paper absorbs light. I would no more have forgotten that scar, or that iris's imploded green, than I would have forgotten my own face in the mirror. I continued to stare at him, until he began to lift his hand.

Without a word I darted past him toward my car. He took a step after me, stopped. I jumped into the Taurus and locked the doors, fired up the engine and the headlights. The windshield was glazed with frozen mist; I waited for it to defrost then peered out.

The man was gone. My hands were shaking so much the steering wheel trembled. I definitely needed to eat something and then try to sleep. My car was halfway out of the parking lot before I realized I'd left my bag in the room.

I swore and glanced back at the motel office. The lights were on, and I could see a figure seated in the alcove—Mackenzie—and another, taller, figure: the guy I'd just bumped into. I sat in the car and waited until he stepped out of the office and walked over to an older gray Volvo sedan, watched as he drove off. Then I hopped out and ran back inside my motel room. I grabbed my bag and *Deceptio Visus*—I wanted something to hide behind while I ate. No more small talk with the natives. I headed back outside to my car then stopped.

The door of the room next to mine was ajar—in the confusion of running into me, my neighbor had forgotten to close it. As I watched, a gust of wind pushed it open another inch.

I hesitated then stepped over and placed my hand on the doorknob.

"Hello?" The hairs on my arms rose as I thought of that green-shot eye. "Anyone there?"

No reply. I pushed the door open.

The light was on and the room empty. I looked back quickly to make sure no one saw me. Then I went inside.

You might think I'd never done something like this before. In fact it was exactly the sort of thing I did.

It was a room identical to mine. Clothes were tossed over a chair. On the bed was a computer case, open, with a laptop inside. A few books were stacked on top of the laptop, along with a small notebook. I picked up the notebook, flipped through lists of names, phone numbers, dates.

No interest there. I tossed it aside then peered into the computer case.

Pens, a calculator, cell phone charger; a thick yellow Rite Aid One Hour Processing envelope stuffed with photos and a CD-ROM. I took the envelope and walked to the window, angling myself so I could see outside without being seen, and looked through the photos.

They were color pictures, overexposed 4x6s. There were two copies of each. Hard to tell how recent they were. I guessed maybe a few years old, though some people still use film and transfer the images to CD-ROM. The photos showed some kind of family gathering—a brilliant sunny day, women in pastel and tropical-bright dresses, men in light-colored jackets or shirtsleeves. A white-haired woman in a broad-brimmed red straw hat held a champagne flute. Two dark-haired women who looked like sisters cocked their heads and pursed their lips in an effort to look disapprovingly at the photographer. A big dog ran past a crowded table, a black blur, its tongue hanging from its mouth.

Everyone looked happy, even the dog. A wedding? No one takes pictures of funerals.

But there was no bride or groom that I could see; no wedding cake or birthday cake or anniversary cake; no presents. A few darting children in the background, but not enough to herald a kid's party. Round tables where people sat and smiled for the camera, their faces shadowed by big striped umbrellas, yellow and green.

Pink blossoms strewn across some of the tables, wine glasses, wine bottles.

Most of the photos were like this. I'd almost reached the last of them before I found one in which I could pick out the figure of the man I'd nearly run into. He stood in a group of men and women, all dark haired, though sunlight and distance made it impossible to discern any other resemblance between them. All were nearly as tall as he was, and there was a similarity in the way they held themselves—squinting, shoulders canted slightly to one side, as though flinching from something—the light? a sudden cold wind?—that made it seem as though they might be siblings or cousins and not just friends. I stared at the photo for a moment, glanced out the window at the parking lot, then looked at the last two pictures.

Both showed the man I'd seen. In one he was sitting alone at a table. Light filtered through a canopy of leaves and splattered his face yellow and black. He seemed brooding, distracted, though maybe he was just bored or tired. Behind him the hindquarters of the black dog could just be glimpsed, its tail an arrow aimed at the man's outstretched legs.

The last photo was different.

It was the same man in the same chair at the same table. The black dog was gone. Now the man's head was turned, looking at someone out of camera range. He'd moved just enough that sun fell full on his face, which was bright but not overlit. His hair had blown back a little from his forehead; his face was split with a smile so rapturous it seemed contorted. It made me uncomfortable, and I looked away.

Then I looked again. I tilted the picture back and forth, as though the unseen thing he stared at might materialize; waiting for that same sense of damage I'd felt outside to rise from the image like a striking cobra.

But it didn't.

I frowned.

What was he looking at? His lover? His child? The black dog? It wasn't just that no one had ever looked at me like that. I'd never seen anyone look at anything like that. His expression changed everything. I went back to the first photo and skimmed through them all again, as though they might now make sense, offer up a shared secret like a shell prised open with a knife.

Of course that didn't happen. It would never happen. I knew that. They were nothing but a bunch of snapshots of someone else's party. I would never know who these people were, or where they were. I would never know what the man saw, or who he was, or why he was in the motel room next to mine.

Only he wasn't in the room next to mine. I was in *his* room. I glanced out the window. The parking lot was still empty. I slipped the pictures back into the yellow envelope, retaining a dupe of the man with that rapturous smile. Then I stuck the envelope back into the computer case and left. I made sure the door closed tight behind me, made sure no one saw me leave. I got into my car and started it, sat for a minute and waited, just in case someone appeared who might have seen me emerge from Room I.

No one did. I turned the heat and defroster up to high and shoved the photograph into my copy of *Deceptio Visus*. I waited until a black streak ate through the frozen condensation on the window-sill, and I could see into the darkness that surrounded me. Then I drove slowly away from the motel, out onto the main road and down the narrow spine of the Paswegas Peninsula, until I reached Burnt Harbor.

8

THE VILLAGE CONSISTED OF a handful of buildings perched on a rocky ledge overlooking the harbor. Maybe it was beautiful in the daytime, in the middle of summer. Now, in the early dark of a November night, it was as desolate as the Lower East Side had been once upon a time. For that reason the place felt—well, not exactly welcoming, but familiar. Like walking into a room full of strangers in a foreign country then hearing them speak my native language.

. . . all that bleak shit you like? Well, this is it, Phil had told me.

He was right.

There wasn't much there. DownEast Marine Supplies, a lobster shack that was closed for the winter. A street lamp cast a milky gleam onto a broken sidewalk. On the hillside above the harbor, lights glowed in scattered houses. There was a small crescent-shaped gravel beach and a long stone pier that thrust into the water, dinghies tied up alongside it. Farther out a few lobster boats and a solitary sailboat. It smelled like a working harbor: that is, bad. I looked for a place that might be the harbormaster's office—a building, a sign—but found nothing.

There was no mistaking the Good Tern, though—a tumble-down structure a few yards from the pier, gray shingled, with a torn plastic banner that read BUDWEISER WELCOMES HUNTERS beneath a weathered painting of a seagull. There were pickups out front, along with a few Subarus, and I could glimpse more cars parked around back. The lid of a dumpster banged noisily in the wind.

I parked, stuck the copy of *Deceptio Visus* into my bag, and got out. The wind off the water was frigid. In the seconds it took me to run toward the building, I was chilled again.

The entrance was covered with photocopies advertising bean suppers, a used Sno-Cat, snowplow services. Yet another flyer looking for Martin Graves, the same faded image of a young man in wool cap and Nike T-shirt. Wherever he'd run off to, I hoped he was warmer than I was. I went inside.

The open room had bare wood floors, wooden tables with miniature hurricane lanterns holding candles, walls covered with faded posters advertising Grange dances. A bar stretched along one wall, where six or seven people hunkered down over drinks. No TV. Blues on the sound system. Several couples sat at the tables, old hippie types or maybe they were fishermen; raw-faced women with long hair, bearded men. A man by himself reading a newspaper. One or two of them glanced at me then went back to their dinners.

I couldn't blame them. The food smelled good. A middle-aged woman wearing a bright Peruvian sweater showed me to a table along the far wall.

"Cold out tonight!" she said, sounding shocked: Maine, cold? "What can I get you?"

I ordered a shot of Jack Daniel's, a beer, and two rare hamburgers. I knocked back the shot and ordered another, sipped my beer. When my burgers arrived, I wolfed them down then ordered another beer. That ache you get after doing crank, the sense that your brain has been walled up behind broken rubble—that began to subside, replaced by the slow pulse of alcohol.

I nursed my second beer. I was in no hurry to head back to the Lighthouse, though the thought of hiding dirty Kleenex from Merrill Libby did have its appeal. A nearly full moon crept above the black harbor. It wasn't yet seven o'clock. I angled my chair so I could catch the light from the hurricane lantern on my table and opened my copy of *Deceptio Visus.*

I turned the pages carefully—it was probably the most valuable thing I owned—until I reached Kamestos's brief introduction.

> I have called this collection of photographs *Deceptio Visus,* "deceiving sight." But there is nothing here that is deceptive. Our gaze changes all that it falls upon. Within these photographs, I hope, the discerning eye may see the truth.

It had been a long time since I'd read those words. Once they had seemed to explain the world to me, the way I saw things; the sense I had that someone, or something, watched me. But I had lost that way of seeing or feeling, if indeed I'd ever possessed it; if it even existed.

Now it all just seemed like shit. I looked around for my waitress to order another beer.

Two of the people at the bar were watching me. One was a solid-looking man with a graying beard and close-cropped brown hair. A rat-tail braid dangled across his shoulder. As he cocked his head, light glanced off a jeweled stud in one earlobe. He wore a red flannel shirt, stained jeans, heavy work boots. He had a cigarette tucked behind one ear and a yellow pencil behind the other.

Beside him sat the man I'd run into at the Lighthouse. He stared at me, frowning slightly. Then he stood, picked up his wineglass, and walked over.

"Can I see that?" He pointed at my book.

Before I could say anything, before I could even remember the stolen photograph inside it, he picked up *Deceptio Visus.*

"No," I said, but he had already opened it. He glanced at the copyright page then handed it back to me.

"My copy's signed," he said.

I grabbed the book and shoved it into my bag beneath the table. When I looked up, the other guy had joined his friend.

"Did he try to steal your book?" he said. "Because I can call the police if you want me to." He plucked the cigarette from behind his ear, bent over my hurricane glass, and lit it. His hands were cross-hatched with scars, and the tip of one thumb was missing. "Smoke?"

"No," I said.

As if by magic, the waitress appeared and set down two more beers and a glass of red wine.

"You know you're not supposed to do that in here, Toby," she scolded.

The bearded man smiled sheepishly, pinched out his cigarette, and stuck it back behind his ear. His friend stood, silent, beside him. The sleeve of his suede jacket had ridden up so that his wrist was exposed, the scar grayish in the dim light.

I looked at him uneasily. I hated that he'd seen me before I saw him. The sense I'd had earlier, that overpowering taint of fear and damage—it wasn't gone, but it was definitely subdued. I thought of how he'd jumped away and cracked his head on the door.

I'd surprised him. Now he'd surprised me. I picked up one of the beers and took a long pull.

"I'm Toby Barrett," said the bearded man. He picked up the other beer and raised it to me. "I hear you're looking to get to Paswegas."

"How'd you know that?"

"Everett told me there was a lady looking to get over."

"Oh yeah? Is he here? He fucking bailed on me when I called him this afternoon."

"You mean he wouldn't take you over in the dark?" Toby Barrett seemed amused. "You're lucky he answered his phone."

He pulled out the chair across from me and sat. "You're from away, aren't you? Not me." Toby cocked a thumb at his friend. "Not him, either."

I finished my beer. "What about Everett Moss?"

"No. Not Everett," conceded Toby. "Everett was squoze from a rock."

"You know her?" His friend pointed to my bag beneath the table. "Aphrodite Kamestos?"

"Yeah. Sure I do."

He stared at me coolly then smiled, his teeth white and uneven. "You're lying."

I set one booted foot atop my bag. He finished his wine, set down the empty glass, and pushed the full one toward me.

"I'm outta here," he said. "You can drink that, if you want. In case all that Jack Daniel's isn't doing the job for you."

I said nothing. He turned and walked away. I watched him hand a few bills to the bartender then head for the door. He had an odd loping pace, his head thrust forward and staring downward, hands shoved into his pockets. At the door he turned and stared at me. He smiled again, his mouth moving silently, but I could read what he said.

Liar.

A blast of cold air rushed into the room as he disappeared outside.

"The fuck," I said.

"I beg your pardon?" said Toby Barrett.

"Nothing." I desperately wanted to leave, but I didn't want to run into that guy again. Whoever the hell he was.

"Gryffin," said Toby. "With a Y. Don't mind him. He's always like that."

"Like what? Fucking rude? And who the hell names their kid Gryffin?"

"It's a respectable old hippie name. He's not rude, really—"

"Oh yeah? He just picked up my book and—"

"Well, he didn't hurt it now, did he?" Toby's voice was low and calming. I imagined he'd be good with fractious children or dogs. "That's just what he does. He's a rare book dealer. What about you? You a friend of Aphrodite?"

"Not a friend, exactly. I'm seeing her on business. Assuming I ever do see her."

He looked surprised, then said, "Well, okay. We'll get you out to the island. Don't worry." He finished his beer. "What's your name?"

"Cass Neary."

"Right. Well, Cass Neary, I'm off too. Got to get up at the crack of dawn. Nice meeting you."

He nodded and left.

I paid my bill then went back outside. Three beers and two shots of whiskey did a lot to neutralize the cold. Gryffin was nowhere in sight. I walked down to the granite pier and looked out across the harbor. I could hear the creak of boats rocking, the thin rustle of wind in the evergreens. The northern sky arched overhead, moon so bright I could read the names of the lobster boats: *Ellie Day, Aranbega II, Miss Behave.*

Somewhere out there was Paswegas; somewhere beyond that a hundred other islands unknown to me, unnamed. I heard a low thrum, turned to see the running lights of a small boat cruising slowly along the shoreline. A green light on one side, red on the other, like mismatched eyes.

Our gaze changes all that it falls upon.

I stood and watched it move through the darkness. Did people here fish at night? Did they ride around in their boats for fun, looking for frozen lobsters?

My eyes teared, from cold and strain. I rubbed them and looked out again.

The running lights were gone, the outboard's thrum silent. Nothing else had changed.

I drove back to the Lighthouse. I went slowly; I'd had a lot to drink, and the road wound perilously between woods and steep hills where the shoulder fell off into sheer rock that slanted down toward the sea. Then it was woods again. Even driving slowly, the car seemed to lunge through the forest. Trees momentarily shrank from its passage then loomed back into place. I gazed into the rearview mirror, entranced. It was a spooky effect but also hypnotic. I looked back at the road in front of me again.

A black form stood in the middle of the tarmac. I swerved to avoid hitting it, swerved again so I wouldn't plow into the trees.

A deer, I thought, my heart pounding, and brought the car to a crawl. But it wasn't a deer.

It was Mackenzie Libby. She had been walking toward Burnt Harbor, but now she turned to stare at my car, her baggy pants flapping like wings, her face a white crescent in the folds of a hooded sweatshirt. Her eyes caught the red glare of my taillights and glowed like an animal's. Her mouth opened. She yelled something I couldn't hear. It wasn't an angry sound, more questioning or pleading. Then my car rounded another curve and she was gone.

Stupid fucking kid! I thought, but at least the encounter had woken me up. I drove the rest of the way without passing another car, or person, and reached the Lighthouse ten minutes later.

I wanted to be nowhere near Gryffin. I considered asking Merrill Libby for another room, but that seemed a little paranoid, even for me. Plus the office lights were off. I hopped out of the car and ran across the empty lot. I entered my room on tiptoe, locked the door and drew the curtains, then angled the room's single chair beneath the doorknob. Security didn't seem a high priority at the Lighthouse—there was no dead bolt, only a flimsy-looking chain.

And, of course, no telephone. But my choices were limited to staying there or sleeping in my car. I'd probably freeze to death if I did that. So I made sure the heat was cranked as high as it would go and got ready for bed.

It was only when I switched the light off that I realized there was no clock in the room and, natch, I had no travel alarm.

I checked my watch. It was just after nine. The last time I'd turned in that early I was ten years old. At least I'd get a good night's sleep and wake in plenty of time to meet Everett. I lay in bed, listening to the plastic crackle every time I moved, half expecting to hear a knock at my door or on the few inches of sheetrock that separated me from Gryffin. But there was only the sound of wind, and mice scrabbling in the ceiling.

The alcohol had done its job. I was drunk and exhausted. But I couldn't sleep. I kept listening for the sound of a car pulling up outside. The thought of Gryffin in the next room wouldn't leave me, like that sick rush when someone else's pain lingers like the after-taste of blood. It wasn't even him I was thinking of, but the photograph of him, that unguarded, reckless eruption of joy on the face of a total stranger.

I switched the light back on and fumbled for the copy of *Deceptio Visus*, took out the photo, and stared at it.

A happy man at a party. Sun, bougainvillea, and a champagne flute. That was all.

Our gaze changes all that it falls upon.

I looked around the motel room. Nothing had changed here in forty years. I slid the photograph back into the book and turned out the light. At some point I fell asleep; I at some later point woke, to the noise of car wheels on gravel just outside my room. I lay there listening to a car door opening and closing, and then as the door to the next room slammed shut.

I held my breath. Would he be able to tell I'd been in there? For a few minutes I listened as someone moved around on the other side of the flimsy wall. There was the sound of a flushing toilet and, finally, silence. I huddled beneath the blankets, telling myself that my anxiety was meaningless, that nothing was different, and that at any rate by the morning I would be gone. Only the last of these was true.

9

I WOKE WITH A blistering headache, reached for my watch then sat bolt upright.

Seven-ten. I was supposed to meet Everett at six.

I stumbled out of bed and pulled on my boots—I'd slept in my clothes—grabbed my bag and ran out to the car, my boots sliding on a sheen of ice. Sunlight streamed across icy puddles; the grass glittered with frost. The Volvo that had been in front of Room 1 was gone.

The door to my car was iced shut. I scraped at it with my room key until I could finally pull it open. Inside, I jammed on the defroster and started backing up without waiting for the windshield to clear. I pulled over by the office, ran inside, tossed my room key onto the desk then raced back to my car. As I started to drive off I saw Merrill Libby yank open the office door.

"Hey!" he shouted. "Did you—"

"I can't," I yelled back. "I'm late—"

He stumbled down the steps as I roared off, his face bright red. Maybe he was mad I didn't stay for coffee.

The road was slick. I drove as fast as I dared until I got stuck behind a school bus. By the time I reached Burnt Harbor, it was seven-thirty. I drove to the waterfront and hopped out of the car.

I saw no one. A few pickup trucks were lined up at dockside.

Gulls circled above the water, keening loudly. The lobster boats were gone.

I shaded my eyes and looked across the harbor. I could see the islands clearly now, bathed in morning light. The nearest one was a slaty blue, its jagged headland softened by golden mist. A small white shape churned toward it from the harbor's mouth.

I hoped that wasn't my ride. I turned and headed for the Good Tern.

It was more crowded than it had been the night before. A different waitress hurried between tables and gave me a brusque nod. "One?"

"I'm looking for Everett Moss." I scanned the room, trying to figure out which burly man in a Carhartt jacket and gimme cap might be the harbormaster. "Is he here?"

"Everett?" The woman frowned. "He was here earlier, but I think he went out. Hey, Toby—"

She called to a man sitting alone at a table by the window. "Where'd Everett go?"

Toby Barrett looked up from a plate of eggs and bacon.

"Everett? He left a while ago." When he saw me, he blinked. "Oh. It's you. You know, I think he was waiting for you—"

"Well, he didn't wait long enough," I snapped.

"Have a seat." Toby nudged a chair toward me with his foot. "You want coffee?"

"Yeah, sure."

I slumped into the chair. Toby paid me the courtesy of turning his attention back to his food. He was wearing the same clothes as the night before, with the exception of a faded T-shirt commemorating the 1975 solar eclipse in Boze, Montana. After a minute the waitress brought me coffee and a menu.

"I can't eat," I said. I held my head in my hands. "God, I can't believe this." I picked up my coffee, grimacing. "So where the hell is Everett's office, anyway? If I had been able to find him?"

"His office? That would be it, there—"

Toby gestured out the window to a red GMC pickup.

"His truck?"

"Yup. He give you his home number? That's the best way to get hold of him, unless you radio him on his boat. Not much cell reception up here."

I drank my coffee miserably, hoping I wouldn't get sick. "I overslept. But I thought he'd at least wait."

"He did. For a while, anyway. He was in here for breakfast— he's here every day." Toby speared an entire fried egg and ate it in one bite. "But then he got another paying customer, so he left."

"Will he come back?"

"Not for a while. He'll make his delivery. Then he'll probably be out hauling traps."

"Shit."

I finished my coffee. The waitress set a fresh pot on the table, along with a plate of toast. I picked up a piece and ate it slowly, fighting nausea.

Now what?

Toby leaned back in his chair. He reached into the pocket of his flannel shirt, took out some rolling papers and a bag of American Spirit tobacco.

"How come you need to get out there so bad?" he asked as he began to roll a cigarette.

"I have a job out there."

"A job?" He seemed taken aback. "On the island? Who you working for? Aphrodite?"

I hesitated. Phil had geared me up with all this cloak-and-dagger stuff about Kamestos and her paranoia, but it all seemed stupid now that I was actually in Burnt Harbor. There was no one here, and certainly no one who seemed to care that I'd arrived.

"I'm supposed to interview her," I said at last.

"Really? She expecting you?"

"Yeah." I wondered if maybe this guy was the friend Phil had mentioned, and asked him.

"Phil Cohen. Nope. Never heard of him." Toby tipped his head, regarding me with calm hazel eyes. "But you do know Aphrodite."

I finished my coffee.

"No," I admitted. "I've never even spoken to her. Phil was the guy set it up for me. Through an editor in London."

I poured myself more coffee. "But you know what? I don't even know what the fuck I'm doing here. I think I better just get back into my goddam car and drive back to New York."

"That would be a long way to come to have a cup of coffee and sleep—where did you sleep last night, anyway?"

"The Lighthouse."

"That would definitely be a long way to come to sleep at the Lighthouse."

Toby tapped his cigarette and tucked it behind his ear, folded up his tobacco packet and rolling papers, and put them away.

"Well, if you still want to get over there to Paswegas, I'll take you," he said.

I stared at him in disbelief. "You can take me?"

"Sure." He pointed toward the harbor. "See that boat out there?"

"A sailboat?" I squinted at the sunlit water. "You can sail in the winter?"

"Sure. Water's same temperature as it is in the summer. You'd just die faster if you fell in now. We'll motor over, unless the wind's with us. It'll take a little longer than Everett's boat, but I'll get you there. I was going over later today anyway."

"Jeez. Well, thanks." I ran a hand through my dirty hair. "I didn't even take a shower."

"That won't bother me. If you're staying with Aphrodite, I'm sure she'll let you take a shower. But we should get going."

He stuck a ten dollar bill under his plate. "How should I pay you?" I asked.

"We'll figure something out." As we headed to the door, he glanced at me. "Those all the clothes you got?"

"Pretty much. You mean, am I dressed up enough to meet her?"

"I mean you're going to freeze your butt off if you don't put on something warmer." He looked at my boots and shook his head. "You better be careful with those—cowboy boots are terrible on deck. I think maybe I got some stuff on the boat you could wear. Come on."

I followed him outside. I retrieved my things, locked the car, then headed after Toby.

Two steps and my gut clenched. Maybe getting onto a boat wasn't such a great idea, after all. But Toby was already halfway down the beach, so I hurried after him.

As he'd warned, my boots were terrible in the damp. The pointed toes caught between rocks and slid on lumps of greasy black seaweed. I walked gingerly to where he bent over a wooden dinghy. A few yards off, waves swept the shingle and left a trail of shining foam.

Toby glanced up. "That all you got?"

I nodded. "Will my car be okay if I leave it for a few days?"

"Should be fine till Memorial Day. Okay, come on down this way—"

He dragged the dinghy into the shallows, waved for me to clamber in. I did. A film of brackish water covered my boots and immediately soaked through to my feet, ice cold.

"Better get down," said Toby.

I sat as he got behind the dinghy and shoved it farther out. A moment later he hopped in, settled in the bow, and took the oars.

"This won't take long," he said. A few strong strokes and we were free of the shingle. A few more and I leaned over the side and vomited.

"Seasick already?"

"Hangover."

I cupped icy seawater with one hand, rinsed my mouth then splashed more water on my face.

I felt a little better. My headache receded. The frigid air and water seemed to purge exhaustion from my blood. My eyes stung, but the pain felt clean and sharp, almost welcome. I sank back onto my seat, making sure my satchel stayed dry.

"See there?" Toby gestured at a small, blunt-nosed sailboat bobbing a short distance from the end of the pier. "That's her. *Northern Sky.* Know anything about boats?"

I blinked into the splintered blue-and-gold light. "No."

"She's what they call a gaff cutter. Twenty-six feet on the waterline. I bought her twenty years ago for a dollar, from the ex-wife of a guy in jail down in the Keys. You know the two happiest days of a man's life? The day he buys his boat and the day he sells her."

Out here the dank reek of the harbor was gone. The air smelled of salt and wet rock, with a faint undertone of diesel fumes. I shaded my eyes and looked for other boats.

"Are you the only boat out here?"

"The only sailboat, this time of year. There's a few lobster boats. Bugs migrate to deeper water in the winter, so it slows down about now. In the summer there's a bunch of people here—yachts, windjammers. But you want to get off the islands in a hurry, you need a power boat. That way you can catch your flight back to Florida."

"Sounds good to me."

Toby laughed. "Oh, it's not that bad. Not nowadays. Fifty or a hundred years ago, then that would be bad, I guess."

"What the hell do people do out there?" I squinted at the islands. "Besides fish. I mean, what do you do?"

"I go back and forth. Bring supplies out to the islands. I'm a carpenter, and I do heating systems. There's a lot of rich people around. Summer people. Used to be everyone left after Labor Day. Now some of 'em stay on till Thanksgiving, but they don't winter over. Summer people, I mean. Islanders live here all year round. But they don't need me to do their work for 'em."

He rested the oars and lit a cigarette, cupping his hands against the spray. "Aphrodite, I've done some work for her."

"How long you been here?"

Toby exhaled a plume of blue smoke. "I came in 1972. Used to be a commune out on Paswegas, it was pretty well known back then. I came and hung out there awhile, ended up staying."

"A commune? How long did it last?"

"Not that long. Few years."

I zipped my leather jacket, shivering. "I wouldn't last a week."

"People been living on these islands a long time," Toby said mildly. "The Micmacs were here for thousands of years. But no, that commune didn't last long. None of them ever do. I guess that's why they decided to rename it an artist's colony. That was more successful. For a little while, anyway. That's why they call it Burnout Harbor."

I made a face, and Toby said, "Hey, I'm surprised you didn't know about that. If you're coming to see Aphrodite, I mean. She kind of started the whole commune thing, her and her friends."

He fell silent, smoking and staring with narrowed eyes across the reach of blue water. Finally he said, "That's what brought a lot of folks here. People from away. Back-to-the-landers. That's why I came, actually. I studied at the Apprenticeshop, boatbuilding, but a lot of the folks I met then, they were real hippies. There was a lot of communal-type living going on. A lot of runaways. College drop-outs. Kids from Boston and New York. Even kids from California. Some from around here. They wanted to, I don't know what—build their own yurts? Raise goats? Whereas Aphrodite was more into art and, well, kind of a spiritual thing, I guess you'd say. Oakwind, that's what she named the commune. That's when I first met her."

"Wasn't she kind of old for the whole hippie scene?"

Toby frowned. "Well, no, I don't think so. And she was really good-looking back then."

I did the math in my head: Kamestos was born in 1936, so . . .

"Well, okay," I conceded.

"There were a lot of artists." Toby took a final drag on his cigarette then began to row again in earnest. "A few photographers. Couple of writer types who were friends of her husband; one of them stayed on. Everyone smoked a lot of weed. There was a lot of acid. Aphrodite owned a big chunk of land on Paswegas, her and her husband. They'd let people squat on their property, build these little shacks and stuff. A few still live there; locals call 'em the cliff dwellers. Aphrodite's husband, he was dead by then."

"Did you know him?"

"No. He killed himself. I never heard the whole story. I guess he was gay, and maybe that was an issue, or maybe it was drugs? Some weird stuff went on at Oakwind, the whole place kind of imploded. Everyone just went their separate ways after that."

I rubbed my arms. "What kind of weird stuff?"

Toby's gaze grew remote. He turned to stare at the green and black mass of Paswegas looming in the distance. "Out on the islands, every couple of years you get a witch hunt. People go crazy, cabin fever. Winter especially. Lot of times it's directed at a schoolteacher, someone from away. Back then there was only about forty people living on Paswegas. Today there's less than that. So the hippies came, and all of a sudden you've got, like, double the population on a place that's not real used to having company, except in the summer. It's a fragile human ecology, just like an animal ecology; you introduce a new species, even just one person, and everything goes to hell. Some bad stuff happened. Afterward most everyone split."

"But not Aphrodite."

"Not Aphrodite," said Toby. "Maybe you could get her to talk about it. But I doubt it. Okay, here we go—"

We'd come up alongside the sailboat. A carved sign adorned the stern; *Northern Sky* picked out in gold leaf. Even beside the dinghy it looked small. I had a flash of panic: how could something so tiny hold two people, let along bring them anywhere safely? Toby grasped *Northern Sky*'s rail and pulled the dinghy against it. I stood and stumbled on board. Toby followed, then began tying off the dinghy at the stern.

"You go put your stuff below," he called. "Just slide that hatch there, I'll be right down. Watch your head."

The boat was a pretty little thing. White paint, gray trim, mahogany accents. Bronze portholes verdigrised from age and salt air. I still couldn't see how two people could move around without bumping into each other or tripping over a million lines, wires, sails, buckets, God knows what.

Not to mention ice—the deck was slick with it. Fortunately it was only three steps across the bridge deck to where the companionway led down. I skidded over and pushed open the hatch then climbed down a ladder into a space so densely packed it was like walking into a broom closet.

I had to stoop to enter, and even then my head grazed the ceiling. Forward, my way was blocked by the mast and, directly behind it, a sheet-metal woodstove roughly the size and shape of a large coffee can. Beyond this was the bow, a V-shaped berth crammed with boxes, milk cartons, power cells, books, ropes, tools, a small chemical toilet.

But where I was—smack in the middle of the main cabin— everything was meticulously, if eccentrically, organized. To either side was a bench covered with frayed corduroy cushions. Above these were amazingly carved shelves, pigeonholes, cupboards, and nooks, some no bigger than the pencils they held, others large enough to support rows of books and manuals. There were hooks carved like fingers, canned goods stacked behind carven filigree. Two copper gimbals shaped like mouths held kerosene lanterns. Crocheted nets dangled from the ceiling, filled with onions and garlic and sprouting potatoes. Tucked into an alcove by the ladder were a tiny alcohol-fueled cookstove and an NOAA weatherband radio beside a bottle of Captain Morgan rum and several bottles of Moxie.

"You okay? Find a place to stow your stuff?"

Toby's bearded face appeared in the hatch. I ran my fingers across a shelf carved with rows of eyes. "Did you do this? All this carving? And this?"

At the end of the shelf hung a mask. Papier-mâché, vaguely Native American–looking: a frog, mottled brown and green and creamy yellow. It had protruding golden eyes, a wide, lipless grin. The papier-mâché was so smooth it looked like plastic, except at the edges where you could see unpainted bits of newsprint. It was beautiful, but also unsettling.

I said, "You made this too?"

"Yup." Toby came down, and I moved to make room for him. "Just put your bags there—"

He pointed at one of the cushioned berths. "We'll motor over. Not enough wind; we'd have to tack back and forth. Just as fast this way."

I turned from the frog mask and put my bag down then removed my camera.

Toby stared at the old Konica. "Boy, that's an antique."

"I'm a photographer." It was the first time I'd spoken those words in a long time.

"Don't most people use digital cameras these days?"

"I don't." I glanced around the cabin. "Do you have a mirror? I feel pretty gross."

"No mirrors." His gaze remained even, but his eyes narrowed as he added, "You don't have a mirror on you, do you?"

"Would I've asked for one if I did?"

He leaned back against the ladder, still staring. Not at me; at my camera.

"There's a mirror in that," he said.

"Yeah? There's a mirror in *all* cameras. This kind, anyway." I was starting to get pissed. "Is this some kind of superstition? No women on board, no—"

"Put it away." His tone was less patient now; vaguely threatening. "Here—give it to me and I'll stow it."

I started to snap back—I hate people touching my stuff—then shut up.

Something in his expression intimidated me. Usually I can tell if someone's going to freak on me; there's that smell of damage, like the smell of a spent match that signals an explosion a few moments later.

There was no hint of that to Toby Barrett.

But there was something else, just as powerful—a sense of occlusion, of an intense self-possession, like an emotional force field. Like the rocks I saw out in the harbor, their edges hidden by mats of seaweed, all their menace beneath the water.

I shoved my camera back into the satchel and handed it to him. Toby opened a cupboard and stashed the bag inside then opened another cupboard that held clothes. He picked up a heavy black wool sweater, gave it a cursory sniff, and tossed it to me. "See if that fits. It's your color."

I took off my leather jacket and pulled on the sweater. It was bulky and mouse eaten and smelled of cedar and lanolin.

But it was warm. I was just able to squeeze my jacket back on over it. Toby rubbed his beard and glanced down at my boots.

"You got some pretty big feet there. But not big as mine. I don't know if I've got a pair of shoes to fit you. Maybe Aphrodite'll have something."

"I like to wear these. They're . . . comfy."

"I bet. Those steel tips look lethal."

"They are." I lifted one foot to display a black full-quill ostrich-leather Tony Lama cowboy boot worn smooth as eel skin by nearly twenty years of wear. I'd had the soles and heels replaced more than once. The steel tips were customized for me, no longer shining but dull gray.

"They won't keep you warm, though," said Toby. "We'll see what we can find for you on the island."

He moved back to the ladder, lifted it, and set it aside, revealing a pair of doors. He opened these then stepped into a small engine room. His voice echoed back to me.

"Got to hand crank the engine. This could take a minute . . ."

I heard the rhythmic sound of a handle turning. There was a small sputter, the smell of diesel. Toby swore under his breath.

I turned and gave the cabin a quick once-over. The portholes were so crusted with salt that only an opaque, pearly light filtered through them. The woodstove was black from use, as was the cookstove. All of the metal flatware was tarnished. Everything had a comfortable sort of glow, but nothing gleamed or glittered.

I frowned. It was weird, but also weirdly methodical, and that was puzzling; as though there were some pattern here that just escaped my recognition. I sat on one of the berths and looked around, trying to filter out all the *stuff*—the shelves, the books, the tools—and concentrate on what, exactly, ordered the space around me. What made it lucid; literally, what made it shine.

Or not.

You learn to do this as a photographer. You're always searching for light—its source, its distance; always measuring how diffuse it is, how long it's going to last. You think about the same thing when you're in the darkroom printing.

As I sat in *Northern Sky*, I began to see more and more darkness around me, despite the fact that there were no curtains drawn, despite the fact that it was early morning of a cloudless early winter day. Another minute and I began to lose a sense of perspective. The cabin seemed larger than it was; the darkness at the bow crept toward me until it enveloped the outlines of berths, bookshelves, the gimbels' copper mouths. Everything blurred to a deep russet-brown, like a sepia image foxed with mold.

Toby Barrett may not have had something to hide, but he certainly cultivated the shadows. At the very least he wanted very much to preserve the illusion that he was safe from scrutiny, even if he was in a tiny cabin with no doors or screens.

A sudden roar shook the boat.

"Got it!" Toby ducked out of the engine room. "For a minute there I was afraid she wouldn't start."

He shut the doors, threw the ladder back into place, and disappeared up the companionway. I clambered after him. He was already in the cockpit, tiller in hand.

"Have a seat," he said. An unlit cigarette protruded from one corner of his mouth. He brought the boat about until the nearest of the islands was ahead of us, lit the cigarette and took a long drag. "Want one?"

"Just give me a hit off that," I said and took it from his mouth.

The cigarette tasted of diesel fuel and hashish. I passed it back to Toby and stared out at the dark bulk of Paswegas and the archipelago behind it. "How come you don't use a powerboat?"

Toby shifted the tiller. He sat straight backed, oblivious of the wind and icy spray, his eyes fixed on the island. "How come you don't use a digital camera?"

"It feels weird to me. Like a step is missing. Or a wall."

"A wall?"

"Well, not a wall exactly. But you get used to having something between you and whatever it is you're shooting. Maybe it's just that you have time to worry if the picture's going to come out or not. With digital it all happens immediately."

"And that's a bad thing?"

"Maybe not bad. But different."

I hesitated. I was surprised to hear myself admitting this. I'd never really articulated it before, certainly not aloud.

"Maybe it was just too much trouble to keep up with it all," I said at last. "Everything changed so fast. I guess I just didn't care enough anymore."

"What kind of pictures did you do? Magazine pictures? Anything I would've seen?"

"I doubt it. I had only one book, and not many copies were

printed. My stuff was pretty dark. Dead people. I shot the downtown punk scene in New York for a while, before it went belly-up."

"A dead scene," said Toby. He flicked his cigarette into the water.

"Yeah, I guess."

"So you must know all about Aphrodite's photography. That's why you're here, right? You must like her work."

"Yeah." I shifted, trying vainly to get out of the wind, and bumped my knee against his. "Her pictures of the islands. She took those forty years before Photoshop, and people still can't figure out how she did it."

"I never got the impression she was that well-known. She just had one or two books, right?"

"Yeah. But they were influential books."

"Maybe your book will be influential someday. Maybe it's influential right now and you just don't know it."

I shook my head. "No. She was a genius, even if she was only a kind of minor genius. I was just lucky. If you can call taking pictures of dead junkies lucky. I wasn't even very good at that."

My back was starting to ache, from the cold and being hunched against the wind. I stood, balancing myself against my seat, and gazed out at the island. It was an unwelcoming sight, thorny-looking evergreens and spiky outcroppings of black and gray stone. The buildings scattered across the rocky hillside looked as though they'd been thrown there and forgotten, falling down houses and gritty trailers.

"So that's where you live," I said. "What about your friend back in the bar?"

"Gryffin? No. He just comes up sometimes on business." He craned his neck to stare past Paswegas. "You ever hear of someone named Lucien Ryel? He was pretty well-known ten or twenty years ago."

"Lucien Ryel?" I looked up in surprise. "Yeah, sure."

"He lives out there—"

Toby pointed to a low gray shape on the horizon. "Tolba Island. I've done some work for him over the last couple of years. He doesn't winter over. *He's* got a power boat, a Boston Whaler."

"Lucien Ryel," I said. "No shit."

In the early 1970s, Ryel had been the force behind the English prog rock band Imaguncula. He was famous for performing in drag, something between that guy in *A Clockwork Orange* and a Balinese temple dancer. He left Imaguncula in 1980 and went on to produce house music in Manchester before becoming an expat in post-Wall Berlin, where, as far as I knew, he had disappeared.

"What the hell's he doing up here?"

Toby shrugged. "He's only here a few weeks every summer. He's another one came to the commune for a while, before my time. He even wrote a song about Oakwind. Liked it here enough that he bought an island too. I was never into his music. I had one of his albums when I was in college, but I never played it."

The boat hit some choppy waves, and I clutched at my seat. "You okay?" asked Toby. "You could go below if you feel bad. You look a little green."

"I told you, hangover." I waited until the sick feeling passed, then said, "What is it with people buying islands?"

"They used to be cheap—you could buy an island for, I dunno, fifty thousand dollars. Maybe less than that. Not anymore. Lucien's place, Tolba—back in the nineteenth century they quarried granite there. Cut columns and blocks for some big cathedral. When that was built, they cut it for houses. You've heard of a company town? This was a company island. One day someone showed up and told everyone they were shutting down the quarry. So everyone had to leave the island."

"You're kidding."

He turned, adjusted the tiller, and blinked into the sun. Ahead of us the harbor of Paswegas opened up. Neon orange and red and green floats bobbed in the water. A small bell buoy clanked as we passed it.

"There were quarries on a lot of the islands here," said Toby. "Vinalhaven, that's where they got the stone for the Brooklyn Bridge. In the 1890s they were paving city streets, New York, Boston. They didn't have asphalt back then, so they used stone. On Lucien's island, you can see all these great big blocks of granite they left and quarry holes everywhere. He bought that place cheap and hired me to do his heating system. A real big modern-looking place—folks call it the Stealth Bomber. But he's easy to work for. And he's got deep pockets, and he only comes at the end of the summer so I see him maybe once a year. He lives in Europe the rest of the time."

"Doesn't this seem like a weird place for someone like that?"

"What's weird about it? *You're* here."

I gave up. After a few more minutes we entered the harbor, passing a solitary lobster boat moored alongside a red float.

"Everett's boat," Toby said.

He brought the *Northern Sky* to a mooring and dropped anchor. I retrieved my stuff from the cabin.

"Weather's changing," Toby said when I got back on deck. He untied the dinghy and motioned for me to climb into it. "See those clouds? That's a front coming in. You're not planning on leaving today, are you?"

"I don't actually have a fucking clue what I'm doing."

"That's the spirit," said Toby.

He rowed toward the pier. The harbor was even smaller and grungier than Burnt Harbor's. Busier, too. Paswegas may only have had thirty year-round residents, but half of them seemed to be hanging around the dock. Two derelict pickups were parked in front of a boarded-up building with a sign that read LIVE BAIT COFFEE. One truck had cardboard covering half its windshield; another had no windshield at all.

"Beaters," Toby explained as the dinghy drew up alongside the pier. Pilings black with creosote poked from the water. Budweiser cans floated past a ladder where a cormorant stood with wings outstretched, its eyes dull as uncut garnets. "No ferry service here, no mail boat anymore cause there's no post office. Everyone shares those trucks. You keep your good vehicles in Burnt Harbor."

"What about groceries?"

"You got the Island General Store. Or you bring stuff back from Burnt Harbor." He lifted his chin toward the men in the harbor. "That's why they're looking at us."

He tied off the dinghy, and we walked down the pier. The men leaned on a rail, observing us as they smoked and talked.

"There's your friend Everett Moss." Toby cocked his head at a burly man with a white beard, wearing stained coveralls and an orange watch cap.

"Toby," the man called. Toby headed toward him, and I followed. "That the young lady I was supposed to bring over this morning?"

"This is her." Toby halted and lit a cigarette. "Cass Neary."

"Hello there." Everett looked at me and nodded. He had bright blue eyes in a sunburnt face, an easy smile. I waited for him to apologize for not waiting for me.

Instead he turned back to Toby. I glanced at the other men. They quickly looked away, stubbed out their cigarettes then wandered in the direction of the closed bait shop. Everett glanced across the dark waters of the reach to the mainland.

"You haven't seen Mackenzie Libby?" he said to Toby. "Merrill called me this morning. She didn't come in last night. My granddaughter Leela told me they'd been e-mailing earlier, Kenzie said something 'bout going into town."

Toby frowned. "Mackenzie?"

"Merrill's daughter."

"Oh." Toby tugged at his braid. "She run off?"

I snorted. "I would, if that was my father."

The two men looked at me, Toby amused, Everett Moss less so.

"Cass Neary," he said, as though he'd just figured out who I was. "You stayed there last night, didn't you. She told my granddaughter she'd been talking to you."

I had a sudden flash of a white face in the night, black branches. I shifted my camera bag from one shoulder to the other and looked at the sky. A wheel of gray cloud had escaped from the dark ridge that was blowing in. As I stared, the cloud began to turn, like a clock's mainspring unwinding. I heard a low buzzing like a trapped fly and dredged up the image of the girl in the Lighthouse, the way she peered shyly into my room, as though I had something special hidden among the shabby furniture and plastic mattress cover.

There'd been no reek of desperation about her, no fear, just a kid's longing for something she couldn't put a name to yet. She was bored; she dreamed of waking up somewhere else. Her father might have been an asshole, but he didn't beat her or abuse her.

That's why she hadn't interested me. No damage.

"Merrill's wicked pissed off," said Everett.

"Yeah. Now *he's* got to clean the motel rooms," Toby said. They both laughed.

"Well, he's all worked up, no doubt 'bout that." The harbormaster slung his hands into his pockets. "John Stone told me Merrill called him this morning too, got him out of bed. John told him she aint't back by sunset, *then* he should call. Or maybe little miss went on down to Florida, see her ma. Anyway, you see her, tell her to get herself home."

He began walking down to the water, stopped and looked back at me.

"You too," he said. His gaze wasn't threatening. It was worried. "You see her, call me or John Stone, he's the sheriff. Don't like these kids running off."

He lifted a hand to Toby and headed off.

"Come on," said Toby. "We better get you up to Aphrodite's house."

We walked through the village. The bait shop, a mobile home with a bunch of large, scary-looking dolls standing in the window. The Island General Store, a clapboard building covered in flaking rust-colored paint, with a low wooden stoop and a gas pump with a trash bag tied over it. A bunch of flyers flapped from the store's walls and screen door.

"That guy," I said. I walked over and pulled at a faded piece of paper. "Martin Graves. I keep seeing these everywhere. What's the deal with him?"

I glanced aside and saw another flyer, curled with damp and age. "Jesus. What's the deal with all of them?"

I smoothed out the second flyer. This one was a color xerox of a smiling teenage girl, her face and hair bleached to a brown slurry between faded words.

"'Heather Pollitt,'" I read aloud. "What happened to her?"

"She ran off." Toby stepped up beside me. "Went down to Bangor, I think. She had a baby or something. That's a real old flyer, that one; we should take it down—"

He tore it down and crumpled it, tossed it into a barrel by the door. "Oh, and look here—somebody's cat is missing too. That's a new one," he added, tapping a handwritten sheet dated a few days earlier. "Poor Smoky! I hope they find him. But that guy—"

He pressed a scabbed-over thumb against the picture of Martin Graves. "I don't know what happened. I heard he just took off or something. Supposedly he had a fight with his girlfriend, or maybe it was his wife? Anyway, his parents keep putting these up. You saw some driving up here?"

"Yeah. I think I read about him online too. This place has a high mortality rate for kids. And cats."

We started back up the hill. Behind us gulls wheeled and screamed above the harbor. The road was dirt and gravel and ice, chunks of broken blacktop. After a few yards it curved and began to climb steeply between scrawny firs and birch.

"Fishers get the cats," said Toby.

"Huh?"

"What you said about kids and cats. Fishers get them."

I looked at him suspiciously. "They use them for bait?"

"Not fisher*men*. Fisher cats. That's what they call them, but they're really just fishers. They're kind of like a wolverine, or a big mink, but they can climb trees. Usually they eat porcupines, but sometimes one will move into a neighborhood and start picking off all the local pets. Cats, small dogs even."

"Kids?"

Toby laughed. "Not that I ever heard. They're not that big— maybe the size of a big coon cat. I think that's why they call 'em fisher cats."

"How do they eat porcupines?"

"They're really smart. Smarter'n a porcupine, anyway. But you don't find them on the islands, usually. Just the mainland. Here, let's go this way."

He turned off the narrow road into a pine grove. There was no path that I could see, but Toby moved confidently among the trees. The shrieks of gulls died into a muffled near silence; the sound of wind in the trees was louder than the ocean. The moss underfoot was so thick and damp it was like walking on soggy carpet, and the moss wasn't just on the ground—it covered everything, rocks, logs, even an empty beer can. If I fell asleep on the ground, it would probably cover me, moss and this bright yellow mold, and some-thing Toby said was old-man's beard, long stringy hanks of lichen that hung from tree limbs like hair. Unlike the rocks by the harbor, these looked soft and plushy with moss. They looked *organic*, like if you stared at one long enough you might catch it breathing.

It was a weird place; what you'd imagine a fairy tale would look like if you fell into one. They gave me a bad feeling, all those trees. When I touched one, the bark wasn't damp but wet and slimy. It seemed to give beneath my finger, like skin.

It creeped me out.

I used to like that feeling. I used to hunt that feeling down. For a second, I thought of getting out my camera and hunting it again.

But I couldn't. The island spooked me. I got the sense here that nothing you did could ever **matter**—not for long, anyway. You could build a house or an entire town and the island would just swallow it and you'd never know it had even existed. Everything would just be eaten away. I kicked at a boulder, and my boot tip snagged in two inches of moss. I had to bend over to yank it out.

Toby stopped to wait for me. "Porcupines like pine trees," he said. "Like fishers do. But porcupines are stupid. Porcupines and skunks. Ever notice how much road kill is porcupines and skunks? They rely so much on being obnoxious, they think nothing can kill them. But a fisher's smart—vicious, but smart. And fast. They come up on a porcupine, bite it on the nose then flip it over and tear its throat and belly out. They'll go right for its head, rip its whole face off, then eat it from the inside out."

I made a face. Toby laughed.

"You don't need to worry," he said. "Like I said, they don't come out here to the islands. And they don't attack people. Not much, anyway. They go for smaller things. I saw one once, in the woods by Burnt Harbor. It was playing with a mouse, like a cat does."

"But what if one did come here?"

"I don't know." He ran his hand along a branch covered with lichen that looked like peeling orange house paint, snapped the branch off and tossed it. "They can swim, I think. Maybe one could swim over. I guess then it could swim back to shore. Or maybe they eat each other. There never seems to be a real long-term problem back on the mainland. People trap them."

He began to walk again. "You getting tired?"

I shrugged. That hangover was starting to rage behind my eyes. It wasn't even ten, and I was ready to crawl back to bed. "Just fried," I said. "I didn't sleep well last night."

"The Lighthouse didn't suit you?"

"It wasn't that. Too wound up, I guess."

"Last I saw, you were knocking back the Jack Daniel's. That would unwind me pretty fast."

We walked on. Now and then I'd spot sea urchins on the moss, their spines the same gray-green as the lichen. I stopped and nudged one with my foot. "How do these get here?"

"Sea gulls drop them on the rocks to crack 'em open." Toby glanced at me curiously. "So'd you see her last night? Merrill's daughter?"

"Just for a few minutes." I picked up the sea urchin. Several spines fell away at my touch, not sharp but soft and brittle, like burnt twigs. "She checked me in. And she came to my room after, to tell me about that place where we ate. The Good Tern. So I guess I can thank her for my hangover."

"I think you can thank yourself for that," said Toby.

I rubbed my finger across the sea urchin until the rest of the spines flaked off. What I held now looked remarkably like one of the small tussocks of moss everywhere. I cupped it in my hand then carefully put it into my bag.

"Those are real fragile," Toby warned. "You want to watch, they break like eggshells."

"I'll be careful." I looked around, shaking my head. "It's so strange. I mean, it's almost winter and it's still green."

"The fog does that. It covers everything, the rocks and trees; then the moss and lichens cover them and feed off the moisture. It's a paradise for parasites."

Ahead of us the pines thinned out. The shadowy green world gave way to a bleached-out stretch of stone and birch, a building barely visible through the trees. I thought of Mackenzie's white face momentarily blazing in my headlights.

She was a cute kid. Probably she'd been running away—or, more likely, running off with some boyfriend or girlfriend. I preferred to think of her on a Greyhound headed south to Boston or New York, meeting a friend in Port Authority, heading west. Who was I to stop her escape? I hoped she was a hundred miles away.

"How much farther?" I asked Toby.

"Almost there."

I blinked as we stepped into milky sunlight. We were at the top of a long slope leading down to the rocky shoreline and a small cove. The slope was scattered with trees—birch, oak, hemlocks. Tucked within the trees were two small gray-shingled buildings. Both looked utterly derelict and abandoned.

"You were asking about the commune," said Toby, and pointed. "Most of it was up at the top of this hill, but people salvaged it or burned it for firewood. Those shacks are all that's left. Denny's old bus is over the hill a ways. And that's Aphrodite's place there—"

Among the trees by the cove stood a clapboard building that looked as though it were attempting to pull itself up the hillside. There were loose and missing boards everywhere. The roof was sunken, the stone chimneys crumbling. The white paint had weathered to a uniform gray and was filigreed with moss, and moss-covered boulders thrust up against the walls.

I looked at Toby. "At midnight does it turn back to rocks and pine needles?"

"Not what you expected?"

"No. It's so dark. Photographers want light."

"Light's better on the eastern side." He gestured toward the black water of the cove. "It's old. Wasn't real big, so she kept adding on to it.

"I don't see any lights."

Toby looked up. Smoke threaded from one of the chimneys, carrying the acrid smell of creosote. "She's here. Someone is, anyway."

He headed for the front door, its granite sill scattered with ashes. An untidy stack of firewood stood beside it, and a snow shovel.

"Hey, Aphrodite." Toby rapped loudly on the door. "You got visitors."

I felt a flicker of real excitement. I thought of the pictures in *Deceptio Visus*, of a Medusa's frozen face gazing from a black-and-white photograph. Then the door opened, and those Medusa's eyes were staring at me.

10

SHE WAS SO SMALL and finely built that I felt huge and ungainly standing in front of her, silver-white hair to her shoulders, white skin, bright red lipstick carelessly applied. Her face was lined, but otherwise she looked remarkably like the woman in the photo. Behind a pair of wire-rimmed glasses the familiar onyx eyes glittered, bloodshot but still challenging. She wore a black woolen tunic, black leggings, scuffed-up moccasin slippers. She looked like a girl headed for dance class, or a wizened geisha doll.

"Who are you?" she demanded.

Without warning a mass of dark shapes surrounded her, growling and whining. I backed away in alarm. "Jesus—"

"They won't hurt you." Aphrodite gestured at me impatiently then crooned, "Runi, Fee—down, get *down.*"

The writhing shadows resolved into three immense dogs, the biggest dogs I'd ever seen. Toby put a reassuring hand on my shoulder.

"Those are her dogs," he said.

"No shit." I pulled away from him. One of the dogs jumped toward me, its head brushing my chest before I pushed it down. Another stood on its hind legs and pawed at Toby's shoulders. It was so tall it looked as though they were dancing.

"They won't hurt you," Aphrodite repeated. The look she gave me was disdainful.

Toby took a step back, toward the trees. "I better get going," he said. "I'll see you later."

"Hey, wait," I said and pushed at a grizzled, narrow muzzle. "I didn't pay you yet."

"Not to worry," he said. "You can catch me another time."

"Get inside," ordered Aphrodite. "Fee! Tara, Runi! *Now.*"

The panting dogs receded. As I followed them inside, one thrust its nose against my hand and stared up at me with moist, imploring eyes.

"I'm Cassandra Neary," I said as Aphrodite yanked the door shut. "Man, those are some big dogs. Are they wolfhounds?"

"Deerhounds."

She hissed a command, and the dogs pattered off. We stood in a narrow foyer, its pine flooring scratched and furrowed, tattered rugs askew. A line of windows on the opposite wall looked across the cove to open water and a gray prospect of islands and gathering cloud. There was a bench heaped with yellow rain slickers and boots, split kindling and old newspapers, aerosol cans of Deet, several big flashlights. Kerosene lamps hung from the ceiling alongside coils of rope and a pair of snowshoes. Aphrodite's small, black-clad figure was incongruous among all this North Woods clutter. She stared up at me imperiously, finally asked, "Who did you say you were?"

"Cass Neary. Cassandra Neary." My mouth went dry. "I'm supposed to—Phil Cohen said he'd spoken to you. About an interview for *Mojo* magazine."

"Never heard of it. An interview?" She made a throaty sound that I realized was a disgusted laugh. "I never give interviews. Who sent you?"

"Phil Cohen."

She continued to stare at me, shrugged and turned away. "Never heard of him."

"You never heard of him?" I asked weakly. I thought of what he'd told me.

She specifically asked for you, God knows why.

Now I knew why. She hadn't asked for me at all. This was another of Phil's screwed-up plans, sending me on a fool's errand because he was too lazy or chickenshit to do it himself.

Another Phil Cohen favor. And I was so desperate, I'd fallen for it.

"Have you had breakfast?" It was the same tone she'd used with the dogs.

"I—I wouldn't mind some coffee." I felt sicker than before but did my best to sound calm. "Thanks."

"This way, then."

I gritted my teeth and comforted myself with images of Phil with his nose broken. Aphrodite moved with small darting steps; that and the Klaus Nomi makeup made her look even more like some bizarre automaton. As we walked through the hall, heaps of kindling gave way to stacks of magazines and books, shoes in varying stages of decay, fifty-pound bags of dog food, cases of bottled water, cartons filled with empty liquor bottles, and baskets of plastic film canisters.

I glanced at one of the baskets then looked up. Aphrodite stood in a doorway with her back to me. I grabbed a film canister, shoved it into my pocket, and went on.

"Do you have your own darkroom here?" I asked.

"No. Sit down." She looked at me irritably. "You should have left your jacket in the mudroom—no, give it to me, I'll do it."

I handed her my jacket but kept my camera bag. As she retraced her steps, I looked around at a big old-fashioned kitchen. A wood-burning cookstove stood in the center, deerhounds flopped beside it like mangy fur rugs. There were fragments of Turkish carpets on the floor, and a trestle table covered with papers and the remains of breakfast. I set down my bag, wandered to the window, and stared out at the cove. A small dark shape loped along the water's edge then disappeared beneath the pines. It was too small for a deerhound. I wondered if it was a fox, or a lost cat.

"I see Toby got you here in one piece."

I turned. A man was beside the stove, pouring coffee into a mug. I stared at him, incredulous, as Aphrodite came back into the room.

"This is my son, Gryffin Haselton." She picked up a kettle from the stove and walked to the sink to refill it. "Do you want coffee or tea?"

"Coffee would be my guess," said Gryffin. He crossed the room to hand me the mug he'd just filled. "I took your berth on Everett's boat earlier. Toby said he'd make sure you got here okay. The way you were putting it away last night, I figured you'd sleep in."

"You figured wrong." I took the coffee.

"Well, you got some local color, anyway."

Gryffin turned to get another mug. The deerhounds moaned softly as he stepped between them, and I reached down to stroke one warily. Its head felt like a skull wrapped in worn flannel. Aphrodite leaned against the kitchen counter and regarded me with those glittering black eyes.

"Tell me what this imaginary interview is supposed to consist of."

I told her, glossing over the fact that *Mojo* was not a photography magazine and I was not, in fact, anywhere on its masthead. When I mentioned Phil Cohen's name again, she frowned.

"Phil Cohen." She stared at her moccasined feet then shook her head. "I never heard of him."

"He said he used to come up here sometimes." I fought to keep desperation from my voice. "He said there was, I dunno, a commune or something."

Gryffin glanced at his mother.

"Denny," he said, as though that explained everything. He stared at me in disgust.

Aphrodite gave him a quick look then turned back to me. "I have to check the woodstove."

She left. Gryffin settled at one end of the trestle table. He pushed up his sleeves, displaying that scrawled scar on his wrist, crossed his long legs at the ankle and surveyed me with bitter amusement.

I drank my coffee and looked more closely at his face for any resemblance to Aphrodite.

Yeah, I should have seen it, I thought. Once, I would have.

That odd sense of recognition I'd felt when I'd first seen him outside the motel? It was his eyes. They were Aphrodite's eyes, oblique, the green spark in his left iris a sort of optic smirk. His smile, too, was hers; though what was cold in Aphrodite's face became wry, even rueful, in her son's. I thought of the joy in his photograph and wondered if he'd inherited that from his mother as well. I doubted it.

But I felt no recurrence of what I'd sensed earlier; no damage.

"He wouldn't have waited for you, you know." Gryffin glanced out the window at the cove. "Everett. I would've gotten a ride with Toby like I'd planned, and you'd still be sitting there in Burnt Harbor."

I took a seat at the other end of the table. "No. By now I'd be on my way back to the city."

"Really? You don't seem like you'd give up without a fight. I would have guessed you'd have started swimming over." He looked at my beat-up cowboy boots and black jeans. "My other guess is you've never been north of the Bowery."

I didn't take the bait. "So. Did she abuse you as a child?"

"Nope. She drinks too much, but I bet you can relate to that. Cassandra Neary. I googled you. You get a few hits. Your book does, anyway. Did you bring a copy?"

"No."

"Too bad. That might have given you some street cred with her."

"Phil Cohen said she knew I was coming."

"She didn't. And I have no idea who this Phil Cohen is. But if he's a friend of Denny's . . ."

His voice trailed off.

"Who's Denny?" I asked.

"You really don't know?" I shook my head, and an expression that might have been relief flickered across his face. "Good. Keep it that way."

He leaned forward and added, "I don't need to tell you she doesn't do this often, right? See people."

"My impression was she didn't do it at all."

"She doesn't." He sipped his coffee. "You're not going to find out anything new, you know. I mean, you're not going to find where any bodies are buried, because there aren't any. You probably wish there were."

"She said she didn't have a darkroom here. Is that true?"

"She told you that? Christ." Gryffin looked annoyed. "Of course she has a darkroom. Downstairs, in the basement. It's been locked for, I dunno, ten years at least. Maybe longer."

He gave a sharp laugh. One of the dogs looked up in alarm. "Aphrodite hasn't taken a picture for years and years. She used to talk about getting another book together, showing in a gallery. But she never did. Maybe you can light a fire under her."

He shot me a look, then shrugged. "My guess is, that ain't gonna happen."

I held my mug so tight it shook. Hot coffee spilled onto my hand. "You can go fuck yourself," I said.

"Yeah? I'll call you if I need any help with that."

He stood as his mother entered the room.

"I'll leave you two," said Gryffin. "I've got some work to do upstairs."

In the doorway he stopped and looked back at me. "Stick around for dinner," he said. "We're having crow."

Aphrodite watched him leave. Her face was flushed, the glitter in her eyes banked to a glow. I caught the burnt-orange scent of Grand Marnier on her breath.

"Let's go into the other room." She started back down the hall. "The fire's going in there."

"What does your son do?"

"He's a rare book dealer. On the internet—he had a shop, but he closed it a few years ago."

I was glad I hadn't mentioned the Strand.

I followed her into the next room, an airy space that looked out across the reach. This was more like I'd imagined Aphrodite Kamestos's home. Twentieth Century Danish Modern furniture, Arne Jacobsen armchairs, a cane and bamboo Jacobsen Slug chair, a beautifully spare Klint dining table that served as a desk. A small black woodstove sat upon a tiled heath.

Surprisingly, there were no photos. But I saw a bookshelf on the far wall, filled with oversized volumes. Some I recognized from my own collection; others were books I had held covetously at the Strand but didn't try to steal—too big, too valuable. There were pristine copies of *Mors* and *Deceptio Visus*; the limited Ricci edition of Lewis Carroll's photos; Cartier-Bresson's *Images a la Sauvette. Pictures of Old Chinatown, Untitled Film Stills*; books by Avedon, Steichen, Arbus; Herb Ritts, Larry Fink, Joel-Peter Witkin, Katy Grannan.

It was a small fortune in photography books—the Cartier-Bresson alone was worth a thousand bucks. And the presence of those last few artists signaled that Aphrodite had kept up with the field. It made the room feel like a museum, or the kind of place where you instinctively remove your shoes. I looked furtively at my scuffed boots.

"Sit." Aphrodite settled into one of the armchairs. "Did you forget your tape recorder?"

"Hmm?" I took a seat and looked at her, puzzled.

"Your tape recorder. Did you leave it in the other room?"

"My tape recorder." I winced. "Shit! I forgot—"

Aphrodite's thin eyebrows lifted. "You left it in your car?"

"Yes." I rubbed my forehead. "Back in Burnt Harbor."

That was a lie: until now, I'd never even thought of bringing one. I rubbed my hands on my thighs and stared at them. My computer was five hundred miles away in my apartment. I didn't even have a spiral notebook.

"Well," I said quickly. "I guess we can do it the old-fashioned way. I can just write everything down." I nodded at my bag. "I have my camera—"

Aphrodite stared out the window. The full daylight on her face showed her age; her white skin looked as though it would tear if you touched it with a fingernail.

"No," she said. "I don't allow myself to be photographed."

She didn't sound angry or disappointed. Her expression was resigned, as though when all was said and done, she'd been expecting no better than this. She turned, and I could see where the corners of her mouth twitched slightly upward in an ironic smile, just as her son's had. For a moment I felt as though this had all been some kind of bizarre, over-elaborated joke. Then she stood.

"I have some things to take care of."

"Wait!" I got to my feet and without thinking reached for her. She recoiled.

"Your photos—I mean, you know what they are." I didn't care if I sounded crazy or just pathetic. "They changed everything for me. When I first saw them—it was like I'd never seen anything before that! It made the whole world look different, everything. *Deceptio Visus*—that book? It's what made me want to be a photographer."

"A photographer." Her lips curved in a thin smile. Her gaze was hateful. "Is that what you think? Every dilettante I ever met was a photographer. Every little vampire. Every little thief."

She spat the last word. "*Deceptio Visus*," she went on. "You never could have seen those pictures."

"The book," I repeated weakly. "I have the book—the original, not the reprint."

"They were all shit." She stared at me as though daring me to argue. "Nothing was like the originals. *Nothing.*"

She slashed at the air so violently she lost her balance. I reached for her again. This time she hit me, so hard I staggered back a step.

"Don't you touch me," she whispered. "I never let them touch me."

I rubbed my arm. Her dark eyes had grown distant. Or no, not distant: they seemed to focus intently on something in the air between us, something I couldn't see. What Phil had said about her paranoia suddenly made sense.

Without another word she turned and headed from the room.

I called after her. "Your photos."

She didn't stop, but I had nothing left to lose. *"Deceptio Visus.* I won't touch them. I just want to see them. Please."

She stumbled in the doorway. It was the first gesture of hers that seemed to belong to an old woman. "Gryffin will show them to you."

She was gone. Bam, just like that.

I'd blown it.

"Fucking hell," I said.

I drew a deep breath. I shook uncontrollably as I sank back into the chair, a chair worth what I earned in six months. I felt the same surge of rage that had come when I'd hit Christine, my hands burning like they'd scorch right through the chair's arms, right through anything they touched. I clawed at my jeans and felt five hundred dollars' worth of fabric tear.

A door slammed. A moment later three sleek gray forms streaked down toward the cove, followed by a slender figure in a barn coat. I sat with my head in my hands until I heard another door behind me. I looked up and saw Gryffin Haselton, carrying a laptop.

"Oh. Hey." His brow furrowed. "Where's my mother?"

"Gone." I stood unsteadily and looked away. "I fucked up. I forgot a tape recorder. I guess she doesn't like that."

"She doesn't like a lot of stuff. I wouldn't worry about it." He set his laptop on the table and plugged it in. "Don't worry, I'm not sticking around. Just recharging."

He fiddled with the computer then glanced at me.

"I don't know what the hell I'm doing here," I said. Something about him made me feel calmer, or maybe I was just exhausted. I ran a hand through my filthy hair. "Christ, what am I doing? You saw me last night! Why the fuck didn't you tell her I was coming out to talk to her?"

He looked at me, bemused. "I don't know you from Adam. But even if I had told her, she wouldn't have let you in."

"Whatever." I sighed. "She did say you could show me her pictures. If you don't mind."

"No. I don't mind." His voice made him sound younger than he was. "I just flew up for a few days to deliver something."

"You live here?"

"Chicago."

"Your mother said you're a book dealer." I hesitated, then said, "I work at the Strand."

"Yeah? I don't do much business with them anymore. Too expensive. The internet's ruined it for everyone. That's why I had to close my shop."

"You don't do photography, then? It's not the family business?"

"Christ no. I've never wanted to know anything about what she does. Not that she's done much of it since I've been alive. She blamed me for it."

"For . . . ?"

"You name it," he said. "Her marriage. Her work. Her drinking. All of it. She needed an excuse. I was it."

I digested this. After a moment I asked, "Why are you here, then?"

"Business," he said tersely. "And just because she's a bitch doesn't mean I have to be."

He turned to stare out the window. Aphrodite's slight figure walked along the water's edge. Behind her, the deerhounds ran and leaped across the mossy slope like figures escaped from a medieval tapestry.

"Wait till after lunch, maybe she'll be better then," said Gryffin at last. "After a few more drinks."

"I doubt it. She seemed a little—paranoid."

"She is. And the alcohol makes it worse. Actually, I was surprised she opened the door. If Toby hadn't been with you, she wouldn't have. But come on. I'll take you upstairs."

He stood.

"So the drinking's a problem," I said.

"Sure is. It's why she stopped working. Or maybe she stopped working and then she started to drink. It changes according to who she's pissed off at. It was after my father killed himself. None of this is breaking news, so don't bother taking notes."

He held open a door for me. "Watch your head—"

The stairwell was dark. At the top Gryffin opened another door, and I stumbled after him into a long, sunlit gallery. At the end of that hall, more steps led up to another narrow corridor.

"Sorry it's so cold," said Gryffin. "No central heat. I think there's a space heater in your room." He stopped in front of a closed door. "The pictures you want are in here."

Cold stale air surrounded us when we stepped inside. On the far wall, two small windows looked across the water to the islands. "I assume these are what you meant. *Deceptio Visus.*"

I nodded. For a minute I couldn't speak.

"Jesus," I finally said. I felt as though I'd been holding my breath for years, waiting for this. I started to laugh. "Holy shit, this is amazing."

They hung on the walls, each photo framed and numbered as in the book. Some had been shot from a promontory looking out across the bay at distant islands; others were views of Paswegas. I crossed the room, shivering again, but not from the cold.

"Amazing," I repeated in a whisper.

Close up, the colors looked like prismatic syrup poured onto paper: indigo and blood red sky, cadmium sunlight smeared across cobalt water, pine trees like emerald stalactites. The paper was thick, and there were tiny flecks of pigment on the white borders, as though someone had flicked a paintbrush. I brought my face so close to the prints that my breath fogged the glass.

"This is fucking incredible." I glanced over my shoulder. Gryffin leaned against the far wall, watching me. "Do you know how she did these?"

"Hey, if you're asking me—"

"I'm not. I know. You don't?" He shook his head. "It's an unusual method. See, this is all really heavy watercolor stock . . ."

I tapped the glass covering one photo. "You coat the paper with gelatin and let it dry. Then you paint over it with layers of pigment mixed with starch. Remember when you were in kindergarten and you colored a page with a red crayon, and then a blue crayon on top of that, then a yellow one or whatever, then scraped it off with a nail or a chopstick so the colors came through? This is the same principle. Once you've covered the paper with pigment, you add a sensitizer then dry it in a closet, someplace dark. It's a really slow emulsion when it's finished, and light sensitive. When it's dry you put your negative on top and set the whole thing outside in the sun for, like, three hours. You need really strong, hot light—I bet she did it on the beach. The sun just boils that emulsion right off. Then you wash it, and . . ."

I peered at the photo. "Well, it looks like she worked over the finished prints. Touched them up with colored pencils, or maybe pastels. It must've taken her forever." I shot him another look. "Didn't you ever wonder about that? How she did these?"

"Not really. She never cared what I thought. And, well, she's my mother. Did you spend a lot of time wondering about what your mother did?"

"No. But I spent the last thirty years wondering how your mother did this."

"Satisfied?"

I took a step back from the wall. The way the photos were hung made the two windows, with their views of the real islands, look like part of the sequence.

I liked the illusory islands better.

"Yeah," I said at last. "I guess I am. But . . ."

I glanced around the room, frowning. "Her other pictures— the ones from the other book. *Mors.* Where are they?"

"She destroyed them."

"*What?*"

"She burned them. Or, I dunno, maybe she tore them up and threw them into the ocean. It was a few years after I was born. I don't remember it, but I remember hearing about it years later. There was some kind of a big scene, with—"

He stopped. I felt as though I'd been kicked in the stomach. "But—why?"

"I don't know." He looked away. "Something bad happened. You know about Oakwind? The commune?"

I nodded, and he made a grim face. "Well, this was after Oakwind split up, but I gather it had something to do with that. There was a lot of bad blood there, between her and—well, her and just about everyone except for Toby. It didn't start that way, but . . ."

"But why would she destroy those pictures? They were taken, what? In the 1950s."

He shook his head. "Cass, I have no clue. I wouldn't bring it up, though, in the unlikely event she talks to you again. Not unless you still want to drive back to New York tonight. You hungry?"

"Not really."

"Well, I'm heading down to the Island Store to get a sandwich. Want to come?"

I wanted to stay, but I wasn't sure he'd leave me alone there. And even if I wasn't hungry, I needed a drink.

"Yeah, sure," I said. "One minute."

He waited as I made a final circuit, looking at each photo. Then we went back down to the mudroom.

"My mother'll be off for a while with the dogs," he said and pulled on a heavy coat. "They won't bother you. Mostly they just sneak around looking for a soft place to sleep. But if you were expecting Aphrodite to make lunch or something—uh, she doesn't do lunch. She barely does dinner. She does cocktails, after-dinner cocktails, pick-me-ups. A lot of pick-me-ups."

He opened the outer door, looked doubtfully at my leather jacket. "You going to be warm enough?"

"I'll be warm when I get back to the city." I swore as the zipper caught in Toby's sweater. "Your helpful fucking friend already gave me *this*—"

I yanked the zipper free then opened my bag, grabbed my camera, and slung it around my neck. "And you know what else?"

We crossed the moss-covered yard, heading back to the harbor. "I could use a pick-me-up too."

11

INSTEAD OF GOING THROUGH the woods, Gryffin cut down toward the water. There was no sign of Aphrodite or her dogs.

"This isn't the way Toby took," I said. I had to pick among wet rocks and clumps of seaweed, my boots slipping when I tried to climb over a granite mound.

"I like to see the water," said Gryffin. He stopped and held out his hand to get me over the boulder. I ignored it, and he shrugged. "That's the whole point of coming here, right? For the water."

"You tell me. Did you go to school here?"

"School? No." He seemed amused. "They only have a one-room schoolhouse here. It goes up to eighth grade. After that, kids used to go live on the mainland and go to school in Machias. I don't think there's any kids left here now."

"Is that what you did?"

"I went to the Putney School. In Vermont."

Nowadays, tuition at Putney will set you back nearly thirty grand. Even back in the '70s, it would have cost a nice bit of change.

"Isn't that where Dylan's kid went?" I asked.

"Yeah, I think so. But that was after my time."

The tide was coming in, covering the gravel beach and lifting black strands of kelp from the rocks. I saw another sea urchin shell, almost as big as my fist. The bottom had cracked open and the shell had filled with sand. I sifted the sand through my fingers then pocketed it.

Gryffin started for where a thin line of birches ran up the hillside. When he reached the first tree he paused to stare out to the islands. His profile was sharp, his dark hair tangled in the collar of his coat. The light showed up more gray than I'd noticed earlier. It wasn't a conventionally handsome face—nose too big, eyes too small, weakish chin—but it was an intense one, eyes narrowed and mouth set tight, as though it were a constant effort not to lose his temper. Deep furrows in his brow suggested this was a habitual expression.

I wondered what he looked like when he really did lose it. My fingers brushed the spiny little mound in my pocket. I thought of hurling it at him, just to see what would happen, but the shell was so fragile it wouldn't do much good. Instead I popped the lens cap from my camera and shot a few pictures. Gryffin looked back.

"What are—hey, stop that!"

"What, is there a family ban on photography?"

He didn't reply, just turned and began walking again. I lowered the camera and followed in silence up the hill, to where the birches joined bigger trees, oaks and maples. Some of the birches must have been really old. They were huge, their trunks charcoal gray. Not much moss here, just drifts of leaves with a film of ice and scattered patches of thin snow. The ground crackled underfoot, like walking on crumpled newspaper.

"So, you come up here a lot?" I asked.

"Not a lot. A couple times a year. Usually in the summer, or earlier in the fall. I had to go to a show in October, otherwise I would've been here a few weeks ago."

He didn't walk particularly fast, but his legs were so long I had to hurry to keep up. He kept his head down and his glasses jammed close to his face. He looked like an overgrown teenager, gangly and wary. "I mostly came to see a friend of mine. Ray Provenzano, he lives on the far side of the island. He was a friend of my father's.

Another poet. Also a book collector—that's the delivery I told you about."

"I know his name. Vaguely," I said.

"Yeah, the Strand's a place you might still find Ray's books. Here, we're at the road again."

He crashed through a clump of underbrush onto the rutted roadway. I picked my way more carefully, watching that my camera didn't snag on anything, finally stomped out onto the blacktop.

"See where we are?" Gryffin pointed. "There's the Island Store."

"How do you get to see your friend on the far side of the island?"

"There's roads—tracks, anyway—all over the place. Not a lot of cars, that's true. Everyone uses three-wheelers or four-wheelers. ATVs. In the winter they use snowmobiles. Hear that?"

A sudden roar like a chain saw erupted from the woods behind us. "That's a four-wheeler. A few of the old-timers, they still have their old beaters to get around in. Ray, he has a four-wheeler here. Not that it goes anywhere unless his flunky, Robert, drives it. Not that he goes anywhere."

"How come?"

"Ray made himself persona non grata a while ago. He was hiring teenage boys from Burnt Harbor to come over and paint his house. I don't know what went on exactly."

He sighed. "Anyway, the kids' families didn't like it much. Next time he came over to Burnt Harbor, he was ambushed. Spent the rest of the summer in the hospital. He didn't press charges, so . . . everything's kinda blown over. But he doesn't go off-island much anymore."

"How does he get his groceries?"

"He has a teenage gofer. Robert."

"You're joking."

"No. Hey, Ray knows if he tries anything again, he's dead. Here we go."

We'd reached the Island General Store. Gryffin held the door for me and we went inside.

Reggae music blasted from the kitchen. An enormous New-foundland dog lay on the floor, sound asleep.

"Hey, Ben." Gryffin reached down to rough the dog's head. Its eyes remained shut, but its tail moved slightly. "Where's Suze, huh? Where's Suze?"

I looked around. A woodstove with no chimney hookup was covered with coffee thermoses and Styrofoam cups. I could smell pizza baking, and stale beer. There were shelves of canned goods and boxes of pasta; in a smaller back room, cold cases of beer and milk. An ice-cream freezer. Behind the wooden counter, cartons of cigarettes; on a high shelf accessible by a stepladder, bottles of rum, whiskey, brandy, sake. An open doorway led into the kitchen.

"Sake?" I said.

"Summer people," said Gryffin. "Suze's got a pretty good wine list too."

I eyed the comatose Newfoundland. "What's with all the big dogs? I thought this was golden retriever country."

"That's southern Maine. This is the Real Maine—Rottweilers and half-breed wolves. You can ask Suze. Hey, Suze!"

A petite woman walked out of the kitchen, wiping her hands on a dishcloth. She was obviously Paswegas Island's groove supply. I pegged her to be about my age, bleached blond dreadlocks streaked pink and green, windburned cheeks, pale blue eyes, a front tooth with a tiny chip in it; gray cargo pants and a multicolored cardigan over a T-shirt that read THEY CALL IT TOURIST SEASON: WHY CAN'T WE SHOOT THEM? She had the kind of milk-fed face that would have seemed open if it wasn't for a deep wariness in her eyes, the web of broken capillaries around her upturned nose.

"Hey, Gryffin. What's up?" She had a raw, husky voice, as though she spent a lot of time shouting. When she noticed me she did an exaggerated double take. "Whoa. Incoming stranger."

"No shit, Sherlock." I went over to a beer case and grabbed a sixteen-ounce Bud. Suze scowled. Then she started to laugh.

"Nice manners." She turned to Gryffin. "She with you?"

"Kind of."

"Figures." She glanced at the counter. A set of keys rested beside a stack of paper plates. "Shit. Tyler left his keys again. He's gonna be wicked pissed if he gets all the way over to town before he notices."

Gryffin looked toward the harbor. "Want me to go yell at him?"

"Nah. He'll figure it out. What you up to, Gryff? Seeing your ma for the weekend?"

"Maybe. A few days."

"Gonna go see Ray?

"Yeah. How's he doing?"

There was a blast of cold air as the door opened. Two guys entered, eighteen or nineteen, wearing Carhartt coats and reeking of cigarette smoke. In the kitchen a phone rang. Suze went to answer it. Gryffin followed her. So did the big dog. The newcomers walked past me, heads down, and went to the beer case. One of them looked curiously at my camera.

"Hey, Suze, you got a pizza going yet?" he yelled.

Suze's voice echoed from the kitchen. "Yeah, in a minute—"

The new customers went into the back room and studied the beer cooler as though it were a Warcraft cheat sheet. Otherwise the place was empty.

I picked up a bag of Fritos and bellied up to the counter. Keeping an eye on the back room, I palmed the forgotten keys, slid them into the pocket with the sea urchin, then set my beer and the bag of Fritos where the keys had been. Then I stepped over to the window and picked up a copy of the local paper.

It wasn't that local—the *Bangor Daily News*—but at least it was that day's news. With no mail boat, I figured Everett Moss must bring the papers over from Burnt Harbor. I scanned the head-lines—national news mostly, none of it good, and some cautiously optimistic predictions about the state's deer season. I flipped to the local section. A bean supper in Winthrop, an investigation into welfare scams, more bad news for the Atlantic salmon fishery.

And, at the bottom of the page, a brief item.

BODY WASHED UP AT SEAL COVE

The body of an unidentified man was found washed up on a private beach just north of Seal Cove in Corea. The body was discovered just above the high-water mark by an appraiser working on a neighboring house. Cause of death will be determined following an investigation by the State Medical Examiner.

"Hey, Suze." One of the customers ambled back to the counter. He plunked down a six-pack and a box of Little Debbie Swiss Cake Rolls. "I'll take a couple slices of pepperoni or whatever you got going."

I replaced the newspaper and wandered toward the register. A glass case under the counter held nothing but bottles of Allen's Coffee Brandy—pints, liters, big plastic gallon jugs. The guy with the beers noticed me eyeing the case and shot me a grin.

I nodded at him, hoping this wouldn't be misconstrued as part of a Maine courting ritual, then crossed to the other side of the room and pretended to look at a shelf of rental videotapes and DVDs. A darkened doorway opened onto a set of stairs. Beside it a curling bit of cardboard read PASWEGAS HISTORICAL SOCIETY. I peered up the steps, but it was too dark to see anything.

A few other customers entered and made a beeline toward the back room. I waited to see if one of the newcomers was keyless Tyler. So far, no. After several minutes Gryffin reappeared.

"I ordered us both a turkey sandwich. That okay? She's making them now."

"Yeah, sure. Thanks." I inclined my head toward the little crowd around the counter. "Lunchtime rush?"

"You got it."

The door opened again. A young woman came in with two small children. The kids ran over to the ice-cream freezer and began rooting around inside it. The woman walked over to one of the young guys.

"Hey, Randy. You seen Mackenzie?"

Randy shook his head. "Kenzie Libby? No. What's going on? I heard she was missing or something."

"Her father hasn't seen her. Someone said she was down to Burnt Harbor last night."

"At the Good Tern?"

"I don't know." She looked over at the kids. They were both facedown in the ice-cream freezer, their feet dangling behind them. "Brandon! Zack! Get your butts outta there—"

The kids extricated themselves and ran to their mother. Suze came back out of the kitchen, carrying sandwiches and slices of pizza. The woman with the kids bought a pack of cigarettes and left. The remaining customers filed over to the register, paid for their food, and did the same. When they were gone, Gryffin placed a bottle of apple juice on the counter.

"You hear about that? Mackenzie Libby's gone missing," said Suze.

"I heard," said Gryffin as he paid for the sandwiches. "I saw her last night, at the Lighthouse. She checked me in. She was there too," he added, cocking a thumb in my direction. "Not with me, though."

"You see her?" Suze said to me. "She's usually in the office there after school gets out."

"Yeah, I saw her. Gothy little Suicide Girl type?"

"Yup. That's Kenzie." Suze took note of my camera. "You from a newspaper?"

"No." I looked at her T-shirt. "I'm a tourist. But I'm out of season."

"Always open season on tourists." Suze shook her head. "I just hope she didn't get messed up with one of those kids running a meth lab over by Cutler."

"You get a lot of that?" I asked.

"Yeah. It's all over the state these days."

"Any around here?"

"Here on the island? God, I hope not."

"Hey, never hurts to ask," I said.

Suze snorted. "Nice." She bagged our sandwiches, a bottle of juice for Gryffin, and my beer. "Well, have fun. That may be work if you're hanging out with Gryffin."

We went outside. "What, you're no fun?" I said.

"Not much." The door banged shut behind us. Gryffin set down the bag and buttoned his jacket. He raised an eyebrow as I snagged my beer. "Isn't it a little early for that?"

"Beer. It's what's for breakfast." I cracked it and took a sip. "Your mother would know."

We trudged back uphill. "What's with all the coffee brandy?" I asked. "Looks like Suze is stockpiling the stuff."

"That's Allen's Coffee Brandy, the Maine drug of choice. It's lethal—70 proof. That's how a lot of people up here get their vitamin D—they mix it with milk and get an extra buzz from the caffeine. Kills more people than heroin does."

I took another pull at my beer. "That's disgusting."

"Pot kettle black."

"I hate sweet shit," I said.

He angled off toward the path I'd first taken with Toby. I let him get a few steps ahead of me, then slid my hand into my pocket. I found the keys I'd nicked, felt around till I located the hole in the bottom of the sea urchin. The keys just fit, though a bit of the shell broke off as I poked **them inside**. I removed the sea urchin from my pocket and held it, a spiky little fist in my palm. Then I set it down at the edge of the road a few yards from the store.

It blended in nicely with gravel and rocks and dust-covered moss. "Bye-bye," I said and hurried after Gryffin.

We walked without speaking, skirting the pine grove and taking a different path toward the water. I finished my beer, reached over to tuck the empty into the paper bag Gryffin carried. A flicker of distaste crossed his face, but he said nothing.

"So," I said. I was feeling better. The beer made me feel warmer, and everything had that benign, soft-focus look it gets when you drink in the middle of the day. "This commune everyone talks about. Any of those guys still around?"

"Oakwind?" Gryffin stopped to shake a stone from his shoe. "Not really. Most of them were clueless as to how to actually build a house, so their places fell apart over the years. There's a couple of them left."

He put his shoe back on and began walking again. "Mostly they got sold when the hippies went back to Wall Street or Juilliard or wherever. Some people went native and stayed here. There's three or four folks around Burnt Harbor. Here on Paswegas it's just Toby and Ray, I think. One or two guys on the outer islands, but they're not people you want to mess with. I'm talking about guys who live in old school buses and survive on blocks of government cheese."

"And Allen's Coffee Brandy."

"And Allen's Coffee Brandy," Gryffin agreed. "Old Toby, now, he's just a few steps ahead of them—he lives on rum and Moxie. He keeps an apartment here down by the harbor, but he stays on his boat until the weather gets really bad."

"What about this guy Denny?"

He fell silent.

"He's a burnout," he said at last.

I waited, and after a minute he went on. "The winters were too hard for most of them, so they split. The ones who stayed tended either to be the most together, like Toby, or the most burned out. Like Denny. Lucien Ryel, he was together. Together enough not to live here year-round, anyway. You know who he is? He owns an island not too far off."

"Yeah, I gather he's a local celebrity."

Gryffin laughed. "Who told you that? Toby? Around here, someone hires you and his check clears, he's a celebrity. Lucien's more like another has-been. We have a lot of them, in case you haven't noticed."

"What about you?"

"I'm a never-tried-to-be-something."

We were high on the seaward side of the island now, near a line of misshapen firs that formed a bit of windbreak. They leaned away from the water crashing far below, as though trying to flee from it. Beside the trees were two huge boulders. Gryffin walked toward them and gestured for me to follow.

"See that?" He stopped and pointed across the reach to a long shadow that seemed to hover just above the water's surface. "That's Lucien's island. Tolba Island. That means 'turtle' in the Passamaquoddy language."

I squinted, but distance and sea haze made it hard to get a fix on the place. I popped the lens cap from my camera and focused, took a few shots then lowered it again. "It doesn't look like a turtle to me."

"Yeah, me neither. I guess when you're on it, it does. I wouldn't know—I've never been there. Toby says he's got a whole compound—recording studio, main house, hermit's cave . . ."

"A cave? Really?"

"No. That's just what Toby calls it. It's where the caretaker lives. Denny."

"I thought Toby was the caretaker?"

"Toby? No. Toby did a lot of the work, but he's never lived there. And Lucien lives in Berlin—he only comes here for a week or two in the summer. He wanted Toby to stay out on the island

and watch the place for him, but Toby said no. So he got Denny to do it."

"Better than living on a bus," I suggested.

"Yeah, I guess." Gryffin gave me a resigned look. "Denny was the guy started the commune. He was around our house all the time when I was little. He and my mother, they had a thing. It ended badly."

"What happened?"

"I don't know. When I was really little, I was always scared of him. When I got a little older he was gone, but by then I thought he was, like, Charles Manson. I could never figure out what the appeal was, for my mother and everyone else."

I thought of Phil. *This guy she was involved with, he and I did a little business, back in the day.*

"Probably he had really good drugs," I said.

Gryffin nodded. "I remember at Putney, this girl—big druggy—she died of an overdose. When they did the autopsy, the medical report said her brain looked like a Swiss cheese. And I thought, Christ, Denny Ahearn's brain looks like that and he's still *alive*."

"Maybe that's what happened to the girl from the motel."

"Drugs?" Gryffin shook his head. "I doubt it. Not Kenzie."

"No. This Denny guy. Maybe he kidnapped her or something."

"Uh-uh. Denny never leaves the island. I mean, he might come over once or twice a year to get some groceries, but that's it. Toby brings him whatever he needs when he's out there provisioning Lucien. Denny's a total hermit. I mean, he's just sane enough to be on this side of AMHI."

"AMHI?"

"Augusta Mental Health Institution. State loony bin. If he were down in Portland or someplace like that, he'd probably be on the street. But here—well, he's pretty normal."

"Normal?" I stared at him in disbelief. "Ever hear of Stephen King? I mean, you were the one who brought up Charles Manson."

Gryffin looked exasperated. "You're from away, so you don't get it. Half the guys in Maine look like Charles Manson. Especially here down east. There's a lot of survivalist types living off in the woods; you can't go arresting them every time someone wanders off the Appalachian Trail. If you could even find them."

"But you know right where Denny is."

"Yeah, and it's a good place for him." He stared out at the bulk of Tolba Island. "Guys like Denny, maybe they know what's best for them. Stay away from the rest of us. Some people just don't play well with others. If they want to hide and waste their lives, that's their business."

I didn't say anything, just stood beside him, gazing at the water. After a minute I peered at his face.

"What?" he demanded.

"The green ray." I extended my finger. He flinched, and I stopped, my finger hovering an inch from his cheekbone. "There—in your eye. That weird speck of green. I've never seen that before."

"Pigment. Too much melanin. Like a freckle, only in my iris."

"It's weird. It's kind of beautiful."

"That's your beer talking. Come on, I'm starving."

We walked to Aphrodite's house. The day suddenly felt old. The sun was already sliding down toward the western horizon, and as we approached the house it all seemed plunged in shadow. I was hungry now too, and tired.

"I'm going to crash after I eat," I said as we went into the kitchen. The house was silent, with no trace of Aphrodite or the dogs. "I didn't sleep well last night."

"I'll get you set for a nap after lunch. Sit."

He cleared aside the papers on the table by the window. We ate without talking. When we were done he cleared the plates, then said, "Okay. I'll show you the guest room. Then I've got to make some phone calls and do some work."

"What about your mother?"

"What about her? She's either schnockered or out in the woods with the dogs. She'll be back at some point. Maybe after you have your little nap the two of you can trade hangover remedies," he said angrily. "She drives me nuts. She always has. We've never really gotten along."

He sighed and ran a hand through his hair. "You want to know the truth? If I were you, I'd just leave and go back to the city. Even if she'd known you were coming, even if you had brought a tape recorder—she would have found some way out of it. And that—?"

He pointed at my camera. "Not in a million years."

I stared at the table. I still hadn't paid Toby for bringing me out; it couldn't cost much more to have him bring me back to Burnt Harbor. If I left early the next morning, I could be home by tomorrow night. I wouldn't be out much more money, or time, and I'd have the rest of the week to—

To what? Scream at Phil? Drink myself to sleep or shuffle around the clubs looking for music and someone to go home with?

That wasn't going to happen. The clubs were gone. I had a better chance of getting laid here in Bumfuck than on the Lower East Side. I had the Rent-A-Wreck for the rest of the week, but not enough money to do something interesting with it.

And there was still the minor matter of Phil Cohen. No matter that he'd screwed this up, he would give me grief and almost certainly do his part to make sure everyone within the Tri-state radius thought it was my fault.

"Shit, I dunno." I looked up at Gryffin. "Listen, would there be a problem with me staying overnight? I mean, this editor arranged this for me, and I don't really want to bail and go back without anything to show him. I'll keep a low profile," I added. "Just for a day or two."

Gryffin sighed. "I guess we can see what she says. Get your stuff, and I'll show you the guest room; you can sleep or read or whatever. Check how your Nokia stock's performing."

He led me back upstairs. We went past the room with Aphrodite's islandscapes, into a narrow ell that led to one of those jerry-built additions, its floor uneven and the windows mismatched.

"Remember what I was telling you about the folks at Oakwind having no idea what they were doing when it came to architecture and building? This is Exhibit A." Gryffin waved in disgust at the walls. "Denny built this—*my* wing of the house, including the guest room. And if you think it's bad now, you should have seen it back then. Snow blew right through the cracks in the walls; there'd be two-inch drifts in here. Nothing was plumb—you could set down a bowling ball at one end of the hall and it would roll to the other. Toby had to come in and basically rebuild it. So it's still kind of funky, but—"

He stopped and opened a door. "You will find no snow in your sleeping quarters."

No heat, either, that I could detect, but I was afraid to push my luck by mentioning that. The room was under the eaves. There was a bed with a white coverlet, a nightstand and lamp, a ladder-back chair and small chest of drawers. Braided rug on the floor, a window overlooking evergreens and gray rocks.

"It's fine." I dumped my bag on the bed. "Thanks."

Gryffin bent to feel the baseboard heater. "This isn't on. And I forgot the space heater. Well, you'll be okay for a while. If you stay, I'll bring you the heater before you go to bed tonight, how's that? But now I have to get some work done. Bathroom's down the hall, there should be hot water. See you later."

He left. I grabbed a change of clothes and found the bathroom. More mismatched windows, a cracked skylight that had become a morgue for moths and flies, clawfoot tub, rust-stained sink.

But there was a nice Baruch rug on the pine floor, and expensive Egyptian cotton towels, and a block of Marseille soap in a brass holder by the tub. All of which led me to peg Gryffin as a closet sensualist.

I took a long bath. There was plenty of hot water. When I

was done I dressed, keeping my expensive jeans but upgrading to a clean black T-shirt. Then I went back to my room, crawled under the blankets, and passed out.

It was late afternoon when I woke. The light seeping through the windows had that trembling clarity you get in early winter, when there are no leaves to filter it and the clouds are the same color as the sky. I exhaled and watched the air fog above my mouth. Then I got out of bed, went to the bathroom, and washed my face. I raked my fingers through my hair and confronted the mirror.

I looked like shit. For the last few decades I'd coasted on good bone structure and good teeth. Right now those were the only things I still had going for me. With my ash-streaked hair and sunken eyes, I looked like a bad angel scorched by the fall to earth. I bared my teeth at my reflection and stepped back into the hall.

The door to Gryffin's room was shut. I knocked on it softly. No reply. I went inside, closing the door behind me.

The room wasn't bigger than mine, though less monastic. There was a more elaborate rug on the floor, a nice Mission-style bed, carelessly made with plaid blankets and a heap of pillows. Dark curtains, half drawn. A small desk with the now-empty computer case I'd seen in his motel room. An open suitcase holding flannel shirts and jeans. A few framed photos on the walls—a fishing trip, friends from Putney, graduation from Bowdoin College. On the desk a heavy old brass candlestick with a thick pillar candle and a Gauloises matchbox; on the windowsill some smooth gray rocks and the carapace of a box turtle.

I went to the bed, pulled back the covers, and ran my fingers across the sheets. No protective plastic here—the bedding was fancy cotton, soft as suede, or skin. Christine had loved expensive sheets too. She'd tried to buy some for me, but I wouldn't let her.

"Why?" she demanded. "This is crazy, Cass. Your sheets are like sandpaper! You sleep on nice sheets at *my* place."

I hadn't said anything. She wouldn't have understood. It *was* crazy. It was like not having a cell phone or a digital camera. The discomfort, the annoyance, reminded me that I was alive. It kept me from feeling completely numb, even as it kept me detached.

Christine had kept me human, barely. I knew that, and it scared me. Sometimes when she'd touched me I'd felt like I was burning, like her bed was on fire. I still felt like that sometimes when I thought of her.

I picked up one of Gryffin's pillows and buried my face in it. It smelled of some grassy shampoo, and faintly of male sweat. It had been a long time since I'd been close enough to a man to smell him. I stood for a moment with my face pressed against the pillow. Then I lay on the bed, pillow crushed to me so I could breathe in his scent, and masturbated, thinking of the way he'd looked in the photo, that green-flecked eye.

Afterward I smoothed the coverlet and headed back to my room. I thought about getting my camera, decided to leave it. I hadn't brought much film with me. I pulled on Toby's sweater and went downstairs.

The house had a strange, late-afternoon calm. Chilly hallways, dead bluebottles on the windowsills; the dull ache, somewhere between anticipation and disappointment, of knowing night was almost here. In the living room a deerhound curled on the couch like a gigantic dormouse, snoring. No other dogs. No Aphrodite. Not much heat coming from the woodstove, though I could see a dull glow through the soot-covered window.

I found Gryffin at the kitchen table, bent over his laptop. He waved tersely at me without looking up. I crossed to the refrigerator and peered inside.

A container of skim milk, another of V-8 juice; eggs and a bag of coffee. Breakfast wasn't just the most important meal of the day around here. It was the only meal.

"I'm going to the store," I announced. "You want anything?"

"Me? Uh, no," Gryffin said distractedly. "Thanks."

Outside, chickadees fluttered in the trees. Something rustled in the dead leaves of an oak then made a loud rattling sound as

I passed. It didn't seem as cold, despite looming shadows and a steady wind off the water.

Or maybe it was like my grandmother always said: You can get used to anything, even hanging. I remembered Phil's words—*all that bleak shit you like? Well, this is it.*

He was right. It made me feel the way the Lower East Side used to make me feel, before the boutiques and galleries and families moved in and the clubs closed and the place became just another sewage pipe for American currency and overpriced clothes. I loved the way it used to be, loved that edge, the sense that the ground beneath me could give way at any time and I'd go hurtling down into the abyss. I had fallen, more than once, but I'd always caught myself before I smashed against the bottom. Back in the day, of course, I was out there taking pictures of people who weren't so lucky. It was terrifying, but it was also exhilarating.

Now all that had changed. Now there were clean wide sidewalks over the pit. Making my chump change last from week to week for twenty-odd years was no longer a sign of being a survivor. It was further proof, not that any was needed, that I was a fuckup.

I was still managing to be a fuckup here, of course. But I was starting to like it. It seemed a good place to be, if you needed something to slice through the scar tissue so you could feel your own skin. At the moment, the cold was doing a pretty good job of that. I zipped my jacket and shoved my hands into my pockets, wind at my back. That beer had been good. Some Jack Daniel's would be better.

I walked through the woods. A small animal burred angrily from a tree. I stopped, thinking of the fisher Toby had mentioned, looked up and saw a red squirrel glaring down at me. I chucked a pine cone at it and went on.

There was no one in the Island Store when I arrived, just the big Newfoundland lying in front of the counter. The air smelled good, garlic and tomatoes cutting through the underlying odors of beer and pizza. Dub music thumped from the kitchen. The dog stood and yawned then followed me as I went to the back room and got another beer from the cooler. When I returned to the counter Suze stood there. She slid a carton of cigarettes behind a Plexiglas window, then locked it.

"Going for another pounder?" She pronounced it *poundah*. At my blank look she picked up the beer and held it in front of my face. "Sixteen ounces?"

"Yeah. And two pints of Jack Daniel's." She raised an eyebrow. "I'm on the South Bend Diet."

"Too quiet for you here?" She dragged over the ladder and got my bottle from the shelf. "Coming from the big city?"

"Seems busy to me. That girl disappearing. Bodies washing up on the beach."

"Aw, that happens all the time. The bodies, I mean. Often enough, anyway. The hungry ocean, it's a dangerous business." She took my money, put the bottles in a paper bag and pushed it across the counter to me. When I started to remove the beer, she shook her head. "You can't drink that in here."

Before I could retort, she motioned behind her. "But you can drink it out here."

I followed her into the kitchen. She grabbed a coffee mug then kicked open a battered wooden door, letting in a blast of wintry air and revealing a rickety set of steps. One of the rails was broken, and there was only room for two people to stand side by side. But it had a commanding view of a Dumpster and a propane tank and, past a ragged scrim of stone buildings and faded clapboard, the harbor. Suze leaned against the intact railing, leaving me to stand with my back to the door.

"Yeah, Mackenzie." She cupped the mug in her hands. "John Stone called me a little while ago—county sheriff—I guess they're waiting till tomorrow to officially call it a missing persons case."

I popped my beer. "Isn't that kind of a long time to wait? If they're really worried?"

"That's what I said." Suze nodded vehemently. "I asked him

why this wasn't an Amber Alert—they practically shut down 95 and close the Canadian border if that happens—but he said she's too old. Under fifteen, that's the cutoff date. Older'n that, you're screwed. And the local authorities, they don't have a lot of manpower. So they don't like going off on a wild-goose chase, which is what John Stone thinks this is."

She shook her head, disgusted. "This is so messed up, man. You're from away, so you wouldn't know, but this kind of shit happens all the fucking time. Kids go missing, no one ever finds them. Or they show up . . ."

Her husky voice trailed off.

"Dead?" I suggested.

"No," she said. "A lot of people just never get found. But I think that's because they don't want to. The rest, mostly they turn up alive, in Florida or South Carolina or someplace like that. Someplace warm. Kenzie's mom, she lives around Orlando. Her and Merrill had a really nasty divorce. Kenzie hasn't seen her mom in two years. I think she headed down there. But in the meantime everyone's all worked up and the cops are pulling over everyone with a broken headlight. Over there, I mean."

She indicated the mainland. "And, I mean, some scary shit does come down, you know? People disappear, you don't find the body for ten years, or maybe ever. And maybe you never find out what really went down. Then you get the critter factor, and you got to bring in forensics from Augusta . . ."

"What's the critter factor?"

"You know—animals getting to the body, eating it. This ain't Disneyland. People forget that. Even people who live here and oughta know better. Like, you don't fuck around on a boat in the winter. You don't get drunk when you go out to get your deer."

She glanced at my leather jacket. "You don't forget to wear blaze orange in November. Anyway, that body in Seal Cove? Maybe they drowned, maybe it was a suicide or drugs." She sighed and drank her coffee. "Our local law enforcement sucks."

"I'm surprised you have local law enforcement."

She gave a croaking laugh. "We sure don't have much. John Stone has to come over from Burnt Harbor whenever a call goes in. That can take hours, if he's up in Eastport or someplace. If you need an ambulance, someone has to take you to Burnt Harbor by boat. If things are really bad they Medivac you out by helicopter. That costs, like, three thousand dollars, so you better be insured. Which of course nobody is."

"So, what—you just don't get sick out here?"

"Pretty much." She smiled, and a sheaf of blond dreadlocks fell across one eye. I reached to brush the matted curls away, waiting for her to flinch or snap at me. But she just stared out toward the shore.

"Sure is slow today." She laughed again and pointed to where a figure in yellow raingear paced slowly along the beach, head down. "Look at Tyler! He's still looking for his keys. Man, he was pissed. He came roarin' back up here, but they were gone, and he starts yelling at me—'*Where's my goddam keys, goddamit, where the goddam hell you put my goddam keys!*'"

She finished her coffee. "I told him he better not be accusing me. You saw them, right? Right there on the counter? I told him he probably came in and got 'em and just forgot about it. He's always wasted. That or one of his friends picked them up for him and he'll get 'em later when he runs into them."

I watched the man on the beach.

"Yeah, I saw them," I said thoughtfully. "They were right there on the counter. Maybe one of those little kids picked them up."

Suze frowned. "Yeah, maybe. I'll ask Becky next time she comes in. Or I'll just sic Tyler on them—that would teach 'em."

She gave her rough laugh and edged past me to the door. "I better get back, before someone else loses something. So, you're a friend of Gryffin's? He's an odd guy."

I finished my beer and followed her back inside. "Odd?"

"Well, you know." Suze pulled her dreadlocks back from her

face and fastened them with an elastic. She looked prettier that way. "His family's kind of weird. Did you know his father, Steve?"

I shook my head. Suze gave me a funny look, as though she was about to say something. Instead she began fiddling with the register.

After a moment she glanced up again. "He was a nice guy, Steve. A poet—he hung out with Allen Ginsberg and those guys, they came up a few times when the whole commune thing was happening. I was just a kid, but I remember; it was very cool. That's how Ray ended up here. But I don't really know what the deal was with Steve and Aphrodite. He was gay, and, I mean, she had to know it. Everyone at that commune was screwing like rabbits. Aphrodite got pregnant, and then Steve and Ray, they began living together. Ray pretty much raised Gryffin after his father died. He's a sweetheart—total opposite of Aphrodite. Who, as you may have figured out, is a total bitch."

I nodded. I took the two pints of bourbon from the bag and shoved them in my jacket pockets, turned to toss the empty beer bottle into the trash.

"Hey!" Suze frowned. "We recycle here!"

"Sorry."

I grinned sheepishly and handed the empty to her. Suze stuck it beneath the counter then lifted her head as a woman walked in. Before she could say a word, Suze had a pack of cigarettes and a lottery ticket on the counter. I looked across the room to the darkened stairway.

"Historical Society open?"

"Yeah, sure. Light switch's on your right. It's pretty rank, no one's been up there in about six months."

I went upstairs. A bare bulb illuminated a sparsely furnished room, cold and smelling of mildew. Two grubby armchairs, their greasy upholstery covered with knitted afghans. A few makeshift cases held arrowheads, fishing spears, rusted farm equipment. Faded photographs on the walls—members of the Paswegas County Grange circa 1932, lobster boats, the Island General Store in palmier days. The island school's eighth-grade class of 1978, seven bright-faced kids in jeans and tie-dyed shirts. I looked at this one closely and recognized Suze, her blond hair and the same puckish grin, flashing a sardonic peace sign.

That was about it for the Historical Society. There was also a shelf labeled LIBRARY that consisted entirely of the collected works of Clive Cussler, and a third-place trophy from the Collinstown Candlepins Bowling League. Beside the trophy was a turtle shell the size of my hand, black with yellow spots.

Something was scratched into the shell. I picked it up and tilted it until the ragged letters caught the light. Letters and something else—a crudely carved eye.

S.P.O.T.

I held it toward the overhead bulb.

"Spot," I whispered and rubbed my finger across the carving. A pet spotted turtle. I turned it over. Someone's initials were carved on the bottom.

ICU

I started to put the turtle shell back on the shelf when something rattled inside. I shook it, turning it back and forth until a small object dropped into my palm. I held it toward the overhead bulb.

It was a tooth. Not a baby tooth, either—a grown-up incisor. The upper part was smooth as ivory, but the long root was discolored, mottled brown and black.

Not with decay. When I scraped it with my fingernail, flecks came off. Dried blood.

I sank into one of the armchairs, set down these mildly gruesome trophies and pulled out one of the pints of bourbon. I took a few sips, again picked up the shell and the tooth and stared at them broodingly.

I traced the letters on the upper carapace—S.P.O.T.—and wondered if they'd been carved while the turtle was still alive. I hoped not. I swallowed another mouthful of Jack Daniel's, then slid my hand beneath Toby's sweater, across the scar tissue on my lower abdomen and the raised lines of my tattoo.

I let the sweater fall back and studied the shell some more. Some kid's pet, I assumed. I peered inside, but I couldn't see anything, so I stuck my finger in and wiggled it around. Something prickly was stuck on the bottom.

I fished it out. I thought it was a wad of cloth, but when I rubbed it between my fingers I realized it was a frizz of human hair, dark brown and friable as a dead leaf.

I flicked it away. I dropped the tooth back inside the shell and replaced it on the shelf. I wiped my hands on my jeans, stuck the Jack Daniel's into my pocket, and went back downstairs.

The place was empty again, save for Suze and her dog.

"I better go," I said. "See you."

Suze leaned on the counter and grinned. "You get bored, you know where to find me."

"Thanks. I'll keep that in mind." At the door I stopped. "You know where Toby Barrett lives?"

"Toby? Yeah—he's right down there in the Mercantile Building—"

She pointed to an old granite structure on the far side of the dock. "His apartment's in the basement. You go round to the back, there's a door there. You have to pound on it and hope he hears you. He's not there now, though," she said, scanning the gray water. "His boat's out, so he must've gone back to Burnt Harbor. He'll either spend the night there or come back here late. You need to talk to him? I can give him a message when I see him. Probably won't be till tomorrow."

"That's okay. I was just curious. I'll catch up with him later," I said and headed up the road. At the crest of the hill, I stopped.

There on the beach was that stocky yellow-clad figure, still looking for his keys. He was a lot higher on the shore than he had been; it must be close to high tide. The sun had dipped behind the far end of the island. Ragged clouds hung above a sea streaked yellow and green as an overcooked egg yolk.

I wished I'd brought my camera. For a few minutes I watched the solitary form pacing the shore, slate-colored gulls wheeling above his head like the black cloud that used to follow Joe Btfsplk in old L'il Abner comics.

Some people make their own bad luck. Others, I help them out.

Finally I turned. As I approached the shadow of the firs, I looked down to make sure the sea urchin was where I'd left it. It was.

12

BY THE TIME I reached Aphrodite's house, it was almost dark. The wind had risen, and my boots squeaked on the frozen ground. But in the kitchen everything was noticeably warmer and brighter than when I'd left. All the lights were on, and someone had stoked the woodstoves.

Aphrodite was nowhere in sight. Neither were her dogs. I heard Gryffin's voice from the next room, looked in to see him pacing as he talked animatedly on the phone. Before he could see me, I retreated to the woodstove and tried to warm up. I did another shot of Jack Daniel's. Then I pulled out the film canister I'd nicked from the basket earlier and opened it.

Inside was a roll of processed film. God knows how many years ago it had been cooked—decades, maybe. I assumed the photographer was Aphrodite, though there was no way to be sure. Whoever it was, he or she hadn't given much thought to conservation.

Film is alive. Too much heat, too much humidity, too much sunlight—these things kill it. Fortunately, the chilly conditions in Aphrodite's mudroom had functioned as a makeshift fridge and protected this roll, at least, over the years. I turned from the woodstove, so the sudden exposure to warmth wouldn't cause condensation. I unspooled the film carefully between my fingers and held it to the light.

It was black and white, Tri-X. I caught its familiar sweetish odor, somewhere between latex and lactose. The negs were over-exposed, maybe deliberately. They showed a naked man lying on his back, the image cropped so the head was out of frame, his torso a surreal contortion of erect cock and hands. All the highlights and shadows were reversed, of course, so that his cock became a lumi-nous wand surrounded by radiant fingers. There were dark shapes in the background that might have been faces, or masks.

Or they might have just been shadows. I continued to thread the negs through my fingers, frowning as I examined each one.

"... great. See you then."

In the next room, Gryffin's voice abruptly fell silent. I curled the film back into a tight spool, replaced it in the container, and shoved it into my pocket just as Gryffin entered the kitchen.

"I'm heading out." He crossed to the sink to dump his coffee mug. "I'll be back in a couple of hours."

He started to go, then leaned against the sink and stared at me. I could see the little wheels turning behind those wire-rimmed glasses. Was I a safe bet to leave alone for the evening? Or would I rob his mother blind?

I stared back at him, thinking *And where the fuck would I go then?*

He must have gotten the message. "Anything edible you can find, help yourself. Or Suze down at the Island Store stays open till six or seven."

"I'll manage," I said.

He studied me again, then beckoned me to the woodstove. "Here. Watch."

He loaded the firebox with wood, adjusted the damper, pointed to more wood in a box by the door. "If I'm not back in a couple of hours, throw some of that on, okay?"

He left. When he was out of sight, I scanned the living room for any sign of Aphrodite then headed into the basement.

The steps were half rotted, and a naked hundred-watt bulb made ominous spitting sounds when I switched it on. Plaster flaked from the walls, exposing wooden lathes and clumps of horse-hair. I heard scrabbling in the shadows as I walked around. Dirt floor, stone foundation; exposed beams curlicued with wormholes. Cobwebs covered shelves of old bottles and rusted tools. An oil drum served as a trash bin.

But nothing that resembled a darkroom setup. I was starting to wonder if Gryffin had lied to me when I spotted a door in the far corner. It was set into a floor-to-ceiling cubicle not much bigger than a closet, made of drywall and two-by-fours. I hurried over and tried the knob.

Gryffin was right. The door was locked.

I tried to jimmie it open. No luck.

I retraced my steps and returned to my bedroom. For a few minutes I sat and watched the sky fade from lavender-gray to indigo to dead black. I didn't put the light on. Instead I drank Jack Daniel's until the darkness no longer seemed ominous but soft, diffuse, as though a heavy black curtain had been replaced with gray gauze. A few stars showed through the trees then disappeared. The fog was coming in.

Finally I got up. I found my wallet and retrieved my credit card and started back downstairs.

The hallway was dark. But at the far end, light spilled from an open door. I walked quietly as I could, until I was close enough to see that the light came from a bedroom. Inside was a TV with the sound turned off. I cleared my throat and took another step, waiting for someone to call out.

No one did. I stuck my head inside.

The place was a mess. Heaps of clothes on the floor, books and papers piled on top of a woodstove that obviously hadn't been used in a while. A space heater hummed noisily. Black-and-white prints hung everywhere, and a double bed was pushed against the far wall. It seemed to be covered with big fur throws—the three deerhounds. I could just make out a small black figure in the middle of the bed.

Aphrodite. She lay on her stomach, silver hair tied back with a black ribbon. Several opened photo books were strewn around her. Her skinny legs in their black tights stuck out from beneath one of the dogs, as though the geisha doll had been tossed in with a bunch of stuffed animals.

I couldn't believe I'd left my camera behind.

I knew better than to go back for it. *The Decisive Moment*—that was the English title for Cartier-Bresson's most famous book. And I'd missed my chance—already one of the dogs was stirring. I went back down to the basement.

In a few seconds I'd sprung the lock with my credit card. I entered and instinctively reached for the safelight switch.

Red light surrounded me, along with the dank smell of mildew and the sour-wine stink of acetic acid. As my eyes adjusted to the faint crimson glow, I felt my neck prickle.

It had been twenty years since I'd been inside a darkroom. I steadied myself against a counter and took stock of what surrounded me.

A plywood table with plastic trays for developer and stop bath, fixer and holding bath; shelves made of cinder blocks; a stainless steel sink. Boxes of photographic paper bleached with mold. Jars of developer. A metal cabinet scattered with curled, moisture-damaged prints so blackened with mildew they resembled fungi. Plastic sleeves for holding negatives, all empty. An enlarger. Above the table, a sagging clothesline for drying prints. A pair of heavy rubber gloves hung from the clothesline. I put them on, grateful to have something between me and the foul air. When I picked up a jar of developer, a bloom of spores rose from it like smoke.

Even thirty years ago, this darkroom hadn't been state-of-the-art. But I didn't need high-tech equipment to do what I'd come down here for. I flipped on the overhead light. The bulb had blown. I'd have to do my prep work under the safelight. It was dim, 15 watts, but I'd manage.

I opened the tap, hoping the pipes hadn't frozen. The faucet gurgled and coughed and finally spat a thin stream of brownish water. I waited till it ran clear, rinsed out the plastic processing trays, then set about mixing the developer, the stop bath, the print fixer. I had no idea if the chemicals would still be lively, but it was worth a shot. I mixed each batch directly in its tray and lined them up on the plywood table. Then I looked for tongs.

No tongs. I'd have to agitate the paper by hand, shaking each tray. Messy but feasible. I did find scissors, and the heavy piece of glass I'd need to flatten the negs. I cleaned and dried it on my T-shirt then dug out the roll of film. I uncoiled the long spool and gingerly cut it into four pieces, careful not to damage any individual frame. The plastic envelopes for holding negs were too filthy to use. Again, I'd make do. I turned to examine the enlarger.

It was a Blumfield, circa 1974 by my guess, British made. An expensive piece of equipment, with a flat easel surface and an upright pillar holding the enlarger itself. It seemed dusty but otherwise in working order. I cleaned off the surface where the negs would go, blew dust from the enlarger lens, then switched on the tungsten diffuser bulb, praying it hadn't blown too.

It hadn't. I switched off the diffuser and searched until I found a sealed box of Kodak paper. The cardboard was buckled and smeared with mold, but inside its foil wrapper the paper was undamaged. I grabbed a sheet and went to work.

I moved fast. I set the negs on the enlarger's easel, covered them with the glass plate, and exposed them for eight seconds. I slid the sheet into the stop bath, shook it and counted to thirty, then transferred it to the rapid fixer and did the same thing again.

Even with the rubber gloves, my fingers were numb when I finally rinsed the sheet under running water. I didn't care. I'd already seen the ghostly images bleeding through, each one an eye opening slowly, irrevocably, onto another world. When I turned the water off my hands shook with cold and excitement. The safelight was so dim I could barely see what I'd just printed on the contact sheet. I needed a loupe.

I found one in the rusted cabinet. The round eyepiece was badly scratched. It was like looking through a submarine porthole, but I needed to see if any of the images warranted an enlargement. If so, I might have something to bring back to Phil, or just keep for myself—my own little souvenir of Bad Vacationland. I squinted at the contacts, and swore in exasperation.

This wasn't *Blow-Up.* There was no body; no dead body, anyway. The nude pictures were lousy, not to mention overexposed and out of focus. A dick is a dick is a dick, and no one was going to be interested in this one.

But three images were different. They showed a young woman, also nude, with light brown hair, head tipped to smile at the camera. She had a hand cupped over each breast, and her hands were holding something, coconuts maybe, or balloons.

Technically, these images were slightly better than the others. They were in focus, and the exposure seemed right. But there was something about the girl's expression that held my eye. She looked innocent and sexy and slightly daft, Betty Boop recast as a long-haired hippie chick.

I spent another minute trying to decide which of the three was best. Finally I chose one, found the matching neg, and made a hasty 8x10 enlargement. Then, just for the hell of it, I picked one of the other negs at random and pulled a print of it too.

Both were sloppy. My buzz was wearing off. I was exhausted. My initial excitement now turned to fear of getting caught. I hung the contact sheet and the two prints on the line to dry, dumped the processing chemicals down the sink, and did my best to clean the place up. The negs went back into the canister in my pocket. I peeled off the gloves and flung them onto the cabinet, grabbed the still-damp prints and contact sheet, switched off the enlarger and safelight. I split, locking the door behind me.

The basement was cold and empty. I waved the prints back and forth for a few seconds. When they seemed dry, I rolled them into three narrow tubes and stuck them down the front of my jacket. I made sure I still had the loupe and went upstairs.

After the basement, the kitchen felt like a sauna. The only sounds were the crackle of wood in the stove and the slap of waves on the shingle outside. I pulled a chair in front of the woodstove, looked around for any sign of Aphrodite or her dogs. All seemed down for the count.

I was starting to feel the same way. I yawned. When my stomach growled, I decided against another shot of bourbon and stumbled over to the fridge.

The pickings, as noted, were slim. I grabbed two eggs and the V-8 juice. I rinsed out a coffee mug and cracked the eggs into it, filled the mug with V-8, and downed it in one long swallow. Then I dragged myself to my room and collapsed into bed.

13

I WOKE FROM A dream of a cold finger touching my forehead, pressing until it felt as though someone were driving a nail into my skull. I groaned and opened my eyes, recoiling when I saw an enormous brown eye staring at me.

I shot upright as the eye resolved into a grizzled head and cursed as the deerhound backed away. Pale light flooded through the window. The dog sat and cocked its head, staring at me. I stared back then started to get up.

My stomach churned; I doubled over and was sick on the floor. I sat shivering on the edge of the bed until I summoned the strength to stagger to the bathroom. By the time I'd showered and stumbled back, the dog had cleaned up for me.

"Nice work." I pushed it from the room.

I dressed, opened the window, and leaned out so the icy wind could scour my cheeks. I shut my eyes and remained there until I felt my hair freeze.

I had no idea what time it was. Midmorning, maybe. I felt lightheaded, with that deceptive lucidity you get from a world-class hangover, the feeling that you've finally purged yourself of everything that made you drink in the first place.

Another spasm of nausea cured me of that. I stayed on the bed until it passed then remembered the prints I'd made yesterday.

They were still tucked into my jacket. I took them out and smoothed them on my knees: the contact sheet and two 8x10s.

In the darkroom, I'd assumed all the photos had been taken by Aphrodite. The first picture—that close-up of a cock surrounded by waving hands, as though it were a theremin—it definitely had the hallmarks of Aphrodite's work. The uneasy juxtaposition of the familiar and the strange had been reduced to a banal attempt at 1960s hard-core, but the same eye had been behind the camera. I recognized it the way you recognize someone in a bad Halloween costume.

Like I said, it was out of focus and the lighting was all wrong. The depth of field was off. But even if it could have been improved by more time in the darkroom, what would be the point? It was crude and banal.

What a waste.

I examined the other photo. This one should have been cheesy, with its wide-eyed subject mugging for the camera, long hair tossed back from her face, hands covering bare breasts.

Yet this photo worked. It wasn't just that the girl was cute and had nice tits, what I could see of them, anyway. It was that the photographer had trusted his instincts, and the girl had trusted them too. Even more, she'd trusted *him*.

And, just as I knew the first photo was by Aphrodite, I knew this one had been taken by a man. Phil used to make fun of me for claiming I could identify a photographer, no matter how obscure, by his or her images. He ranked on me even worse when I once drunkenly announced I could identify the gender of a bunch of unknowns whose pictures hung at a small gallery in DUMBO.

But I did it. I nailed every single one.

"That's amazing, Cass," Phil said. "Another remarkable if totally useless skill."

Even now, I couldn't tell you how it works. It's like me picking up damage, like there's a smell there, or a subliminal taste. And you'd think that would be an easy call to make with this picture, because it sure looked like it would taste like cheesecake.

But this photo was weirder than that. When I'd first glimpsed the contact sheets under the safelight, I'd noticed the girl was holding something over each breast. I thought they were coconuts, which would fit in with the whole kitschy vibe this little hippie chick projected.

Now that I looked more closely, I wasn't so sure. Even when I got out the loupe and peered at them, I still couldn't tell. She was holding something, and from the shit-eating grin on her face, it was something funny. But what?

I had no clue. Whatever it was, though, it made me queasy. The girl trusted whoever was behind the camera. That came through, in her smile and the way she'd tilted her pelvis toward him, which seemed less of a come-on than a welcome. She looked about nineteen or twenty. There were tiny furrows to either side of her mouth, and tinier lines around her eyes.

And the photographer had done a sharp thing there too. You couldn't see it in the frame, but he'd set a lit candle in front of her then positioned her so that the flame was reflected in each eye, making them sparkle. A simple effect, but a good one.

For a few more minutes I sat and stared at the photo. Then I put away the loupe and slid the prints and contact sheet into my copy of *Deceptio Visus*. I needed coffee and something other than Jack Daniel's as a nutrient.

Downstairs, the living room woodstove was dead cold. The one in the kitchen had nearly burned out. I wadded up some newspapers and tossed them inside, along with a few sticks of wood, and hoped for the best. Then I made coffee, trying to convince myself that my hands trembled from the cold and not because I had the shakes. The deerhounds heard me and came skittering into the room. They looked hungry, so I gave them some water and filled their bowls from one of the sacks of dog food in the mudroom. They ate voraciously and afterward shambled over to where I sat by the window with my coffee and a piece of dry toast.

"Poor old dogs," I said. Their heads were almost on a level with my own. "Doesn't anyone ever feed you?"

"That's the way they're supposed to look."

In the doorway stood Aphrodite. The dogs turned and raced toward her. She put a hand to the wall to steady herself from the seething gray mass.

I stood awkwardly, pointing to my chair. "Do you want to sit?"

"In my own house? I'll sit where I choose."

She walked toward the sink. In the thin morning light she appeared ancient, her skin dull and her hair disheveled, eyes bloodshot behind wire-rimmed glasses. I felt a pang. She looked so frail. It seemed impossible this wizened doll could have shot the pictures in that upstairs room, let alone the grim, hallucinatory images in *Mors.* Her hands trembled as she pulled a coffee mug from a shelf.

"I made coffee," I said.

"So I see."

She reached into a cabinet and withdrew a bottle. A minute later she joined me at the table, steam threading from her mug, and the smell of brandy.

We sat in silence. I wondered if she'd rail at me again, or acknowledge that we'd met the day before. Did she even remember?

Finally I said, "Gryffin showed me your photos. The island sequence. They were—it blew me away, seeing them for real. I mean, I waited my whole life to see them, and then, last night . . ."

My voice died. "They're just incredible," I said at last.

"I was never happy with the transfer process." Aphrodite sipped her coffee. "That whole book. I was never happy with it. The colors were muddy. Today, maybe they could do a decent job. But back then?"

She shook her head. One of the dogs whined and thrust its nose at her. She stroked its muzzle absently. "They ruined it."

I stood to refill my coffee. "Do you want some more?" I asked.

She gazed out to where thin eddies of mist snaked across the water's surface.

"Sea smoke." She drank what was left in her mug and slid it toward me. "Thank you."

I filled both mugs and handed hers back.

"The other pictures," I said tentatively, settling in my chair again. "From *Mors*. I didn't see them up there. Do you—are they here?"

"They're gone."

"Oh. Jeez. I—"

I stopped, afraid I'd said too much already. She seemed not to have noticed I'd spoken.

"I saw them," she said after a moment. "Your pictures."

I looked up in surprise. "My pictures?"

"Yes. When your book came out. A long time ago. Twenty years, I suppose."

"More like thirty."

"Thirty." She nodded slightly without looking at me. "Yes, that would be right. Some of them—you had a good eye. One or two, I remember. The rest, though—"

One thin hand waved dismissively. "Derivative. And late. You weren't the only one who saw *Mors*. You know that."

I stared at the table. Everything went white. There was a sharp taste in my mouth, that pressure against my forehead. It was a moment before I realized she hadn't stopped talking.

". . . his were just grotesque. Tabloid fodder. He stole from me like the rest of them did, and it was all shit. *Just shit*."

I looked up. Aphrodite's eyes shone with a hatred so pure it was like joy.

"You little thief." She jabbed at me. "Cassandra Neary. You think I didn't see? But you were the least of it. The least."

One of the dogs barked as Gryffin walked into the kitchen.

"This the breakfast club?" he asked, yawning.

I shoved my chair back and stormed outside, the door slamming behind me.

I didn't stop until I reached the gravel beach. I paced along the shore, kicking at rocks. The wind tore at my face, but I hardly noticed. I headed to a stand of small, twisted trees and boulders. Driftwood had fetched up against the rocks. I grabbed a branch and smashed it into a boulder, again and again until it splintered into dust and rot. Then I leaned against a barren tree, panting.

"If only we could harness this power for good." Gryffin stepped gingerly up the path from the rocky beach. "I come in peace," he added and raised his hands.

I drew a long breath. "Fuck off."

"Here." He held out something wrapped in a paper towel. "Ray made this for dessert last night. I brought a piece back for you."

I hesitated, then took it: a slab of apple pie.

"He's a good cook," said Gryffin. "Those are his apples too. Fletcher Sweets, they're called. They only grow here on the island."

"Thanks."

"A Yankee is someone who has pie for breakfast. That's what Toby says."

Gryffin watched me eat. "You were really whaling on that tree," he observed. "What'd she say to you?"

"Nothing."

"She's a monster. But you knew that. It's why you came here."

"I came because I needed a fucking job and Phil Cohen lied to me that he'd set up this interview." I finished the pie and started walking back along the beach. "And because I wanted to see those pictures. Most of which, I gather, she destroyed. So instead of this goddam trip earning me money, it's costing me money."

I picked up a rock and threw it into the waves. "Which I don't have."

"Well, she's gone off, for a while, anyway. Her and the dogs."

"What does she do all day?"

"Beats me. Usually she makes a circuit of the island." He swept his arm out, drawing an imaginary circle. "Along the shore. She picks up stuff that washes up. She'll be gone for a while, unless the weather gets really bad."

We walked toward the slope that led back to the house. A raven hopped across the dead grass and let out a gravelly cry at our approach.

"I'm going to the Island Store," said Gryffin. "Want to come?"

"No. Not this minute, anyway." I sighed. "You think I'll be able to get a ride back over today?"

"Today? Well, you missed anyone who'd be going early this morning. But someone'll probably head back later in the afternoon."

"What about your friend Toby? Will he take me?"

"Probably. If I see him, I'll mention it."

"That'd be good."

He started up the hillside. I jammed my hands in my pockets and watched him go. The steely light burned my eyes, and my feet ached from the cold. But I couldn't stand the thought of seeing Aphrodite again. When Gryffin was out of sight, I began climbing the hill myself.

Once I reached the pine trees, the path split. One trail bore off to the left and angled downhill again, toward the village; the other wound upward among more trees and jagged outcroppings of stone. I took the right-hand path, scuffing through a mat of pine needles and fine snow.

It was a steep climb. After a few minutes, I began to sweat. My fury diminished, bitten away by the cold. For the last few years I'd carried on conversations in my head. Well, not conversations, really: arguments. Now the voices fell silent. I found myself focusing on things I didn't usually notice, like the vapor clouding my face with every breath, the way sounds seemed to carry from far away. Seagulls, a diesel engine, waves tugging at the shingle beach below.

As I neared the top, the hill's crown emerged, a granite dome surrounded by oaks with a few dead leaves still clinging to them. A weathered sign dangled from a lopped-off bough.

OAKWIND EST. 1973

Boards and buckled plywood poked up between rocks and burdock stalks, all that remained of the commune. I picked my way between scrap metal, broken bottles, old tires, a fire pit. A man-sized standing stone reared from the wreckage of weeds and winter-killed saplings, flecks of white paint on its granite surface. I crouched in front of it and pushed away dead ferns to get a better look.

Someone had painted three concentric circles on the stone, like a target. The central circle—the bull's-eye—had been filled in with white paint. There was a smudge of metallic green pigment in the middle circle.

I touched it. The stone was rough and cold. When I withdrew my hand, specks of pigment and lichen stuck to it.

I felt a sudden wave of dizziness, stumbled to my feet and backed away.

From the far side of the hill a raven clacked. A late cricket clung to the standing rock, rubbed its legs then crawled toward the earth.

I kicked at the ground, then, for good measure, bent and dug at it with my fingernails. A scant half-inch of turf came up. I rubbed it between my fingers and stood again, relieved.

There was nothing buried under the stone, not unless the hippies had jackhammered their way into the hill's granite dome. It was just a rock with a bull's-eye painted on it. The commune had probably used it for target practice. I started back down the hillside, but only got a few steps before I stopped again.

Tucked among the oaks was the mottled bulk of a large vehicle. An old International school bus, painted in a camo pattern with candy colors—pink, lime green, orange—that time had turned splotched and sickly. Branches burst through the broken windows. What looked like lime green paint was splattered against the glass, but as I got closer I saw this was some kind of mold, its edges curled and black.

I pushed through the underbrush until I reached the cab. Above a wooden platform that served as a step, the door hung in two pieces. I pushed it open.

It was like being in a fish tank where everything has died. Light streaked through windows hung with blackened plastic curtains that had once been green. All the seats had been removed, and wadded rugs had been chewed to fuzz by rodents. There were beer cans and condoms, signs of more recent occupation; splintered chairs, a plastic bucket crusted with brown. An exploded futon. A jagged face hung from the ceiling, lantern-jawed and with huge hollow eyes.

It was another mask, like the frog I'd seen on Toby's boat. Green, with a beaked mouth and a stiff ridged collar like some kind of horned dinosaur, only this thing had no horns. The glossy paint had peeled, revealing swatches of newsprint. I touched it. It felt pulpy and soft, like an enormous mushroom.

I walked to the rear of the bus. Here a few windows were intact. A raised plywood platform held a foam mattress covered with the remains of an india-print spread, chewed to a paisley filigree. Above the bed, moisture-swollen paperbacks lined a small bookshelf.

What the Trees Said. The Forgotten Art of Building a Stone Wall. Walden Two.

The only hardcover was an old edition of Mircea Eliade's *The Sacred and the Profane.* Its frontispiece was stamped *Andover-Harvard Theological Library* above a name written in faded blue.

D. Ahearn.

I opened it. The spine was broken, its pages heavily annotated in the same blue ink.

UNDERTAKING THE CREATION
OF THE WORLD

GENERATION THROUGH <u>RETURN</u>
<u>TO THE TIME OF ORIGINS</u>   !!!!!!

recovering this *time of origin* implies ritual repetition of the
gods' creative act.
!!!!!!!! The *marine monster Tiamat* !!!!—symbol of darkness, of the formless, the   non-manifested—

Excitable boy, I thought.

There was also a New Directions paperback of Stephen
Haselton's poetry, with a picture of him on the back. A thin guy,
fair haired, clean shaven, blandly handsome. Photo credit: Aphrodite
Kamestos.

I flipped through this book but found nothing. No name on
the frontispiece. No marginalia. I tossed it onto the shelf and wandered back to the front of the bus. The place looked and felt as
though it had been stripped of everything that might have been of
interest or value. Not even a torn Grateful Dead poster remained.

So much for the counterculture.

I went outside. Dun-colored clouds crowded the sky. The
wind rattled stalks of burdock and dead goldenrod as I headed
toward the path. As I entered the stand of trees, I hesitated, feeling
that someone was watching me. I turned and looked back at the
clearing.

A gray stone loomed among rubble and dead ferns. That
was all.

14

NO ONE WAS IN the house when I got back. I paced between the kitchen and the living room, anxious for Gryffin to return and tell me I had a ride to the mainland. I killed time by cracking the second bottle of Jack Daniel's. I considered calling Phil to ream him out but decided I'd rather do it in person.

Finally I decided to take another look at Aphrodite's island photos. I'd spent my life dreaming of them. Maybe for just a little longer, I could pretend I was in my own private museum, with the pictures all to myself.

The upstairs hall was cold and smelled of ash. I retrieved my camera and went into the room, leaned against the wall and stared at the photos.

After a few minutes I shot a few frames. It felt good to handle my camera again without someone yelling at me to put it down. I knew I'd never get anything worthwhile—I was fighting nightfall, exhaustion, Jack Daniel's on a nearly empty stomach. I stumbled around anyway, struggling to get enough distance, enough light, a focus.

The sound of the shutter release was like a moth beating against glass. I took a dozen pictures then slid down to the floor. I began to cry.

Those photos . . . They were so fucking amazing. It was like she'd thrown open a window and let you look into a perfect world, the most beautiful place you could ever imagine, but you could never get inside it. No matter what I did, I would never be able to produce something that good. I would never make something *great*. Even at my best, for fifteen seconds thirty years ago, I wasn't capable of it. Aphrodite had been right.

Bile and the afterburn of bourbon rose in my throat. I lurched into the hall and ran right into Gryffin.

"Jesus!" He caught me and shook his head. "Can't you walk out a door without knocking me over?"

"No." I pushed past him.

"Hey, wait up—"

He followed me to my room. I shoved my camera into my bag, avoiding his eyes.

"What happened?" he said. "Did Aphrodite get back?"

"No." I fought to keep my voice even. "Did you find Toby? I really need to get out of here."

"He wasn't around. Suze said he had a job in Collinstown and he stayed over there."

"I have to go! Isn't there someone else? The harbormaster, the fucking Coast Guard—I don't care who it is. Just get me back to my car!"

"Hey, I wish I could, okay? But no one's around. Merrill Libby's daughter never came home last night. Everett's helping organize a search party."

"Then why aren't you there?"

"I'm city folk now. They don't want me."

He leaned against the door. "I came to see if you felt like celebrating." He grinned and suddenly looked remarkably like the guy in the snapshot. "I just made fifteen grand."

I snorted. "Stock market?"

"I sold a first edition to a guy out in L.A. That's what took me so long. Suze has a better internet connection at the store, so I was working from there. I've been waiting till the market was right. I paid ten pounds for it—about fifteen bucks—at a shop in Suffolk a few years ago."

"Nice turnaround. What is it?"

"*Northern Lights.* The original title for *The Golden Compass.*"

"What's *The Golden Compass?*"

"I thought you worked at the Strand?"

"Not in the stacks. Stock room."

"It's a children's book—that's where the big money is. The English edition predates the American, so . . ."

"Is it a good book?"

"You think I have time to read these things? You didn't answer me—you want to help me celebrate?"

"How? Where do you spend fifteen grand around here?"

He started down the hall. "I'm going to dinner again at Ray's. I told him last night, if I came back I might bring another guest—I figured if you were still around you'd need to get away from this place. He's a good cook. He has a decent wine closet. But I'm leaving now, so—"

I followed him downstairs into the kitchen.

"So either you come with me or you're on your own, dinner-wise," he finished.

He went into the mudroom, pulled on his coat and picked up a big flashlight, dashed into the kitchen and returned with a small book that he stuck into his pocket.

"For Ray," he explained. "You coming?"

"Yeah, what the hell." I glanced down at my T-shirt and leather jacket. "I'm not dressed for dinner."

"For Paswegas, you're overdressed."

"How far is it?"

"Not that far. Come on."

He walked outside, heading for the water, then turned to where a line of white birches glowed ghostly in the early dark. "Less than a mile. There's a path through here, just watch your step."

He switched on the flashlight. The birches flared as though they'd been ignited, and Gryffin disappeared into a thicket.

"Is Ray another book collector?" I said, hurrying to catch up.

"Not really. He's just . . . a collector. All kinds of things. Books, junk, stuff he finds at the dump. Folk art—he's big into folk art. Primitive art."

"Like Cohen Finster?"

"Not that classy. Ray likes his art down and dirty. Not pornographic—well, not necessarily pornographic—but he likes an artist with dirt under his fingernails. You know, guys who build a model of the Sistine Chapel out of old carburetor parts. Life-sized cows carved out of soap. That kind of stuff. But you'll like his place—Toby helped him build it. Ray's one of the original cliff dwellers."

After about ten minutes the path began to climb more steeply. I grabbed at trees for balance. The wind raged up from the water, bitter cold, and sent dead leaves whirling around us. Finally we reached the top.

"This is it." Gryffin stopped. He pointed the flashlight to where the ground abruptly disappeared. "See that? Don't go that way."

The boom of waves echoed up to us, the relentless wind. He waved the flashlight, and its beam disappeared into the darkness. I turned and saw lights showing through the mist.

"What the hell is that?" I said.

"That's Ray's place."

It was made entirely of salvage. Clapboards, barn siding; car hoods and bumpers; washing machine doors and a satellite dish, as well as cinder blocks, corrugated metal, blue sheets of insulation. There were dozens of windows, no two alike. Solar panels covered the roof. A row of propane tanks was lined up alongside one wall, and a Rube Goldberg contraption that looked like it might have something to do with water.

Weirdest of all was that it had all been fashioned to look like a castle, complete with a shallow moat filled with dead leaves, a footbridge made of two-by-fours, and a turret. Sheets of plastic flapped from the walls, as though it were a snake shedding its skin.

"Boy, Sauron's really fallen on hard times," I said.

"He built it all himself, and it didn't cost a thing," said Gryffin. He strode across the footbridge to a door that had once belonged to a walk-in freezer. "Hey, Ray! Company—"

The steel door swung open, revealing a teenage boy, maybe seventeen or eighteen. Tall and heavyset, with sandy hair and beautiful, almond-shaped blue eyes in a pockmarked face. He gave Gryffin a perfunctory smile, but when he saw me the smile faded.

"Gryffin, hey." The boy lifted his chin in greeting and stepped away from the door. Around his neck he wore a necklace like the one Kenzie had made, of sea glass and aluminum tabs. "S'up?"

I followed Gryffin inside. The boy gave me a hostile stare. His mouth parted so that I could see a black stud like a boil on the tip of his tongue.

"Nice," I said. "You oughta have that looked at."

We walked into a large room filled with freestanding bookshelves. Faded banners hung from the ceiling like flypaper, emblazoned with mottoes in the same lurid colors as the old school bus.

```
VENCEREMOS!
THE MILK OF HUMAN KINDNESS HAS NO EXPIRATION
DATE
TEMPIS FUCKIT
```

The books leaned heavily toward the Beats, mangled paperbacks of *On the Road* and *Junkie* and *The Dharma Bums,* but also some that were valuable. And there was artwork, if you could call it that: a couple of paint-by-number pictures in homemade frames; a series of paintings of fanciful dirigibles on small oval canvases; a poem composed of words and phrases cut from newspapers then glued on a sheet of cardboard and signed by Brion Gysin and William Burroughs. That would be worth what the whole house cost to construct, plus a small retainer for Lurch back by the front door.

There were framed photos, too, on the wall beside the kitchen, where Gryffin had disappeared. I heard a whoop, and Gryffin stepped out.

"Well, glad you're pleased," he said. "I told you I might bring someone? Here she is. Cass, this is Ray—"

A figure came bustling toward me. A stocky man in green drawstring pants and voluminous purple T-shirt, his white hair long and wild, eyes glinting behind purple-framed glasses repaired with duct tape. His face looked as though it had been dropped then reassembled by someone who'd never done it before. The hand he thrust at me was missing the middle finger.

"Hello, hello!" he exclaimed in a hoarse Brooklyn accent. "So glad to have anuthah visitor. Ray Provenzano."

He shook my hand vigorously. "You didn't mind coming to dinner, did you? Aphrodite's a terrible cook. Robert! Robert!"

He shouted, and the boy who'd let us in lumbered back into view. Ray clapped a hand on his shoulder and looked at me. "What would you like to drink, Cassandra? Wine? I just opened a great Médoc."

"Sounds good."

"Robert, get another bottle, wouldja please? Here—"

Ray stepped into the kitchen. There was the sound of stirring, a burst of fragrant smoke, and he reemerged holding two full wineglasses.

"Shalom," he said, thrusting one at me. "I know who you are—the photographer who shoots dead things. I googled you. I'll hafta see if I can get some of your stuff. Your book, maybe. You still taking pictures?"

He kept talking as he ducked back into the kitchen. "You can see, I'm a big collector. All kinds of stuff. If I'd known you were coming, I'd of gotten your book. How's that wine?"

"Good," I said.

"You like cassoulet?" He poked me with a wooden spoon. "Not in the kitchen! Gryffin, get her outta here. Go sit or something, I got stuff to do."

I went into the main room. Robert sat on a sprung couch, listening to an iPod through a pair of earbuds. Gryffin stood perusing the bookshelves. I made a dent in my wine, then inspected those photographs.

He had a good eye, this friend of Gryffin's. There was a signed early Caponigro; a Bobbi Carey cyanotype; an image from Kamestos's island sequence that I'd never seen before.

But it was the next photo that made me catch my breath.

It reminded me of Aphrodite's stuff. Threads and fuzz protruded from the hardened emulsion, and a stew of pigments bled through the image. Colors you normally wouldn't see in the same frame—magenta, crimson, a sickly psychedelic orange; acid green, spurts of violet and leathery brown. The rush of colors was disorienting but also purposeful, like one of those untitled de Kooning paintings that seems to hover just beyond comprehension.

Somebody knew what he was doing here. But I sure as hell couldn't figure it out: I was at a total loss as to what I was looking at.

To make it worse, the picture had been messed with after processing. I could see brushstrokes and the marks of a fine-point drafting pen, or maybe a needle, and there were bits of leaves or feathers just under the emulsion surface. It all distracted from the image itself, that abstract mass of color and texture; and while there was a real painterly quality in the use of pigment and brushwork, it was definitely a photograph and not a painting. All the post-production stuff—brushstrokes, dirt—made it impossible to get a fix on what the original image had been.

Perversely, that's also what made it hard to look away. It was weirdly familiar, like Aphrodite's pictures, but like something else too. What? I kept feeling like I almost had a handle on it—a face, a dog, a branch—feeling like I *knew* what it was. I'd seen it before.

I'd bet cash money that whoever shot this picture had looked a long time at *Mors*, maybe too long. And I'd bet my life it was the same guy who'd shot those peekaboo pictures of the little hippie chick.

The weirdest thing was how it *smelled*.

You had to be practically on top of it to notice, but it was there—a pungent, indisputably *bad* smell, like nothing I'd ever encountered before. It smelled like a skunk, only much, much worse, musky and intensely fishy at the same time. It smelled horrible and rank without smelling like something dead—whatever it was, it somehow smelled *alive*. I've been around corpses. I've seen a body hauled out of the East River. I've taken pictures of a severed arm.

None of them smelled good. And none of them smelled like this.

Gryffin came up behind me. "What're you looking at?"

"This picture here," I said. "Who took it?"

Gryffin squinted at it. "I dunno. Ask Ray."

"It's not by Aphrodite, right?"

"Definitely not. Although . . ."

He peered at the corner of the print, then tapped it. "Look at that."

I had trouble seeing it at first, but then I made it out—a tiny word, in black ballpoint ink, printed carefully as though by a kid. S.P.O.T.

"'Spot'? What's that?" I remembered the turtle shell I'd seen in the Island Store. "What, is it a pet?"

"It's a joke. It's got to be one of Denny's."

"Denny Ahearn?"

"Yeah. Ray would know. Want more wine?"

We sat at a table set with candles and heavy old silver, also two more bottles of wine. I refilled my glass and said, "So Denny—he was a photographer too?"

"Oh sure." Gryffin rolled his eyes. "Drugs, sex, photography— Denny's a Renaissance man."

"Robert!" Ray's blistering voice rang from the kitchen. "Get in here, I need you. Now!"

Robert stood, still jacked into his earbuds, hitched up his pants, and sloped into the kitchen. I leaned across the table toward

Gryffin. "What's with the kid? Does this guy like getting beaten up by the natives?"

"Robert's eighteen. Ray pays him to help out. I don't think they sleep together—Ray just likes to have someone to boss around."

"Helps out with what?" I looked at the skeins of dust trailing from the ceiling and walls. "Is Robert in charge of the duct tape?"

"Voila!" Ray made his entrance, carrying a majolica tureen. "Cassoulet!"

There was also home-baked bread and pickled string beans. The wine was great.

And there was a lot of it. The cluttered space began to take on a warm glow. If I let my eyes go out of focus, I could almost imagine what our host might see in Robert, who ate in silence, earbuds dangling around his neck.

Mostly, though, I looked at Gryffin. There was nothing special about him. He was nothing like my type, unless you consider too much melanin in one iris to constitute a type.

But I couldn't tear my eyes from him. I kept waiting to see him look the way he did in that stolen photograph.

It wasn't happening. Occasionally he'd glance at me, that oddly furtive look. When we finished eating, Robert cleared the table then brought in more glasses and a bottle of Calvados before flopping back onto the couch. Within minutes I heard him snoring softly.

"Ray." Gryffin pointed to the photo we'd examined earlier. "That picture—who took it?"

"That one?" Ray's broken face twisted into a frown. "That's Aphrodite's."

"No," I said. "The one next to it."

"This?" Ray stumped to the wall and removed the photo. "This is one of Denny's."

He blew on the surface. A fume of dust rose, and he began coughing. "Ugh—Robert! You're falling down on the job! For chrissakes."

He shook his head. "Yeah. Denny's—this is one of his. I paid a lot of money for this."

Gryffin laughed. Ray glanced at him irritably and turned the frame over. It was backed with a piece of stained cardboard.

"He needs to work on his presentation," Ray said. "I told him that. He never listens."

"Denny's incapable of listening to anything except the UFO voices in his head," said Gryffin. "May I?"

Ray handed him the photo. Gryffin stared at it, finally pronounced, "I still think it's crap."

"You Philistine," moaned Ray. "It's *beautiful.*"

Gryffin looked at me. "What do you think?"

"I think it's good," I said as Ray poured Calvados. "But—what is it?"

Ray handed me a glass. "Who knows? I like it."

"Yeah, me too." I sipped my Calvados, still staring at the photo. "Does he do a lot of these?"

Ray leaned back in his chair and stroked his beard. "I'm not sure. Not a lot, I don't think. She started him on it—Aphrodite." He pointed at Gryffin. "He doesn't like to hear this."

Gryffin stood. "No, I don't. Excuse me for a minute."

He left the room. Ray shrugged. "Don't mind him. Aphrodite, she and Denny were involved, back in the old days. This was before Gryffin was even born, but there was always bad blood between him and Denny. Who fucked everything, I might add. Everything in skirts, anyway."

He hesitated, his expression pained. "Gryffin's father, you know, Steve—the love of my life. We were together seventeen years. Steve lived here, Gryffin was always around. I mean, when he wasn't off at school. Aphrodite was never much of a mother. Actually, Steve was never much of a father either," he said. "Whereas I love kids—and don't you look at me like that, I never touched him. *Never touched him.*"

He sighed, staring across the room to where Robert snored on the sofa. "You know, I never touched those others, either. I did *look*, though," he added and laughed again. "But you know what that's like, right? You photographers. You like to look and not touch. Voyeurs."

"No," I said. "Voyeurs need to feel protected. I like to feel threatened."

"Seems like you'd be able to find a lot of work these days."

"Hasn't worked out that way. Denny—how come he didn't sign his name?"

"Didn't he?"

"There." I pointed at the corner of print. "It says 'Spot.'"

"Oh yeah. That's him."

"Spot? What's that mean? Gryffin said it's a joke."

"A joke?" Ray held out his hand, and I gave him back the photo. He looked at it then replaced it on the wall and settled back into his chair. "I guess it's a joke. Tell you the truth, I don't really remember. It was something weird, though. Denny, he was into that kind of woo-woo stuff. That commune of his, they got into all kinds of ritual shit. Well, *they* called it religion. I called it ripping off the Indians. Native Americans, I mean—they were crazy for that kind of stuff. After they finished the Buddhists and the Hindus and the God knows what else. All those off-brand religions. But those kids, none of 'em was any more Native American than me."

He sighed. "Denny, he was way into it. He was smart too—he flunked out of Harvard. He was studying comparative religions or some such. *Gilgamesh*, that was one of his big things. Babylonian stuff. He was a beautiful young man, Denny. You wouldn't know it now. Let's face it, living here takes years off your life. That's why everyone drinks like a fish. It's the winters. Heating with wine. Look at me! Aged before my time."

He downed another shot of Calvados. "But that photo—what think you, huh? His stuff is starting to get picked up. Lucien Ryel, he bought some. That one there, I paid a grand for it a year or so ago. It's probably worth more now."

"A grand?" I gave him a dubious look. "That's a lot of money for someone no one's ever heard of."

Ray shrugged. "Hey, I'm a collector. You know how it works. Everyone wants to bet on the new kid. Even if he's an old new kid. The photography market's crazy these days, you know that. I don't think Denny gives a rat's ass about that kind of shit, but Lucien, he's got an investor's eye. He turned on his rock star friends—Pete Townshend, he bought some of Denny's stuff. Townshend goes for outsider art. I guess this qualifies as outsider photography."

"Pretty good for someone who used to live in a bus."

"Did Gryffin tell you about that?" Ray gave his braying laugh. "Hey, don't knock it! This is one of the last places in the country where people can still live between the cracks."

It didn't seem to me that Ray would fit between a crack smaller than, say, Chaco Canyon. But I kept my mouth shut as he went on.

"They're all one-offs, his stuff. Does he do a lot of these? I don't know. I've never seen where he lives. But he obviously spends a lot of time on them. Like Aphrodite used to, you know? Making her own paper and stuff."

"And emulsion," I said. "He must prepare his own emulsions too. That's what it looks like to me. If they're really one-offs, then he's producing some kind of monotype. Or monoprint, if he uses the neg more than once. Interesting."

"That the kind of stuff you did?"

"No. I would've been happy to sell lots of copies of my stuff. If anyone wanted to buy them. But—"

I pointed at the photograph. "What it means is, that's an original work of art. Like if this guy was Robert Mapplethorpe, that picture would be worth a ton of money. Probably you've already figured that out."

"That it's worth a lot of money?"

"That this guy ain't Robert Mapplethorpe." I finished my Calvados. "So, what about her? Aphrodite. How come she stopped taking pictures?"

Ray ran a hand across his scarred cheek. "Hard to say. Those early photos—she never really had a success big as that again. I think part of it was she took so long with each one. And there wasn't a market back then for photographs, like there is now—she couldn't make money at it. She refused to do commercial work when they wanted her to, and after a while no one wanted her to. And the drinking—that's been going on a long time. When she and Steve got involved—well, you know, she really loved him. And he loved her too, in his way. But it was different then; for a long time he couldn't really admit to himself what he was. That he was gay. Unlike me, who never had a problem."

He laughed.

"They must've gotten along at least once," I said. Ray looked at me, puzzled. "Gryffin. They had him."

Ray made a face. "Oh yeah. Gryffin. The miracle child. That was Denny's idea. Like I said, Aphrodite never really took to it— being a mother and all. But things went bad between her and Denny early on. They got real competitive, he started taking pho- tos, Aphrodite encouraged him—like, here's this beautiful young guy, she takes him under her wing, you know? But then they got competitive, and then it got weird. *He* got weird. Aphrodite, she's accusing him of stealing stuff—"

"Like what? Camera equipment?"

"No. *Stealing her soul.* Stealing her pictures! Not the photos— stealing what she did. You know, ripping her off. Her ideas. Her 'vision.'"

He laughed and wiggled his eyebrows. "Totally insane! Like how people used to think you'd steal their soul if you took their picture? That kind of thing."

I frowned. "She couldn't believe that."

"Nah. *She* didn't believe it. But Denny did! He was very convincing, too." Ray looked at me and shrugged. "I guess you had to be there. Anyway, nowadays she spends all her time drinking with those damn bony dogs."

"Are you two done?" Gryffin stood in the hall, watching us.

"Yeah," I said. "Bathroom that way?"

He nodded.

Compared to the rest of Ray's jerry-rigged palace, the bathroom was luxurious. Mexican tiles on the floor, a small Jacuzzi.

Best of all, a well-stocked medicine cabinet.

I locked the door then perused the contents: Percocet, hydrocodone, Adderall. I pocketed some of the Percocets, but I was more interested in the Adderall. At 25 milligrams apiece, they'd provide a nice little blast of Dexedrine. I popped one then added a handful to what was already in my pocket. Ray wouldn't miss them.

When I returned, Gryffin was staring stonily out the window. Ray looked at me.

"I thought maybe you decided to use the Jacuzzi," he said. "You can if you want."

"No thanks." I sat down. Immediately a phone began to ring. Ray turned and bellowed at Robert, still sound asleep on the couch.

"Robert. ROBERT. Get the frigging phone!"

Robert stumbled to his feet. I glanced at Gryffin. He raised his eyebrows, silently framing a question: Leave? I nodded.

"Hey, Ray." Robert stuck his head out from the kitchen. "It's John Stone."

"John Stone, John Stone," Ray muttered. "Now what."

He shuffled off to get the phone. Robert came out and sat at the table.

"She was looking for you." He ran a finger across the sea glass necklace.

"What?" I said.

"The other night at the Good Tern? Kenzie—she was looking for you."

"That girl from the motel?" I frowned. "I don't even know her. Why would she be looking for me?"

"I dunno." He stared at his feet. "But she told me. She said there was some lady from New York City staying there. She said you were nice."

He shot me a baleful look. Gryffin glanced at me then leaned across the table to ask, "So you saw her, Robert?"

"No. We were IMing. I was going to meet her later, but she never showed up. She said you were going to give her a ride."

"A ride? To where?"

"New York, I guess."

I stared at him then laughed in disbelief. "Jesus! Poor kid. She must really be hard up."

"That's what I said."

I looked to see if this was a joke, but his face had already shut down. From the kitchen Ray's voice rumbled on into the telephone.

"Did you know her?" I asked Robert.

"Yeah. We hung out. She gave me CDs to rip."

He stopped as Ray came back into the room and announced, "That was John Stone. He wants to talk to you guys—not you, Robert, I told him you were here. You have an alibi, though he said he might need to talk to you if she doesn't show up. But you—"

Ray pointed, first at Gryffin, then me. "And especially *you*—"

He sank back into his chair. "He wants to question you."

"Me?" I felt a small hot flare inside my skull, the Adderall's opening salvo. "What the fuck does he want to talk to me for?"

Ray began to sing, "*'Sheriff John Stone, why don't you leave me alone . . . ?'*"

"This guy's the sheriff?"

"Hey, Cass," said Gryffin. "Relax. John's a good guy, he won't give you a hard time. What'd he say, Ray?"

"He said they were starting to question people. Her father filed a missing persons thing a few hours ago, and now they have to follow up on it. Even though John told me in great detail how Little Missy's probably headed off to Lubec or Bangor or someplace with a boyfriend no one knows about, which personally I also think is probably the case, but John has to do his job.

"But he doesn't have to do it tonight," he added and laughed again. "'Cause he don't want to come over here from Collinstown unless somebody has something of interest to tell him. Which I said I'd ask. So, do any of you have something of interest to tell him?"

Gryffin shook his head. "Not that I can think of."

"I already told him I was IMing with her last night," said Robert.

All faces turned to me. The red flare inside my head mushroomed into something white and hot. "Not without a fucking attorney."

Ray slapped his thigh. "That's the spirit! Stick it to the man!"

"Shut up, Ray." Gryffin looked annoyed. "You're overreacting, Cass. If you don't have anything to tell him, just say that tomorrow. You don't need to get paranoid; no one's accusing you of anything. Anyway, I saw you at the Good Tern."

I could see Robert watching me with those blank cold eyes. A song went through my head: *I was just gonna hit him, but I'm gonna kill him now.*

"I gotta go," I said, and stood.

"Yeah," said Gryffin. "We better get back."

As I passed the couch, I looked down and saw several CDs scattered across the cushions. Green Day, Mosque; and something else.

I held the CD toward Robert. "This yours?"

"Nope. Kenzie's. I told you, she gives me stuff to download."

"Huh." I looked at it again: Television, *Marquee Moon.* "She has good taste."

Robert shrugged. "She likes that old shit."

I tossed it back onto the couch and followed Ray and Gryffin to the door.

"Well, very nice to meetcha, Cass. Maybe I'll get hold of your book." He embraced Gryffin. "You be back tomorrow?

"I doubt it. Got to get back to Chicago."

Robert stayed where he was. When I looked across the room, I saw him nodding, earbud cords dangling from his ears, his eyes fixed on me. I stared back at him, then turned and followed Gryffin into the night.

15

WE WALKED BACK MOST of the way without talking. We were both pretty loaded; it took most of our energy just to keep our footing in the icy mist. I had a nice shiny feeling from the Adderall, and after a few minutes I popped a second to boost it.

But something kept gnawing at the glow: the memory of Mackenzie Libby's white face in the headlights.

She was looking for you. She said you were going to give her a ride.

Wishful thinking, but why not? I was probably the first person she'd ever seen who might have heard of *Marquee Moon*. I thought of Patti Smith's "Piss Factory," *sixteen and time to pay off.* Leave home, sleep in the gutter, find yourself a city to live in.

I should have picked her up. Though then, of course, the locals would be coming after me with pitchforks.

"Be careful," Gryffin warned as the path narrowed. "It's slippery—"

I felt impervious to anything short of a bullet to the head. When we came to the final stretch leading to the house I began to run. I tripped and fell, hard.

"Hey." Gryffin hurried to my side. "I said be careful! Are you okay?"

He crouched beside me. I pushed him away, but he grabbed my hand and trained the flashlight on it.

"Jesus," he said. "Doesn't that—"

"Hurt? Yes." My palm was slick with blood. "Shit."

I staggered to my feet, got the Jack Daniel's and took a swig. Gryffin watched me with a kind of intrigued disgust. I laughed.

"What?" he demanded.

I couldn't speak, just kept laughing as I wiped my bloodied hand on my jeans. Gryffin turned and walked on. I ran after him, an amphetamine surge knuckling behind my eyeballs so that the darkness splintered into sparks.

"Aw, don't go away mad," I yelled, but he ignored me.

"I'm going to bed," Gryffin said when we got inside. He hung up his jacket and started for the kitchen. "You and my mother can sit up doing Jell-O shots if you want."

"Wait," I said.

I leaned forward, grabbed his chin, and kissed him. He didn't pull away. His cheek was unshaven, his mouth tasted of Calvados. I let my hand trail down his neck, my fingers resting for a moment in the hollow beneath his windpipe. I felt his pulse, then drew my mouth down to his throat and kissed it.

"Gryffin," I whispered. "What kind of a name is *Gryffin*?"

He pulled away and left the room. When he was gone I started laughing uncontrollably.

The Adderall had kicked into high gear. I love speed, that black light you see alone at three A.M., when bottles shimmer like cut glass and everything reminds you of a song you once loved. This is when everything comes into focus for me, when what's inside my head and what's outside of it become the same thing.

What can I say? Bleak is beautiful. I stared at my reflection in a darkened window, pressed my palm against the cold glass. I thought of my camera in the spare room.

The house was dead still, the woodstove barely warm. Two deerhounds lay on the couch but didn't stir when I walked past.

Aphrodite was still conspicuous by her absence, though she'd left the radio on, a DJ whose voice droned into John Coltrane. I turned it off, found an empty film canister and dropped my stolen pills into it, and went upstairs.

The door to Gryffin's room was closed. Mine was open. I went in and sat on my bed for a few minutes, my legs twitching. To blunt the speed, I drank some more Jack Daniel's. The bottle was almost empty, so I killed it. I picked up my camera and checked the flash.

It was dead, and I hadn't brought a spare battery—I couldn't think of the last time I'd needed one. I thought of a recent argument I'd had with Phil.

"Get a digital camera, Cass. Anyone can take a great picture with one of those. Even you."

"Screw that," I'd said. "It's too easy. It's degraded art—no authenticity."

"Oh, right." He looked disgusted. "The last word on Degraded Art, from Ms. Authenticity 1976. You know what your problem is? You're a goddam dinosaur, Cass. You're fighting a culture war that ended thirty years ago. And you know what? Your side fucking lost."

I started, hearing a voice in the spare room. I'd been talking to myself. It happens. I made the mistake once of mentioning it to Phil. He suggested I try Ecstasy.

I cradled the old Konica against my chest. It wasn't even that late—a little past midnight. The drugstore speed would keep me going for a few more hours.

I felt pretty good, in between spasms of speedy paranoia. Kenzie Libby's face, an outboard engine droning into voices that whispered my name. I wondered what Kenzie had said about me when she'd been online with Robert. I remembered what Toby had said about the islanders.

Every couple of years you get a witch hunt.

I pushed the thoughts aside. Time to move.

"Hey ho," I croaked.

I went to the bathroom and drank from the tap then stared at my reflection in the mirror.

I looked like I'd crawled here from the city. I popped the lens cap from my camera and took a picture of myself. A great photographer could make something of all this, night and speed and that raw face in the mirror, shaky hands holding a cheap camera and a black T-shirt riding up to reveal a faded tattoo. A great photographer would see past that, all the way back to shadows in an alley and a car wreck in the woods.

I thought of Aphrodite.

Our gaze changes all that it falls upon.

I needed to talk to her again. I needed to make her see me; I needed to tell her how her photos had changed me all those years ago. I needed her to understand that I'd come here now hoping they would change me back.

The door to her room was open and a light was on. I listened for the television, the sound of voices, or dogs.

But the TV was off. If any dog was in there, it was asleep.

And Aphrodite? I peeked inside.

No dogs. No drunk. The rumpled bed was empty, still strewn with photography books. A lamp cast a piss yellow glow across the floor. I stood in the doorway and listened in case she was just out of sight, in a closet maybe.

But everything was silent. I went inside, stepping around a pile of black tights and underwear, a shapeless cardigan felted with dog fur, an empty bottle of Courvoisier. The cast-iron woodstove was cold, but the space heater worked overtime, cooking the room's scents to a stew of dogs and brandy and unwashed laundry.

I stepped around heaps of clothes until I reached a wall of photos. Aphrodite when she was young and beautiful, a hybrid of Lizzy Mercier Descloux and Liz Taylor. A faded photo of a tall bearded guy, very handsome, glancing at the camera through lowered eyelashes. He held a toddler on his knee, the little boy's head turned from the camera. Gryffin and his father.

Steve Haselton looked different from the photo I'd seen on that New Directions paperback: edgier, less blandly patrician. I guessed it was the long hair and beard and manic smile. He looked kind of like Hunter Thompson, right before or right after the drugs kicked in. There was a picture of Gryffin too, standing on the rocks by the ocean; maybe ten years old, gawky and wild-haired, holding up a starfish. Unsmiling. A somber kid.

And there were photos of the Oakwind commune at what I guessed must be a clambake. It looked more like the down east version of an acid trip. Long-haired people in gypsy clothes gamboled on the beach. It was raining. Smoke rose from a pile of stones covered with black gunk—seaweed? Mushrooms? In one photo, a naked little boy poked grimly at smoking rubble with a stick. Gryffin again.

It was less Summer of Love than it was Lord of the Flies. The photos were underexposed and out of focus, like the negs I'd processed downstairs. The kind of artsy stuff an ambitious high school photographer might shoot.

But each bore Aphrodite's signature in the lower right corner. I turned away.

It was true. Something had been stolen from her. She'd had it, and she fucking lost it.

My foot nudged an empty bottle. It rolled beneath the bed, and I noticed something beside it, a stack of three oversized portfolios, expensive black leather Bokara cases.

They didn't seem to have been moved for a while. The leather had a dull green bloom of mildew. I gingerly picked up the first portfolio, sat on the bed, and opened it.

Inside were clear vinyl sleeves. Not the kind any serious artist would use today—chlorine gas leaches from the vinyl and turns your photos yellow.

But these pictures were old. More middle-class hippies playing at a freak show; a sad photo of Aphrodite with her arms around her younger husband, his head turned from her, long hair covering his face. I replaced the portfolio and pulled out the next one.

This was more interesting. The vinyl sleeves held color land-scapes, not the hand-worked images of *Deceptio Visus* or *Mors* but stark views of distant islands. With these photos she was almost onto some-thing, but the pictures were all too literal: a stormy sea, some jagged rocks, forbidding clouds. There wasn't the imminence that irradiated her earlier work, the sense that she'd witnessed something unearthly and terrible yet lovely, something that had only revealed itself for that hundredth of a second and would never be glimpsed again, except here, now, in this image. There were so many photos crammed into this second portfolio—not just photos but contact sheets, negs, even faded Polaroids—that I could almost imagine her desperation, shoot-ing hundreds of frames in hopes of nailing just that *one.*

From what I could see, she never did. I reached for the last portfolio.

These photos were different.

For starters, they were all shot on SX-70, the famous One-Step film developed by Polaroid in the early 1970s. The SX-70 camera was a huge innovation, and the first model, the Alpha, was hugely expensive—three hundred dollars, which these days would equal almost fourteen hundred bucks. SX-70 film came in individ-ual sheets, each containing its own pod of developer, covered by a layer of transparent polyester. After the film was exposed, it would slide between little rollers inside the camera, like the wringers of an old-fashioned washing machine. These rollers burst the pod and spread the developing chemicals across the film. Once it developed inside the camera, you had what Polaroid called an integral print.

But the SX-70 had a feature that the folks at Polaroid hadn't counted on. The exposed film took a long time to fix. So you could use your finger or a pencil or just about anything you wanted, as long as it wasn't too pointed or sharp, and manipulate the devel-oping chemicals in their polyester sheath. This produced cool, if simple, special effects—halos, silver and black dots, penumbras like solar flares. They looked like those blotches you see when you hold a piece of Mylar up to the sun. If you really wanted to work with an image, you could extend the time it took to fix by warming then cooling the print, over and over again.

It was like a very primitive form of Photoshop. Some people played with the chemicals on purpose and declared the results a new art form. Most people, of course, did so by accident, made a mess of their snapshots, and complained. Almost immediately Polaroid rushed to make cheaper versions of the Alpha, "improving" the film to something called Time-Zero, so that the problem wouldn't exist in later camera models.

Some artists still use SX-70s—you can buy the film through Fuji. But these weren't recent photos. I'd guess they'd been taken around the time that the cameras first appeared, in the early 1970s, roughly the same time as the Magic Clambake. I recognized some of the people, commune members I assumed: a couple of skinny guys in overalls and flannel shirts; Aphrodite, looking far too imperious to be hanging out with a bunch of longhairs ten years younger than she was; little Gryffin.

And then, a series of pictures that made my neck prickle. They showed a pretty, freckled girl with long hair—the same girl in the 8x10 I'd processed in Aphrodite's darkroom. In the SX-70 photos, she was sleeping, or pretending to. The pictures were in extreme close-up, and the film had been manipulated so that little wiggly shadows ran across her face, giving the images a spooky, submarine quality. I couldn't tell if her eyes were open or shut. Someone had gone over them with a needle-sized stylus, so that in some photos it looked as though they were covered by silvery green coins. In others her eyes seemed wide open with amazement.

Same deal with her mouth—the chemicals had been moved around so that her lips were distorted and discolored. It looked as though something were protruding from them, a snake's head, or maybe a finger.

This will make the pictures sound grotesque, and they were. But they weren't *just* grotesque. Small as they were, they seemed outsized and even kind of funny, the way R. Crumb drawings are, their creepiness outpaced by audacity. Why would someone do *that* to a Polaroid picture?

Someone wanted to do it a lot. There were dozens of photos, most of the same girl, her face altered so that she resembled a broken statue, mottled green and black. But a few pictures seemed to be clumsy self-portraits. One showed a mirror and the flashlit reflection of a figure holding the SX-70. The others showed portions of a face, badly out of focus. A scalp, a nose or ear, a toothy grin. Someone had gone to the trouble of taking these photos. And someone else had taken the trouble to save them.

None of these photos were signed. They didn't need to be. I knew it was him.

Denny Ahearn.

Those Polaroids pumped out damage the way that little space heater cranked out BTUs. I could taste it, a tang like biting into an old penny, like the taste you get from speed that hasn't been cooked enough. I wanted to recoil, but the images drew me on. I looked at one after another, impelled by the eye behind that camera, a presence so strong it was like it was in the room with me.

And then, there really *was* an eye, staring out at me from the last page. It was the only photo that hadn't been manipulated. A single amber eye, gleaming as though it had been coated with glycerin. The cornea wasn't white, but a custardy yellow, threaded with red filaments. I could see the pale reflected outline of a camera in the iris.

That was creepy enough. What made it worse was a blotch of green pigment like the one in Gryffin's eye. Only this was a bigger flaw, and it was in a different place, just below the pupil.

I couldn't look away from it. It was like staring at a painting where the canvas has been torn: if you could only rip away the ruined canvas, another painting would be revealed: the *real* painting. I felt the same vertiginous horror I'd experienced as a girl, looking into the sky to see a great eye gazing down at me.

Now I felt that jagged bit of pigment was the *real* eye, the realest eye I'd ever seen. I brought the photo to my face to get a better look, and grimaced.

It stank. Not the musty, doggy smell of Aphrodite's room, but the smell I'd detected on the photo back at Ray Provenzano's house, a reek like someone had dumped rotting fish on top of a dead skunk.

It was faint, but unmistakable. And it was coming from the Polaroid. I held it under my nose and sniffed.

I replaced the photo, sat on the floor and stared at the unmade bed, soiled sheets, dog fur, all those expensive photo books, Roberto Schezen, Rudy Burckhardt . . .

"Shit," I whispered.

I stood and grabbed a book, the familiar Runway colophon on its spine beneath the title and photographer's name.

DEAD GIRLS CASSANDRA NEARY

On the title page was an inscription.

'ONE BECOMES HUMAN BY IMITATING THE GODS'
FOR A WITH LOVE
D

"What are you doing?" For a second I thought I'd imagined the voice. "*What* are you *doing?*"

I looked up.

It was Aphrodite, the deerhounds at her sides. A twig was stuck to her leggings; her lipstick was faded and her silvery hair flattened as though she'd just woken up.

But by the way she swayed back and forth, red eyed, I figured that she'd been up—though maybe not upright—for a while, and keeping the same kind of company I had; no speed, maybe, but plenty of cognac or whatever it was that made her look like a skeletal marionette.

"Aphrodite." I blinked. "Wow. I—"

Before I could move she was on top of me. I fell back as she yanked the book from my hands and smashed it against my head. I cried out and fell backward, struggling.

"Hey!" I gasped. "Stop, I was just—"

A dog whined as she smashed the book against my face again. I kicked out violently and struck her shoulder. She staggered backward and the dogs growled, as though this was a game they'd played before.

"Get—*out*—" The book dropped to the floor. Aphrodite beat at the air as though there were another, invisible assailant between us. "Get—*out*—get—*out*—"

I crouched on the bed as the dogs pawed at each other and Aphrodite swiped madly at nothing, like someone practicing a deranged form of Tai Chi.

"*Get out, get out . . .*"

Whoever, whatever, she was fighting seemed to have nothing to do with me. She didn't even seem to remember I was there. I edged off the bed.

"Get—*out!*" Aphrodite's voice rose to a strangled cry. Abruptly she grew silent. She lowered her hands, panting, and looked around.

Now she did see me.

No, not me: my camera. She gazed at it then lifted her head and stared right at me. When she spoke, her voice was calm.

"Amateur. Thief." She smiled a horrible broken doll's smile. "You're nothing but a little amateur. Both of you—*nothing.* You think I didn't know? You thought I wouldn't know who you were? You—"

She lunged and grabbed at my camera. "You're *nothing . . .*"

I covered the Konica with one arm and pushed her away. She reeled back, the dogs dancing around her as though this, too, were part of the game. One of them leaped up, its paws grazing her shoulders. Aphrodite gasped, still staring at me, then fell.

I had no time to stop her, only watched as her head struck the corner of the woodstove. I heard a *snap*. Not like a dry stick breaking, more the sound of something green that doesn't want to give way.

Her body hit the floor. The deerhound backed away and slunk toward the bed. The other two dogs surged forward, tails wagging, and nosed at her crotch.

I clutched my camera and held my breath, listened for the sound of footsteps and Gryffin's voice: sirens, shouting, God knows what.

But there was nothing. The room was still, except for the snuffling dogs and the hum of the space heater. I drew a breath and ran my hand protectively across my camera.

"Go," I whispered. I swatted at the dogs. "Go, go on—"

They backed off, mouths split in white grins.

"Lie down." I gestured toward the bed. "Go on, lie *down*."

They leaped onto the bed, padded across the covers, and settled down, long gray muzzles on their paws. I made sure there was still no sound from the hall then went to the body.

Her head lolled to one side. A skein of spit ran from the corner of her mouth to the floor, mingled with blood from a deep cut in her temple. The cut formed a shape like a tiny inverted pyramid, glistening pink at the sides, deep indigo at the deepest point. I glanced at the woodstove. A small chunk of flesh was impaled on one corner, a few hairs protruding from it, like a daddy longlegs snagged in a bit of bloody Kleenex.

I looked down again. One of Aphrodite's eyes was fixed on me. A pinkish glaze sheathed the cornea, like a welling tear. As I stared, the eyelid dropped in a wink then slowly rose, the tear darkening to scarlet as it spilled onto her cheek. A red bubble appeared in one nostril and popped. Tiny red specks appeared across her cheeks, a flush.

She was still alive. I took a step toward the door.

And stopped. I turned back, got onto one knee, popped the lens cap from my Konica, and began to shoot.

I had shit for light, but I didn't care. There was enough for an exposure. That's all I needed. Tri-X doesn't pick up as many details in the gray area as something like T-Max. It doesn't have as fine a grain, it's a colder film, it can be raw. It's perfect for what I do. It was perfect now.

What mattered was what was in front of me at that moment: the matte bulk of the woodstove, ash on the floor; the macabre doll with her head twisted. She was beautiful, it was all beautiful, her spill of silver hair and the play of blood beneath her skin.

I got a series of close-ups. At one point I worried that her breath might fog my lens. But by then she hardly seemed to be breathing at all.

I don't know at what point she actually died. But gradually the flush on her cheeks took on a violet tinge. A strand of hair fell across her face, obscuring one eye. I moved it aside, shot two more frames before checking the camera.

I only had four shots left. I stopped, suddenly aware of my body clammy with sweat. I looked at the bedroom door then scrambled to my feet.

On Aphrodite's bed, the dogs slept. A body lay on the floor, and a leather portfolio.

Otherwise nothing was out of place. It looked like an accidental death. To me, anyway. Even kind of a natural death, all things considered. I tugged at my T-shirt so it covered my hand, grabbed the copy of *Dead Girls* and stuck it on a bookshelf, lining it up so it looked as inconspicuous as possible. Then I got the portfolio, did my best to clean it with my T-shirt, and shoved it back under the bed.

Would that be enough? My fingerprints were probably all over it, and the other two as well. But I couldn't waste time trying to clean up. I'd have to hope no one would bother with it. I glanced around the room for any hint I'd been there.

All seemed as untidy and forlorn as when I'd entered. I used my T-shirt to polish the doorknobs, swiped the fabric across the doorjamb for good measure. I felt surprisingly calm, as though I were cleaning up from a party.

Had I touched anything else?

Nada.

I was safe. Maybe.

16

PHIL USED TO SAY my motto should be *Born to Lose*. At that moment, *Nothing to Lose* seemed just as good. I gave one last look at Aphrodite's room. Would she have left the door ajar? The light on?

I decided yeah, sure, if she didn't know she was going to be dead. I headed for Gryffin's bedroom.

His door was shut. I stood and tried to get my nerve up.

I was wasted, but I wasn't stupid. I wasn't sure exactly what had happened back there in Aphrodite's room—did she fall or was she pushed?—but I knew it didn't look good.

I needed to cover my ass. Getting rid of the film in my camera would be a start, but I didn't want to do that. Those pictures . . . maybe no one else could ever see them, but *I* wanted to see them. I *needed* to see them, to prove that I wasn't like her, not yet. To prove that I hadn't lost it.

The hall was black. But gradually my eyes adjusted. There's always a gray scale, even in what seems like total darkness. I went into Gryffin's room and closed the door behind me.

The bedroom was warm. I could hear him breathing deeply. Not snoring, which was good. I don't sleep well with other people in the room.

Not that I could sleep yet. I crossed to the far wall. There was enough light that I could see Gryffin lying on his back. One arm rested on his forehead. His head was tilted. The sleeve of his T-shirt had hitched up so that I could see the hollow beneath his arm.

He looked beautiful. Otherworldly, I would say, except that what was so lovely about him was his very ordinariness, the fact that he could be in the same room with me, breathe the same air; and know nothing of me at all. As though I were a ghost; as though Aphrodite had been right, and I was truly nothing.

But for as long as I stood there, for as long as he didn't wake, our worlds occupied the same space, the way a photograph can create a secondary world that exists within the real one. I felt as though I had stepped inside a photo—not one of my own pictures but someplace calm, someplace suspended between waking and sleep, the real and the ideal. A place my work would never belong, any more than I would.

Gryffin belonged there. Dark as it was in that room, I could imagine he slept somewhere else, sunlit. A beach, a green woodland. Sun, a man smiling; always out of reach. I would never be able to touch him.

Grief hit me then, the image of Aphrodite's sad small body sprawled beside the woodstove, and horror at the darkness around me. I turned and groped around the room until I found Gryffin's desk, the brass candlestick and box of wooden matches. I struck one, not caring if he woke, lit the candle then extinguished the match.

The flame seemed blinding, but he didn't stir. I stood at his bedside, candle in my hand, and gazed down at him: his mouth parted slightly, as though he were on the verge of speaking to someone in his dream. His eyes moved behind his eyelids. His breath was warm and smelled of toothpaste and alcohol. He was beautiful.

Everything is random. That's what I used to believe. Nothing happens for a reason, nothing happens because we will it. I never believed in gods. I believe in Furies. I think there are beings, people, impelled by the power to do harm. Sometimes the impulse is momentary. Maybe in some instances it's eternal. And maybe that's the one thing in the universe that isn't random.

When I was raped, I ran into one of those Furies. Over the years, I became one myself.

But if there is an opposite to whatever I am, it—he—was lying there in front of me. As I stared at him I realized that what I had first sensed outside the motel room, that black roil of damage . . . it had nothing to do with Gryffin Haselton, nothing at all. He'd looked at me, and I'd seen a glimpse of myself in his eyes. My own rage and fear had come back at me like bullets bouncing from a wall.

Nothing else.

I shot the last four frames. I steadied the camera on the edge of the desk so that my shaking hands wouldn't ruin the exposure. Even so, I knew the images would be blurred. Like when you're outside shooting the moon without a tripod—no matter how hard you try to remain still, you move, and the moon moves, and the earth moves. And the camera captures everything.

Now, in Gryffin's room, very little seemed to be moving: but I knew the photos would show differently. They would show how everything changes, a fraction of a second at a time. *Death is the eidos of that Photograph*, Roland Barthes wrote, but not even death is static like a picture is. If you look at a corpse long enough, you see things move beneath the skin, as real and liquid as the blood in your own veins.

Now I saw a sleeping man, motionless. Four frames. When I was done, I rewound the film inside the camera then removed the roll. I needed to hide it.

Gryffin might find it in a drawer, or under the mattress. I saw the turtle shell on the windowsill and remembered what I'd found in the room above the Island Store. I picked up the shell, pressed my finger against the bit of carapace that formed a trap door where the turtle's head had once retracted. It moved to reveal an opening big enough for the roll of film.

I slid it inside then shook the shell. The film didn't move; it was wedged tight. I put the shell back on the windowsill, turned and watched Gryffin sleep.

Our gaze changes all that it falls upon . . .

I never wanted my gaze to change him.

But, of course, it already had. I blew out the candle, removed my boots and leather jacket, wrapped my camera in the jacket, and set it on the floor.

Then I pulled the blanket back and slipped beneath the covers. Gryffin made a small questioning sound and shifted onto his side.

"It's me," I whispered. "I'm cold."

"What?" He mumbled and turned toward me. "Huh?"

"Cass. There's no heat in my room. I'm freezing."

I could see him frown. Then he shut his eyes.

"Whatever," he said, and put his arms around me. "Just go to sleep."

Gradually the cold ebbed from my body; gradually the room grew light. I listened to the humming in my head and the sound of Gryffin's breathing.

Finally I slept. It wasn't exactly the sleep of the just. But for those few hours, it was enough.

part two
SHADOW POINT

17

"GET UP."

I buried my face in the pillow and groaned.

"Get *up*." The voice came again, louder. The bed shook. It was a moment before I realized this was because someone had kicked it, another moment before I figured out the someone was Gryffin. I rolled onto my back and stared up at him, blinking in the morning light.

"What?"

"My mother." He was fully dressed but looked terrible: unshaven, eyes bloodshot, his face knotted with grief. "You have to get up. My mother's dead."

"What?" I sat up and felt as though someone had jabbed a steel rebar through my skull. "Oh *shit*."

"For God's sake." He lowered himself onto the bed. "Something happened, she fell or something. She—"

He covered his face with his hands and began to shake.

"Your mother?" I didn't have to mime shock as memory overwhelmed me, her pallid skin, the pinprick froth of red on her lips. "Gryffin . . ."

He didn't look up. I touched his shoulder. "I'm sorry," I whispered, so softly I wasn't sure he heard me. He turned, and I leaned against him. His entire body shuddered as I stroked his arm.

At last he pulled away. He removed his glasses and wiped his eyes. "It's terrible." His voice was raw. I wondered how long he'd been awake. "I heard the dogs in there whining. She—it looks like she fell. By that goddam woodstove, she never even uses it—"

He choked and got unsteadily to his feet. "You better get dressed and come downstairs. The sheriff's on his way over."

"What?"

But he was gone.

I got up and dressed. I have as many words for "hangover" as an Inuit has for snow. None of them did justice to how I felt. I tried to make myself look presentable. I hadn't imagined I could feel any worse, but the thought of being questioned by a cop pushed me close to panic. I popped another Adderall and hoped it would kick in before the sheriff arrived.

I went downstairs. The door to Aphrodite's room was shut.

I found Gryffin in the kitchen. The deerhounds loped across the room to greet me, whining. I looked at Gryffin.

He sat staring out the window. It was overcast—high, swift-moving clouds but no fog, just an endless expanse of steely water and sky. A raven pecked at something on the gravel beach. On the horizon hung a ragged black shadow. Tolba Island.

"There's coffee," he said at last. He gestured toward the pot but didn't look at me. I poured myself some then sat by the wood-stove. After a minute, he turned.

"I went up to let the dogs out. Usually they come downstairs if she's not awake. It looks like she hit her head on the woodstove." His voice cracked, and he took a gulp of coffee. "I—I guess she was drunk and she tripped. I mean, every time I come here, I think I'm going to find something like this. And now . . ."

He squeezed his eyes shut. "God. Do you remember what time it was when we came in? Was it around midnight?"

"Yeah, something like that."

"And you didn't see her, did you? Before you—before you came in to get warm."

"No." I cupped my hands around my mug.

Tears fell onto his shirt. He rubbed his eyes. One of the dogs turned and raced toward the mudroom and began to bark. The others followed, yelping. Gryffin ran a hand across his face.

"That'll be him." He went to get the door.

I waited in the kitchen. I thought of when Christine had died, and how the fact that we hadn't gotten along or even recently spoken just made it worse. Any chance of making things right was gone.

I pushed the thought away, tried not to think about what lay on the floor upstairs. I heard the door open. The dogs' barking rose to a frantic crescendo then diminished. There was the sound of male voices, a rumble of sympathy. Gryffin walked back into the room, trailed by a uniformed policeman and Everett Moss. Moss looked at me in surprise.

"I forgot you had company," he said to Gryffin. "Well, I just needed to escort the sheriff over here. Marine Patrol will take over, I guess, when you need to get back. And other arrangements—"

He shook his head. "I guess State Office'll deal with that. I'm sorry for your loss, Gryffin. Let me know if I can do anything to help."

He left. Gryffin restlessly smoothed back his hair. He looked young and vulnerable. Frightened.

"I'm so sorry about all this, Gryffin," said the sheriff. He nodded at me. "I'm John Stone, Paswegas County Sheriff."

He was short, gray-blond hair, slight paunch, a worn face with a kindly expression. The kind of cop who, after retirement, becomes a school bus driver and remembers everyone's birthday.

"I know this isn't the ideal time to ask you questions," he said, "but I'll have to do that."

He took out a notebook and a pen, set a camera on the table.

"Go ahead," said Gryffin.

"It shouldn't take too long. I was coming over anyway to question you about Merrill Libby's girl. Which I'll have to get to after this."

He sighed. "The dispatcher's already called in about your mother. They're sending down someone from Machias, but it'll be a little while before he gets here. So I'll try to finish this up as fast as I can."

"Who's coming from Machias?" asked Gryffin.

"Criminal investigator. Homicide. I'm sorry, but this is all routine, Gryffin. What you have here is what we call an unattended death. So we have to do this. I'm real sorry. I'll start with you, then your friend."

He sat at the table and began filling out a form. I took a seat and drank my coffee, trying to stay calm as he went down his list: Who was there, Where did Gryffin find the body, What time. Had her doctor been notified.

"Any sign of forced entry?"

"No."

"Purse missing? Any money missing? Any valuables?"

"No. No. No."

"Keys gone?"

"Sheriff, I have never seen a set of keys in this house."

John Stone leaned back. "Well, you know, yesterday Tyler Rawlins had a set of keys disappear down at the Island Store. So these things do happen." He glanced at his clipboard again. "You said you were here last night."

"Yes."

"Did you see your mother?"

"No. Not since sometime in the afternoon."

"Do you usually see her?"

"No. Usually she takes the dogs out, she's gone most of the day. We're not close. I was just here on business. You know she drinks, Sheriff."

The sheriff gave a brief nod. "But you were here last night?"

"No. We went to Ray Provenzano's for dinner."

"Your mother with you?"

"No. Just me and her—" Gryffin indicated me. "You can check with Ray."

"Okay, I will. What about when you got home? You do anything? Go right to bed?"

"Yes."

"Your bedroom's upstairs? Did you hear anything unusual? Before you went to bed. Or later. Did you look into your mother's room?"

"No. I don't come up here much. I—"

He stopped. John Stone wrote down something then asked, "Were you by yourself? When you went to bed?"

For the first time Gryffin hesitated. "No." His face reddened. "I was—she was with me."

He pointed at me. John Stone sucked at his upper lip, made another mark on his sheet. "Okay. Anything else you can think of? Anything out of the ordinary? Those dogs—"

He looked out to where the deerhounds ran along the rocky beach. "Did they bark?"

"No." As quickly as he'd blushed, Gryffin paled. "Excuse me, I'm not feeling well. I—"

He bolted from the room. John Stone drew a long breath then looked at me. "Boy, I really hate this. Now I have to do the same with you."

He put a new sheet onto his clipboard. "Can you spell your name, please."

A flicker of panic went through me. But as the minutes passed I felt more confident. The Adderall kicked in with its laboratory glow of invincibility, and I had to remind myself that this was police procedure and not a job interview. The dogs chased a seagull on the beach. John Stone's radio crackled. He checked it, turned to me again.

"So, why'd you come here?" He sounded genuinely curious.

"To interview Aphrodite Kamestos. For a magazine."

"That's right, she was supposed to be famous at some point, wasn't she. I never knew her." He frowned. "You knew her, then?"

"No. Not personally, not before I came here yesterday. Someone set it up—an editor. At the magazine."

"What about Gryffin? You know him? He a friend?"

"No. I never met him. Not before yesterday."

"What about Mrs. Kamestos? She seem sick to you? Anything out of the ordinary?"

"I never met her before yesterday. She seemed fine, I guess. She seemed . . . drunk."

"So I gather. They'll do a toxicology report, we'll see what that says." He made another mark on his clipboard and put down his pen. "I guess that'll do it. Unless you can think of anything else?"

I shook my head.

"Don't you go far, now," Stone went on. "I still have to question you about this other thing. That girl from the motel you stayed at the other night. But I got to finish this matter here first."

A shadow fell across the table. I looked up to see Gryffin. His hair was wet, he'd shaved and changed into a white oxford-cloth shirt and corduroys, a brown jacket.

"You finished?" He slid into the chair next to mine.

"Just about," said John Stone. There was another crackle from his radio. He picked it up, spoke briefly before turning back to us. "That was the dispatcher. Marine Patrol just left Burnt Harbor, they should be here in a few minutes."

Gryffin toyed with his coffee mug. "Then what?"

"He'll ask you some more questions and take a look around. They'll arrange for someone to bring the deceased over to the funeral home, and the State Medical Examiner will take over."

"Christ." Gryffin closed his eyes.

Stone glanced over his notes. "Well. What I need to do now is take a look at the deceased."

They went upstairs. I poured the rest of the coffee and drank it, slung on my jacket, and went outside. The dogs ran over to me then raced off into the pine grove.

"Nice display of grief," I said, and threw a stick after them.

The sky was gray and unsettled, not a brooding dark but a bright pewter haze that stung my eyes. I shut them and bright phantom bolts moved behind the lids, shapes that became a face tangled in dendrinal knots, branches, blood vessels, Kenzie Libby running along the road.

I opened my eyes. Wind hissed through dead leaves, a sound like sleet. A few tiny white flakes blew past my face.

Who could live here? I wondered.

I thought of Kenzie, of Aphrodite dead, and the flyers I'd seen everywhere. Dead cats. Missing kids. A new one now.

HAVE YOU SEEN KENZIE LIBBY?

I shivered. Maybe this was one of those places where people weren't meant to live, like Love Canal or Spirit Lake.

Yet it was beautiful. Not just the trees and water and sky, all those things you expect to be beautiful, but the rest of it— stoved-in clapboards and flyspecked modular homes, beer bottles in the harbor, houses cobbled from stuff that everyone else threw away, a light that seemed to leak from another world.

I could live here, I realized. It wasn't exactly a comforting thought.

There probably isn't a bigger way of blowing a story than what I'd just done. Like, if you were to take a photograph of Paswegas at that moment and ask, *What's wrong with this picture?* the answer would be pretty clear. There was no way I could stay.

I thought of the film I'd hidden in the turtle shell and the stolen picture in my copy of Aphrodite's book. I thought of Aphrodite herself, and how it wouldn't take a crack team of investigators to dust for fingerprints under the bed and find mine.

I assumed John Stone wouldn't bother. Aphrodite had been lit up like Las Vegas when I'd last seen her alive; the toxicology report would prove that. End of story, unless I tried to write something up for *Mojo*.

But I kept thinking of Kenzie Libby, making jewelry out of broken glass and beer cans; a kid in the middle of nowhere who knew the words to "Marquee Moon." What must it have been like to hear those guitars for the first time, here on a rock in the middle of the winter, everything around you black and white and that music like a message in a bottle tossed to you from a city five hundred miles away?

What was it like to be so desperate to escape your life that someone like me looked like a way out instead of a way down?

I hunched against the cold and swore, and wished I had another bottle of Jack Daniel's. I wasn't crazy about the idea of hitching a ride back to the mainland with a cop. Or a corpse. I'd wait till everyone left then head down to the harbor and see if I could find Toby. I already owed him money for the ride over. I'd make it a round trip and call it even and get the hell out of Dodge.

I glanced back through the window to see if Gryffin and John Stone had come downstairs. The kitchen was still empty. I jammed my hands into my pockets. My feet in the cowboy boots were already freezing. I headed toward the pine grove, hoping to warm myself by moving.

That was another bad idea. The wind blasted me, and the trees offered little in the way of shelter as a flurry of snow whirled up. My ears throbbed from the inside, like someone had jabbed a pencil in there. I swore again.

Above me, something growled. I looked up.

An animal crouched in a pine tree—cat sized, with blackish brown fur and glittering eyes and a small red mouth, a sleek furry tail. It glared at me, teeth bared in a hiss. I stared back, too stunned to run away. I'd seen foxes and coyotes in the woods back when I was a kid, and once even a bobcat, but nothing like this, all rage and teeth. It looked like the Tasmanian Devil in the old cartoons. It crept to the edge of the branch, its back reared like a cat's about to spring. For a moment it was silent. Then it snarled.

I've never heard anything like that noise. It didn't even sound like an animal. It sounded like a human, like a person growling in pure rage. The snarl grew louder, the fur around the animal's face fanned out in a brown-gold halo. It moved forward, gaining better purchase on the tree limb. It was going to jump.

I took a stumbling step backward, heard a flurry of barks, and turned.

Aphrodite's deerhounds ran along the top of the hill. Behind them strode a tall figure in a police parka. Sighting me, one of the dogs broke away and raced down the hillside. I looked back at the pine tree, but the animal was gone.

The man walked toward me. "These your dogs?" He sounded pissed off.

"No. They belong to them." I pointed at the house.

The dogs rushed past us, sniffed hopefully then loped toward the beach.

"You part of the family?"

"They're inside."

The man nodded. He was broad shouldered, with a square face and blue eyes, close-cropped blond hair and a nick on his chin from shaving. Tom's of Maine meets Tom's of Finland. His name tag read Jeff Hakkala.

"I'll be doing the investigation," he said. "You said next of kin's in there? And the sheriff?"

"Yeah."

He headed toward the house. I let him get a few yards ahead of me then followed.

Gryffin opened the door. Hakkala introduced himself and went into the kitchen to confer with John Stone. Gryffin remained in the mudroom with me.

"You look pretty bad," I said.

"I am. God, this is awful."

I hesitated then asked, "Do they have any idea what happened?"

"'They?' Who's 'they?'" He glanced into the next room. "There is no *they*. There's John Stone, and now this guy. He'll call the medical examiner, they'll do an autopsy. I have to arrange some kind of funeral . . ."

He buried his head in his hands.

"I'm sorry." I felt a real pang of grief—not for Aphrodite but for him. I touched his shoulder. "Really. It's—well, I'm just sorry, is all."

He nodded and put his hand on mine, just for an instant.

"Yeah," he said at last and looked away. "I gather this guy is going to ask us a few more questions and then do whatever he does up there at the crime scene."

The back of my neck went cold. "Crime scene?"

"That's what they call it. An unattended death—they treat it like a homicide. He didn't think it was anything but her falling, three sheets to the wind, as usual. That's what the autopsy will tell them, anyway. I guess it takes a few weeks before they sign off on everything."

"Do I need to wait around?"

He shot me a grim look. "No. This guy'll question you, and the sheriff wants to question us about the girl in the motel. Then you can go, I guess."

For a minute we stood in silence. Finally I said, "Me being here . . . I guess I made it worse."

"No, Cass." He started for the kitchen. "You just made it weird."

18

THE DETECTIVE DIDN'T SPEND much time with me. I answered his questions, he wrote everything down. Then he went to see Gryffin in the living room. I remained with John Stone in the kitchen, watching as he fed the woodstove.

"Been up here before?" He nudged the stove door shut with his foot.

"No."

"Probably won't be in much of a hurry to come back, now."

I shrugged. "I dunno. I kind of like it, except for the cold."

"Not much besides the cold. For the next six months, anyway."

He looked up as Gryffin stepped back into the room.

"He's on the phone," Gryffin said. "This could take a while."

John Stone glanced from him to me. "Mind if I ask you a few quick questions about Merrill Libby's girl?"

Gryffin sank into a chair. "Go ahead."

"Well, did either one of you see her the other night? I gather you did—Everett said his granddaughter was on the computer with Merrill's girl. She said she'd seen you at the Lighthouse." He turned to me. "And that Robert Stanley, the one works for Mr. Provenzano—he said you was talking to Merrill's girl. That's what she told him, anyway."

"Mackenzie," I said. The sheriff looked confused. "Libby's girl—she's got a name. Mackenzie."

John Stone blinked. "Well, yes, of course she does. But she—did you see her?"

"She checked me into the motel. Afterward, she came to my room—I'd asked her father if there was someplace to eat. He said no, but she wanted to tell me there was a place, that restaurant down at the harbor. The Good Tern."

"She enter your room?"

"Yeah. For, like, a minute. It was freezing, I didn't want to make her stand outside. She told me about the restaurant. Then she left. End of story."

"Some of the kids—well, one of them, Robert, he said that the girl—that Mackenzie told him you were going to give her a ride somewhere."

Fucking Robert. I felt myself grow hot. "I didn't tell her that. I didn't tell her anything. I said about five words to her, and that was it."

John Stone allowed himself a wry smile. "Five words, huh? Well, Miss Neary, we picked up a lot of chatter—teenagers talking, you know. They may confiscate her computer, see what shows up on there."

My mouth went dry. "What do you mean?"

"Computer records. We had a incident last year, a juvenile met someone online and was abducted. Picked her up down in Portsmouth."

He shook his head. "Least she was alive. Me, I wouldn't let my kids do that stuff. God knows who they meet up with. So you were at the Good Tern that night? Did you see her there?"

"No."

Stone stared out the window again, brooding. "I talked to Toby Barrett yesterday evening, he said you'd been there with him and Gryffin here."

He looked at Gryffin. "You were at the motel too, right? You and Miss Neary—you were in adjacent rooms? And Toby said you were at the Good Tern afterward. But Miss Neary, you said you only met him yesterday."

I stared at John Stone. So did Gryffin.

"I forgot," I said at last. "I mean—I saw him at the motel. I bumped into him."

"*Really* bumped into me," said Gryffin. "Outside my room."

"What does this have to do with Mackenzie Libby?" I said. "Because my father's an attorney, and if you're going to do any kind of questioning, I'm going to call him right now."

John Stone lifted a placating hand. "No, no—Merrill Libby said he hadn't seen the two of you together when you checked in. He said he always rents those two rooms out in the winter, something about the heat. We just—he's obviously concerned about the young lady. Mackenzie. He says she's a good kid. A good girl."

He sighed. "These kids . . . I got a grandson that age, you don't want to think of what can happen to them. Right now they've got the game warden searching for her."

"Game warden?" I broke in. "An old lady dies of natural causes and you send out a homicide detective, but this kid disappears and she gets a freaking game warden? Like she's a dog?"

John Stone looked taken aback. "Well, it's standard procedure. They're starting to organize people to search for her. Merrill Libby, he'll mobilize the whole town. But I'll tell you the truth, Miss Neary—you wander off into the woods, you're a lot better off having the warden service look for you with trained dogs. He knows those woods better'n anybody."

"But you just said she might have taken off with someone. Not that she's lost in the woods."

John Stone shrugged. "Well, probably that's all that happened. Probably she got ticked at her dad and run off. Then it got cold, it got dark, she started back but she got disorientated and she's out there now. I just hope she didn't take a fall somewhere, like if she went down to that pier at Burnt Harbor."

He made a grim face. "Probably not cold enough for someone to freeze to death, long as she didn't go in the water, not a young person in good health, anyway."

He turned to where Hakkala was putting away his phone. "Well, I think that's about it. Time to go find Everett, take me back over. You think of anything else about Merrill Libby's girl, you let me know, okay?"

"Kenzie," I said, but John Stone didn't hear. He set down his clipboard and headed into the next room. Gryffin went with him.

I looked at the table. Stone's ballpoint was lying on top of the papers he'd filled out. It was a nice pen, dark blue with gold lettering on the barrel. I picked it up and read PASWEGAS COUNTY POLICE DEPARTMENT: PROUD TO SERVE. I glanced to where Stone and Gryffin were talking, their backs to me, then slid the pen into my jacket pocket.

"Sorry again for your loss," the sheriff said. He shook hands with Gryffin, stepped over to have a word with Hakkala. Gryffin walked back to me.

"Well," he said.

"I better get going too." I shoved my hands in my pockets and stared at my feet. "Look, I—"

"Stop." He turned to the window, blinking away tears, then glanced back at me. "How're you getting back to Burnt Harbor?"

"Toby, I guess. If he'll take me."

"Oh, he'll take you. If you can find him. Know where he lives?"

"Yeah, I think so."

I stared at him, that green-shot eye, and, inexplicably, thought of Christine. Grief took me, the irrevocable knowledge that I was seeing him for the last time and I would never, ever be able to make it right.

I looked away. "I better go get my things. Will they let me go upstairs?"

"I already brought them down."

He ducked into the next room, and I had a flash of panic, recalling the turtle shell with my film in it. Before I could say anything, he'd returned.

"Here." I tried to look grateful as he handed me my bag and camera. "Hope you get home okay."

"Yeah, me too. Gryffin—I'm really sorry."

I turned to go. He stopped me and drew me to him. For just an instant he held me, his chin grazing the top of my head. Then he pulled away and walked into the next room.

I zipped my jacket, grateful I still had Toby's sweater, slung my bag over my shoulder then looked up to see Hakkala watching me.

"You're leaving?"

"Unless you need me for something."

"Is there a way to contact you—cell phone, local number?"

"I don't have a cell phone. I'm going to Burnt Harbor to get my car and drive back to New York. You have my number there."

He nodded. "Thanks for your assistance," he said and rejoined the others.

And that was it. As abruptly as Aphrodite had dismissed me during our aborted interview, I'd been cut loose. I really was free to go.

The realization should have been a relief. Instead I felt a stab of hopelessness that not even speed could blunt. I took a deep breath, went outside and started walking, stooped against the frigid wind. I'd buy another bottle of Jack Daniel's and then find Toby. As I headed through the evergreens I scanned the trees, looking for signs of the animal I'd seen earlier. But there was nothing there.

19

THERE WAS A LITTLE crowd inside the Island Store when I arrived. Five young guys in Carhartt jackets stood by the beer cooler, talking. As the door slammed behind me they glanced up. One of them was Robert.

"Hey," Suze called as I approached the counter. "What's going on up there? I heard Gryffin's mother died."

"Yeah, n'she probably killed her," muttered Robert.

Suze glared at him. "It's Sunday! No beer till twelve!"

"Isn't that one underage?" I cocked my thumb at Robert.

"What, just because he's still in high school?" She shook her blond dreadlocks then lowered her voice so the others couldn't hear. "They're looking for trouble. Actually, they're looking for you. So stick around here after they leave, okay? You guys ready?" she yelled.

They shuffled over. They were all built like Robert, heavyset and leaning toward muscle, with cold, challenging eyes. They bought cigarettes and Slim Jims and a couple bottles of Mountain Dew, took their change and left, brushing past me as they headed for the door. After they'd gone, Suze's big black dog ambled out from behind the counter, tail sweeping the floor in a lazy wave, and snuffed at me.

I scratched his ear and looked at Suze. She wore a lime green hooded sweatshirt and baggy cargo pants, earcuffs shaped like silver lizards.

"So you heard," I said. "She died in the night, I guess. Gryffin found her when he got up. It looks like she fell and hit her head."

"Poor Gryffin. I never really knew her. She didn't come in much, and she wasn't real friendly when she did. Like I said, a bitch. Want some coffee?" She filled a Styrofoam cup. "Here. You look like you could use it."

"Thanks."

"Yeah, I saw John Stone go up there, and that state cop. It's no surprise—you know that, right? She was a mean drunk; she got picked up a few times over the years when she'd go over to Burnt Harbor and drive. She finally had her license revoked. I think Gryff got the car."

She went into the kitchen. A moment later I heard PiL coming from the boombox.

I wondered what she did for fun around here. Wait for people like me to show up? I drank my coffee and glanced down toward the harbor. Robert and his cronies stood beside an abandoned building, smoking.

"What's his problem?" I said when Suze came back out.

"Robert? He thinks you had something to do with Kenzie taking off."

"What?"

She raised her hands. "I know. But that's Robert. He's not the sharpest knife in the box."

"She his girlfriend?"

"Nah, they're just friends. All the kids here, you know—they fight like cats, but they look out for each other. And people from away, they're not too popular here. I mean, the lobster fishery's in trouble from shell disease, there was a red tide last year killed the clamming season. The Grand Banks are fished out. I saw some underwater pictures this guy took, an urchin diver? The whole bottom of the ocean's scraped clean. Like a fricking desert—nothing's there. Scallop trawlers did that. So the fish are gone, and the paper mills are shut down, and everyone's buying their timber from Canada 'cause it's cheaper. You see those logging trucks heading south, they're not from here. Ten years ago, MBNA came in, hired people to work as telemarketers, and everyone thought that was the best thing ever happened. Then MBNA pulled out and everyone's out of work again, only now they're carrying a shitload of credit card debt. It sucks. Meanwhile, the tourists come and think this is fucking Disneyland. You own property here or Burnt Harbor, doesn't matter if your family's been there for a hundred years. Our taxes went from one or two thousand bucks a year to ten or twelve thousand. A lot of people don't make that much in a year. So they have to sell their houses for teardowns, or their land, and all of a sudden you have all these rich assholes complaining that they can't get a moccachino."

I finished my coffee and tossed the cup into the trash. "Your point?"

"We don't like people from away."

"What about you?" I leaned against the counter. "You don't like me either?"

Suze set her elbows down and leaned forward until her forehead touched mine. I cupped her chin in my hand, speed fizzing in me like champagne, then kissed her, her mouth small and warm.

"I like you just fine," she said in a low voice. "I was hoping you might stick around for a while. But now—"

She withdrew, glanced out the window, and shook her head. "Those boys, they'd just hassle you. And me. And if Kenzie doesn't show up soon, it could get ugly. If I were you, I'd split."

"What, frontier justice?"

"Pretty much. Doesn't matter what the cops say. If they don't find her, they'll start looking for someone else."

"Seems like you'd have some likely candidates without going too far out of the gene pool."

"We hang together here. Like, we beat our wives and kids and shit, but we still don't like people from away."

"What about those flyers? And people disappearing and washing up on the beach? Did they all run into someone from away?"

"Hey, it's nothing personal."

She turned and climbed up the ladder. She had a cute ass, what I could see in those cargo pants, anyway. I said, "While you're up there, get me another pint of Jack Daniel's."

"Sure." She stepped down and over to the register. "That it?"

I nodded. "I saw something back there by Gryffin's place. In those woods leading up to the house, those pine trees? There was an animal up in one of them."

"Did it look like Robert?"

"No. Really. I never saw anything like it before. It was about this big—" I held out my hands. "Dark brown fur. Kind of a long fuzzy tail. It was *fierce.* I thought it was going to attack me. It growled, and I could see its teeth, these white sharp teeth—it was mean."

Suze frowned. "That's weird."

"I think it was a fisher. Toby told me about them—the ones that eat all the cats."

"A fisher?" She slid my Jack Daniel's into a bag and handed it to me. "If you were over in Burnt Harbor, yeah. But not here. Fishers never leave the mainland."

"Toby said they can swim."

"Technically, maybe. But they're pretty big, and their fur is so heavy that if they swim, it just weighs them down. I know, 'cause one of my uncles used to trap them. You take a rooster and cut its throat and hang it from a tree, alongside a steel trap. It's illegal now. My uncle, he once saw one on the ground and it jumped, like, twenty feet. From here—"

She pointed to a far corner of the room. "—to there. Bang, like that. Jumped right into the tree. Those things are vicious as a wolverine. What you saw, that was probably somebody's cat. Was it gray? Maybe it was Smoky."

"This was big," I said. "And it wasn't a cat."

"Well, maybe. But I doubt it was a fisher. I've been here my whole life, and I never heard of a fisher here. There's nothing for them to eat—no rabbits or porcupines or anything."

"That's why it ate Smoky." I picked up my bag. I was getting pissed off; I definitely needed something to slow me down a little. "Is Toby around? I need to talk to him about a ride back to Burnt Harbor."

"He's probably still in bed." She peered down at the harbor. "Yeah, his boat's there. You know where he lives, right? Just go round back and knock real loud. He'll be bummed about Aphrodite—not for her, for Gryff. They're good buds."

I stuck the bourbon into my pocket and said, "Gryffin was telling me about that guy Denny Ahearn. He seems kind of weird. To me, anyway. Like, if this was the United States of America, Homeland Security or someone would be asking *him* questions about this girl, and not me."

"Denny?" Suze smiled. "Nah. He's pretty harmless."

"Do you know him?"

"Sure. I used to hang out with all those guys when I was sixteen, seventeen. Denny was really charismatic. Plus, he always had the best dope."

She laughed. "He was fucking crazy! The mirror game, that was one of his big things. When you were tripping. Some people totally freaked over that shit. I always thought it was fun. For a while, anyway. Then some sad shit came down, Denny's girlfriend died. He never really got over that."

"How'd she die?"

"Car accident."

The door banged open and the same woman with two small kids barged in. "Listen," I said quickly to Suze. "You have a phone

I could borrow? It's long distance, but I really need to make a call down to New York. Here—"

I started to pull out my wallet, but Suze stopped me.

"Don't worry about it." The kids started smacking the ice-cream cooler as Suze handed me a phone. "Here, go upstairs, it's quieter."

I hurried up to the second floor and dialed Phil's cell phone. It rang, I heard the noise of downtown street traffic, then his voice.

"Phil Cohen Enterprises."

"Phil, it's Cass—"

"Hey hey! Cassandra Android! How's it going up there?"

"Not good." I paced the room nervously. "You sent me here. Why?"

"Why?" His voice edged up defensively. "Whaddya mean, Cassie?"

"I mean you told me that Aphrodite wanted me—that she specifically wanted me to come up here to interview her. Then I got here and she says she never fucking heard of me. Or you."

"No shit." The background noise grew louder. Phil shouted at someone, then said, "Well jeez, Cass, I—"

"Don't fuck with me, Phil." I leaned against the wall and wiped sweat from my cheeks. "She had no clue about any of this. She never even knew there was an interview."

"I—"

"You said there was some guy up here you knew."

Silence. Car engines droned into the bass thump of a radio.

"Phil! *Who was it?*"

"The guy I used to do business with," he said at last. "Guy named Denny Ahearn."

"Denny Ahearn." I stared across the room at the shelf with the bowling trophy and the turtle shell. "Did you ever talk to her at all? Aphrodite?"

Another silence.

Then, "No. I mean, I couldn't, I didn't have her number or anything. I e-mailed Denny, we went back and forth a few times. We started batting around names of people who might go up there to see her, and I mentioned I knew you, and suddenly he got all hepped up. So I figured I'd do you a favor."

"Goddam it, Phil! Why'd you fucking lie to me?"

"Listen, Cassie." He sounded aggrieved. "I woulda suggested you anyway—"

"I don't care about that! I don't know who this guy is! Why did he ask for me? What did he say?"

Phil sighed. "Well, okay, let me think. He said he liked your book—he said you were very simpatico. I guess he's an artist or something these days. And he knows her—Aphrodite. He just wanted you, that's all. I thought he was like doing you a favor, huh? He said he wanted you to see his work. He said he thought you'd see eye to eye."

Eye to eye.

"Fuck," I said. I hung up.

"Hey, Cass?" I turned and saw Suze's face framed in the doorway. "You okay? I need the phone."

"Yeah, sure." I handed it to her. "I'll be right down."

She left. I dug out the Jack Daniel's and drank until my hands steadied, walked over and picked up the turtle shell.

S.P.O.T. That crudely carved eye.

And, on the other side, the letters ICU.

Not a set of initials, not the intensive care unit.

"I see you too," I whispered, and put it back.

I went downstairs. Suze was alone again.

"Why doesn't he go off that island?" I knew I sounded wired and drunk, but I didn't care. "Denny. And how would anyone know if he did or not?"

Suze stared at me curiously. "I hardly see him. Once or twice a year, he'll come over to get supplies. Toby always brings him. Toby says he's gotten kind of, I dunno, just weird, I guess. Like an agoraphobe. And he and Aphrodite, they kind of hate each other. So in a place as small as this, you just keep your distance, you know? But I don't think Denny could hurt someone."

"I have one word for you, Suze: Unabomber."

"Really, that's not Denny." She sounded pissed off. "He's more like—"

"Charles Manson? John Wayne Gacy?"

"No! He's more—well, spiritual. The commune, it wasn't just smoking dope and stuff. After it busted up, I was, what, sixteen? Denny organized this guerrilla street theater, we'd go around and protest. Down to Bath Iron Works where they built those battleships; we threw pig blood on them and got on TV. After that Denny really got into the mystical shit. He was reading all these books, eating a lot of acid. You're about my age, you remember what it was like, right? He was playing the mirror game once, he thought he had a vision or something. Like a vision quest."

She turned to shove a carton of cigarettes onto a shelf. "So then we all had to get spirit guides. Totem animals. We made these beautiful masks out of papier-mâché—they were amazing. I still have mine, up there—"

She looked at the ceiling. "In my apartment. You want to see it?"

"Maybe another time." I started for the door. "I really have to find Toby."

"Boy, you're suddenly in a hurry." She cocked her head. "You think you might be back?"

"I doubt it. I couldn't afford the taxes."

"Cheaper if you share," she said and grinned.

At the door I paused. "So what was your spirit animal?"

"A dolphin. Fun in the sun, endless summer. What about you?"

"Dee Dee Ramone," I said, and left.

I took a few steps toward the harbor, then stopped. I searched the road until I found the sea urchin I'd set down the day before. I looked around, saw no one, put my boot on top of the shell and pressed until it cracked.

The keys were there, glinting in the drab light. I nudged them with my boot's pointed toe then kicked them so they landed near the Island Store's stoop.

"Be more careful next time, Tyler," I said. I headed for the water.

20

IT WAS LATE—past noon. A ragged cloud bank hung above the mainland. The wind shifted, smelling more of smoke than the sea. I turned down the narrow alley that led toward the Mercantile Building.

It was like a northern ghost town. Dead ivy covered a wall made of granite. Near the water stood three clapboard houses, abandoned and falling into disrepair. All had FOR SALE signs on them. Abutting them was a wooden structure, shingles flaking off like fish scales. BOULDRY'S CHANDLERY was painted in white letters on the side. It had high, narrow windows, most of them broken, empty doorways that opened onto a cavernous space that smelled of turpentine. Next to this was the Mercantile Building.

I walked quickly, bent against the wind. The alley was so narrow it seemed like a building might fall on me, if someone gave it a good shove.

"*Junkie bitch.*"

Two figures stood in an empty doorway of the Chandlery. Robert's cronies. One took a drag on his cigarette then tossed it at me. I flinched as it struck my arm.

"You're going the wrong way," he said. "If you're leaving."

I had no time to run before they surrounded me.

"Did you hear that?" said the guy who spoke first. "You're going the wrong way."

They weren't much taller than me, but they were heavier. And there were two of them. The bigger one, a guy whose Carhartt jacket read Dewey's Garage, pointed at my bag.

"That your stash in there?" He reached for it.

I stared at him, holding his gaze; drew my foot back and with all my strength smashed it into his shin. My boot's steel tip connected with something hard as he shouted then crumpled, yelling.

"Oh shit oh shit oh shit."

"What the fuck!" His friend stooped beside him.

"I'm not a junkie," I said.

I took off for the Mercantile Building. The back door was off the alley. Tacked to the wall was a yellowed index card with Toby's name on it.

I hammered on the door. "Toby!"

The guy I'd kicked had gotten to his feet. He clung to his friend, both of them staring at his leg.

"Toby!" My knuckles hurt from pounding. "Open the door!"

I could outrun these guys, but could I outrun the whole town if they got their friends after me? "Toby, goddam it—"

The door swung open. I pushed past a bleary-eyed figure and shoved it closed.

"Two guys just jumped me out there. Can you lock that?"

Toby turned a dead bolt and looked at me. He wore a Motorola T-shirt and wool pants, a pair of slippers.

"Good morning." He rubbed his eyes, yawning. "Is it early?"

It would be hard to tell if it was—we might have been in a cave, or a subway tunnel. There were no windows that I could see, nothing but stacks of lumber and old furniture.

"Noonish," I said. "Thanks for letting me in."

"No problem." He regarded me curiously. "Somebody tried to beat you up?"

"Yeah."

"Did you do something to annoy them?"

"Besides walk down the street? No."

"That's a bit unusual. Did you know them?"

"I saw them earlier at the general store. I think they think I kidnapped that girl or something."

Toby raised an eyebrow. "Really? Why would they think that?"

"Who the hell knows? Everyone here is paranoid. Including me, now."

He tugged at his beard. "Well, my apartment's down by the boiler room." He pointed at a stairway. "This is all just storage up here."

The stairway was dark. The room we emerged into was even darker, until Toby pulled a string and an overhead bulb flared to life.

"Boiler room," said Toby. He walked past a contraption that looked like something out of *Metropolis*. "My apartment's there."

He pointed at a door covered with a pirate flag. "Welcome."

There was something very different about his apartment, and it took me a minute to figure out what it was. It was warm. It was *hot.* I unzipped my jacket, plucking at Toby's sweater.

"That's one of the good things about living by the boiler room," he said. "In the summer, I just switch it off and the whole place is so cool you wouldn't believe it—those brick walls are a foot thick. It's like what they say about Maine women."

"Which is?"

"You want a big woman with tattoos. Shade in the summer, warm in the winter, and moving pictures all year long."

His place was a cross between a machine shop and a roadside museum. There were boxes everywhere, jars full of nuts, bolts, drill bits. Racks of antique tools hung from the ceiling, bolts of sailcloth. A vintage Triumph motorcycle peeked from beneath a Naval Academy Sailing Squadron flag.

Toby called to me from farther back in the warren. "Come here, I'll show you something."

I followed him to his sleeping quarters, a bunk in the back corner. It was like being inside a submarine captained by Pee-wee Herman. Semaphore flags dangled from the ceiling. There was a brass hookah and a bunch of old computers and dozens of empty bottles of Captain Morgan rum.

I ducked beneath a chart of Paswegas Bay. "This is amazing."

"Why, thank you." Toby smiled. "Check this out."

On a table beside the computers was a black rotary phone, a cheap Radio Shack microphone attached to its handset. The lunar-landing *ping* of a satellite connection came through the mike while a laser printer spat out sheets of paper. Toby bent to peer at one of the computer screens.

"See that?" He pointed to a grid of lines and numbers, tapped the second monitor, which showed a series of sine curves, and finally the third, which displayed a gray-and-white whorl that, when I squinted at it, resolved into a satellite map of the Atlantic Ocean and Eastern Seaboard. "That's a northeaster."

He picked up one of the printed pages and handed it to me. It showed a higher-definition version of what I'd seen onscreen, with CLASSIFIED slashed across it in white letters.

"Naval weather satellites," he explained. "I had the Arabian Gulf earlier."

"You hacked into this with a rotary phone?"

"It's not that hard. You want some coffee?"

"Some water."

He lit a cigarette and moved methodically about the room. I felt as though my face was starting to peel back, just above my eyes. When Toby appeared again, I started.

"Here——" He moved a roll of charts, revealing a chair, and handed me a glass of water. "Have a seat."

"Thanks." I drank gratefully.

Toby pointed at my boot. "You got some paint there on your shoe." He tossed me a roll of paper towels, unscrewed the top from a bottle of rum. "Want some?"

"No thanks." I cleaned the blood off the tip of my boot and tossed the paper towel into a wastebasket. "Listen. Things haven't been going so good. Aphrodite—Gryffin's mother—she died last night."

Toby's eyes widened. "What happened?"

"I'm not sure. I think she was drinking and fell and hit her head."

"Jesus. How's Gryffin taking it?"

"As well as can be expected."

"I better call him."

He hurried to the front of the apartment. I fidgeted and fought my paranoia with more Jack Daniel's. It helped, but not much.

"He doesn't sound too good." Toby returned and sat across from me. "Coroner or someone's on the way over; they're taking her body to Augusta. Gryffin's got to do something about a service and cremation. What a shame."

He looked upset but not surprised. "She had kind of a drinking problem for a long time. Like I said, I never knew her that well, but—that whole crowd from back then, for a while there we were pretty tight. Someone should tell Denny."

"Are you going to help Gryffin?"

Toby sighed. "I wish I could. But that northeaster—I got to get over to Lucien's place and make sure everything's battened down. Denny's supposed to have closed everything up for the winter, but Lucien likes me to run backup."

"I've got to get back to the city. I really need a ride back to Burnt Harbor. Can you bring me before you go?"

"I can't. Sorry. I should have checked Lucien's place last week, but I got caught up with another job. And now the weather's supposed to come down. Can't let the pipes freeze."

"Couldn't you just run me over first? Like, just a real quick trip there and back?"

"I'm sorry." His dark eyes glinted. "Any other day, I'd be glad to. But I can't let this slip. First thing tomorrow, though, I'll be out."

"Shit. Well, is there someone else? Like Everett? Can I call him?"

Toby sucked at his lip. "Boy, you're in a spot. I don't know if you could find anyone today. They'll be out looking for Kenzie Libby."

"So why wouldn't one of them give me a lift?"

"Well, I don't know as I'd ask them. If I were you, I mean. Maybe you should just lay low till tomorrow morning. Kenzie'll show up by then, everyone will be all pissed off at her for scaring 'em. They'll fall all over themselves to help you. If the weather's not too bad, I mean. This is the first big northeaster of the year."

"I don't give a fuck. I want to get the hell out of here—"

Toby shrugged. "Well, you can go down to the harbor and take your chances, I guess. I wouldn't. Tempers running high already, and now this thing with Aphrodite. But you can stay at my place if you want."

He gestured vaguely at a corner. "There's a futon."

"I have to leave," I said.

Toby's phone rang. "'Scuse me," he said and ducked into the shadows.

I stared at the row of monitors. They now appeared to be clocking atmospheric disturbances somewhere east of Subar.

I got up and started pacing. I searched for a mirror, to see if I looked as crazy as I was starting to feel, but of course there were none, not even a window.

The bathroom had a shower stall. But no mirror.

I went to the kitchen and got some more water. Toby stood in the doorway, phone pressed to his ear, and stared into the boiler room, talking to Gryffin again, I assumed. He lifted his hand to me, and I turned away.

I wandered toward the back of the room again and passed a cluttered table. From underneath it peeked a mask. I stooped and pulled it out, another brightly colored confection made of papier-mâché and chicken wire and acrylic paint.

It was a frog's head, like the one I'd seen on *Northern Sky.* This one was even more eerily totemic. Also surprisingly heavy, as I discovered when I lifted it. I put it over my head, knocking a book off the table as I did.

Inside, the mask smelled like library paste and hashish. I took it off and put it back where I'd found it then picked up the book.

Mircea Eliade, *The Sacred and the Profane.* The same book I'd seen in Denny's bus. I set it on the table, frowning.

Something else had fallen over, a photo in a cheap plastic frame. I picked it up.

It was an SX-70 close-up of a naked girl lying on her back, hands splayed beside her face. The film emulsion had been manipulated so that fizzy lines exploded around the edges of the picture. Her hair formed a dark corona around her head, and an eye had been drawn on each of her open palms.

You couldn't see her face. It was covered by a tortoise shell that had two more eyes painted on it. In one, someone had painted a tiny green star.

"What the hell," I said.

Toby came up alongside me. "Whatcha looking at?"

"Where'd you get this?"

He took it and held it to the light. "Denny. Sort of experimental, isn't it?" He handed it back and pulled meditatively at his pigtail.

"Who's the girl?"

"That was a girl named Hannah Meadows—'Hanner.' She had a real strong Maine accent. You can't tell from that, but she was real good-looking."

"You can't tell from this if she was even alive."

"Oh, she was alive. She was one of Denny's girlfriends. He had a bunch of them back then. Bunch of women, bunch of kids. He got into all that tribal stuff."

He pointed at the mask beneath the table. "Like that. That took me forever to make. And God, did I sweat in it."

"You made that?"

"Sure. We all had to make our own masks—that was part of the thing. You chose your spirit animal, and then you made the mask, and then we had a ritual, and you were filled with the mask's energy. That was the theory, anyway," he said and laughed. "But Hannah, she was a nurse—she worked the night shift at the hospital up past Collinstown. She was beautiful, and something about her—well, a lot of those girls were cute, but Denny just loved to take her picture. She used to model for him all the time. He even talked about marrying her."

He whistled. "And boy, Aphrodite, she wasn't happy about that. And she sure didn't like him taking all those pictures."

"What happened to the girl?"

"Oh, that was terrible. Really sad. She got into a car accident driving home one night. In the summer; it was after she got off work. She flipped over the guardrail and went into a lake. She got out of the car okay, but then she never made it to shore. They got the car out of the lake, but she wasn't in it. Took them almost a week to find the body. Denny was the one found her, he was with the crews out looking. She'd gotten tangled up in some alders along the shore. I guess it was pretty bad. Something had been at the body, some kind of animal. He kind of went off after that, accused Aphrodite of cutting her brakes, though I don't think they ever found any proof. It was a bad scene. Hey, you okay?"

His face creased with concern. "You look like you're going to pass out."

"C'mere." He steered me to a chair and made me sit. "Put your head between your knees," he said. "That's it. So you don't faint. Just stay there for a minute, I'll be right back."

He went and got a cold washcloth, pressed it to my forehead. "There. Boy, you look a mess. Maybe you should try to take a nap. Sounds like you had a rough morning over there."

"I haven't eaten anything," I said, though the last thing I felt like was food. "Do you have some crackers or something?"

He got me some stale Uneeda Biscuits, also a glass of something cold and brown. "Here, see if this helps."

I ate a cracker, took a tiny sip of the brown liquid. "Christ, that's disgusting! What is it?"

"Moxie."

"It tastes like Dr. Pepper laced with rat poison."

"That's the gentian root."

I shoved the Moxie back at him and finished the crackers. Toby raised an eyebrow. "Better?"

"Yeah. Thanks."

He puttered into the kitchen. A few minutes later he returned, carrying something. "Denny gave me this last time I saw him, back around Labor Day, when I brought his supplies to Lucien's house. This is what he's doing these days."

It was a large color photograph, 12x24, in a handmade frame, like the one at Ray Provenzano's house. From an upright black shape, like a rock or tree, something protruded. A truncated branch, or an arm. Leaves surrounded it, silvery green. It was impossible for me to tell if the color was real or if the emulsion had been tampered with.

But in other places, the photograph had definitely been distressed, with needles and brushes, maybe a fingernail. Layers of pigment bled through. Handmade color separations, I would bet my life on it: a brilliant serpent green, a murkier, brownish jade, brilliant scarlet, dull orange, porcelain white. A muted, flaking shade of rust, like old iron.

I ran my finger across the surface, feeling countless little whorls and bumps and scratches, then held it beneath the lamp.

"There's leaves in there. And insects," I said, squinting. "And, I dunno, some kind of bug. A baby dragonfly, maybe?"

"Where? Oh—yeah, you're right." Toby ran his finger along the outline of an insect's thorax, with tiny, oar-shaped wings. "That's a damsel fly. A darning needle, we called them when I was a kid. They were supposed to come into your room at night and sew your lips and eyes together while you slept. Denny was scared of them."

I looked at the damsel fly. Beside it were scraps of paper, each with a letter on it.

$S_T 2^9$

Part of an address? I brought the print to my face. "Jesus, this is like the other one! It stinks."

"Denny's not much of a housekeeper."

"It smells like dead fish, only worse. Skunky."

"Well, he sets out a few traps, for lobster. And I know he goes ice fishing in the winter."

I was going to ask how you went ice fishing in the ocean, but then I saw something written in the margin.

Some Rays pass right Through S.P.O.T.

"'Some rays pass right through.'" I looked at Toby in surprise. "That's from a Talking Heads song."

"Denny's big into music. I don't know it."

"It's about exposing a photograph—that's what happens, you expose the emulsion paper to the light. Some rays pass right through."

I tapped the edge of the photo. Tiny particles rained from it.

"Ray told me these pictures are worth a lot of money," I said. "Denny just gave it to you?"

"It was payment for some work—I built him a new darkroom a while ago. I do a lot of jobs on barter. I live here free, in exchange for keeping an eye on things. Thinking of which—"

He crossed the room. "I've got to get ready to go."

I sat for another minute, examining the photo. A flake of rust-colored pigment came off and stuck to my hand. Where it had been, I could clearly see a torn piece of paper that had been embedded into the emulsion. A fragment of another, a black-and-white photograph of a bare foot with the ghostly outline of a street sign and something scrawled across it in blue ink.

ICU

My foot. Canal Street.

It was a detail from one of the photos in *Dead Girls.*

I stared at the flake of pigment then sniffed. It had a faint whiff of that same fishy odor. Cupping it in my palm, I walked to the wastebasket, fished out the wadded-up paper towel I'd just tossed, and smoothed it on the desk.

You got some paint there on your shoe.

The smear of blood from where I'd kicked Robert's friend wasn't the exact same shade as the flake of dried pigment. But it was close enough.

I threw the fragment and the paper towel into the wastebasket, ran into the kitchen. Toby was filling a gallon jug from the tap.

"Listen," I said. "After you finish your work at this other island—are you coming back here? Or heading straight over to Burnt Harbor?"

"Depends on the weather. Probably I'll be back. Unless it really comes down, in which case I'll drop anchor over at Tolba and stay in Lucien's house. Why?"

"Maybe I could ride out with you to the island. Then later, if you do go over to Burnt Harbor, you can drop me off. If not, I'll just come back here with you."

"You really want to get out of here, don't you? Okay. I guess, if you don't mind getting cold and wet. I just thought you might want to take a nap or something. You looked pretty whipped, to tell you the truth."

"If I fall asleep now, I'll never wake up."

"Don't want that." He picked up the jug and headed for the door. "You got much to carry?"

"No." I slung my bag over my shoulder. "Just this. My camera."

"Good. You can help bring some things down. Then we won't have to make two trips."

He gathered a canvas bag of extra clothing, a toolbox, two water jugs. He stopped by the door and pulled on a parka.

"Cold out there." He eyed my leather jacket and cowboy boots. "You're not going to be warm enough."

"I still have your sweater." I unzipped my jacket to show him, and the sweater rode up, exposing my stomach.

"That a tattoo?" He stooped to peer at the scroll of words entwined with a scar. "'Too tough to die.'"

He gave me an odd look. "Looks like you earned that."

I didn't reply. I thought of a girl walking toward a car beneath a broken street lamp; of another girl walking down a darkened pier where a boat drifted, its engine cut and running lights switched off.

"Did it hurt?" asked Toby softly.

"It all hurts," I said and turned away.

For a moment he was quiet.

"Here," he said. "Take this—"

He opened a cupboard and tossed me a blaze orange watch-cap. "You lose ninety percent of your body heat through your head. Not that it'll do you much good if you go overboard."

He picked up the toolbox and the canvas bag, gestured at the gallon jugs. "Can you handle those?"

I pulled on the watchcap and picked up the jugs. "Yeah."

"What about this?"

He reached into the shadows and grabbed a wooden pole about six feet long, tipped with a lethal-looking bronze spike that had a hook like a talon welded to it. He hefted it, eyed it measuringly, then handed it to me.

"What is it? A harpoon?"

"Boat hook. For grabbing stuff that falls overboard. Among other things. Like if we run into your friends again outside. You know how to use a boat hook, don't you? You just put your lips together, and—"

He mimed smashing someone. "Run like hell. Come on."

I followed him outside. I tightened my grip on the boat hook, but the alley was empty.

"We'll go this way." Toby headed around the corner. "Shorter walk."

It also avoided that sorry little main drag. A small crowd had gathered at the far end of the beach. I recognized Everett Moss and a few of the other men I'd seen when I first arrived, but not the guys I'd encountered by the Chandlery. Two black dogs played on the rocky beach. There were more boats in the harbor, including a Marine Patrol vessel.

"Guess that's how they'll get Aphrodite back to shore," said Toby.

We headed toward the pier. No one seemed to have noticed us yet. They stood in a tight group, heads bent. Now and then someone looked across the reach to the mainland. "'Less they're waiting for an ambulance boat or something."

The sky had grown darker and more ominous. Clouds and sea were the same charred gray. A cold wind seemed to blow from everywhere at once. The black dogs were the same color as the clots of kelp they snapped at. The gulls were like white holes in the sky. Everything seemed to be part of one thing here, even the men in their slate blue coveralls and dun-colored coats and blaze orange vests: They were all like pieces that had broken off from the island but could be made to fit again, if you knew which jagged part went where.

I used the boat hook like a walking stick and tried not to lag behind Toby. A dog spied us and ran across the shingle, barking. The men all turned. I half expected someone to shout at us—at me—but they said nothing. Their silence unnerved me, but after a minute they turned away again.

Toby waited for me on the pier. "How you doing?"

"I'm okay."

He held out a hand, steering me up the granite steps, and we walked to the dinghy. I felt exposed and went as fast as I could, my boots skidding on the slick surface. We reached the dinghy and climbed in. Toby rowed to where the *Northern Sky* was moored, climbed up on deck, and set down his things. I handed him what I'd brought, and he helped me on board.

"You get this stuff stowed below while I tie up the dinghy. Those water jugs go under the sink down in the galley. The rest of that stuff, just put it so we don't trip on it."

I started for the companionway then paused.

"I might want to take some pictures out here. You going to let me use my camera this time?"

Toby loosened a line from a cleat. "I don't have a problem with that."

"How come you had a problem with it yesterday?"

"I wasn't sure yet whether or not *you* were going to be a problem."

I felt oddly pleased and gave him a wry smile. He looked at me. "You still don't have a mirror, do you?"

"Nope." I stared back, then asked, "The mirror game. Suze told me that was something Denny used to do with everyone."

He said nothing.

"What was it?" I prodded. "Was it something about that girl? Hannah?"

"No." He sighed. "It really was a game. We'd get really stoned, then you'd just stare into the mirror until your face started to look all weird, like it was melting or something. The way if you repeat the same word over and over, it starts to sound funny? Like that. It was silly. But then Denny started to do some other stuff. He was reading a lot about primitive religions; he started making up these rituals. That was pretty silly too, at first. But then it just started to get bizarre. He started believing in the stuff he'd made up. He'd force people to do things—look at yourself in the mirror for an hour, three hours. He did it once for a whole day. All day, all night. It—"

He shook icy rain from his parka and shivered. "I was with him. I did it too—stared at myself in this big mirror. Every time I started to nod off he'd poke me. After a while he stopped, but he wasn't asleep. He just sat there and stared at himself, and then he started whispering to himself. Just kept saying the same thing over and over. Like Chinese water torture." He glanced at me. "That was when I knew I'd had enough. I got the hell out of there and got a job at Rankin's Hardware for a few months, just to kind of normalize myself. I know it's stupid, but I can't stand it now, seeing myself in a mirror."

He stared at the sky and shook his head, as though remembering.

"What was he saying?" I asked.

"'I see you.'" He shielded his eyes from the rain. "'I see you, I see you. I see you.' That was all."

Abruptly he turned and clapped my shoulder. "Go on now. You better get that stuff below."

I climbed down the companionway and stowed the boat hook and water jugs and my bag. Toby joined me a few minutes later.

"I've got some extra foul-weather gear." He rooted through a cupboard. "You'll ruin those cowboy boots of yours, sliding around in the salt water. See if these fit."

The anorak fit, but the Wellingtons were way too big. I said, "I think I better stick with my boots."

"Suit yourself. Just be careful. Give me a hand with the rest of this stuff."

It took me a few trips to get everything stowed below. Toby moved quickly and efficiently across the deck, seeming impervious to cold and sleet. When he finished, he beckoned toward the companionway.

"We'll motor past the point there. Going straight into the wind like this, it would take us three times as long to sail. If the wind changes direction, we might motorsail."

He squinted as icy spray gusted across the deck. "This could be rough. Think you'll be okay?"

"I'll be fine."

"You sure?" He looked me up and down. "You feel bad, you can try going below. I don't think that helps much, myself. You're better here on deck where you can feel the wind. There's life jackets there—"

He cocked his thumb at several orange vests and a life preserver. "Not that they'll do you much good. You go overboard, you've got eight minutes before hypothermia kicks in. That's how they train kids down at the yacht club—they throw 'em in the harbor and toss 'em a life preserver to help get 'em to shore."

"They get them back out, right?"

"That's what the boat hook's for."

I huddled in the stern while Toby went below. After a few minutes I heard the rumble of the engine turning over. Smoke spewed across the water. Toby hopped back up on deck and stood beside me at the tiller as the *Northern Sky* nosed away from the pier. I tugged the watchcap over my ears and looked across the harbor to the beach.

The men stood in that same small group. A few watched us pull out. The others had turned to watch four dark figures walking slowly down the road from the crest of the island. Two of the figures carried a stretcher. Behind them walked a heavyset man in a black overcoat, and a tall lanky figure. Ray Provenzano.

And Gryffin.

"Look," I said.

Toby turned. He ran a hand across his brow then raised it in a wave.

On shore, the tall figure stopped. He lifted his head and gazed across the water then slowly lifted his hand. His voice came to us, garbled by wind and the throb of the engine.

"What'd he say?" I asked Toby.

"'Be careful.'"

I watched as the figures on shore grew smaller and smaller, until they were no bigger than the rocks and, at last, became indistinguishable from them, disappearing completely as we rounded the point.

21

YOU CAN GET USED to anything, even hanging. Even cold. Still, I thought longingly of the little woodstove I'd seen down in the *Northern Sky*'s cabin. When I asked Toby about it, he looked at me dubiously.

"Think you can get a fire going? It's tricky. Time you did, we'd probably be there."

I reluctantly agreed. We'd left the point behind us. Now Paswegas was a green-black hump, like a breaching whale. There was no real chop, but a lot of long swells. It didn't make me feel sick, more like being in a gray uneasy dream that I couldn't quite wake from. Now and then a big wave would catch us sideways, flinging frigid water over the bow. I started counting these to see if there was a pattern, and yeah, every third wave was big, and every twelfth wave was *really* big. I helped Toby pull up the dodger, a small awning that covered the cockpit, and ducked under it as another wave slapped the boat. It wasn't much protection, but it kept the worst of the spray from us, and some of the wind. My feet were swollen inside my boots. My face felt as though it had hardened like cement.

Churning sea thrust against roiling sky. The sky pushed back. We fought both of them. A few gulls beat feebly against the clouds. I went below and got my camera, returned to the relative shelter of

the dodger and did my best to keep my balance while I shot that unearthly expanse of gray and white and sickly green. Islets rose from
the water, some little more than big black rocks, others crowned
with salt-withered spruce or birch. I saw tangles of bone white driftwood on rocky beaches, and dead seabirds, creosote-blackened pilings ripped from God knows where. I thought of photos I had seen
of Iceland, of volcanic islands rising from the sea.

Who would ever live here? I thought. And answered: *I could.*

"Cass." I capped my camera and put it back beneath my jacket.
"Come here, I'll teach you how to keep a heading. The currents are
okay for the moment."

He showed me how to read the compass, its face tilting beneath a transparent plastic dome; how to hold the tiller steady.

"I'm going below for a second." He raised his voice above the
wind and pointed. "That's where we're headed—"

A long black shape skimmed the broken surface of the water.
"That's Tolba. We're sailing a line of sight—not sailing, motoring.
So you just keep heading in that direction, okay?"

I minded the tiller while he went below. It was like fighting
with a live stick, but I figured Toby wouldn't leave if he didn't think
I could hold my own. He returned a minute later with two coffee
mugs, a liter of Moxie, and a bottle of Captain Morgan rum.

"See if this warms you up."

He poured Moxie into each mug, added a slug of rum, and
handed one to me. I took a sip and nearly spat it out.

Toby looked hurt. "You should try it with a little squeeze of
fresh lime. Nothing finer."

I fished beneath my anorak until I found my Jack Daniel's.
Toby finished off his mug and set it down. The deck was treacher-
ous with spray, but he moved easily, keeping the tiller steady. The
freezing mist had turned to a fine, steady rain. After a few minutes,
Toby shook his head.

"We're dragging," he yelled above the wind. "The dinghy.
Here, I'll need you to take over again—"

He opened a storage box and removed a bleach bottle that had been cut to make a scoop, turned and placed my hands on the tiller. "I've set it so we're going into the wind now. That'll slow us down while I bail. Keep that heading."

He ducked out from the cockpit and headed toward the stern. I watched him lower himself down into the dinghy and begin bailing then turned my attention back to the tiller.

Ahead of us, Tolba Island rose against the mottled sky. It was like watching a photograph develop: bit by bit, details grew clear. The finely etched tips of spruce on the island's heights; slashes of white that were ancient birches; a sweep of blood red stone that gave way to a pale, red-pocked strand; a granite pier projecting into the water.

It was big; far bigger than Paswegas.

I looked back to check on Toby.

He shouted, "How you doing?"

"Okay."

"Almost done here! Hang on—"

Exhaustion seeped through me like another drug. My gut ached from coffee and speed and alcohol. If I crashed now, I'd be down for the count. I fingered the film canister in my pocket that held the stolen pills. I had enough speed to last me another day or two if I rationed it. I had the Percocet for when I needed to sleep. If I held off till I got back to Burnt Harbor, I could hit the road and get as far south as Bangor that night, find a Motel 6 and crash there. Not exactly deluxe accommodations, but better than the Lighthouse.

The Lighthouse . . .

I thought of that first night in Burnt Harbor, of Kenzie's white face disappearing into the shadows, like a moth.

She was looking for you, Robert had said. *She said you were nice.*

Well, that was her first mistake.

She said you were going to give her a ride.

My stomach turned over, but not from the swell. I fumbled for the bottle of Jack Daniel's.

She wasn't running away. I knew that. Robert knew it too. She'd been looking for me, but she'd run into someone else. I thought of the boat I'd glimpsed that night in Burnt Harbor—its running lights, one red, one green; then darkness, its engine silenced. I remembered the animal crouched in the tree, its wild maddened eyes.

Fishers never leave the mainland.

"Whooee! Wicked cold out there." Toby ducked beneath the dodger, shaking sleet from his anorak. He stuffed the scoop back into its bin and patted my shoulder. "You seem to have done okay. Here."

He took the tiller and angled it slightly. The *Northern Sky* turned toward the far end of the beach. "Now we're not going into the wind, we'll make better time. If you can handle it for a few more minutes, I'll go down and fire up the Coleman stove and heat us up some coffee, how's that?"

"Sounds great."

He grabbed the mugs and went below. I stood, brooding, as we drew closer to the island. Great reddish boulders were scattered on the rocky shore. On the cliffs above the beach, spindly stands of evergreen and birch. A glitter among the trees indicated a house or outbuildings.

Toby returned with two steaming mugs. "Here you go."

I stared at the island. "It's so big."

"Don't forget there was a whole village once."

I raised the mug to my face, pressing it against my cheek until it burned. "I can't believe you just come and go from here."

"Not often. Fishermen do it all the time."

"Yeah, and freeze to death for a living."

"You think we have a choice? Places like Paswegas, we're like Custer's Last Stand. People from away, developers—they're killing us. They move here from New Jersey and New York and they don't want to let us hunt our own land anymore. The fishermen can't catch fish. Red tide kills the clammers. We get your Lyme ticks, and your Nile mosquitoes . . . every bad thing we used to hide from, finds us now. Away isn't 'away' anymore. It's here."

He didn't sound angry the way Suze had: only resigned and sad. I sipped some coffee and scalded my tongue. Didn't feel bad at all.

"I saw something," I said. I backed up against the dodger, out of the wind. "Back on Paswegas. An animal, in those pine trees by Aphrodite's house. I think it was that thing you told me about. A fisher."

"What'd it look like?"

"Kind of big, or biggish. Black-brown, like a little bear but with a long tail. A lot of fur. It snarled at me."

"Was it on the ground?"

"It was in a tree. Aphrodite's dogs came running up, and it climbed away or jumped off or something. I'm sure it was a fisher."

"Huh." Toby sipped his coffee and steered the boat toward a long pier that seemed to be made of rusty metal. As we drew closer, I saw that it wasn't metal but stone, the same bloody color as the boulders on shore. "It does sound like a fisher."

"When I mentioned it to Suze, she thought I was crazy. She said it was impossible for a fisher to get out to one of the islands."

"Well, that's true. But if you saw it . . . people see things all the time. Wolves, mountain lions. Not on the islands, but back there—"

He cocked his head toward the mainland. "People report them to Fish and Wildlife, but the feds don't want to admit they're back in Maine. Once they admit we got mountain lions and wolves living here, you have a whole lot of issues about endangered species. Also a whole lot of pissed-off farmers and hunters, 'cause the wolves and cougars eat their livestock, and they thin out the deer herd. But they're here, all right."

I felt a faint tingling on my neck. "So it's theoretically possible for a fisher to be there, even if no one's ever seen one before?"

"Sure. I mean, moose have swum out to the islands, and coyotes and foxes. Back a hundred years ago, there was one or two winters so bad there were places where the reach would freeze, and animals could walk over. You don't usually find big pine trees on the islands anymore—they were all cut for lumber, or to make masts. Plus they don't like the salt air. But there's a few big pines on Paswegas, and there's a couple of really big ones here on Tolba. So you could have porcupines, and maybe you could have a fisher. Anything's possible."

I finished my coffee. "You got any food down there?"

"Yeah, go and poke around in the galley, you'll find something."

I went below. It wasn't exactly warm, but it was out of the wind and rain. Quiet, too. Well, not quiet, exactly, but the sounds were different. Rain slashing against the porthole windows, mildly ominous creakings, the drone of the engine. I sat and pulled a blanket around my shoulders. After a few minutes I went to the galley to see what I could find to eat.

There was enough rum and Moxie to qualify as an alternative energy source, but not a lot of what you'd call food. A few sprouting potatoes, a couple cans of tomato sauce. I found a half-full bag of green apples that seemed okay, also a box of blueberry Pop-Tarts. I ate an apple then wolfed down Pop-Tarts while rummaging through cupboards to see what more there was.

String, a corkscrew, plastic condiment packets. A bottom drawer held a first-aid kit, fishing line and hooks, matches in a waterproof tin. Aspirin, ipecac, Benadryl. I shoved them aside and saw something else.

A flare gun.

I picked it up. About five inches long, made of plastic, with a black barrel and orange trigger. I checked the barrel. There was a single red canister inside. I held it, thinking, put it into the drawer and went back up on deck.

"Find something?"

"Some Pop-Tarts."

"Yeah, I bought a case of those for Y2K."

I stood beside him at the tiller and watched black water slop against blocks of rose-colored stone. In the sleety mist it was hard to tell where the pier ended and the beach began. Granite blocks blended into boulders, boulders faded into reddish sand indistinguishable from stunted trees killed by salt and cold. A line of spruces well above the waterline glowed a green so deep it was almost black. Here and there, a black gleam as of eyes gazed back from the trees. A house.

"Is that where we're going?" I asked.

"That's it. Mr. Ryel's Dream House."

I thought we'd pull up to the pier. Instead, the *Northern Sky* angled off toward a pair of round floats. A lobster buoy bobbed nearby.

"Take this," said Toby, leaving the tiller to me. "I'm going to cut the engine. Try to keep us from drifting away from those floats."

He went below. The engine died. The only thing I could hear was the roar of the wind and the crash of waves on the rocky beach.

"This is a good mooring," Toby shouted as he headed toward the stern. "We'll tie up here and take the dinghy to shore. The boat'll be safer if the weather gets rough."

"Will it get worse?"

"Don't know. It seems to be dying down now, but that could just be the eye. Whyn't you get your stuff from below. That way if we end up staying over at Lucien's place you'll have it."

He started to tie off the boat. I climbed down to the cabin and got my bag, put my camera back inside, checked to make sure my copy of *Deceptio Visus* was still safe. I opened it, flipping through the pages until I found the prints I'd made in the basement, the contact sheets and the other two. Aphrodite's photo of the naked man I now knew must be Denny Ahearn, and Denny's photo of Hannah Meadows. I looked at them then put them aside and stared at the snapshot of Gryffin.

I shut my eyes and recalled his face as I'd first seen it, the emerald flaw in his iris. *The green ray.* I thought of the photo in Aphrodite's room—a different green-flecked eye—and the larger picture of Hannah Meadows in Toby's apartment. Painted eyes, one with a green star inside it.

I couldn't make sense of it. There *was* no sense to it, not to anyone except the person who'd shot those pictures.

I've heard alcoholics say they can recognize another alcoholic without ever seeing them take a drink, that they can read a book or hear a song and know that the person who wrote it was a drunk. I'm not crazy 24/7, but I've been crazy enough that I recognize someone else who's nuts.

Especially another photographer. Like Diane Arbus. She was a genius, and maybe I'm not. But I know what she saw out there when she looked at the world through her viewfinder. I know what she saw when she killed herself. Just like I know what I saw when I watched Aphrodite die, what I felt: the stench of damage like my own sweat, and my own reflected face like a flaw in her iris.

I rode a wave of grief that left nothing in its wake, not memory or remorse or rage. When it passed I looked down and saw Gryffin's photo still in my hand. I slid it into *Deceptio Visus* and put the book into the bag with my camera. I went back on deck.

"We're all set," announced Toby. His cheeks were white with cold. "You got everything? Grab one of those life jackets."

The rain had nearly stopped, but the sky remained nickel colored, swollen with cloud. I fished out another Adderall and washed it down with a mouthful of whiskey. There was something behind those clouds, something behind that black lowering bulk of granite and stunted trees, something I couldn't see yet. I got the life jacket and waited in the stern by the dinghy. Toby returned with another life jacket, the canvas bag, and a toolbox.

"I think this is everything. You sure you're okay?" His brow furrowed.

"I think so." I picked up the boat hook. "What about this? Can it come along?"

"Yeah, sure, go ahead and bring it. Just don't leave it behind."

We loaded the dinghy then rowed to shore. It was rough but not scary. Or maybe I was just getting used to it. I scanned the sea for signs of another boat, saw nothing but a few floats. No planes in the sky, no sign of the mainland; just a few black shapes that seemed to flicker above the dark water. Fish, I thought, or maybe dolphins or seals. Toby said they were rocks.

"Another reason Denny never leaves," he said, pulling at the oars. "Summer it's okay, but winter—forget it."

We reached the shore and got out. I helped him pull the boat well above the highwater mark, kicking through tangles of seaweed encrusted with dead crabs. When we were done, he straightened and shaded his eyes, staring out to sea.

"I don't see Lucien's boat." He frowned. "Huh. Denny must've moved it."

I hoisted my bag and the boat hook. Toby dug a cigarette from his pocket and looked at me. "So. What do you think?"

It was beyond desolate: it was where desolation goes to be by itself. Stone pilings reared from the water, skeletal remains of a dock. I couldn't see a house. Surf-pounded stones lay on the beach between skeins of weed and blackened driftwood. Farther up, those huge blocks of blood red granite were the only jolts of color in a scoured gray world. My entire body ached with cold and fatigue, but somehow that seemed like the right way to feel here. It was a place that had the flesh stripped from it. Just above the shoreline reared a stand of dead trees—cat spruce, said Toby—trunks bleached white and every needle stripped from their branches. Overturned tree stumps surrounded them, roots exposed like tentacles, and the wing of a seabird, its feathers eaten away so it resembled a shattered Chinese fan.

And everywhere, red granite. Not boulders or rocks but immense blocks and overturned pillars, Greek columns covered with lichen, poison green, blaze orange, white, half-carven angels and a monolithic horse and rider.

"This is incredible." I walked to an angel whose face was veiled with black mold and ran my hand across its eyes. "It's not all rotted away."

"That's why they call it granite." Toby took a drag from his cigarette. "Back when everyone left here, they just packed their clothes and what they could carry. Obviously they weren't going to cart off the granite. They left things you wouldn't believe. When Lucien built his place, I found saw blades and drills. Beautiful stuff; I've got some of 'em back in my place. Not to mention the carvings. They had a hundred guys out here quarrying the stuff, but there were men stayed in the sheds and just carved stone. You know how you see all those memorials from a hundred, hundred-fifty years ago? Well, a lot of them were carved here then shipped out to Boston and New York. Angels, statues . . . if the carvers made a mistake, they'd just leave it here."

"It's amazing."

"Wait'll you see Lucien's place."

We began walking up a narrow gully. I was glad I had the boat hook to help steady me against the slick rocks underfoot. As we climbed, the gully widened into the remnants of a road.

"That story you told me before," I said. "About Denny's girlfriend. The one who died."

"Hanner."

"Right, Hannah." The gale picked up. I looked back to where the *Northern Sky* bobbed in the water like a gull at rest. "Those masks everyone made—did she have one? Did she have a totem?"

"I don't think so. I think she just went along with whatever Denny did."

"Your totem animal? It was a frog?"

"Yeah. Because they're amphibious. They live on the land and the water both. Like me."

I hitched my bag from one shoulder to the other. "What about Denny? What was his totem?"

"Denny?" Toby drew thoughtfully on his cigarette. "Good question. It was a long time ago, but—"

He pinched the cigarette out between his fingers then flicked it onto the slick stones at our feet. "I think it was a snapping turtle."

22

LUCIEN RYEL'S HOUSE SHOWED what you could do with Ray Provenzano's scrap-metal ethic and several million dollars. It resembled an ancient temple crossed with the remains of a lunar lander, built in the lee of a granite dome above the ocean and surrounded by a stand of massive pine trees and withered rosebushes. A cantilevered deck made of steel girders and I beams ran the length of the building, all glass and weathered metal, inset with blocks of carved granite: huge feathered wings, a colossal arm, an immense, preternaturally calm face. Solar panels carpeted a roof bristling with satellite dishes. The windows were pocked with silhouetted cutouts of flying birds.

"First summer Lucien was here, we had so many dead birds we had to pick 'em up with a shovel." Toby paused to catch his breath. "They'd fly right into the windows. So he put those stickers up. Kind of messes with the view."

The road wound toward the back of the house. Two large propane tanks were set alongside the wall. I stared at the roof. "He looks pretty plugged in."

"That's nothing. Lucien comes all the way out here and then he never leaves the house, just spends all his time in the studio or online. He got a digital switch so he could get high-speed Internet.

Paid a bundle to run it here. He keeps talking about getting a wind-mill, but right now everything's powered off batteries. I've got to make sure they haven't drained. Denny's supposed to check them, but he forgot once. He comes up here to use the phone and Internet but never bothers to check the goddam power."

He stopped and stared at a small outbuilding tucked into the trees. A modular utility shed, its doors flapping in the wind.

"That shouldn't be open." Toby walked over to peer inside. "Huh. He took the tractor out too."

He shut the doors and fastened them with a padlock. "Okay. Now we can get inside and maybe get you warm again." He pulled out a key ring. "Eureka."

After the onslaught of wind and cold, inside was eerily silent, save for a soft, rhythmic ticking sound.

"Solar batteries," said Toby, shucking his rain gear.

We were in a long, open room, its vaulted ceiling crisscrossed by steel I beams. The polished wooden floor shone like bronze. No rugs, no cushions, but a lot of 1980s furniture made of welded copper and steel. The standing lamps resembled carnivorous in-sects. A Viking stove lurked behind a wall of industrial glass, along with a freestanding wine closet. The effect was of being on board the battleship *Potemkin*.

"So." I wandered over to the window. "Did he really build all this? Or was it delivered directly from the gulag?"

Toby dumped his toolbox on the floor. "You wouldn't believe what this place cost."

"Yeah, I would. Taste this bad, you have to be so rich no one ever argues with you."

"It's very fuel efficient. See that south-facing window? You get incredible passive-solar gain from that."

"When? On the Fourth of July?"

"No, really—it stays pretty warm in here, relatively speaking. Speaking of which, I got to go drain the water tanks. You try and warm up, I'll be back up in a bit."

"Here." He fiddled with a dial on the wall. "That'll make it easier. Heat."

He got his tools and went downstairs. I peeled off my anorak, then my boots and wet socks. My feet felt like frozen lumps of meat. I warmed them as best I could with my hands, found some dry socks in my bag, and put them on. I stuck my boots on top of the heater and set off on a quick circuit of the house.

It wasn't exactly a party pad. The wine closet was locked. Other rooms contained yet more minimalist furniture, a plasma-screen TV, small recording studio. A powder room—no medicine cabinet—where I tried to clean myself up. The water was brackish, but it was warm. Right then I wouldn't have traded warm water for the best sex or drugs I'd ever had.

I emerged feeling, if not appearing, a bit more human. I forced myself to stand in front of the mirror, staring at a face that looked more like Scary Neary than it ever had. I resembled my own skeleton, tarted up with bloodshot eyes and windburned skin.

I bared my teeth in a grimace and wandered into the master bedroom suite. It seemed to float among giant pine trees. Lucien Ryel had sunk a ton of money into building this place and heating it all winter long, not to mention keeping a caretaker on retainer.

Now I understood why. There was a fortune in artwork on those bedroom walls. And not the usual stuff your aging rock stars collect, Warhols and Schnabels and Koons and Curtins.

Ryel had a taste for the art equivalent of rough trade, or what had been considered rough trade up until about ten years ago, when, like bondage equipment, outsider art became mainstreamed. There were two Chris Mars canvases, a Joe Coleman, paintings by artists whose names I didn't recognize but which were the sorts of things that would give you bad dreams, if you're susceptible to them.

The stuff was amazing. Some, like a Lori Field collage of women with animal heads and pencil-thin limbs, were ethereal. Others, like a Nick Blinko drawing of a skeleton eating its own skull, were nightmarish.

There were photographs too. A couple of eerie Fred Resslers where you could see faces in the trees. An early Mapplethorpe portrait of Patti Smith. A vacant lot by Lee Friedlander. Works by Brian Belott, Branka Jukic . . . I would have been happy to take whatever could fit into my pockets, if I'd had room.

Then I saw the photos beside his bed.

There were three of them. Oversized color prints, handmade frames, no glass. Monotypes, like the photos at Ray Provenzano's place and Toby's apartment. All three had the same childish signature.

S.P.O.T.

Nothing else to identify them. No title. No song lyrics.

Yet I knew they formed a sequence with the others. And even though I still couldn't pin down what these were photos *of*, I knew they were linked, somehow, with the older photos I'd seen in Aphrodite's room—those crudely manipulated SX-70 prints—and Toby's picture of Hannah Meadows.

I couldn't tell how they fit. The pattern was there, but because it wasn't my own craziness I couldn't put a finger on what held them together. But I knew they were all images of the same thing.

What?

From some angles it resembled a body, from others an island, or the humped form of some kind of animal. The colors were murky greens and browns and viscous blues, shot through with glints of red and orange. Like the others, these used handmade emulsion paper distressed with a needle or fingernail. In spots the dyes had flaked or been rubbed off. Stuff was embedded in the layers of pigment—a fly's wing; hair; shreds of newsprint. Messy, but it gave the prints a strange depth, as though they'd captured some of the real world the photo sought to hold on to.

They reminded me of daguerreotypes. When you look at one of those head-on, even the darkest parts throw light back at you, so you get a reverse image. It's like a photographic negative and positive, all in one.

But then you tilt a daguerreotype just right, and the shadows and light fall into place, and what you're looking at becomes a 3-D image. It's an effect impossible to reproduce in a book or print, or even with computer imaging technology: the purest example of generation loss I can think of. A daguerreotype portrait always seemed like the closest you could come to actually seeing someone who had died a century and a half ago.

I tried to puzzle out the scraps of newsprint embedded in the photos.

U_S T^2 SEE
EN

The letters reminded me of the ransom-note typography on 1970s album covers and band posters.

S^T 2_9

Street 29? Saint 29? Maybe it wasn't an address. Maybe it had some bizarre religious meaning. I took the first photo from the wall and sniffed it.

I gagged. That same sick, rank fishy odor combined with the worst dead skunk you can ever imagine.

"Uh, Cass?" Toby stood in the doorway. "What are you doing?"

"Come here. I want you to smell this."

"What?"

I handed him the photo and went to the next two.

"Whoo boy!" Toby thrust the print back to me. "That stinks!"

"No shit. These do too."

"I'll take your word for it." He tugged his pigtail. "Did they go off or something? Can a photograph go bad?"

"I don't think so." I hung them back on the wall. "I think it's something in the pigments he used to make the emulsion."

"Do they use stuff like that? Stuff that spoils?"

"Not usually. Not at any photo lab I ever hung out at, anyway."

Toby peered at the prints, his nose wrinkling. "It smells like, I don't know—cod liver oil or something. Only worse. Like a skunk."

"That's what I thought too."

"Is there a kind of fish that smells like a skunk?"

"You tell me."

He wandered the length of the room, looking at the other paintings. "I forgot he had this stuff. Kind of dark for my taste."

He stopped by the window, stared out at the sea then glanced at his watch. "It's getting pretty late. We're not going to make it back tonight, not if we don't hurry. I still have to check a few things here. And I need to go see Denny . . ."

He sighed. "I don't want to be the one to tell him about Aphrodite, but I guess I'll have to."

"Were they still close?"

"No. But I think that makes it worse. Gryffin—"

He fell silent and looked away.

"We better keep moving," he said at last.

He left. I hurried to a nightstand, rifling the drawers till I located a piece of stationery. Then I got out John Stone's pen and my film canister with the stolen pills and removed four Percocets.

PROUD TO SERVE read the pen, and it did. I rolled it back and forth on top of the pills, pressing with the heel of my hand to crush them to a powder. When I was done, I scraped the powder into the slip of folded paper and stowed it carefully in my pocket.

I was almost to the door when I saw a bookshelf nearly hidden behind a metal bureau. Its oversized art and photography books were organized by size, not artist, but I knew where I'd find *Dead*

Girls, lined up neatly between *Untitled Film Stills* and Roberta Bayley's *Blank Generation.* I pulled it out and looked at the title page.

> *For Lucien*
> *A shot in the eye! This one's the REAL THING.*
> *Denny*

I left without looking at Denny's photos again. I didn't want to get any closer to them than I already was.

23

TOBY WAS IN THE kitchen, putting away his tools. I sidled toward the counter.

"You mind if I give that rum and Moxie thing another try?"

"Go ahead." He smiled wearily. "Help yourself."

"You want one too?"

"Thanks, yeah. Not too much rum." He rubbed his forehead. "I'm going out to have a cigarette. Lucien doesn't like me smoking in the house. Right back."

I found a glass in a cupboard and tipped the crushed pills into it. I could see Toby through the window, smoking on the stone steps. I poured a shot of rum into the glass then filled it with Moxie.

I sniffed and took a tiny sip. The stuff tasted so foul to begin with, I couldn't tell any difference with the Percocet chaser. To be on the safe side I added more rum.

I needed this to work fast if it was going to work at all, but I didn't want to kill him. Toby was a decent guy. He was also my only ticket back to Burnt Harbor.

Someone told me once that there's no such thing as luck. You make decisions all the time without being conscious of it—like, you move before you realize you're darting to avoid an oncoming truck. Or you walk toward a car before you realize the voice you hear is a stranger's, and it isn't whispering your name.

So maybe these things aren't accidents at all. Maybe they're just the beginning of a long chain of events that you set in motion yourself. Maybe you set it in motion before you were even old enough to remember. Playing in the car while your mother's driving. Hearing what happened next. Opening your eyes when they should have remained closed. Seeing something you should never have seen. Moving when you should have stood still. Standing still when you should have run.

I watched Toby through the window. When he put out his cigarette I grabbed another glass and sloshed some Moxie into it.

"Hey," I said as he walked back in. "Here—"

I handed him the doped glass. He looked approvingly at my nearly empty one.

"See? It grows on you." He took a sip. "You know, it's going to be an hour or two till I get back from Denny's. If I'd thought this through better I wouldn't have drained the hot water tank. You could've taken a shower."

"That bad?"

He smiled and drank some more. "No, no. I just thought, you must be tired. I know you're cold."

"I'm better now." I looked around and tried to determine which piece of barbed-wire furniture would be the most comfortable for someone to pass out on. I decided on a chaise that looked like a head-on collision, pulled a chair beside it and sat. "So where does ol' Denny live?'

Toby settled on the chaise. "Other side of the island, past the little quarries. His place is by the biggest one. Maybe a mile. There's an old road where they used to haul granite down to the harbor."

He pointed toward the empty beach. "Hard to believe now."

"Mmm."

I waited impatiently. I was so wired I felt like smashing through those nice big windows. That would fit right in with Ryel's aesthetic. I choked back a mouthful of Moxie and poured myself some Jack Daniel's.

"Cheers," I said, drinking. "I'm reverting to type."

Toby finished his cocktail. "You sure you don't want to take a nap?"

"Toby," I said. "Listen to me: I don't want to take a fucking nap."

I prayed those Percocet weren't controlled-release. Best-case scenario, Toby would start feeling drowsy within a few minutes. I banked on the alcohol boosting that.

"You're the one doing all the work," I said. "Rowing and stuff. Why don't you chill out for a few minutes? I'll wake you."

Toby leaned back on the chaise. "Too much to do, if we're going to get back to Paswegas tonight." He yawned.

"Go on, rest for five minutes," I urged. "I will if you will."

"Yeah, okay, maybe. But . . ."

He looked at me, dazed. Faint comprehension crossed his face. "Hey. This is kinda . . ."

He tried to stand then sank back, staring at me with glazed eyes. "You."

"It's okay, Toby." I poured myself some more Jack Daniel's. "I can wait."

He closed his eyes. I waited.

It didn't take that long. When I thought he was out, I crouched at his side.

"Hey, Toby," I whispered then raised my voice. "Toby, man, wake up."

I shook him gently. He snorted, and I lowered him onto the chaise.

Down for the count. I folded my anorak and slid it under his head. His eyes fluttered open. He gazed at me blankly then began to snore.

I looked outside. It was almost three o'clock. The sun would set in an hour. I had ninety minutes before nightfall, tops. I went into the kitchen and yanked open drawers and cabinets until I found a flashlight. I pocketed it, got some water and swallowed one more Adderall. I only had two left.

My instinct was to bring the Konica. But I didn't want to risk losing it. If I made it back safely I could retrieve it then. If not . . .

I stood and zipped my leather jacket. I pulled on the orange watch cap, grabbed the boat hook, and headed for the door. As I did, I caught a glimpse of myself in a dark window: a gaunt Valkyrie holding a spear taller than I was, teeth bared in a drunken grimace and eyes bloodshot from some redneck teenager's ADD medication.

"Hey ho, let's go," I said, and went.

24

CHRISTINE ONCE SHOWED ME a quote from Nietzsche: "Terrible experiences give one cause to speculate whether the one who experiences them may not be something terrible."

"That's you." She shoved the book at me. "What happened to you in the Bowery that night—"

"Shut up," I said.

"I'm right! You know I'm right! You can't let go of it, you can't even *think* of letting go of it or grieving or doing any goddam thing that might help! So you better just hope nothing else bad ever happens to you. Because you know what, Cass?"

She stabbed a finger at my portfolio on the table: *Hard to Be Human Again.* "You've got so much rage in you, you're hardly even human now."

I walked until I found the road Toby had spoken of, an earthen track covered with chunks of stone. Far below, the wind roared off the gray Atlantic; to either side, cat spruce thrashed and moaned like something alive.

The speed made me even colder. My fingers on the boat hook were almost numb. I slid on wet rocks and struggled to keep my balance as the sky darkened. It was difficult to believe there had ever been sunlight at all. My lower abdomen burned as though I'd been branded. I slipped my hand beneath my T-shirt and felt the familiar ridge of scarred skin.

I thought of Kenzie Libby. Studs in her chin and ear, a necklace of weathered glass and aluminum. That childish face and the bad dye job on her cropped hair.

People make themselves spiky for a reason. Maybe being stuck in Burnout Harbor was enough, watching the trickle of rich strangers grow to a torrent and wash away your world, with no hope of anything for yourself but a job at Wal-Mart or—maybe, if you were lucky—someone from away who'd take you with them when they left, spikes and all.

But those spikes don't do anything to protect you. I remembered what Toby had said about the fishers—how they'd flip a porcupine over then rip its belly out.

They think nothing can kill them.

Fishers never came to the islands, but I'd seen one.

Denny never leaves the island.

I kept climbing. It felt strange to walk along a road without houses or telephone poles or utility lines. Ragged thickets covered the thin soil, along with dead ferns, scattered birch and maples. Bushes thrust from cracks in moss-covered granite. A crow flapped up from a tree, screaming, and disappeared into the shadows.

But after a while I began to see signs of former human habitation in the underbrush. Crumbled stone foundations; fallen chimneys; cellar holes filled with rubble. A few minutes later I reached the first quarry.

It was set off from the old road, a miniature lake cut into the hillside. The water looked solid and cold as obsidian. Wiry, leafless trees clustered at the water's edge.

I used the boat hook to keep from sliding on loose scree, grabbed one of the trees, and bent it toward me. It had smooth, silvery brown bark covered with tiny bumps that looked like insects.

Dozens of blood red shoots sprouted from its trunk, like a hydra. It looked malevolent, and more alive than anything in that frigid landscape.

I clambered back up the slope and kept walking. I passed two more small quarries, and more cellar holes, but nothing that even a hermit could have lived in.

Eventually the road curved. I found myself looking down across crowns of cat spruce to an expanse of rose-colored rock that gave way to a muddy beach. Blocks of granite were scattered across it, like giant dice. In the center of the beach stood a ramshackle wooden pier. Tied up at the end was a motorboat: Lucien Ryel's Boston Whaler.

I saw no other signs of people. My forehead grew clammy with sweat. I swallowed a mouthful of Jack Daniel's and kept walking. A few more minutes, and I reached the big quarry.

It was about the size of a baseball diamond. Sheer rock walls rose thirty or forty feet above the waterline. I didn't want to think how deep it was. A crow swooped down, flew croaking above the black surface, and landed in a dead tree on the opposite shore. I stared at it and frowned.

There was something in the tree, a ragged mass like a squirrel's nest, but with something snarled in it, something blue and white. A plastic bag, maybe, or a balloon. It was impossible to tell from where I stood. But if I wanted a better look, I'd have to walk all the way around the quarry then fight my way through the underbrush. I didn't want to do that.

I continued on up the road. It was nearly full dark, but I was afraid to use my flashlight and draw attention to myself. Beyond the quarry, I could just make out the remains of several buildings, worksheds or barns. Still nothing that looked like where someone might live now. An icy mist blew up from the shore. The air grew hazy, the ruins insubstantial as paper cutouts. I couldn't stop shivering. A few minutes later, I stood on the crest of the hill.

Around me the island dropped down to the sea. Fog rolled across the water and up the hillside. I could just make out the Boston Whaler. I turned to where the road began its descent.

Through the dusk, lights gleamed. A group of small buildings stood behind the quarry, tucked between spruce and more remnants of Tolba's abandoned industry—broken statues and granite columns, piles of rubble that gleamed in the yellow glow from a small house with smoke coiling from its chimney.

The sight of those glowing windows made me sick. I clutched the boat hook, leaned over and spat up a thin string of bile, waited for the feeling to pass.

It didn't. I swallowed another mouthful of Jack Daniel's.

Fear and whiskey, I thought. *Run, Cass, run.* Light guttered from a broken street lamp. *So you're really from New York, huh? That must be really, really nice.*

I saw her stumbling through the cold dark toward Burnt Harbor, then down toward the beach, hands shoved in the pockets of her hoodie. Trying to get up the courage to go into the Good Tern and talk to a stranger from the city.

I would love to go to New York.

Yeah, well maybe I could fit you in the trunk on my way back.

Whose voice did she think she'd heard as she walked on the beach by the Good Tern?

My fingers tightened on the boat hook. I took a few steps toward the lights when I heard the crow again. I looked up.

Several yards from the road, a single pine reared from a black thicket of underbrush. The crow sat in the tree's uppermost branches. It stared at me and gave another harsh croak, lifted its wings, and flew down toward the beach.

I watched it go then squinted at the tree's lower branches, at a dark tangle like what I'd seen in that other tree overlooking the quarry: a shapeless mass like a squirrel's nest.

Only this was way too big for a squirrel's nest. I tugged my jacket tighter and headed toward the tree. Between the failing light and the thicket, it was difficult to see clearly.

The tree was huge. In its shadow, a mossy area had been meticulously cleared of everything save a few sticks and dead leaves. Here a number of small, flattish objects had been set in a circle about eight feet across.

I crouched and turned on my flashlight.

At first I thought they were rocks, maybe as big as my hand. But they weren't rocks.

They were shells. Not seashells—turtle shells.

I picked one up and grimaced.

It was a baby snapping turtle. I used to find them as a kid in Kamensic; they'd fall into swimming pools and you'd have to retrieve them with a skimmer. The most vicious little things I'd ever seen—after you rescued them, they'd run at you hissing, tiny jaws wide.

It had been a while since this one had attacked anyone. I tipped it back and forth. It seemed empty. But I caught a whiff of something, a musky reek like rotting fish and skunk.

I set the shell back down and stared at the others: a dozen baby turtle shells in a circle. In the center of the circle, four small indentations formed a square.

That circle had a definite ritual appearance. The indentations looked more like holes left by tent pegs. But the area was too small for a tent, only the size of a Porta Potti. I straightened, saw a small white object beside one of the turtle shells.

A candle nub. I rolled it between my fingers, thinking, and put it in my pocket.

The sky was nearly black. Icy rain spattered my face as I slowly traced the flashlight's beam across the circle. A few tiny objects shone white against the ground, like bits of broken crockery. I picked one up.

An eggshell. Not a turtle egg or something exotic, just the

broken shell of an ordinary egg. I chucked it away, continued searching the ground until I saw a faint gleam, as though my light struck glass.

I got on my knees, searched until I saw a glint like gray metal. A nail head, I thought; but when I tried to pick it up, there was nothing there.

What the hell?

I pointed the flashlight at the ground. The reflected light was gone.

But when I looked at my finger, I saw a grayish smudge. Not dirt, more like the residue left when you kill a silverfish, greasy and dark. I sniffed my finger: no smell. I wiped my hand on my jeans, stood, and trained the flashlight on the tree.

The jumble of sticks was about ten feet above me, caught in the crotch of two large branches that splayed into smaller limbs, their stiff needles shaking in the wind. The tree held other things as well. A torn bag, hanks of dead grass.

I walked toward it. When I stepped outside the circle of turtle shells, something cracked beneath my boot. I bent to pick it up.

An antler, mottled white, thin and slightly curved, with tiny ridges along one edge where it had been gnawed by an animal. I ran my finger along it, felt hardened shreds of tissue like splinters of wood, then held it to the flashlight.

My mouth went dry. I'd spent enough hours thirty years ago photographing myself with a life-sized model of a human skeleton to know this wasn't an antler.

It was a human rib.

I turned it to clearly see the crosshatch of teeth marks at one end, panicked and flung it into the darkness. I spat on my fingers and rubbed them frantically on my jeans. Then, clutching the boat hook, I walked the last few steps to the pine tree and slowly raised my flashlight until, at last, I saw what was there.

A body. What remained of it, anyway, caught in the crook of the branches like a burst trash bag. A T-shirt and ragged jeans still clung to it, the shirt dangling so I could see the faded Nike wing emblazoned on the chest. What I had taken for sticks was a tangled mass of bones, blotched with dried shreds of sinew. Part of the rib cage protruded through the T-shirt. What I had taken for dead grass was black hair, matted with leaves and hanging from something that resembled a deflated soccer ball.

I backed away, my boots sliding on slick rock and moss.

I'd just seen Martin Graves.

25

I STUMBLED BACK TO the road. I'd seen bodies before—I'd sought them out, back in the day—but nothing like this.

No animal could have dragged that body into the crotch of a tree. Denny Ahearn had—but why?

The wind whipped up from the sea, carrying gusts of rain. I took a few deep breaths then swallowed, tasting salt and blood. I spat, leaned on the boat hook and willed the throbbing in my head to stop. A few hundred yards below me, buildings yawned black in the gathering dusk—all save that one house with its malign yellow windows. I thought of what I'd just seen in the tree, and of the other tangled mass by the first quarry's edge.

Yellow light pulsed. Someone whispered my name.

Cass, Cass.

It never ends. It's always 4 A.M. beneath a broken street lamp. And afterward every step, every drink, every person whispers the same thing: You didn't fight.

Until now.

I swallowed some whiskey and gulped another Adderall, hefted the boat hook, and started toward the house.

Denny's compound consisted of several outbuildings scattered between stunted trees. A few buildings had been repaired with plywood or driftwood. Others were little more than cellar holes patched with drywall and plastic sheeting, roofed with sheets of blue Styrofoam.

One building, an old barn, had been more carefully renovated. Its doors were open. I shone the flashlight inside and saw a small tractor and stacks of plastic storage containers, a chainsaw.

I moved on. The ground was slippery. There was rubble everywhere. Granite obelisks and broken columns, an arm as tall as a man. Cemetery figures of angels and grieving women. On each the same symbol had been painted: two concentric circles with a dot in the center.

I realized then what I had seen on the standing stone by Denny's abandoned bus.

Not a bull's-eye: an eye. And every single one held a blotched green star.

Sleet rattled against the outbuildings. I crouched alongside a low shed with a wire run. A gleam showed through windows covered with blue tarps, and I could hear the low murmur of birds roosting inside. A henhouse.

The main house was about fifty feet away. At the back stretched a small, windowless addition, its shingles raw and unstained. I recalled what Toby had said about building a darkroom. There were solar panels on the roof, and a jerry-rigged water system—plastic tubing, oil drums, a large metal holding tank. I headed toward the rear of the house.

As I drew close I could hear music. Wood smoke wafted through the icy rain. I approached one darkened window and then the next, and tried to peer inside.

It was hopeless. Sheets of plastic opaque with grime had been nailed across each window. Everything stank of urine and that now-familiar reek of musk and fish. At the back of the house I found a liquid propane tank and a woodshed. I continued to the other side.

Windows boarded up with plywood; flapping bits of plastic. Something crunched beneath my boots—a pile of eggshells. I took a few more steps and halted by a big wooden box, about five feet tall, no lid. I shone the flashlight inside and shaded my eyes, dazzled. It was filled with splintered plate glass.

I killed the flashlight and headed for the front of the house. I clutched the boat hook as tightly as I could, and edged toward the steps.

A figure stood in a pool of light by the open door.

"Hello," he whispered.

He was a good six inches taller than me, broad shouldered and muscular, his face gaunt, clean shaven. He wore a brown tweed jacket with frayed sleeves, wool pants tucked into gumboots, a white cotton shirt pocked with tiny holes. His white hair hung in two long, tight braids to his chest. Around his neck was a heavy silver disk inlaid with turquoise and threaded on a leather thong.

He said, "Are you looking for someone?"

He had the face of an aging WASP ecstatic, with high cheekbones and deep-set eyes, wide mouth, sharp nose. I felt sucker punched, not just by his beauty but by the sudden dreamlike sense that I knew him, that this had happened already and something—drugs, drink, my own slow spin into bad craziness—had kept me from seeing the obvious.

Then he lifted his head, and I knew.

He had eyes the color of dark topaz. In the left one, just below the iris, was a spray of green pigment like a tiny star.

Stephen Haselton wasn't Gryffin's father. Denny Ahearn was.

No one had bothered to tell me. And of course I had never asked.

"I—yeah," I stammered. "I'm, uh—are you Denny? I'm a friend of Toby Barrett's."

"Toby." He repeated the name in a whisper; a cultivated voice, less Maine than Boston Brahmin. His big hands shook in a slight palsy as he looked past me into the rain. "Is Toby here?"

"He's—he's on his way. He had to do something at Lucien's

house." I remembered Aphrodite's death, and nausea gave way to a rush of adrenaline. "We—I—have a message for you."

"Come in out of the rain." He held up a hand. "But you must leave your staff outside."

He pointed at the boat hook. I hesitated, then leaned it beside the door.

"You're a friend of Toby's?"

I nodded. He bent over a stack of firewood beside the door, picked up three enormous logs as though they were made of Styrofoam.

"I thought he closed up the house a few weeks ago," he said and straightened. "I wasn't expecting him." He stared at me, licked his lips, then whispered, "And you are . . . ?"

"Cass." My voice broke. "Cassandra Neary."

"Cassandra Neary?"

His mouth parted in a smile. My skin prickled. There was a dark blue line along his upper and lower gums, as though he'd outlined them in indigo Magic Marker.

"Please, please—come in," he whispered. He stood aside so I could pass.

Everywhere were mirrors. Big mirrors, small mirrors, beveled mirrors in gilded frames, tiny compacts and those big convex eyes you see at the end of driveways. They covered the walls and hung from every corner. Mirrors, and hundreds of snapping turtle shells. Music played on a turntable, Pink Floyd, "Set Your Controls for the Heart of the Sun." A hurricane lamp was the only illumination.

"This is where I live." Denny dropped the logs beside a woodstove, then gestured at the ceiling. "Do you see?"

The ceiling was covered with CDs, silver side down so that I stared at my own reflected face in hundreds of flickering eyes.

"From AOL," he explained. "I go to the post office in Burnt Harbor a few times a year. They always have lots of them. Do you know what a dream catcher is? Those are light catchers."

He stared at me, mouth split in that awful livid smile. He tilted his head to gaze at the ceiling, and his face reflected beside mine in those myriad eyes.

"I see you," he whispered.

"Yes," I said. "I see you too."

I crossed the room. On one wall hung a turtle shell the size and shape of a shield, painted with two almond-shaped eyes. A carefully drawn green star gleamed in one of them.

"They're sacred," said Denny. He picked up a small snapping turtle shell. His palsied hands trembled as he touched it to his forehead, reverently. "All turtles, but especially these."

I noticed that the turquoise in the silver disk he wore was carved in the shape of a turtle. I said, "They—they must mean something."

He nodded. "The turtle is the bridge between worlds, earth and sky. They carry the dead on their backs. It's my totem animal."

"You chose it?"

"No. It chose me."

"Where do you find them?"

He replaced the little shell on a table covered with others just like it. All faced the same way, to where an 8x10 was propped against a piece of driftwood, a faded black-and-white photo of a beautiful young man, long haired, smiling. His arms were around a fresh-faced girl in a much-patched denim shirt covered with embroidery, her dark hair falling into her eyes. She gazed at him with such unabashed joy that I had to turn away.

"They live in the quarries here," whispered Denny. "Lakes and quarries and swamps. They eat the dead, did you know that? So that they can be reborn."

I glanced around. I didn't know what would be worse—to see some sign that Kenzie had been here, or not.

There was a sofa and armchair, a few tables, an old turntable and rows of LPs. A wooden drying rack hung above the woodstove. Tucked into a corner was a propane-fueled refrigerator, a slate sink with an old-fashioned hand pump. A stale smell hung over everything, sweat and marijuana mingled with wood smoke and the underlying stink of fish and musk.

There were lots of books. Joseph Campbell, Carlos Castaneda, Terence McKenna. *The Whole Earth Catalog, The Anarchist Cookbook.* Photography books. A copy of *Deceptio Visus.* I opened it and saw Aphrodite's elegantly penned inscription inside.

For Denny, who longs to see the Mysteries
With love from One who knows Them

There were other photography books, and numerous tomes on folklore and anthropology—including, of course, *The Sacred and the Profane.* I picked it up.

"You know that book," said Denny. It wasn't a question.

He touched the volume with a trembling hand. I Iis fingertips were dark pink, as though they'd been dyed.

"To emerge from the belly of a monster is to be reborn," he whispered. "The beloved passes from one realm to the next and is devoured to be reborn. When I found her they had been at her already for a week. But there is no death. You understand that. I always knew that you understood."

He bared his teeth again in that blue-veined smile. "I told him to send you. Because you're the girl who shoots dead things. So I knew you would come."

He lifted a shaking hand and pointed to another book. As though sleepwalking, I knelt and drew it from the shelf.

DEAD GIRLS
PHOTOGRAPHS BY CASSANDRA NEARY

The pages were soiled and worn from being pored over. I turned them slowly, while Denny stood above me and watched.

"Hannah gave me that," he whispered. "As a present. She thought it was better than Aphrodite's book."

I stared at all those portraits of my twenty-year-old self, all those speed-fueled pictures of my friends. On every page, in every one, he'd effaced the eyes with Wite-Out then drawn another pair with a tiny green star in each.

I turned to the last page. There, beneath the Runway colophon and a small black-and-white photo of me in torn jeans and T-shirt, were three carefully formed letters in black ballpoint ink.

I C U

I fought to catch my breath. What I felt was so beyond damage it was like a new color, something so dark and terrible it left no room for sight or sound or taste.

I put the book back on the shelf and stood. Denny stared at me. His eyes shone, childlike.

"I'm a photographer too," he said.

"I know. Toby—he told me. I saw—he showed me a couple of your pictures. Ray Provenzano too. And I saw the ones at Lucien's place. They're—they're beautiful."

"We have the eye." He looked at the ceiling, his face everywhere, and laughed. "When I saw your pictures, that was when I knew. Aphrodite began the process, but she stopped. You and me, we carry the dead on our backs. We write on the dead. Thanatography—we invented that."

"I don't think I invented it," I said. "Mathew Brady, maybe. Or, uh, Joel-Peter Witkin."

"No." He shook his head. "Just us, Cassandra. You and me."

I looked around, fighting panic. Other than the single picture enshrined on that table, there were no photos anywhere.

"That girl." I pointed at the photograph. "Who was she?"

He said nothing; just stared at me.

"Your pictures," I said. "Don't you have any of your other pictures?"

"Of course." He turned and shuffled toward a door. "It's why you're here."

He held the door for me, switched on a fluorescent bulb to reveal a tiny windowless room with no furniture, only a small round prayer rug on the floor. Around its circumference was a circle formed of turtle shells.

"Be careful." Denny picked up a turtle shell, pressed it to his forehead then replaced it on the floor. He straightened. "These are what you came to see."

Photographs covered the walls, all in handmade frames: color prints on handmade emulsion paper, worked with pen and needle and ink. They had the same eerie, highly saturated glow as Aphrodite's archipelago sequence.

But seeing these, I knew why Aphrodite had stopped working, and maybe why she'd started drinking.

Because they weren't just better than her photos. They were better than almost anything I'd ever seen. Every comparable artist I could think of, all those so-called transgressive photographers—the ones who pretend to push the envelope, then before you know it they're signing a deal with Starbucks and doing the Christmas windows at Barney's—this guy wiped the floor with them. Those photographers would take you to the edge of something.

Denny went the rest of the way, to a place you didn't want to go. And once he got there, he jumped.

Aphrodite had pulled back from there, and from him. Wisely, I thought, now that I could see what he'd been doing all these years.

But it was too late for me. I was already falling.

I wanted to touch them, I *could* touch them. I could smell them too—the entire room reeked of musk and rotting fish. I gagged and covered my nose with my sleeve.

Denny seemed to have forgotten I was there. He stood in front of one picture and stared at it. I forced myself to breathe through my mouth then shoved my hands in my pockets so he wouldn't notice how they shook.

Based on what I'd glimpsed in the tree outside, I now had a pretty solid idea as to what they were pictures of. But I might have a hard time convincing anyone else, unless they'd seen what I'd seen by the quarry. These images were so murky and strange, so tied into Denny's own, incomprehensible mythology, that they defied any simple description. They didn't shout out *Dead Body!* They shouted *Beautiful,* and *Weird.*

Beside the door hung a black-and-white photo that seemed older than the rest, the only picture that wasn't in color. It showed the arching limbs of a leafless tree, its bark striated black and white against a gray sky. A large animal crouched in the crux of two limbs ten feet above the ground. I immediately thought of the fisher.

But when I peered at it more closely, I saw that it wasn't crouching. It was dead.

And it wasn't a fisher. It was a dog, a black Labrador retriever. Its front legs dangled so that I could see where the fur had been eaten away. Where its eyes had been were two coronas of bone, and a tendril that might have been an insect or a bit of tissue. The flesh had drawn away from its muzzle, giving it a snarling rictus. Its loose pelt appeared to be sliding from its body.

"That's my dog, Moody." I jumped as Denny breathed in my ear. "He was a good old dog."

I stared at the words on the bottom of the print: S.P.O.T 1997 and a title.

"'Sky Burial,'" I read aloud.

"That's what they do in Tibet," said Denny. His eyes were huge and nearly colorless in the fluorescent light. "Excarnation. A bridge between the worlds, we carry the dead to be reborn." He smiled, flashing blue-lined gums. "The first step."

"Right," I said. "Thank you for letting me see these."

I edged toward the door, and something broke beneath my boot.

I'd stepped on one of the turtle shells. Denny looked at it then ran his tongue along his lip.

"Wait for me in the other room," he said.

I did. The turntable had gone silent. I thought of Toby, snoring on Lucien's chaise, and of Kenzie, God knows where. I fumbled for my Jack Daniel's, heard myself saying *Fuck fuck fuck* beneath my breath.

Denny stepped back into the room. "What?"

"Nothing." I ran a hand through my hair, stalling. "Just, I'm sorry."

"Sorry? For what?"

"The—the turtle. Your turtle shell. It seemed, they all seemed . . . special. The dog too." I hesitated. "And her. The dead girl. Hannah."

"Nothing really dies. You understand that. Cassandra. *Cass.*" My name came out as a soft hiss. "Your pictures—you understood. You know what happens. You've seen it."

I remembered being in a car in the woods, headlights shining through trees then fading into darkness; something I saw but could never look at.

"No," I said.

He flexed his hands, tugged the cuff of his shirt as though it irritated him. Above his wrist were three raw red lines where he'd been scratched. He glanced up and saw me staring.

"You said you had news." He went to the woodstove, picked up a log, and shoved it inside. "What is it?"

"Aphrodite. She's—she's dead. Last night, there was an accident. She, it looks like she fell."

He stood, silent, as though he hadn't heard. Finally he whispered, "Aphrodite. She told you to come see me?"

"No—no, she's dead. Because—"

"Because what?" His head tilted and his eyes went black. "What happened?"

"I came here to talk to her," I stammered. "To interview her. That's how I saw your pictures. I—"

"*I* brought you here." His voice rose hoarsely, and he lifted his hand as though to strike. Abruptly he covered his eyes. "Oh, Aphrodite, oh, oh…"

His voice dropped so I could barely hear him. "Does the boy know?"

"Yes."

Denny's eyes opened.

"It was you," he whispered.

Everything contracted to a pinprick of pure black. The room was gone, he was gone. There was nothing but the memory of light, and myself plunging into a void. My hand shot out to keep from falling. Something grabbed it, cold and horribly strong. Within a guttering street lamp I saw an eye, the eye, turning upon itself until it swallowed everything.

"No." I blinked and pulled away. The eye belonged to Denny, not me, green flecked, staring. "No. It was an accident. She fell. That was all."

Denny gazed at me. At last he said, "You watched."

"Yes," I said. "I watched."

He picked up a poker and looked at it contemplatively. Then he walked to the rows of records, withdrew an LP and placed it on the turntable. After a moment, vinyl hiss and pop gave way to a sound like a heartbeat. Harry Nilsson, "Jump into the Fire."

"Such a beautiful song," he whispered.

He stood between me and the door and ran his hand along the poker. My voice broke as I asked, "Do you—could I use your bathroom?"

"It's right in there." He gestured toward the back of the room. "It's a composting toilet."

He walked to the front door and stared outside.

The composting toilet reeked of fresh sawdust, shit, spoiled meat, and musk. There was no lock inside the bathroom, no window, no sink. Just a plastic bucket on the floor and a metal shower stall with a heavy canvas curtain.

But there was a second door with shiny new brass hardware. The addition: the new darkroom that Toby had built. I slipped inside and closed the door behind me.

It was pitch black and smelled of sulfur and almonds. I trailed my hand along the wall until I found a switch that bathed the room in red safelight.

Shelves held bottles of pigment, processing chemicals, sheaves of watercolor stock; a five-pound bag of granulated sugar. A table with three sinks was recessed into the wall alongside a plastic water barrel and foot pump, a metal garbage can with a lid.

A second table looked as though it had been set for a macabre dinner. Feathers and dead leaves surrounded a single large sheet of paper. Fanned around it were locks of hair arranged by color—black, gray, pale gold—and what appeared to be slivers of dried fungus.

And something else. An oversized scrapbook, its cover made of much-patched and heavily embroidered denim, its title picked out in ransom-note lettering.

EYE

AM

WITH_{IN}

DENNIS AHEARN, S.P.O.T.

Photos spiraled around the title, fragments of snapshots, SX-70 Polaroids, pictures ripped from magazines and newspapers. Every one was an eye.

I touched the raised medallion that surmounted Denny's name. It was a snapping turtle carapace no bigger than a quarter. Where its head should have been was a minute braid of human hair.

The book was so heavy, I needed both hands to open it. The pages were crowded with Denny's handwriting and Denny's

photographs, retouched with paint and decorated with dried leaves
and flowers, dead insects, feathers, scraps of fur, and human hair, a
toenail. There were pictures of a girl with long brown hair, mugging
for the camera with a spotted turtle shell in each hand: covering her
breasts with the shells, covering her face, laughing. I turned to a
Polaroid of Denny and Hannah Meadows, naked and lying side by
side, a caption inked beneath in painstaking blue letters.

Sacred and Profane Order of the Turtle

I thought of the awful irony, to play at ritual then have your
rites become horribly real, when you discovered your lover's decom-
posing body attended by your totems.

When I found her they had been at her already for a week.

I thought of lying facedown on the backseat of a car in the
dark; of kneeling in an empty street beneath a broken lamp as another car sped away; of erasing a voice from an answering machine
a few hours before the sky filled with ash.

You and me, we carry the dead on our backs.

I stared at the pictures before me, photographs of the dead
and collages made of hair and human skin, a fringe of pale eyelashes like a tiny feathered wing, fingerbones and teeth strung on a
length of silver cord.

I shivered. Not because I was afraid.

Because it was beautiful. And because I recognized it.

It was like neurons firing inside my own skull, like something
I'd dreamed in childhood. I have no idea how long I stood there,
turning those pages, but for those moments nothing else mattered.
There was only me and a book of photos illustrating rites only I
would ever understand, heroes and heroines only I knew. A girl
in a white nurse's uniform, a brave black dog, a schoolbus like a
tortoiseshell palace. Lovers dressed in carapaces of bone and dried
flesh and hummingbird pelts. A trapdoor had opened in the world
and I'd fallen through, onto a bridge built of bone and flayed skin

and eyes, the wings of dragonflies and a snapping turtle's shell. I couldn't look away.

I turned the final page. A piece of crumpled paper dropped to the floor.

HAVE YOU SEEN MARTIN GRAVES?

I closed the book. Music still swirled from the living room. I went to the shelves above the sink, grabbed a packet covered with brown paper and ripped away one corner.

Sheets of plate glass.

I covered my nose then pried open the metal garbage can. It was filled with eggshells and a putrid syrup of rotting yolks. I shoved the lid back in place.

Albumen: egg white. It's what the earliest photographers used to create a glass negative. It was low-tech, perfect for someone living off the grid. Perfect for someone with time on his hands. You take egg whites and sugar—that's what the sugar was for—water and potassium iodide, beat them to a froth and decant them. You pour this over a glass plate, then fix it by suspending it above a heat source. A woodstove would be ideal. Afterward you soak each plate in a bath of silver nitrate and gallic acid, rinse off the excess silver, repeat the entire process and let them dry.

I'd read about this stuff, but I'd never known anyone who actually did it. I searched until I found the last part of Denny's fantasy factory—an unwieldy contraption of black canvas and long wooden poles.

A dark tent. Beside it stood a homemade box camera.

He was making daguerreotypes. The dark tent's legs—that's what caused the indentations I'd seen in the ground by the corpse tree. He'd slide the glass negative into the box camera, go outside and set up the tent with its black curtains to keep the light out. He'd shoot.

It would take a long exposure time, a quarter-hour if overcast. That's why the people in old daguerreotype portraits always have such fixed expressions—they couldn't move, or the negative would register a blur.

This wasn't a problem with Denny's subjects.

And after the neg was exposed . . .

I looked quickly among the shelves until I found a very old glass prescription bottle.

```
BOLTON-LIBBY DRUG CO.
BURNT HARBOR, MAINE
```

I tilted the bottle toward the safelight to read the last word.

```
MERCURY
```

Daguerreotypists developed their negs inside the dark tent, holding the glass plate above a bowl of mercury and a spirit lamp. As heated mercury vapor whirled around the plate, the image appeared.

Denny must have done this hundreds of times, for years and years. It's why his hands shook, and why his gums had turned blue; it explained why everyone said he was such a sweetheart.

He had been, once upon a time. Then Hannah Meadows died, gruesomely, and to memorialize her he revived a lost art, without bothering to learn about its dangers. Otherwise he'd have known that what drove nineteenth-century hatters mad, with brain damage and psychosis, had driven daguerreotypists mad too.

Denny had mercury poisoning.

I put the mercury down and looked until I discovered another century-old bottle, the reason why Denny's darkroom smelled of bitter almond.

```
CYANIDE OF POTASSIUM
```

Daguerreotypists used it to clean glass negs, so they could be reused. I remembered one of my NYU instructors reading an 1856 text on the subject.

I feel a little unwilling to recommend this mode, as it involves the use of the deadly poison cyanide of potassium; but as every man who photographs must necessarily use what we call dangerous chemicals, I can only caution the beginner.

I replaced the bottle, turned off the safelight, and stepped back into the bathroom.

And froze.

The black canvas shower curtain was moving—the slightest ripple, as though from a faint breeze.

But there was no wind, only the wail of music in the next room. I drew the flashlight from my pocket and stepped toward the shower stall; grabbed the curtain and yanked it back.

She lay on her side in five inches of black water, her head above the scummed surface, hair plastered against white skin, her hooded sweatshirt and jeans soaked with filth. Dried blood webbed her cheeks. Her wrists were bound with duct tape, her knees drawn to her chest. There was duct tape across her mouth; duct tape across her eyes, where he had drawn circles in Magic Marker. A scrawled star was in one of them.

She didn't move. The water did.

A black shape emerged from the muck and began to crawl across her face, claws scratching her cheeks, its shell black with slime.

The girl moaned. She was alive.

I grabbed her shoulder and pulled her up. The baby snapper fell as dark forms suddenly bobbed everywhere, scrabbling at her head and arms.

"Kenzie—it's me. Cass," I whispered. "From the motel. Hold still, for Christ's sake—"

She struggled to kick me with her bound legs. Turtles slopped over the stall's lip and scrambled across the floor. I dragged Kenzie from the stall, pulled a corner of the tape covering her eyes.

"You have to shut up!" I breathed. "Kenzie, *please*—"

The wet tape slid off easily. Beneath, her eyes were blood-red slits in oozing skin. I thought she'd been blinded, but then her eyes widened. She began to shake her head frantically.

"Listen!" I hissed. *"Don't scream.* I'll take it off your mouth, but you can't fucking scream—"

She nodded, and I peeled the tape from her mouth. She leaned over and vomited, bile and bitter almond. On the other side of the door, Denny's voice rose with the music, singing wordlessly.

A baby turtle cracked beneath my boot as I grabbed Kenzie and dragged her into the darkroom. I shut the door and turned on the safelight. Kenzie leaned against the sink, gasping. I jammed the dark tent's legs beneath the doorknob, grabbed the bag of sugar, and poured some into my palm.

"Eat this!" Kenzie gagged as I shoved my hand into her face. *"Eat it!"*

She retched but kept it down. Glucose is an antidote to cyanide—Rasputin survived poisoning because of sweet pastries and Madeira. I had no idea if it would help, but Denny obviously hadn't given her enough cyanide to kill her; not yet, anyway.

She wiped sugar onto her filthy shirt, and I reached for her hand. Her fingers were scraped raw, her knuckles black with bruises.

"You fought," I said. "Good girl."

"There's a gun." She began to sob. "He—"

I clamped my hand over her mouth. *"Shhh."*

The music had stopped.

"Get under there," I whispered. "Cover your eyes."

She scrambled beneath the table. I grabbed the largest bottle on the shelf and turned off the safelight.

There was a soft knock on the bathroom door. "Cassandra?"

In the next room the door opened.

"Oh no, oh no . . ."

His cries were like a bird crooning. I heard something skitter across the bathroom floor. Denny swore under his breath and gave a guttural shout. The darkroom door shook as an object was flung against it. I heard stomping as he crushed one shell after another beneath his feet.

Then silence.

I could see nothing. From beneath the table came Kenzie's ragged breathing. I braced myself against the sink and pried the cork from the bottle.

There was a rustle of cloth, the scrape of wood as Denny pushed against the darkroom door. The dark tent's legs snapped. The reek of dead fish and musk filled the room. Kenzie whimpered.

He was inside.

I grasped the bottle in one hand, with the other found the flashlight in my pocket. Phantom shapes swam in front of me in the darkness. I began to shake, imagining each of these was Denny. The floor creaked a few feet from where I stood.

"*Cass,*" he whispered. "*Cass, Cass . . .*"

Nausea overwhelmed me, a darkened street.

"*Cass, Cass.*"

I couldn't move. The sound of my own name bound me, formless horror and Aphrodite's voice in my head.

Both of you—nothing.

Something brushed my foot.

No, I thought. *Not this time.*

I turned on the flashlight. Denny's dazzled face hung before me, his mouth a gaping hole as I shouted, "*Kenzie! Run!*"

I flung the mercury at his eyes.

With a scream he fell. Kenzie bolted for the door with me behind her.

"Run!" I yelled as we stumbled into the living room. "Run and *don't stop!* Here—"

I thrust the flashlight at her. She took it and stared at me blankly until I pushed her roughly toward the front door.

"Get the fuck out of here!"

She fled outside. Behind me Denny's screams rose to a howl as he staggered from the bathroom.

"Come—BACK!"

Kenzie was right. He had a gun.

Mirrors exploded as a shot went wild, then another. Denny clutched his eyes with one hand then aimed the gun at me. I turned and ran out onto the front steps, icy rain slashing at my cheeks.

Kenzie was gone. I grabbed the boat hook, whirled to see Denny's face, gray splotched with mercury. The gun's barrel thrust against my temple.

"You can't go." His breath was cold and stank of rotting fish. "I see you, Cass. I know."

He twisted his hand. I cried out as metal bored through the skin beside my eye.

"Tell me what you saw," he whispered. "You saw them. I know you saw them."

I didn't move.

"I know what you saw." He licked his lips. "Tell me. Tell me."

I swallowed. My hand tightened imperceptibly around the boat hook.

"All of them." My voice came in a hoarse whisper. "I saw all of them."

"Where?"

"In the quarry."

"Where else?" He dragged the gun's barrel across my cheekbone and I moaned, feeling my skin tear.

"The photos," I gasped. "All your photos—I saw them too."

"And the mirrors?" His voice was so soft I could barely hear him. "What did you see there?"

"I—I don't know."

"Yes, you do. You saw me." I heard him breathing faster. "You saw me, Cassandra. And you saw—"

I struck his shoulder glancingly with the boat hook then staggered backward. Blood streamed into my eye as I caught my balance, grasped the boat hook with both hands, and swung it like a club.

The bronze end struck his hand. There was a deafening retort. Fire lanced my upper arm, and I screamed.

Denny stood at the edge of the granite step, his long white braids spattered with blood.

"I see you," he whispered and laughed.

I screamed again, beyond rage and pain, beyond everything.

"You *fuck*." I hefted the boat hook and with all my strength smashed it into his face.

I heard a sound like a jack-o'-lantern hitting pavement and swung again. Denny roared and dropped to his knees. The gun spun into darkness. I kicked him, felt my boot's steel tip dig into his chest as though it were loam. He tried to roll away, and I kicked him again and again then raised the boat hook and rammed it against his skull. He tried to raise his hands as I struck him repeatedly, half blinded with weeping and my own blood.

Finally I stopped. I leaned on the boat hook, panting, and looked down.

He lay on his side, staring at me. A black stain crept across his forehead like a spider. One eye bulged like a crimson egg, a white petal of skin folded beneath it. As I stared, his other eye opened. His mouth parted in a wash of red and indigo as he gazed up at me. He smiled.

"*I see you.*"

I backed away as he began to get to his feet. Another voice echoed faintly through the rush of rain and wind.

"*Cass!*"

I clutched the boat hook and fled down the steps and into the darkness, past the granite sentinels with their green-flecked eyes, until I reached the road.

26

KENZIE WAITED NEAR THE quarry, her white face glowing in the flashlight.

"I told you to keep going!" I grabbed her roughly, spat a mouthful of blood, then snatched the flashlight from her hand. "Come on."

She stared at me wide-eyed. "Oh my God, your face. Are you okay?"

"I'm fucking great."

"Did you kill him?"

"No."

She began to sob. I whacked her with the butt-end of the boat hook.

"You want to go back and finish for me? Come on, there's someone at Ryel's house; we have a boat, if—"

"If what?" she wailed.

"If you keep your goddam mouth shut."

I dragged her after me, still sobbing. For several minutes we stumbled along the road in almost total darkness, following the flashlight's wan beam. Then I stopped. Kenzie stared at me.

"What is it?"

I killed the light and clapped my hand over her mouth. Beneath the rattle of wind in the trees and the crash of waves I heard another, fainter sound on the road behind us.

"It's him," I breathed.

Kenzie moaned. I found her hand, icy cold, and pulled her to the side of the road. I turned on the flashlight, just long enough to pick out a break in the trees, then moved as quickly as I could, feeling my way with the boat hook with Kenzie right behind me.

We struggled through a tangled hell of brush and whiplike trees, icy stones and frozen earth. My face burned where sleet slashed it; my right eye was swollen shut. Not that I could have seen much of anything. I listened for more sounds behind us but heard nothing above the rising wind.

I had no idea where we were but figured we couldn't be too far from the road, with the smaller quarries between us and Denny's compound. After a few minutes the trees thinned and I halted, panting. Kenzie drew up beside me as I leaned on the boat hook and fought to catch my breath. I strained to see something, anything, that might signal safety, finally gave up.

"Can you see?" I whispered hoarsely.

"I think there's a light," Kenzie said.

She pointed, and I could just make out a blurred point that might have been light, or maybe just a break in the trees. But I thought it was the right direction for Lucien's house.

"All right. Here—"

I fumbled for her hand in the darkness, thrust the flashlight into it. "You take this. Stay right in front of me and don't move too fast. Keep the light close to the ground and listen for me, I'll tell you to put it out if something happens. Go on, I'm right behind you."

She nodded then went on ahead, the flashlight's beam so feeble that more than once I lost it among the wind-thrashed trees and underbrush. I followed her as best I could, lurching clumsily, my boots sliding across stones and fallen tree limbs as sleet lashed at my face. My feet were so numb it was difficult to move. I jammed the boat hook against the ground with every step, feeling my way in the dark.

There were fewer trees here but more rocks. Several times I tripped and nearly fell, catching myself with the boat hook at the last moment. The wind shifted again; the hiss of sleet against dead leaves fell silent. I breathed on my fingers, trying to warm them; then held my hand out, palm up, and felt a touch like another, colder breath. Snow.

Through the trees I saw a pale glimmer, like the moon but moving, slowly, resolutely: Kenzie.

Good girl, I thought.

I kept going, head down, when a thin wail drifted back to me. I looked back but saw nothing and staggered on toward the sound.

I found her standing at the edge of a large clearing, the flashlight turned so it blinded me.

"Put it down!"

She ignored me, just moaned and pointed the light into the clearing. I came up alongside her, grabbed the light and swept it across the ground. Snow sifted down, flakes fine as dust, but enough to leave a thin white tracery across several dark, humped forms. I handed the boat hook to Kenzie and walked toward them slowly then stopped.

Three huge turtle shells had been arranged in a rough circle. Each was so large that my hands, extended, would not have encompassed it. Instead of legs and tails, grayish shapes like driftwood protruded from the shells. Large white fragments were scattered where the heads should have been. I thought of tiny shells being crushed beneath Denny's feet then bent and picked up a cusp of jawbone as long as my finger. Between two teeth, long white strands of hair were snagged, like fishing line.

I dropped it and stumbled to where Kenzie waited.

"What—" she began.

"Just go," I said and pushed her. "Faster."

We stumbled on across the island. Snow changed to rain again; the wind rose and fell. My heart felt like a fist pounding at my chest. Kenzie whimpered; I pulled her to me and held her, murmured until her voice stilled and I drew away, and we both moved on. We saw no further sign of Denny Ahearn, heard nothing but wind and then, gradually, a noise that I recognized as waves beating against rock.

"There . . ."

I pointed at a phantom light that seemed to waver ahead of us. I coughed, spitting blood, touched my swollen eye and winced. The light remained, and I began to run.

Ahead of us, Lucien's house loomed into view. A single light shone from the kitchen.

"Toby's there," I said, but Kenzie had already raced ahead of me.

I staggered inside after her, locked the door, and turned to see Toby standing unsteadily in the living room.

"Cass?" His voice was thick. He looked down, saw the glass of Moxie on the floor, and reached for it.

"No." I kicked the glass away. "We have to get out of here." I grabbed his arm and pulled him into the kitchen.

"Is that Kenzie?" He stared at her in disbelief, then at me. "What the hell happened to you?"

"Denny Ahearn happened." I flinched as he reached to touch the corner of my eye. "Your harmless hippie friend."

"Let's go, let's go." Kenzie looked at us wild-eyed. "Why are you *waiting*?"

Toby blinked, uncomprehending. "Kenzie? Were you—was she here? In this house?"

"Toby. We have to go. Now."

He shook my hand from him. "Cass. You did this, didn't you?" He didn't sound angry, just confused and stoned. "You . . . drugged me, right? Like a roofy?"

"Yes! I'm sorry! I'm a shit! We still have to leave!"

He glanced back at Kenzie. "Jesus Christ."

"It was bad, okay?" I said. "I'll tell you when we're on the boat. Right now *we have to get out of here.*" I pounded the door in frustration. "Can you sail that fucking boat or not?"

"I guess." He ran a hand across his face. "I don't feel too good, but . . ."

He looked at me, holding the boat hook like a lance, then at Kenzie's bruised face. "But I guess I'll take my chances."

He put a hand on Kenzie's shoulder and rested it there for a moment. "Come on. Let's get you home."

They went outside. I grabbed my camera, ransacked kitchen drawers till I found some dish towels. I used one to stanch my bleeding arm; with the other made a bandage for my eye. I bound it in place as best I could then hurried after them.

A stiff wind sent curtains of freezing mist up from the water's edge. Toby and Kenzie had already dragged the dinghy into the shallows. I clambered in beside them, using the boat hook to push off as Toby rowed us out to the *Northern Sky.*

"We'll have to motor," he yelled above the wind. "It'll be rough. Kenzie, you better stay below."

We boarded the sailboat. Toby tied off the dinghy and pulled on his foul weather gear, then turned to Kenzie.

"You wait below like I said, okay?"

She shook her head fiercely. I thought of the bound figure on the floor of that filthy shower stall. Toby started to argue, and I cut him off.

"Just give her a life vest. She'll stay out of your way."

Kenzie shot me a grateful look. Toby frowned.

"If you say so. Here—" He tossed a life vest at each of us. "You too, Cass. I need you to help navigate."

I started to pull it on, wincing as it snagged my wounded shoulder, then gave up. It wouldn't fit over my camera, anyway.

Toby began coiling lines. "You going to tell me what the hell happened back there?"

I did. When I was finished, he shook his head.

"I can't believe it," he said. "I mean, I *do* believe it, but . . ." He glanced at Kenzie huddled in the cockpit. "It's hard."

I snorted. "Yeah, well, I don't know what you guys were smoking thirty years ago, but I think Denny got some of what Ted Bundy was having. Aren't you going to call someone? Like the Coast Guard?"

"The Coast Guard rescues people," said Toby. "Is our boat in distress? Do we need to be medivaced to a hospital?"

He glanced at my bandaged eye, then at Kenzie, and shrugged. "Yeah, but by the time they got here we'd be on shore. They'd tell me to radio the police. We're better off just getting out of here fast as we can."

He held up two oversized flashlights and tossed me one. He shielded his face from blowing sleet, pointed past the bow to a distant gleam like a dim emerald star.

"See that light? It's a buoy. There's a bunch of them between here and Burnt Harbor. Some are lighted, some aren't. We need to follow one to the next, point to point. Use the flashlight to find them. I'll tell you where to look, right or left."

He switched on the running lights. A dull green glow illumined the right side of the cabin, red on the left, white at the stern. "Think you can handle it? I've got spreader lights up there on the mast, but they mess up my night vision. Plus, if Denny's really out there looking for us, it'll be like a billboard. You stay in the bow and I'll yell out to you. Once we get past Paswegas it's clear sailing to the mainland, and we should be able to see the lighthouse up to Togus Head."

His voice was calm, but he moved quickly and nervously, ducking beneath the rigging and pausing only to light a cigarette. "Get Kenzie settled, I'll be another minute."

I joined Kenzie in the cockpit. She sat, staring at her knees. Beneath the orange life vest she wore the same clothes I'd found her in. She looked much older than fifteen; like someone who'd crawled out of a burning building only to find the rest of the world bombed to rubble.

I fumbled in my pocket till I found the Jack Daniel's. There was hardly any left. I gazed at the dark hulk of Tolba Island and drank a mouthful then passed it to Kenzie.

She took a sip and coughed. "That's nasty."

"Damn straight." I finished the bottle and set it down then glanced at her white face, the crosshatch of claw marks across her cheeks. "Hey. You okay?"

"Yeah." She didn't look at me.

"Did he—"

"No."

Sleet rattled the dodger's awning. I looked across black water to where Paswegas waited, lost in night and fog.

"What were you doing?" I finally asked. "That night. When you went down to the harbor."

From below came the engine's stuttering roar. The boat rocked and moved forward. Kenzie stared silently into the darkness.

"I just wanted to talk to you," she said at last. She sounded defiant, but then I saw she was crying. "That was all. I just wanted to talk to someone else. From away."

"From away. Well, that makes sense."

"I hate it here." She kicked out furiously, and the empty whiskey bottle went flying. "I fucking *hate* it."

I smiled. "Hold that thought," I said. "I'm going to help Toby. Here—"

I handed her my camera and the boat hook. "Keep an eye on these, okay?"

I stepped across the icy deck to the bow.

"That lighted buoy's the first one," Toby shouted as he hurried toward the cockpit. "After a hundred feet, start looking left—"

I stood in the bow and swept the flashlight's beam across the water until it picked up the second buoy.

"There!" I yelled.

"Good. Next one's about three hundred feet, still to the left—"

It was like a dream, the *Northern Sky* drifting through a world where all color had been burned away; a world of nothing but black water and black sky, with a shifting scrim of gray between and the occasional shaft of black where ledge emerged from the water like an island being born, the flashlight's beam insubstantial as a white straw flung across the channel. The cold wind made it hard to hear the clanking of the buoys, but Toby kept directing me where to look, and we fell into a kind of restless dance, the flashlight sweeping through the night, the *Northern Sky* shifting right or left as she bore inexorably away from Tolba Island, the engine's drone like my own steady breathing. We might have traveled for miles, for hours; I might have fallen asleep, exhausted as I was and no longer able to tell where one world ended and another began, sky and water and stone and blood.

Then Kenzie's cry cut through the wind like a gull's.

"*Cass!*"

She pointed behind us, toward Tolba Island.

"That's his boat!" she shouted. "That's him!"

Toby peered through the dodger's window. I stepped to the side of the bow, squinting through the mist. I couldn't see anything.

But I could hear it—the roar of a powerboat. Kenzie screamed.

"Get below!" commanded Toby. He pushed her toward the companionway. "There's a radio; see if you can get it to work and put out a Mayday signal. Stay down there till I get you—"

She disappeared down the ladder, and I stumbled into the cockpit.

"Shit." Toby stared at the silvery shape arrowing across the water. "He's got Lucien's Boston Whaler. Thing's got a twelve horse-power engine, we can't outrun him."

The roar grew louder: the boat was a hundred yards off, heading straight at us. Denny stood in the stern by the outboard motor. I couldn't see clearly through the sleet and fog.

But he could.

"I see you!" His voice rose to a ragged shriek. I swore and turned to Toby.

"What do we do?" I demanded. "He's got a fucking gun—"

I remembered the flare gun below. As Toby hunched over the tiller, I darted to the companionway and climbed down. Kenzie held the two-way radio and the NOAA band. The boat hook and my camera were on the bench beside her.

"Is that radio working?"

"I don't know." She punched a button. I heard a blast of static. "I think so. Maybe."

"Keep trying." I flung open the drawer, grabbed the flare gun. As I passed Kenzie I hesitated, then grabbed my camera and climbed back up on deck. Toby stared at me from the cockpit, his face taut. He gestured angrily at the flare gun.

"That's useless!"

"Not if I nail him."

The distance between the boats had narrowed to about fifty feet. Denny's arm dangled limply at his side. He had a gun but showed no sign of using it. His head looked misshapen, his features blackened and smeared across his face like tar. His jaw sagged, and I could see where the flesh had been torn away, like a peeled fruit.

He was smiling.

"I see you," he cried thickly.

"He's coming right at us." I shook my head in disbelief. "Like he's going to ram us."

"Look out—" Toby swung the tiller, and the sailboat tacked sharply to the right. "Watch your head!"

I ducked and grabbed the rail as the Boston Whaler shot toward our stern. There was a grinding sound, and the *Northern Sky* lurched.

Toby's face went dead white. "He's going for the rudder—he's trying to shear it off—"

The outboard's roar became a furious whine. The Boston Whaler circled then swept toward us again, Denny crouching over the motor.

"By his feet." Toby called to me and pointed. "There's a plastic container, it's usually got fuel in it. You only have one flare. See if you can hit it."

I braced myself against the rail. It was hard for me to take aim with one eye bandaged, but I did my best. Denny straightened to stare at me. His mouth opened in a wordless shout.

"I see you too," I said, and fired.

There was a low *whoosh*, and a white ball rocketed toward the Boston Whaler. Around us the world glowed as a bright plume like a meteor's tail split the sky in two. Denny lifted his face, arms outstretched, his shirt blinding white. The flare plummeted soundlessly to his feet and continued to burn, not fiercely but steadily, while brownish smoke rose around him. I dimly heard Toby behind me, cursing. Then the *Northern Sky* arced smoothly away from Denny's boat and began to churn across the reach.

I clung to the rail and stared at Denny. The flare's light still glowed in the Boston Whaler's stern, but he made no move to put it out or kick it away from the fuel container, only stood with arms lifted and face tilted to the night, as though welcoming something. I could see the dull glint of the gun in his hand. Then his fingers opened. The gun fell, disappearing into the water. Denny lowered his ruined face until he stared at me then stooped for something at his feet. The flare, I thought.

But then he straightened. His eyes trapped the flare's dull glow as he shook his head, slowly, sorrowfully, and his mouth split into an anguished smile as he held something out to me, a large, flat, rectangular object that flapped in the freezing wind and billowing smoke. His book.

There was a hiss like air escaping from a valve. Denny's legs bloomed orange and black.

"Get down!" shouted Toby. "That's the fuel line!"

A column of flame shot into the air. Denny screamed, a terrible high-pitched sound like a child's cry, and the engine exploded.

I stared transfixed as gold and argent pinwheels spun from the boat's stern. Black smoke ballooned and momentarily obscured everything as I grabbed the camera around my neck and clawed off the lens cap. I braced myself against the rail, shielded the lens from sleet, and coughed as oily smoke enveloped me then dispersed, windblown, as Denny burned.

I shot him as he died, his clothes ragged wings and his hair ablaze, his hands beating at the flames as though they were swarms of fiery bees. His face blackened and collapsed; one arm twitched rhythmically as the boat began to dip below the water's surface; and still he burned, a man like a dancing ember. I pressed the shutter release and angled myself along the rail, coughing as smoke coiled around me and my eye streamed, until a dome of black and gray erupted from the water's surface and the Boston Whaler disappeared. Gray eddies washed toward us, the stink of diesel and melted fiberglass and charred meat.

The *Northern Sky* drifted, slowly, its engine a soft drone. As in a dream I replaced the lens cap on my camera, pulled it from my neck, put it in my bag, and shoved it out of the way. I stood against the rail and stared across the black swells.

A life preserver floated a few yards off, yellow nylon line, a clotted white shape that might have been part of the outboard engine: scattered wreckage that was too far off for me to see. Freezing rain beat against my face. It was a moment before I realized I was crying. I wiped at my one good eye, touched the sodden bandage on the other, and gazed back out at the water.

The life preserver had drifted out of sight, but the swells brought other things closer: sheets of oversized paper, some torn but others miraculously intact, or nearly so: Denny's book, its pages ripped from the homemade binding. I stared in disbelief as a sheet floated past and disintegrated before my eyes, its layers detaching themselves—leaves, hair, green pigment, ochre, albumen, blood, all dissolving into a bright slick upon the surface of the sea then disappearing into flecks of foam and brown kelp. A tiny shard like an arrowhead seemed to crawl across a page floating past. A swell lifted it, and a torn photograph curled from the sheet. I had a glimpse of eyes blurring into mouth and hands, a turtle's shell.

I gasped and leaned forward with one hand, reaching for a sheet that seemed intact. My fingers closed around one corner, the heavy paper sodden but untorn. Another swell nearly tugged the sheet from my grasp. I stretched out my other hand to grab it, winced as my hand closed on it and my legs suddenly shot out from under me. My boots slid across the icy deck as I pitched forward, and overboard.

The water slammed me like a wall. My mouth opened to scream, and I kicked out frantically as I sank. Frigid water filled my mouth and nostrils. I kicked again, frantic, pinioned by utter darkness. Freezing water crushed me; I saw nothing, felt nothing but that terrible weight and then the shock of light, air, my name.

"*Cass! Cass!*"

I gasped then choked as air filled my lungs, felt a dull pressure against my cheek. Something glinted then struck me again, on the shoulder this time. The boat hook. I tried to grab it but my hands were numb, then dimly saw a figure reaching from the stern. Kenzie.

"Hang on!" she shouted.

Another shape appeared behind her. "We got you, Cass, hang on there—"

Toby grabbed me by the shoulders as Kenzie dug the boat hook beneath my arm. Together they pulled me on board. I knelt, puking up seawater, as Toby draped a blanket around me.

"Come on, girl, let's get you below. Come on," he urged. "You're gonna freeze to death."

He half-carried me below deck, giving instructions to Kenzie beside us. "Try to get her warm, whatever you do keep her warm—"

Kenzie forced me onto one of the bunks and peeled off my clothes, wrapped me in more blankets, then lay beside me. Most of the grime was gone from her wan face, and she'd put on one of Toby's heavy sweaters over her filthy sweatshirt.

"Are you okay?" she whispered.

I nodded but said nothing. The two of us lay there in silence, listening as Toby spoke calmly into the radio and then climbed back up on deck.

When he was gone, the cabin seemed to contract around us. The lamp guttered to a dull glow as I listened to the creak of wood, a noise like someone scratching at the hull. The hiss of sleet sounded like my name. After a while Kenzie and I sat up, still without speaking. We crouched side by side on the bunk, with Toby's worn blankets wrapped around us and his voice echoing faintly from above, and stared out the porthole into the darkness until the first lights of Burnt Harbor shone through the night.

27

WE WERE MET BY John Stone and Jeff Hakkala, two ambulances, and a number of state troopers. A crowd had already gathered outside the Good Tern. I recognized Robert and the two guys who'd set upon me earlier; also Merrill Libby; Everett Moss, the harbormaster; and a small white TV van, headlights blazing through the fog.

"My camera," I said.

Toby gave me a funny look.

"It's safe," he said. "I put it below. Out of sight," he added.

I swore as someone started running toward us from the news van.

Toby put his arm around me and walked me toward the ambulance. When the reporter drew up beside us, Toby shook his head fiercely.

"Can't you see this lady's injured?"

"That ain't no lady," a voice yelled as the reporter fell back into the crowd.

I glanced over to see Robert standing beside Kenzie and her father. He grinned at me, tongue stud glinting in the headlight, then turned away.

At Paswegas County Hospital, Kenzie was examined and treated for trauma and poisoning; there was no sign of sexual assault. My arm was cleaned and bandaged. I got fifteen stitches and a temporary eye patch.

"You're going to have a scar there," the ER doctor told me.

I stared into the mirror, at a black starburst of stitches and dried blood beside my right eye.

"Souvenir of Vacationland," I said.

I was released around three A.M. They kept Kenzie overnight then released her the next morning to her father and the ministrations of local law enforcement.

I spent the rest of the night with the state police. So did Toby. There were a lot of questions, especially for me, and I gathered there'd be more once the FBI arrived and investigators saw what was in the trees on Tolba Island. I didn't want to think about what they'd find in the quarry, or that clearing.

I was beyond exhaustion. And I felt a sick pang, that I hadn't saved Denny's book. All that terrifying beauty, lost. Only glimpses would remain, in the pictures Ray had, and Lucien Ryel.

But they were like postcards of the Taj Mahal. And I'd seen the real thing.

Denny Ahearn had created an entire world out there with his turtle shells and daguerreotypes, his mangled home religion and tormented attempts to reclaim something from the death of the girl he had loved all those years ago. It was a horrifying world, but it was a real one. How many of us can say we've made a new world out of the things that terrify and move us? Aphrodite tried and failed.

Monstrous as he was, Denny was the real thing. So was his work. He really had built a bridge between the worlds, even if no one had ever truly seen it, besides the two of us. Now it was up to me, to carry the memory of the dead on my back.

It was dawn when Toby finally drove me to the Lighthouse.

"Here." He handed me my camera. "I figured you'd want this."

As I turned it to the light, he added, "No one's seen it. Didn't seem like it was their business."

The sign in front of the motel now read NO VACANCY. Merrill had arranged for us to be given cabins in the woods behind the motel, rather than the rooms near the main road.

"In case reporters start showing up," explained Toby. He looked drawn and exhausted, but also immeasurably sad. "Be a little harder for them to find us there."

"That's thoughtful of him."

"Merrill's not a bad guy. I told you that. I should have, anyway." He looked at me and shook his head. "You should get some sleep."

"Yeah. You too," I said and stumbled inside.

Sunlight leaked through the blinds as I locked the door. I kicked my boots off and set them atop the heater, downed the last two Percocets, and fell into bed. I slept like the dead, dreamless, mindless. When I finally woke, it was night again.

I spent the next two days in a daze: no booze, no drugs. A lot of time giving statements to various law enforcement officials. A background check brought up the time Christine had called the police on me for domestic assault, but as she'd never pressed charges no one could run with that. Toby and Suze vouched for my whereabouts and everything I'd done during the time since Mackenzie Libby went missing. Toby made no mention of me slipping him a Mickey. There were a few raised eyebrows and some unpleasant moments—I've never been good at interviews—but there was no arguing with the fact that Kenzie was alive and safe, and that she wouldn't have been if I hadn't intervened. I gave all my pertinent contact information and was told I could go, for now.

The press had a field day. Within hours the incident had leaked to the national media, with headlines like PHOTO FINISH and SILENCE OF THE SNAPPING TURTLES. Denny's story had nearly everything—

murders, abductions, madness, art. Best of all, a teenage girl who survived to tell the tale—though not, it turned out, to the tabloids. Merrill Libby surprised me again by taking a relatively hard line with any exploitation of his daughter. There was an exclusive interview with the *Bangor Daily News*, and that would be it. For now, anyway. Kenzie was in counseling; she'd been sent to stay with relatives near Collinstown for a few days. Merrill had been in touch with her mother for the first time in several years.

The wreckage of the Boston Whaler was recovered. Denny's body was never found, despite divers who searched the frigid waters off Tolba Island. This further complicated things as far as the investigation went.

All this must have been terrible for Gryffin. I still hadn't seen him. Toby said he was caught up with the details of his mother's funeral, as well as with the nightmare of learning his father was a compulsive murderer. It was unnerving to think that, in the space of a few days, I had effectively orphaned him.

I'd also insured that the youth of Paswegas County would be provided with a campfire story for years to come. Toby told me the locals were already referring to Denny as The Mad Hatter, after I'd explained to the investigators about the contents of Denny's darkroom. All artists crave some kind of immortality. Denny Ahearn had achieved his. Unless, of course, he really was too tough to die.

The night after Kenzie's rescue, I finally called Phil Cohen back in the city.

"Cassandra Android! There's a horrible picture of you in the *Daily News!* What the hell happened up there?"

I gave him a thumbnail account. "Thanks for doing me another favor, Phil."

"Jesus," he said. I could hear the city around him—traffic, voices. Even at this distance, it sounded impossibly loud, compared to the wind and crying gulls above Burnt Harbor. "Hey, Neary— tell me there's no causal relationship between all this shit and your being there?"

"No causal relationship whatsoever."

I could tell from the silence that he didn't believe me.

"So," he said at last. "Did you at least get an interview before the old lady kicked?"

"Nope."

"Photos?"

"Uh-uh."

"So what the hell did you do up there? I mean, other than saving the kid."

"Not a lot, Phil," I said. "Listen, does this mean I don't get a kill fee?"

"A kill fee?" He laughed. "I'll see what I can do, okay? You could bank this story, you know that, right? You and the girl, that's real Scary Neary shit, you could really—"

"Forget it," I said. "I've gotta go. I'll be back in a few days; I'll call you."

"Wait—!"

I hung up.

The following morning, Merrill Libby came to my cabin and said that Kenzie wanted to see me.

"What you did." He stood outside the door, sweating even though it was starting to snow. "That was a good thing, Mrs. Neary."

"It's Ms. Neary." I took his outstretched hand and shook it tentatively. "But thanks."

Late that afternoon, Toby drove me to Collinstown. Heavy wet snow splattered the windshield as we crept along a gravel road. The pickup's tires were bald, so we went very slowly. The house was a new modular, surrounded by scraped earth sifted white and starred with children's footprints. Kenzie opened the door.

"Hey," she said shyly.

Her aunt and cousins looked just like Merrill. But they were friendly and didn't ask me any questions.

"Kenzie's staying in Shannon's room," her aunt said. "I told Shannon to give you some privacy."

She turned and told the kids to keep it down. Toby settled with them on the couch to watch TV.

"Thanks for coming," Kenzie said as we walked down the hall. "I'm going kind of crazy here. They're nice, but . . ."

We entered a small room. Pink walls, pink cartoon-patterned sheets, one bed and a sleeping bag on the floor. I sat on the bed. Kenzie flopped onto the floor and picked up a black vinyl CD case. She wore a new red hoodie with Tinker Bell printed on it. The fretwork of scars on her face had already begun to fade, and while there were dark circles under her eyes, her cheeks were pink. When she looked at me, she smiled.

"I really want to go down to Florida to see my mom."

"They won't let you?"

"No, they will. In a few days, I think. It's just boring."

"You have a high threshold for excitement."

She pointed at my eye patch. "Does that hurt?"

"Not really."

"Are you blind?"

"Nah. They just don't want the stitches under it to tear. The skin there's really sensitive."

She smiled that sweet kid's smile. "It looks really, really cool."

"Yeah?" I touched the corner of the patch gingerly. "Maybe I should keep it."

"You should."

She stared at her knees. I reached for the CD case and began flipping through it. "Shit. Is this what you listen to?"

"Pretty much. My mom says she's going to get me an iPod when I'm down there."

I read some of the CD titles and grimaced. "Jesus. Well, these are okay—" I tapped *Fire of Love* and volume two of the Ramones anthology.

"I like their early stuff better."

"Yeah, me too." I stared at the case for another moment then handed it back to her. "Listen, when I get back to the city I'll send you some CDs to rip. You like Patti Smith?"

"I love her! 'Dancing Barefoot' . . ."

"Forget that. Her first album, you have that one? No? I'll send it to you. You're online, right? Give me your e-mail address, I'll write and tell you some other stuff you should be listening to."

"Really? That would be so great."

I stood. "I better get back. Toby's truck, it doesn't do too good in the snow."

I stepped to the door of the bedroom. Kenzie followed, hands shoved in the pockets of her cargo pants.

"Here," she said. She withdrew her hand from her pocket and handed me something. "I made this for you."

It was a bracelet of braided string and fishing line and sea glass, beer tabs and red glass beads.

"Thanks." I looked at her and smiled. "It's beautiful. Really."

She hesitated, then said, "They said you did a book? Like, photographs of stuff? I'd like to read it."

"I would've thought you had enough of photography."

"No. I mean, yeah, but not this kind. I'm going to get a digital camera. My father said I could, with the money we get from the article."

"Yeah? That's really cool. You do that. Send me your stuff. I'd like to see what you come up with."

She walked me to the front door. Toby got up, and we walked outside.

"Thanks, Cass," Kenzie called as we picked our way through the snow.

"I'll send you those CDs," I said and got into the pickup.

Toby backed into the road. I stared at the house. Kenzie had followed us out into the darkness and stood there, snow swirling around her pale face and settling onto her black hair. I rolled down the window.

"Bye Kenzie," I said. She waved as we drove back to Burnt Harbor.

28

THE NEXT AFTERNOON THERE was a memorial service for Aphrodite at the Burnt Harbor Congregational Church. I didn't go, though Toby thought I should. He'd returned to the island after dropping me off the night before, and spent the night with Gryffin. Now it was two-thirty in the afternoon.

"You really should come to the service. You should say good-bye to Gryffin, at least." Toby stood in the door of my cabin, wearing dark wool pants and a pinstriped jacket that smelled of mothballs. He'd trimmed his beard and rebraided his pigtail. "We're going to dinner afterward at the Good Tern. You should come. You need closure."

"Closure? I've had enough closure to last a lifetime." I shook my head. "I already feel like the bad fairy at the christening. I need to get on the road."

My car remained parked down in Burnt Harbor. I still hadn't been back to it. I'd been sleeping way too much—I had a sleep deficit going back at least a week—but I figured if I left before dark I could get as far as Bangor, find another motel, then hit the road again first thing next morning.

This time tomorrow I'd be in the city again. It felt like I'd been gone a year.

Toby's face creased. "Can't you wait till after the service? So we can at least say good-bye? You'll need a ride down to get your car at the harbor, anyway."

I sighed. "Yeah, sure. Whatever."

"Good." He brightened and stepped back outside. "We'll come by afterward. See you then."

"Toby." He stopped, and I said, "I—well, just thanks, that's all. For everything."

"Oh, sure." He stared at his feet, reached down to wipe snow from his boots, then with a sigh straightened. "Jesus. What a horrible week. Poor Gryffin. Poor Aphrodite. And Denny . . ."

"Poor everyone."

He looked at the sky. "It's supposed to snow later. A big storm. I heard eighteen inches," he added. He waved at me and left.

It was almost three o'clock. It had been a flawless day, new snow glittering like broken glass and the evergreens green as malachite against the cloudless sky.

But already the light was failing. I didn't believe it was going to snow—there was a thin ridge of clouds to the west, but otherwise it was the nicest day I'd seen since arriving in Maine. I watched through my cabin window until Toby drove off. Then I sat on the bed and stared at my camera bag. Finally I withdrew the copy of *Deceptio Visus* and opened it.

Our gaze changes all that it falls upon . .

Denny's gaze certainly had changed things. Aphrodite's too, I supposed; though as I looked through *Deceptio Visus* now, her photos seemed calculated and overdone.

And too easy. She'd photographed beautiful things—islands, clouds, the rising sun—and made them more beautiful. Whereas Denny had striven to capture something horrifying and make it beautiful, beautiful and eternal. For him, Hannah Meadows had never really died. Or maybe it was that she had never stopped dying. In all the years since he'd found her drowned corpse by that quarry, he'd never been able to look away.

I found the stolen photograph of Gryffin.

"I see you," I whispered.

I closed the book and put it in the bottom of my bag. Then I got my camera, removed the exposed film and loaded it with my last roll of Tri-X, and went outside.

The dying light sent long, thin shadows across the snow. The pines were still sheathed in white. I walked into the woods that bordered my cabin, found a small clearing, and began to shoot.

I wasn't trying for anything special. I just wanted to feel myself behind the camera. I wanted to see if my eye, injured or not, had changed.

And I guess I wanted to see if the world had changed as well. I shot most of the roll before I lost the light, black branches and the shadows between fallen leaves, a pile of punctured acorns like tiny skulls, gaps in the underbrush where it seemed that small faces stared back at me. Once I thought I heard something moving in the crotch of a tree overhead, and I stumbled backward and nearly fell.

But when I looked up there was nothing there, only a flickering shadow that might have been a squirrel or crow, or maybe something larger.

The light was gone when I walked back to my cabin. I went into my cabin and cleaned up for the last time and replaced my bandage. I checked to make sure I hadn't left anything behind, then sat to wait for Toby.

It was past five when someone knocked at the door. I stood and opened it.

"Cass. Hi."

It was Gryffin. He looked down at me, his face pale and eyes red. "Toby's got Suze and Ray and Robert all crammed into his truck. So I said I'd get you. You have everything?"

"I think so." I struggled to keep my voice calm as I put on my jacket, wincing as I stuck my bad arm through the sleeve. I picked up my bag and my camera. "This is it."

We walked to where he'd parked his old gray Volvo, outside the motel office. I went inside—the door was open—and left my room key on the desk. Merrill was gone. There was a note he'd be back that night. As I returned to Gryffin's car I saw that the sign now read CLOSED FOR THE SEASON.

A few scattered snowflakes melted against the windshield as we headed toward Burnt Harbor. After a few minutes Gryffin glanced at me.

"That looks like it hurt."

"Yeah." I took a deep breath. He looked awful. Not merely exhausted but ravaged by grief and, I knew, something worse. "I—I don't know what to say. Just, I'm sorry about everything."

He was silent for a moment. Then he sighed.

"Thanks. It's bad. Denny—well, you know. My mother was so enraged when he dumped her for that girl Hannah, his name isn't even on my birth certificate. But I knew. Everyone knew. And the way they do things up here—well, no one ever talked about it. I haven't had any contact with him since I was really young, but the police have been talking to me now, I can tell you that. It's horrible. Beyond horrible. But—"

He peered out through the thin snowfall to the dark road winding ahead of us. "He's gone now. I guess. I hope so, anyway. Now it'll just be forensics and trying to figure out who all those other people were."

"Will you be leaving too?"

"Leaving? I wish I could. I've got to stick around and go through my mother's stuff. The state office is calling it an unexplained death with alcohol as a factor. But I still have to deal with her estate. And the police. And lawyers. Try to figure out what they can and can't confiscate as part of the investigation. It's a mess."

We rounded a turn too fast; the car skidded toward the woods before Gryffin eased it back onto the road. He slowed to a crawl, reached into his pocket, and tossed me something. "Here. I think this belongs to you."

I caught it and looked down: a roll of Tri-X film. Before I could open my mouth he said, "My box turtle shell—it had been moved, I noticed first thing when I got up that morning. I picked it up and I could feel something inside. I meant to give it to you then—I guess it was some sort of joke, right? But then I found my mother, and . . ."

He looked away. "I forgot about it."

I ran my fingers across the roll then tucked it into the pocket of my leather jacket. "Well," I said. "Thanks. I, uh—"

"Forget it." For a moment he was quiet. Then he said, "That box turtle shell . . . it was the only thing he ever gave me. Denny."

He glanced out the side window at snow slanting through the trees. "When I heard, I took it down to the beach and threw it into the water. It's gone now. They're all gone."

He downshifted as we approached a curve. "These old Volvos are terrible in the snow. Rear wheel drive. Every year I tell myself I'll buy a new car. Why'd you come after her?"

"Kenzie?"

"No. My mother. Why'd you come here to talk to her?"

I stared outside. "Because I loved those two books," I said at last. "*Deceptio Visus* and *Mors*—they changed my life. When I saw them, that's when I decided I wanted to be a photographer."

"What made you stop?"

When I didn't reply, Gryffin said, "I found a copy of your book online. I ordered it from ABE. It goes for two hundred dollars now. Did you know that?"

"Really? No shit? Two hundred bucks?"

"No shit. With all this stuff going on, I bet you could get a reprint deal if you wanted." He gave a harsh laugh. "Good career move, Cass, all this."

He glanced at me. "Cass. Listen. Why don't you stick around here for a while?"

"I have to get back to work."

"Oh yeah, right. The stockroom at the Strand. Like they're going to miss you? Look, I've started going through my mother's stuff. Her photos and letters and things like that. She kept everything. I'm already getting calls from dealers and collectors—this horrible thing with Denny, all of a sudden everyone is interested in Aphrodite Kamestos again. Not to mention Denny's stuff. Some agent contacted me about a book.

"But I can't stand to look at any of it. So I was thinking. If you were interested, if you could stand it—you could stay and help me collate things. Get a catalog together. I know about rare books, but I don't know enough about photography, and it seems like you do. I couldn't pay anything right off, but you could stay at the house, and then if we got a deal we could work something out. What do you think?"

I stared out the window into the woods, thinking. I shook my head. "No. Thanks, but—"

"But what?"

"Well, for starters, I don't think I could hack living here."

"Really? Seems to me you've hacked it pretty good so far." He gave me that odd furtive look, shot with annoyance but also regret. "Well, okay. I thought it was a good idea. Keep it in mind, all right? I'm probably going to end up hiring someone. It would be good if it was someone like you."

Ahead of us the lights of Burnt Harbor began to shine through the snow. We coasted down to the Good Tern and parked alongside Toby's red pickup. A few people stood by the pier, looking across the water and talking. As we got out they turned—Toby, Suze from the Island Store, Ray Provenzano, and Robert.

"Hey," Suze called. She kicked through the snow to join us, hiking her long peasant skirt above clunky boots. A knit cap covered her blond dreadlocks. "That was a nice service, Gryffin. You did the right thing. As always."

She hugged him then looked at me. "How're you feeling?"

I shrugged. "Okay, I guess. Under the circumstances."

She smiled. "You're a local hero. You know that, right?" She tipped her head, indicating my eye patch. "That looks nasty. Will you be able to see?"

"Yeah. It's just till I pull the stitches out."

She stood on tiptoe to kiss Gryffin's cheek. He smiled wanly, and Ray put an arm around him.

"You'll be okay, Gryffin. We'll take care of you," said Ray. He looked at me then added in his hoarse voice, "Well, you've had quite a little visit."

Toby lit a joint and held it out. I shook my head. He passed it to Ray then said, "So. You got everything, Cass?"

"Yeah. I guess so."

Suze rocked back on her heels and stared at the snow whirling down. "You oughta stick around. They already got eight inches in Portland, had to close 95 cause a semi went off near Bangor. 'A tombstone every mile.' Just like the song."

Robert nodded. "We're gonna get hammered."

"Come on." Gryffin touched my elbow and gestured to my car, parked in the shadows a few yards off. "You better get going if you're going to beat the storm."

We walked, my boots sliding on the greasy blacktop. I kept my head down so no one could see my face. We reached the car.

"Uh-oh," said Suze.

I looked up. "What the fuck?"

The Rent-A-Wreck sagged, its carriage resting on the ground. I crouched to stare at the front tire. It had been slashed.

"Looks like they got 'em all," said Toby. He walked to the rear, shaking his head. "Huh."

"Robert?" Ray's braying voice echoed across the empty harbor. "*Robert!*"

"It wasn't me! I swear to God, it was Bip—"

"Bip?" I stared at him in disbelief. "Who the fuck is Bip?"

"That guy you beat up. He was wicked pissed," he added, and shrugged sheepishly.

Ray punched his shoulder. "You're gonna fix her tires, understand? You and frigging Bip! First thing tomorrow. Or well, whenever the storm lets up."

"Shit." I stared at the car. Suze came up beside me.

"Hey, don't sweat it," she said. "This kind of stuff happens all the time. We'll get you fixed up."

I turned and looked out across the whorl of white and black, to where the lights shone on Paswegas Island, all but indistinguishable from the falling snow.

"Come on," said Gryffin. He put his arm around me and pointed at the Good Tern. "I'll buy you a drink."

The others started toward the bar. I watched them go, then looked up at Gryffin.

He smiled, and for a fraction of a second he looked exactly like the young man in the photograph—not ecstatic, maybe, but still open to the possibility of happiness.

The possibility of something, anyway. I stared at him then slung my camera bag over my shoulder.

"Oh, what the hell," I said, and we followed the others inside.

Acknowledgments:

First and foremost, my gratitude to my agent, Martha Millard, and to Kelly Link, Gavin Grant, and Tina Pohlman, my editors at Small Beer Press and Harcourt.

Heartfelt thanks to those who read and commented on various drafts of this book: Jim Baker, John Clute, Ellen Datlow, Russell Dunn, Tess Gerritsen, Richard Grant, Bob Morales, Eddie and Tracee O'Brien, Peter Straub, Paul Witcover, Gary Wolfe.

To Steve Dunn, for the loan of his island.

To Russell Dunn, for exploring it with me, and for 30-plus years of seeing beauty in the bleak stuff.

For photographic expertise, Norman Walters.

For all things nautical, and for letting *Magic Ghost* stand in for *Northern Sky*, Bruce Bouldry.

For his experience of homicide investigative protocol, Raymond Jeffery Greene.

Most of all, love and thanks to John Clute, compass and True North.